Rav

Copyright © 2024 by H. C. Kilgour and Owl Talyn Press

ISBN: Paperback   979-8-218-47596-3
        Ebook   979-8-218-47597-0

All rights reserved. No part of this book may be reproduced in any form on or by electronic means, including information storage and retrieval systems and artificial intelligence, without permission in writing from the publisher, except by a reviewer who may quote brief passages in a review.

This work is fiction. Names, characters, places, and incidents either are a product of the author's imagination or are used fictitiously, and any resemblance to any actual persons, living or dead, events, or locales is entirely coincidental.

First paperback edition October 2024

Front cover design by Aleksa Kirsten
Map by "aja"

OWL TALYN PRESS
First published in the United States by Owl Talyn Press in the United States
www.owltalynpress.com

Ravliean

H. C. Kilgour

*For Loraine,
For always being willing to read and edit,
no matter how rough it is.*

Westorlines Mountains
Xieng River
Javin Lake
Upper River Fort
Whendell
Tratolek
Suilenroc
Agrielha Castle
Tatat River
Lake Romann
Agrielh
Drath
Grena
Bouyne
Middle River Fort
Revod
Suttan
Ohvenail
Greya
Bowtilmer
Aylentowne
Móverth
N

Albiera River
Averit Volcanoes
Wynsh River
Icchota Lake
Glensung Plains
Port Ligola
Edreba
Yarav Forest
Illeria Mountains
Port Clire
Nueweba River
Haggard Land
Igress
Eastern Ocean

Chapter 1

Nine days. Nine bovestun days since had Kolt upended everything. Where Braxton was, not much had changed, but he knew everyone must be on edge trying to gauge the alterations that were coming—if they had not already.

All in all, he was not entirely upset with the situation. He had no worries or responsibilities. The cell was not terribly cold. The cot was a cot, but it could be the ground. He was given three meals a day from the king's own table. Kolt's upheaval might actually be a blessing.

A rat squeaked, hidden in the impenetrable darkness shrouding most of the cell, and the momentary lapse in judgment fell away. His hatred for the cell, the situation, and *Kolt*, returned and magnified.

Diving into his mind, Braxton found the earth paika—though, for all his anger and determination, was unable to break the blood-red gem. Kolt had done something at the coronation to rob him of his magic.

The golden bracelets he now bore were the source of the block, but he could not understand how they so *completely and unfailingly* inhibited his magic. The only solace they offered was that they had also stopped his visions of the future.

"Hello, brother," a voice from the hallway said.

Braxton rushed to the bars, knuckles instantly turning white from the force of his grip. He would give *anything* to stop that voice from ever speaking again. "What do you want?"

Kolt was shrewd enough to stand outside of reach. "Many things, dear brother."

"Why? Why did you do this?"

"Because you are weak. You would have allowed peace. Right now, we are feared—we are strong."

Braxton saw too much of Caius, who was brazen but had at least known where to draw a line. Kolt was going to obliterate that along with who knows what else. "No. We are weak, splintered, and afraid. You are going to take us into a war that will ensure we never stand as a nation again."

Kolt examined his nails. "I doubt that. I have taken some precautions to guarantee we are victorious." When Braxton remained silent, he goaded, "Do you not wonder why you have become ordinary or why I was father's favorite?"

He spat at Kolt's feet. "You were father's favorite because you are cruel like him."

"No, I was father's favorite because I am spellcaster like him."

Braxton balked at the thought. "Impossible. You are as ungifted as they come." It was a low blow. "If not more so!"

Kolt's face soured. "That is what I would have people think. It is true I was ungifted until I was eight. I find it so unfortunate spellcasters must wait to get their powers, unlike elementals who cannot remember life without them."

"You give no proof."

"Buna." Fire engulfed Kolt's hand.

Catching the malice of the dancing flame reflected in his brother's eyes, Braxton pushed back from the bars. "Why would you hide your gift?"

"When you are normal, no one expects great things of you." There was hurt in the words. Had it been anyone else, Braxton might have felt sympathetic.

"You cannot suppress my magic forever."

Kolt laughed. "I already have with those slajor manacles."

For the first time, true fear lanced through Braxton. Slajor manacles meant Kolt could effectively render any elemental he captured useless. There were only two ways to remove the bindings: they could be removed by the one who made them or at the wearer's death. "The last set was destroyed at the beginning of father's reign," Braxton argued.

"I made more. And tested them on you. They seem to be doing the job."

"Why visit me now? Why wait so long?"

"Let us just say I have been reaping the benefits of being king."

Knowing Kolt, Braxton had a fair idea of what that entailed: women and wine. And a lot of both.

"Now, I have a proposition for you," his brother continued.

"I would rather die," Braxton told him without hesitation.

"See, I knew you would say that! Which is why I will not touch a hair on your fat head. I cannot say the same will be true for the griffins and the boy. Serve me or I will *personally* make them suffer."

Braxton kept his face as neutral as he could, but there was no hiding. His one weakness had been found.

"I see I have hit a nerve. Do not worry, I will give you time to think things over. Just know, when you do bow, you will become the Vosjnik archer." Kolt walked away, giving an antagonistic wave.

Ravliean

There was no way to defy his brother and protect the few beings he had come to care for. It was either sacrifice them or sacrifice himself.

《《《 》》》

Kade finished climbing the stairs to Bernot's office in the Gortlin Tree and leaned against the wall. He wasn't happy to be pulled away from training with Elhyas but, as always, had little choice in the matter. The sounds of huffing drew his attention, and he glanced over the edge of the stairs.

Trudging up the final steps, Keegan panted, "Remind me to take the elevator next time."

"Elevator?"

His twin waved at the empty space beside the landing. "The basket thingy."

Aron arrived next and Kade couldn't help but note the way Keegan began to fidget. He knew the two were close, but something had changed between them recently—drastically. From the way they interacted now... he sincerely hoped his guess was wrong because, if he wasn't, Aron wouldn't be in great shape—and he was just starting to not imagine killing the prince every time he saw him.

As Jared arrived, the door to the office opened, revealing a grim-faced Bernot. "In." Once they were settled, he turned to Aron. "It is about your brother."

The color drained from the exiled prince's face. "Which one? What happened?"

"It involves both of them," Bernot said slowly. "Kolt staged a successful coup nine days ago."

Keegan glanced over her shoulder at Kade, an eyebrow raised as if asking for permission. When she turned back around, she snipped, "And it took you this long to tell us?" She crossed her arms. "We already know."

"I am aware. It is not polite to eavesdrop."

Kade almost laughed. Keegan had no remorse—and neither did Bernot.

"It's not polite to withhold information," Jared said in Keegan's defense. "Why didn't you tell us sooner?"

"Because it is at my discretion when *and* what information I share," Bernot answered coldly.

"Cut the bullshit," Keegan said. "You tell us things when you find out, or I peace out."

The Lazado leader gave her a baffled look.

"Or I leave."

Bernot pursed his lips in response.

Had anyone else demanded the same, the result would've been drastically different. Keegan made sure they weren't left with their thumbs up their arses, but Kade found it aggravating that only *she* had this power.

"I thought you were going to try the diplomatic approach; what changed?" Jared asked.

Kade snorted. "With Braxton, no problem. You can't reason with Kolt. You'd have better luck arguing with a brick."

Bernot pulled a package and letter from a drawer. "It is more so I do not take threats lightly." He passed the note to Jared, and they crowded over his shoulder.

Keegan finished reading well before the rest of them and Kade could feel anger spiking in her blood. She reached toward the package, unwrapping two simple, golden bracelets.

He quickly slapped them from her hands. "Those are slajor manacles. I don't royiken need them magically wrapping around your wrists."

"Kade's explained what they do," Keegan said, "but I don't get how they completely inhibit magic."

Bernot explained, "A spell. And spells do not have to be actively maintained like elemental magic. Makes slajor manacles quite useful."

"Provided you're not the one wearing them," Keegan mumbled.

"Caius was the only spellcaster in Agrielha, as far as I know," Kade said.

"He must've made them before he died then," Keegan surmised. "Which means they have a limited, diminishing supply. How do you get them off?"

"You don't—that's the point." Kade mumbled the last part.

Bernot added, "The person who made the bracelets can remove them, or the person wearing them must die."

Keegan thought for a moment, lips pulling into a thoughtful frown. "I can work with that; we just kill you temporarily."

Bernot's mouth dropped, displaying what Kade assumed they all were thinking. "Dead is dead. No magic can fix that."

Keegan shrugged. "There's dead and then there's... *dead*. Dead from drowning, heart attack... that kinda stuff can be fixed. *Dead* like seven years dead, yeah... that's dead."

"You can't bring someone back to life," Jared argued. "Dead is dead."

Keegan laughed. "Dead ain't dead until you're warm and dead."

Kade didn't agree, but Keegan tended to have the knowledge—and gumption—to prove them wrong. But even if her idea wasn't far-fetched, he had no desire to be the one to test it.

"So, we go to war?" Jared said tentatively.

"Yes," Bernot answered tersely. "I truly wish there was another way."

"There was *never* going to be another way," Aron said bitterly.

Sighing, Bernot leaned back in his chair. "The other nations have agreed to join us, and though war is a turtle, you are all going to have to become warriors... and quickly."

"Give us the right tools and we'll surprise even ourselves," Keegan said optimistically.

"All your guards are apt swordsmen so I would prefer you work with them to minimize risk. As for elemental training, you will have to wait for the other races to assign tutors. Jared, Aron," Bernot continued, "you will also utilize Keegan's guards."

"I expect Carter to have the same opportunities as I," Jared blurted. "And Lucas... when we find him."

"Of course. And Kade, as you are already working with Elhyas, I see no need to change that."

Kade's eyebrows furrowed as he questioned how Bernot knew just about everything.

Seeing his expression, Keegan whispered, "Dude, Elhyas is one of my guards."

Why didn't you tell me this? he snapped, talking telepathically so only Keegan could hear him.

I didn't know you'd met him, she returned.

Kade clenched his jaw to keep his anger back. He'd been fooled and that wasn't something he took lightly.

"The dragons will be here by week's end," Bernot said, "and I am sure I can track down Okleiy to get him to assign you a life tutor."

"Why not just let Mahogen help me?" Keegan suggested.

"I would not seek to overburden him. Now, there is still plenty of daylight—I suggest making use of it."

Taking the cue, Aron briskly walked from the room. Keegan and Jared followed without a word.

Alone, Kade confronted the Lazado leader. "Why did you send Elhyas to spy on me?"

Bernot casually shuffled some papers. "I did nothing of the sort. It was of Elhyas's own volition he kept his connection to your sister to himself."

Kade didn't like the answer, but knew it was the best he was going to get. Giving Bernot a parting scowl, he stalked from the room, letting the door slam behind him. It wasn't often he let people close to him—in any capacity. Halfway down the Gortlin Tree, he realized something—if this was how he felt about a small omission, how had Keegan and Jared felt about all of his secrets?

It was a wonder they still wanted anything to do with him.

«««« »»»»

Keegan glowered as she watched Aron race down and out of the Gortlin Tree. Since they'd spent that night together, he'd been avoiding her. She *at least* deserved an explanation as to his behavior now. And while she wanted to knock Aron about the head and demand such, that would only make the situation worse.

Not possessing the strength, as she was still recovering from the Ramilla, nor in the mood to explore the Gortlin Tree, she pensively made her way down the stairs. At the bottom, Zavier, one of her new guards, was fighting an invisible opponent, gracefully dodging, slashing, and parrying.

"You winning?" she asked, letting her frustration slip away.

Zavier lunged, stabbing his ghost opponent. "Always."

Shoving her hands in her pockets, Keegan left the confines of the tree. They could've taken the elevator to the treetop city, but she hated feeling restricted—plus, this would help speed her recovery and give her ample time to dwell.

The trip to the children's home was quiet, she mulled over the looming war and Aron's shift in behavior while Zavier was on the lookout for nonexistent dangers.

When their destination was in sight, Zavier said, "Bernot wants to see you."

"What the hell?" she said exasperatedly, "We *literally* just left."

The guard shrugged and headed back to the ladder before she could say anything to convince him to disobey an order.

"Let's take the basket." The quicker this was done, the quicker she could go back to stewing.

"He wants to see you at the training field. It's quicker to climb."

"Why?"

Zavier gave a look that said he hadn't been informed and wasn't going to ask.

As they reached the field, many heads turned. Most returned to their opponents quickly.

Bernot waited for them on the far side of the field, the area around him cleared of sparrers—a not so clandestine spot for a meeting that apparently warranted privacy.

Keegan placed her hands on her hips. "Whatcha want?"

"I thought I would see how you are coming along with your water training," Bernot answered.

"You got some water?"

He tossed her a waterskin.

Unstoppering it, Keegan drew the water out and morphed it into fantastic shapes that danced through the air in a silent ballet. When she got bored with the shapes, she molded the water into a replica of her shadow and froze it, letting it shatter on the ground.

"Excellent," Bernot said casually. "Now, let us see what you can do without water in its pure form."

She raised an eyebrow. As kickass as she thought it would be to take control of a person using water magic, she couldn't imagine anyone would be particularly happy about becoming a puppet. Keegan considered creating a cloud, but that seemed too easy. So, she harnessed the plants beneath her feet, easily bending them in a nonexistent wind.

Bernot bore a wide smile. "Let us try something bigger."

It didn't take a telepath to know what he wanted. "That's just... no... I'm not doing that."

"Me, you will be controlling me. I would never ask my men to become your experiment."

Keegan shook her head. "And if this works, you'll ask me to do it against Kolt's men."

"If you can do this, lives might be spared."

"Why not have Atlia do this? Or an Alvor, who I'd hazard to guess are damn good at manipulation."

"Because, at most, an Alvor can manipulate a few people at a time. Merfolk can do it but find it difficult for some reason. Something about impurities."

"Cause blood isn't just water," she muttered.

"Keegan, please," Bernot pushed, placing his hands on her shoulders, "just try. I just want to see if it is possible. We need to use whatever we can against Kolt."

Anger rose in her chest, making its way to her throat like bile. She scrambled to hold it back, but it was like trying to catch a tiger by the tail. Magic burst forth against her will and she felt the men nearest them fall under her control like keys under a pianist's fingers. She could feel their blood circulating, delivering oxygen, fighting pathogens. She could feel them fighting against her with every fiber of their beings.

Fear was prominent as the men's bodies betrayed their minds. She willed her puppets to surround her and Bernot, their weapons rising shakily.

It didn't take long for others to come to defend Bernot, but once they realized their comrades were being controlled, they backed away.

"Is this what you wanted?" Keegan asked, holding out her hands as an invitation for Bernot to witness his request.

"Keegan," Bernot said, uncertainty tinging his words while disgust hid in the corners of his mouth, "I need you to calm down."

"I'm completely calm," she snarled. "*You* wanted me to do this. Just not to your men." She looked about, studying the faces around them. Realization slammed into her like a freight train and her ire stumbled away, replaced with revulsion.

She released the men and most staggered over their own feet as they fled. Those on the sidelines stepped forward, weapons prepared, though all held their distance as if praying there was a boundary to her wrath and magic.

"Is this what you wanted?" She didn't give Bernot time to respond before sprinting away.

《《《《 》》》》》

Aron hated himself for what he had done to Keegan, and nothing could relieve that burden—that *stain*. He had defiled her in his moment of need. And would do it again given the chance. He had to stay away, for her sake.

Keegan had come to his door, and he had keenly felt the torrent of emotions rolling off her. But he had to stay away; for her sake.

Yet, Jared's harsh words circulated in his mind. Was it possible he was only hurting her more?

"No," he muttered, feeling the way he had that night. He must steer clear. But something nagged at him.

There had been so much to the emotions coming from Keegan—bubbling anger, cascading sadness, oppressive self-loathing... Even now he could feel betrayal slicing into his heart with every beat, cutting a little deeper each time.

Aron clenched his fists as his resolve continued to crumble. He had to stay away. He had to... but Keegan... needed him. And he *needed* her, as much as he tried to tell himself otherwise. He was not sure when he had released Shiloh to the old gods, but he had. And he could not say when his heart had gone to Keegan.

Grumbling, he slipped from his room, cursing Jared's name for instilling that grain of doubt. As he left the children's home, he realized he had no easy way to find Keegan. A pang of frustration ripped through his gut like a painful cramp, making his steps falter. Left behind was a mass of misery that made him want to retch, but this was not what he felt.

It took him a moment to realize he was being physically affected by *Keegan's* emotions. He knew he should be concerned that her thoughts were extending so far and so deep, but that was a matter for later. The emotion was distant and as he began to walk, it grew stronger.

After traversing the treetop city and the forest floor, he found her sitting by the Royal Koi Pond. Above the clearing, dark clouds threatened to spill their tears.

"Keegan," he said quietly.

Her head whipped around, semi-dried salt streaks running down her cheeks.

Carefully, he took a seat beside her, wrapping an arm around her shoulders. *This is for her*, he reminded himself.

Keegan was slow to reciprocate, but when she did, her head buried into his chest and tears began to flow once more.

Pulling her closer, Aron felt a raindrop on his head and looked up. The clouds had darkened to a threatening shade of black. Another drop fell, landing on his cheek. More followed and together they sat in the downpour, Keegan's tears mingling with the pooling rainwater.

Slowly, the storm subsided, and the clouds lightened, though did not part.

Keegan pulled away, wiping her eyes with the heel of her palms. "You're an ass!"

"I know and I am sorry. I was… ashamed I gave into temptation. That can never be undone."

Keegan gave him a puzzled look and a strained laugh. "That's what you've been kicking yourself over? Really?" There was a pause. "You're not my first."

Heat rose to his face. "Even so, I took advantage of you."

"You didn't take advantage of me. I wanted it as much as you did."

He tucked a wet strand of hair behind her ear. "I care for you—a lot." Dull rays of sunshine began to pierce the straggling clouds. "I promise I will never do something like that again."

"You'd better not." Keegan leaned her head against his shoulder, seeming to understand he meant the abandonment.

"I was asked to control people using their blood."

She said it so casually that it took Aron a moment to process the words. He shuddered at the thought. "Did you?"

Keegan tensed and the clouds pushed together, shutting out the sun once more. The fact she was controlling the localized weather spoke volumes to how upset she was. "Yeah. I didn't mean to though."

"I am sure Bernot knows that."

She looked up at him, anger flickering in her hazel irises. "He's the one who suggested it in the first place. And now that he knows it's possible, he'll make me do it in battle."

"And you will tell him no," he said soothingly. "Bernot, nor anyone else, can make you do something you don't want to."

Pain and doubt rode on her words. "I'm not so sure that's true. He was right when he said it could save lives."

Chapter 2

Flashes of color streaked across the little windows of the tree canopy. Jared smiled as wind buffeted the branches, sending leaves skittering about like late summer snowfall in the far south. The dragons had arrived.

He had planned to train, but… so much for that. Racing back to the children's home, he found Keegan, Aron, and Carter, followed by Ezekhial, rushing out the door.

Keegan grabbed his hand, pulling him along. "The dragons are here!"

They practically flew through the treetop city and Keegan descended the ladder so fast he was sure she was going to miss a rung and plummet down.

On the forest floor, a mass of people had gathered, and Keegan pushed through, using her small stature to her advantage. The rest of them pressed through the throng less effectively to find a line of soldiers keeping the tide of spectators back.

"What gives?" Keegan asked, pulling her arm from a man's grasp.

Jared guessed she'd tried bullying her way past.

"No one is permitted further," the soldier snapped.

"Good thing I ain't no one!"

"I don't care who you—"

"Let them through," Ezekhial ordered.

"What are you doing here? I thought you were guarding the Child of Prophecy."

Ezekhial scratched his head. "I am."

The man quickly stepped aside. "Oh, royik."

They continued through the forest unhindered, anticipation hanging in the air like static. It wasn't long before they reached a clearing bursting with color.

While the rest of them gawked, Keegan plowed forward, causing them to chase after her. She led them to where Bernot, Atlia, and Okleiy were talking to a dragon he presumed was Tahrin. Truth be told, dragons of the same color were almost impossible to tell apart, so he wasn't entirely sure it was Tahrin.

Bernot said with mild surprise, "I was just about to send for you. Where is your brother?"

Keegan shrugged. "Probably sparring." There was a hint of soreness in the words; Kade and Keegan's familial relationship was still a tender topic.

Tahrin lowered her head to look them in the eyes, sending a warm puff of air from her nostrils. *I am glad to see you managed to keep out of trouble.*

Jared was unsettled by the kind tone, which was drastically different from how he remembered Tahrin. The last time he'd seen her... or any of the leaders aside from Bernot, tensions were high to say the least.

Keegan scoffed. "I wouldn't go that far."

Tahrin motioned with her head to another red dragon nearby. The tips of knife-like teeth protruded from its lips and each of its toes ended in a hooked talon that could rip through flesh easily. *That is Raelin; he will be your fire tutor. Your training begins as soon as you reach the borderlands.*

Before Keegan could respond, Tahrin emitted a roar that reverberated in Jared's bones. He clamped his hands over his ears as the other dragons took up the call, scaring birds from their roosts and making squirrels chatter angrily. A sudden downdraft knocked him to the ground, and he watched as the horde of dragons took to the sky—all except Tahrin.

"Where are they going?" Keegan asked, watching the confusion of color disappear over the treetops.

Everyone else was slower to pick themselves up and spit the dirt from their mouths.

"To the border," Bernot said, dusting grass off his pants. "Same as you."

《《《 》》》

Bernot watched Keegan, Aron, and the two Sieme boys who had made it to the Lazado, walk away and breathed a sigh of relief. He had nothing against them, but they, Keegan *especially*, had a precocious habit of causing unexpected anarchy. At the thought, his eye gave a slight throb, a reminder of her last uproar.

After Keegan's display of blood manipulation, Atlia had physically and verbally assaulted him for being so careless. Apparently, he had not understood just how dangerous that type of magic was—nor that it was a secret very few knew about. Atlia had not been inclined to let Keegan continue with the skill, but eventually reason won out—though, he had to swear only the Merqueen would work with her on it.

Bernot returned his attention to Tahrin and the man with her. He was unassuming at best, thick around the middle, though it was not entirely fat. His face—though it seemed more like his entire head—was flat, which was only accentuated by his shorn, brown hair. Blue eyes were sunken into his face, divided by a nose that started slenderly then became squat and wide.

She has gotten much stronger, Tahrin commented, including the stranger in their conversation. *There is the heart of a dragon in that one. I hope her time was put to good use.*

"It was. She has practically mastered water magic," Bernot said.

The stranger laughed. "She not learn zat in three veeks."

Noticing the calculating look Bernot was giving the man, Tahrin introduced him, *Nikita Sokolov, man from a land where alcohol is water.*

"Zat is Russia," Nikita said with a satisfied nod. "Vhy you never remember her name?"

Same reason I do not eat you, Tahrin said, playfully nipping at Nikita. *Too difficult.*

Bernot shook Nikita's hand. "You must be a Pexatose."

"You vould be correct. I heard you vant me to fight. I miss fighting; it hard to fight dragons. Chertov scaly bastards."

"Everyone will be fighting," Bernot assured him, "we are going to war." *He seems a bit... bloodthirsty,* he noted, speaking only to Tahrin, Okleiy, and Atlia.

No more than any dragon, Tahrin countered. *There is a reason we like him.* She reopened the conversation to Nikita. *Now, what were you saying about Keegan mastering water magic in what, three weeks?*

"She has done exactly that," Bernot claimed. "She can already..." he trailed off, catching the glare from Atlia.

Tahrin threw her head back, giving a roaring laugh that spat fingers of flame. *Merfolk struggle to do that.* Atlia must have finished the conversation privately.

"She took control of eight men. Not only that, but this was done in anger," Atlia informed the dragon.

"Then girl not actually do zis," Nikita argued, even though he did not know exactly what they were debating. "It like vhen voman lift car off baby. No normally possible."

"Keegan is the exception," Bernot said, "if she can do it in anger, you should watch yourself when she is calm."

Nikita was silent for a moment. "Scary cyka."

"What are your abilities, Nikita?" Okleiy asked, speaking for the first time.

"I fire retardant," Nikita answered proudly.

Okleiy gave him a puzzled look. "Fire retardant?"

The man motioned toward Tahrin, and she released a stream of yellow and orange flames over him. When the flames subsided, Nikita was left standing as if nothing had happened despite the curls of smoke that lifted off his body.

"Fire not burn me," Nikita clarified, grinning.

What about the other elements? Tahrin asked, returning the topic to Keegan. *Has she begun training in any of them?*

"No," Bernot answered. "I did not think she would master water so quickly and did not want to push her."

Let us hope she masters the others as fast, Tahrin said, shuffling her wings. *You humans need a fall war. There is no fire in you, and you tend to freeze.*

"With Keegan, I have no doubt this war will be short. And we do have fire within us, just not *actual* fire." He turned to Nikita, "Would you be so inclined to aid in training Keegan?"

"No now," Nikita said, "Maybe soon. I vas promised fighting."

"There will be fighting—later," he said, disliking the man's bloodthirst, "but Keegan has to be trained first."

"No, Nikita has to train first," the Pexatose said stubbornly. "Jesus girl has Raelin."

Bernot was prepared to continue pressing when a soldier handed him an envelope silently. He normally would have thought nothing of the letter, but upon seeing the wax seal embossed with the Alagard crest, tore it open feverishly.

Inside was a single sentence: *Your time has run out.*

《《《 》》》

Braxton rose to his feet at the sound of footsteps and prepared to face his brother. Almost as soon as Kolt had given him the choice, he had known what he was going to do. There really had not been another option. But that had not stopped the king from letting him stew and fret for another week.

"Have you made your decision?" Kolt asked, coming into view.

"I have. I will serve you, but only if Nico is allowed to return home." The stipulation was a shot at a small target.

"No. You will serve me, and I will allow the boy to *live*."

"He will be allowed freedom in the castle."

"Meaning you want him to be able to visit your pets." Kolt looked at him with a blank yet haughty stare. "Fine. And he will continue to train them for battle, too. I want them ready within a month." Kolt pulled a key from his pocket and twirled it through his fingers.

"The griffins will never fight for you."

The key came to a stop. "You will make them. Also, if you or Nico tries to run, I will make the boy the Vosjnik earth elemental."

Braxton felt the corners of his mouth upturn and quickly schooled his features. It was a double-edged sword, but he could protect the boy better if he was part of the Vosjnik as well.

"Do not get so excited," Kolt sneered. "It is a death sentence currently. Until Kade Tavin is killed, anyone branded as the earth elemental will die. Quickly. And usually not painlessly."

"How do you know that?"

"It is in the wording of the spell," Kolt began. "Father chose to ignore that and brand Evard Poukyn anyway and we saw he did not make it a week. There have been a few more loses after him as well."

"Why not just kill us now? Make everyone's life easier."

Kolt unlocked the door, then gave a taunting smile. "Because you are still useful. But outlive your usefulness and I will. And since I am in a giving mood, you will not be branded as the Vosjnik archer, only bear the title. Disappoint me, and I will make you a target for Lunos."

"What about the manacles?" Braxton called after him. "How am I supposed to defend myself without magic?"

"Like any normal person. I would invest in some good armor though!"

Braxton desperately wanted to hurl insults but doing so would only worsen his position. Knowing Alyck would have been monitoring his situation, he decided to first seek out Nico and the griffins.

When he entered the stable, there was a cacophony of noise. The griffins all spoke at once, plying him with questions. Anger spiked in his chest when he realized Ima and Harker were chained in stalls. He quickly undid their bonds, and they began to rub against his legs, much like cats, relief radiating from them.

What happened? Myrish asked as Braxton wrapped his arms around his neck. The bronze griffin returned the embrace in his own fashion.

He began explaining, sending the words out telepathically, unable to bear giving them voice. When he was done, the griffins stared as if he had not said a word.

Are you going to tell us? Crowlin asked, concern glinting in her glossy black eyes.

He cursed, realizing the slajor manacles allowed thoughts to be pushed into his mind but prevented him from returning in kind. "A lot has happened."

When he was done with his tale—again—Phynex gnashed her beak angrily. *We will tear him to shreds!*

Braxton said quickly, "Kolt is a spellcaster, no doubt he has safeguards in place." He gulped knowing what he was going to ask next would be difficult… if not impossible. "I need you to fly into battle and then return… here."

How can you ask that of us? Oxren asked. *We would be free before we are even forced to spill blood.*

Braxton carefully explained the threats Kolt had made.

The only reaction from the adults was stunned silence while fear panged from Ima and Harker.

The hatchlings nestled against Crowlin's legs and from the way she bent her head to them, as if saying soothing words, he could only hope the adults had come to care about the boy too.

There is no good choice, Niyth commented finally.

"I know. I wish there was something, *anything*, I could do."

It seems our fate is to fight for the Alagards, Crowlin said.

"I promise we will find a way out of this. Eventually."

No one can escape their fate, she said calmly. *It is best to accept it and fly forward.*

《《《《 》》》》

"Braxton has been released," Alyck said.

Thaddeus sighed, relieved. "I assume your nephew is on his way to see us."

"Unfortunately," Alyck grumbled, taking a seat in his usual chair.

It had been the same thing every day since Kolt had taken the throne. The "king" demanded Alyck serve him, and the Blind Prophet refused.

"You have to make concessions," Thaddeus pleaded.

"I *will not* bow to him."

Alyck might have no desire to do so, but sooner or later Kolt would find a way to hurt them. It was better to concede now before someone got hurt. And when they could make demands of their own.

There were a few moments of silence before the door opened and Kolt strutted in. "Are you ready to serve me, Uncle?"

"No," Alyck said bitterly.

"I released Braxton."

"I know."

Kolt gave an exasperated sigh. "What will it take?"

"Abdicate."

"No."

"Then rule without my knowledge."

Thaddeus shook his head silently, disappointed and frustrated.

"What if I could guarantee Braxton's life?" Kolt had to be desperate to be willing to give so much.

"What do you mean?" Alyck said cautiously, sitting a little straighter. Given he could not see Braxton's future, he was willing to go to extremes to protect the prince. Why though, the Blind Prophet had not deigned to explain yet.

"I am a spell—"

Alyck cut him off. "You act as if I am unaware."

"I could place a spell on him that will ensure no weapon can harm him."

"And if that is not enough?"

"Then I will make sure he dies," Kolt yelled. "I have already made him the Vosjnik archer but had enough sense to not brand him. I will if that is what it takes."

They all knew that brand was a death sentence—sooner or later.

Alyck was silent. "You made slajor manacles." It was an accusation.

"I did, and Braxton wears a set."

"Remove them, now! You leave him completely helpless."

The boy was doing all he could to hold back a sneer. "He is an apt archer. Serve me and I will put a spell on Braxton to shield him against weapons. Otherwise…"

The muscles in Alyck's jaw tightened and Thaddeus worried he might crack a tooth.

"Fine," Alyck growled. "But you will make a Death Deal."

"And I will be allowed to roam the castle," Thaddeus spoke up, taking advantage of Kolt's vulnerability. Unlike his father who believed a simple locked door could hold them, Kolt had the sense to place a spell over their chambers so neither of them could leave.

"No."

"Thaddeus regains his freedom," Alyck pressed.

Kolt angrily debated with himself. "Fine, but if he leaves Agrielha he dies."

"I accept," Thaddeus said quickly before Kolt could realize his mistake. By not specifying the castle, he was free to roam the city, too—provided he could find the means to get there. He did not imagine he would make the trip often, but the city would always have things he could not find in the castle… like Lazado agents.

"I do not know the spell for a Death Deal," Kolt said. "I will need some time."

"I know it," Thaddeus spoke up. "And I can perform it."

Kolt's eyes darted about, as if trying to find an escape. "You never told us you were a spellcaster."

From the look Alyck gave him, they were going to have a long discussion about this omission after dealing with Kolt.

"No one asked," Thaddeus told them. "Come here and grab each other's forearms."

Alyck and Kolt did so reluctantly, acting as if the other was disease-ridden.

"Before I begin, construct the contract you will be agreeing to."

"Alyck will serve me if I place a spell on Braxton to protect him from deadly attacks," Kolt said.

"No," Alyck growled, "that is not what you said."

"I will place a spell on him to protect him from deadly and debilitating attacks."

"No."

Kolt gulped; the boy was beginning to learn the power of words. "I will place a spell on him to protect him from all weapons."

"Acceptable," Alyck said. "In turn, I will serve you as the Blind Prophet. Thad, proceed."

Thaddeus gave a curt nod and began weaving the spell. Golden cords flickered into existence and wound themselves around both men's arms. "O moudise resy sa jonx ghæ æeyi rhæpn cabre æayi vilet soth evait naya rahm. Alyck Alagard woth sesuna wixne tyth ri ayþ forsae. Kolt Alagard woth herzo o dognath ce Braxton Alagard u proytyct æayni qalx zodonvs poegenox. Yiam woth quirse venot vilet cler jurvet ayþ agno azoles sa jonx. Dæ korbæne xye wedlonst resy." The lines along their arms faded into their skin. "It is done."

"I should start on that spell," Kolt said softly, face pale, as he backed toward the door.

Once the door had shut, Thaddeus turned to Alyck. "You know you have to help him now?"

"I always intended to. If I did not, many more people would die than needed. I may have a heart of stone, but I am not heart*less*." There was a moment of silence. "How did you keep your abilities hidden from me?"

"They only just returned," Thaddeus said, "and I do not make it obvious I have them. I still forget myself."

"We could have used your powers to do something, or be miles from here," Alyck snapped.

"You know as well as I there was nothing we could have done to stop Kolt. And that our place is here—whether we like it or not."

Chapter 3

Keegan had forgotten how strenuous riding could be and her lower back ached with every step Bastille took. It had been a blessing their first "day" of travel only lasted a few hours. But it had not prepared her body for the second day in the slightest.

Aron came to help her off Bastille, stumbling a little under her weight. She might've made a joke at her own expense had she not known he'd never needed to lift anything more than a bow until two months ago. Making sure no one was looking, she gave him a quick kiss on the cheek. Then couldn't help but smile coyly as she noticed the color spreading on his cheeks.

The others began setting up camp and while she insisted on helping, her guards refused—and with four against one, she was outvoted. Even when Kade sided with her saying it was only fair.

It only took a few minutes before she became bored. Out of habit, she closed her eyes and studied the variously colored paikas in her mind's eye. Each one was different and seemed to call to her like old friends—except the one pulsing alongside her heart, warning against arbitrary use. Before leaving Edreba, Atlia had warned her against practicing elements she hadn't mastered without a trained user nearby. But she couldn't see the harm in testing her abilities; it had never been a problem before.

In her mind, she picked up the blue gem and watched as flames began to swirl hypnotically within. A faint warmth came from it, but it was a hostile heat, a warning. This was the fire paika.

Taking a breath, Keegan crushed the jewel. When nothing happened, she remembered each magic required a different process to access its powers. After a moment of thought, she covered the paika with both hands, as if to keep it warm.

Heat spread across her body instantly as she gained access to the magic. She imagined a small ball of fire in her hand, and, when she opened her eyes, there it was. But something was wrong; there was a searing sensation. After a moment, she realized why her hand felt like it was burning—*it was*.

Yelping, she shook her hand, releasing the magic. The fire instantly dissipated. Her palm was red and raw and stung like hell. With her other hand, she pulled moisture from the air, creating a layer of water over the afflicted skin. It only partially soothed the pain.

She curled her fingers, confusion herding her thoughts. Magic—well, *her* magic—had never injured her before.

When you play with fire... she thought.

Swallowing her hurt, Keegan made her way to where the horses were tethered. By the looks of it, no one had noticed she'd been playing with fire. Rifling through her saddlebag, she found a cloth strip of bandage.

"What are you doing?" Aron asked, making her jump.

Spinning, Keegan shoved her hand into her pocket, refraining from cursing as her burnt palm scraped along the cloth edge. "Uhh... nothing," she stammered. "Just looking for something."

Aron raised an eyebrow. Stepping forward, he pulled her hand from her pocket. "How did you burn yourself?"

"How—how'd you know I burned myself?"

Aron rubbed the back of his neck guiltily. "Uhh…. walk with me."

"How did you know?" she repeated once they were well into the forest, safe from prying ears. A sense of panic sat tight in her chest, though she couldn't explain why.

Aron slowly collected his words, "Since… I actually do not know when it started, but… I… have this connection with you—like we are linked. Like there is this string of emotion, but it is more than that."

Her eyebrows furrowed.

"I have been… feeling what you do. I think. I felt you getting burnt. And back in Edreba I knew how you felt when I… when I ignored you."

She'd been doing well with not broadcasting her emotions—except for a few justified instances—so it… likely… wasn't her. "Strange."

"It is not all the time though," Aron added quickly. "I mostly notice it when it is a strong or sudden emotion."

"Keep this to yourself. The burn… and the other thing," Keegan said brusquely. Something told her, whatever this was, would lead to little good.

«««« »»»»

Jared watched the dancing tendrils of the campfire as the others made merry banter, despite the tension. Kade had developed a sudden hatred for Elhyas back in Edreba—and it had finally come to a head with Kade losing a sparring match that was also a bet. Kade had stormed off into the woods, Quin, one of their guards, following.

Groaning, Keegan stood up. "Well, I'm headed to bed. Anyone care to join?"

She meant nothing by it, but Zavier, who was about their age, was still unaccustomed to her teasing mannerisms, and started to stand, only stopping when Ezekhial placed a hand on his shoulder.

It wasn't long before Aron retired as well, making a big show of going to his own tent. Sooner or later Jared knew he'd find his way into Keegan's. With Kade as angry as he was tonight, Aron was going to have to be doubly careful not to get caught.

The bushes across the campsite rustled and parted to allow Quin back into camp, a bloodthirsty look in her eyes. Taking a seat by the fire, she pulled a whetstone from her pocket and a knife from her boot. The angry way in which she sharpened the blade suggested she might be preparing it to slice into Kade—if she hadn't already.

Carter was the next to bid them good night.

The only sounds came from the chorus of crickets and the crackling fire, interjected occasionally by the call of an owl. Jared rose, preparing to retire, when Quin looked up, a hint of scheming in her gray eyes that overtook her irises like a thunderhead.

"Take a walk with me," she said, putting away her dagger and whetstone.

Jared looked to the other men, uncertain. "Are you talking to me?"

"Yes," Quin said, an edge of steel in her voice as she snatched his hand.

He let her lead him into the forest, deciding she shouldn't be intending harm; he wasn't nearly the prize Keegan was. "Where are we going?"

"Wherever I want." Quin stopped and pushed him against a tree.

At first, he thought she meant foul and cursed his trusting nature, but quickly found while she did in a sense mean harm, it was a passionate kind.

Quin's lips pushed against his.

He thought they lacked passion, but he might be wrong—this was his first kiss after all. Jared wanted to do more than just stand there but couldn't move past the shock of the moment. And even if he did do something, what was it he *should* do?

As Quin continued to kiss him, she pushed harder, begging for a different response. Wrapping her arms around his neck, she pulled him away from the tree and reversed their positions. Jared was vaguely aware of his hands moving to her hips. She nipped at his bottom lip, and he felt a stirring in his loins.

Then, the moment passed, and Quin gently pushed him back. Through the gloom, he could tell she was giving him a shy, seductive smile—and could tell there was disappointment drifting in her eyes like a storm that hadn't managed to spill tears.

With a parting squeeze of the hand, she left him to think.

Leaning against the tree, Jared worked to take in everything, touching his lips as the sensation of her kisses lingered. But try as he might, he couldn't figure out what had been going through Quin's head.

Knowing it was impossible to understand a woman's mind—and not sure he wanted to—he headed back to camp. Quin sat laughing with the other guards, like she'd never left.

She gave him a small smile as he turned in for the night.

He was never going to understand women.

«««« »»»»

Bernot slowly placed his last shirt in the trunk and looked around his home. Sadness filled him; he was saying goodbye—maybe forever. He pushed the thought away; they would be triumphant. Clothes packed, he closed the trunk, the noise of the latch having a sense of... finality about it.

"Where do you think you are going?" Lyerlly asked from the doorway.

"To the border, to the battlefront, to war," he answered with a sigh. "Take your pick, they are all one and the same. I can only hope it is not to death."

She came forward, placing her hands on her hips. "Let me rephrase that, where do you think you are going without me?"

He smiled. Lyerlly was... intangible, always willing to be in the thick of it, regardless of the danger. "It will not be safe for you."

"Safe is relative. It is what we tell ourselves to *feel* safe. I will be no less protected at the border—with you—than I will here." She gave a coquettish smile. "In fact, I think I would be better protected at the border. What with the army and all."

He took his wife's face in his hands. "You and I both know that is not true. War is a bloody, bloody mess. Filled with terror and death." Even as he said the words, he knew in his heart he did not want to leave her behind.

Lyerlly placed her hands over his. "And I can fill it with less horror and loss. That is what doctors do."

"How will the hospital run without you?"

"I have already appointed Elia temporary head." She once again proved why he loved her so much; she thought of his objections before he did.

"And what will you do at the border?" he asked, realizing the decision had been made long before the conversation.

Lyerlly raised an eyebrow, knowing the game they were playing—and that she always won. "I will heal the wounded, I will make the sick better, I will be your council. I will be your wife."

"And if I were to order you to stay here?"

She huffed, barely hiding a smile. "Then I would have to do some ordering of my own! Neither of us can command the other."

He chuckled. "That has never stopped us from trying, has it?"

"Promise you will not stop me from coming with you."

He gently kissed her. "I promise. I just wish you would not have waited until the last minute to do this."

"I had my reasons. There were a few things I needed to take care of, be sure of. But I am glad to be going with you; I am not sure I could do this alone."

Bernot took a step back. "Do *what* alone?"

The ends of Lyerlly's lips pulled into a grin. "Childbirth."

His heart paused and he slowly sank onto the edge of the bed, too many emotions flooding over him. "Are… are you sure?" How long had they been trying to start a family? He could not say the timing was perfect by any means, but if… if this was the moment he started the path to fatherhood, he honestly did not care.

"Positive."

Bernot reached forward and pulled his wife into a hug, head resting on her stomach. Tears began to slide down his cheeks. They had finally been blessed by Sola.

Chapter 4

Harker swooped into the stable, talons screeching across the floor. Dismounting, Nico looked back through the opening to watch Braxton continue flying with Oxren. A stab of anger shot through him though it quickly subsided. He would never forgive Braxton for agreeing to serve Kolt... but he understood. The prince had been given a horrid dilemma in which there were no good choices.

Ima bounded over to them and playfully pushed Harker over. The male practically rolled onto his back in submittal, likely exhausted from flying.

"You are soft on them," Kolt said, stepping into the light.

Ima and Harker righted themselves instantly and took on agitated stances, feathers bristling on end.

"I assume Braxton warned you against escape," Kolt said, lazily studying his nails. When Nico didn't respond, he snarled, "Answer me."

"Yes, he warned me."

"Yes, he warned me, *your majesty*."

Braxton had forced him to make certain concessions, but Nico would only bow so far. "Yes, he warned me."

Deciding to pick another battle, Kolt continued, "Did he tell you *what* would happen?"

"Not specifically..." And Nico hadn't asked. The fact that just thinking about the consequences caused

Braxton to blanche was enough to warn him the consequences would be dire.

Kolt's lips pulled into a gruesome smile. "I will brand you."

Of everything Kolt could possibly do… Nico could think of worse. He was certain he'd endured worse.

"Not in the way you think. I threatened to brand you as the Vosjnik's earth elemental. While that still holds, there has been a slight change in plans."

A sinking feeling formed in Nico's gut.

"You will be given the title, but I will withhold the brand. Same deal as Braxton. And, of course, should you do what you are not supposed to… well, branding is an easy procedure."

Ima and Harker hissed from behind Nico at the naked threat.

Kolt laughed at the griffins' display. "It is not a death sentence. Yet."

Nico dared to look Kolt in the eye and hold his gaze, which only made the king laugh louder. Suddenly, Kolt screamed and was thrown to the ground. Harker's beak clamped down on Kolt's calf.

Nico's first instinct was to help. Once that passed, he stood back and watched. It was only when Harker took a sharp kick to the side of the head that he released, backing away into the shadows, wings half-unfurled. Blood splattered the hatchling's teal feathers and dripped ominously from his sharp beak.

Fury and agony painted Kolt's face as he struggled to his feet, his eyes darting between the griffin and Nico. "Control your beasts," he yelled, attacking the weaker target, pushing Nico to the ground. Then he hobbled over and raised a fist to strike again.

Low growls surrounded them and Harker and Ima half-came from the shadows on either side of Kolt. The adults might have been chained to the wall, but their ire was enough to unnerve the king.

A gust of wind buffeted him as Braxton and Oxren returned.

"What the nastor happened?" Braxton questioned, taking in the smears of blood and agitation of the griffins. There was a pause. "I was already aware of that," Braxton said, though to whom he was speaking, Nico didn't know. Red flooded Braxton's face as he turned on Kolt. "You swore not to make the boy one of the Vosjnik."

"No," Kolt argued, "I promised not to brand him."

"You dare renege on our deal?" Braxton fumed.

It seemed to suddenly occur to Kolt that he was drastically outnumbered. "I am doing the same to the boy as I am to you: he will not be branded but will bear the title."

Braxton relaxed a little.

Kolt fed off that. "Now, for your punishment."

"There will be none," Braxton challenged. "Nico cannot control the griffins any more than you. Harker and Ima are akin to children and responded in the only way that made sense to them."

Kolt snarled, "Then this will serve as a reminder to refrain from such behavior in future! Nico will receive five lashes by your hand no later than three days from now."

Ima let out a ghastly screech and lunged at Kolt. Braxton had the sense to grab the scruff of her neck and there was a sickening click as her beak snapped shut on air.

Kolt blanched, and turning quickly, limped from the stables, drops of blood trailing him.

Braxton struggled to hold Ima back, only releasing her once the door had closed, into which she crashed headfirst. Bouncing off the wood, she sat back on her haunches, a glazed look in her eyes as her head swayed.

As the hatchlings' anger subsided, Nico felt regret from Harker. He wanted to tell the griffin none of this was his fault, but…

"You will not be getting whipped," Braxton said, crouching in front of him. "Get everything here back in order while I deal with Kolt."

««« »»»

Nico was not to blame, Kolt was—but Braxton knew his brother would never admit it. That did not mean he could not try to make his brother see reason. He was amazed at how far Kolt got on his ravaged leg, drops and pools of blood making him easy to follow through the halls.

When Braxton caught up to him, Kolt was mumbling under his breath. Be it curses or something else, he could not tell.

"You cannot make me whip Nico," he started. "The boy did nothing wrong."

Kolt lashed out, punching him in the gut, but other than that, gave no response.

Had Kolt been in a better state, the blow might have landed where intended and Braxton would have been winded. But as Kolt was, the punch glanced his ribs. Still, it was enough to make him take a step back.

Wanting to avoid further discussion, Kolt continued limping through the halls, still muttering under his breath.

"You deserved what you got," Braxton dared to say plodding along behind him.

"Would you be quiet!" Kolt snapped. "I will deal with you in a moment."

Following, Braxton strained to hear what Kolt was muttering; by the sounds of it, a healing spell. Glancing at Kolt's leg, the gash looked remarkably better—at least what he could tell through the mangled and bloody mess of his pant leg.

When Kolt reached his destination, Braxton was surprised to find they were outside Caius's chambers. He had not imagined Kolt moving in, though supposed it made sense. It was the *king's* chambers after all.

The room was nothing like he remembered. The once meticulously clean and organized apartment had become chaos. Clothes were strewn across the floor as if they had been hastily removed—in Kolt's case, that was highly likely, as he was not known for his celibacy. The austere decorations had been traded for ones of rich fabrics and colors. There was enough seating for an entourage and the smell of heavy perfume and sweat hung cloyingly in the air. The only thing that remained the same was the portrait of their mother. To Braxton, her eyes seemed sad now.

"You will give the boy his punishment," Kolt said, shutting the door, fully standing on his leg without wincing. The only evidence of his injury was the rip in his trousers and the blood.

"No, the boy did nothing wrong."

"Do it, or he gets thirty lashes."

"Thirty?" Braxton exclaimed. "You are being absurd!"

Kolt picked up a book from his desk and weighed it like a decision. "Do not push your luck."

"At least let me take the punishment; I am the one who truly oversees the griffins," Braxton pleaded. "There is no reason for this except cruelty for cruelty's sake."

"Do not question me," Kolt roared, swinging the book.

The volume caught Braxton full force in the temple. His world blackened and when his vision dizzily returned, he was lying on the floor, head throbbing. He shut his eyes in an attempt to block out the convoluted world, but even in the darkness, colors swirled in a confusing blizzard. Opening his eyes again, he could just make out Kolt standing above him.

His brother spoke, but the words were garbled like his vision. Nor did it help that he faded in and out of consciousness.

Done berating him, Kolt walked away, and his vision fully faded to black.

There was the strange sensation of floating. Then, nothing. When he came to again, he was in his bed, the sky outside inky in color.

Nico sat at his desk, wringing his hands.

Braxton reached up to feel the side of his head and was surprised to find it was not tender. Nico must have called the doctor.

"I am sorry," Braxton croaked, catching Nico's attention. "I could not change his mind."

Looking out the window, Nico tensed. "We still have three days to change his mind."

The words came before he could check them, "I do not think we can."

To his credit, Nico did not cry.

《《《《 》》》》

The door to the anteroom opened and the boy slipped in. "I did it." Kolt was not proud of what he had done by the flat tone he used.

Alyck nodded slightly in response, a grin concealed in the corners of his mouth. "What was the spell you used?"

"Do you not trust me?" Kolt scoffed.

"No."

Huffing, Kolt recited his spell, "Kaythe dæ undegthi wixne proytyct aæyni. Naya zodonv poegenox fayo undegthis ri xao deyfn soth cabre aæyi huschk cler granklos cler tansred. Kaythe dæ undegthi wixne proytyct aæyni iruh ube bokel ube az malink kunyi."

Thaddeus immediately spotted the mistake—and it was not a little one. Kolt had used undegthi, meaning male—rather than undegths, meaning persons—which would only protect Braxton from attacks by *men*.

Alyck was on his feet in an instant, the chair toppling backwards. "You bovestun fool!"

Kolt was perturbed by the outburst. "What are you mad about?"

"He is protected from *males*," Alyck snarled. "The entire other half of the world can still harm him."

Kolt looked confused. "That should not be. I tested it myself and the spell holds."

"What does undegthi mean?" Alyck barked.

"Man."

"No, it means male. Halnson means man and you should have used undegths meaning persons."

"The spell still works."

"By specifying male, any *female* can still harm him, you fool. It half works!"

The king paused, clearly not enjoying being called a fool. "I upheld my end of the bargain." Kolt shrugged unwilling to admit he was wrong. "It is your turn."

"Not until you amend your mistake."

Kolt thought for a moment. "When Thaddeus wove the Death Deal, he said I had to 'place a spell on Braxton to protect him from weapons wielded'. He never said *who* to protect him from weapons wielded by."

Alyck began to argue but Thaddeus cut him off. "He did as he promised, even if only technically."

"Fine. Two can play that game," Alyck sneered. "You want to know the future? Then know this: before the winter snows have melted, another will take the throne."

««« »»»

The camp wasn't what Jared expected; there was hardly more than two hundred men. A flag bearing the Lazado standard—a bleached ram's skull with flowers winding around the horns on a brown background—marked the center.

At the edge of camp, Ezekhial said a few quiet words to the sentries before dismounting and leading them to the command tent. Two soldiers were stationed outside, and one quietly pulled the flap open for them. Inside was stuffy, lit by small torches.

In the center was a large table with a raised-relief map. Jared assumed the colored blocks represented the troops from the different races. From what he could tell, the other races would be a long time coming—which meant *they* weren't going anywhere anytime soon. Jared could tell the man studying the map had once been a great fighter, though judging by age, complacency had corrupted him.

Elhyas gave a subtle cough.

"I see you 'ave managed t' not kill this lot," the man said, without looking up.

Keegan furrowed her brows. "You talkin' to us or them?" Jared surmised the "them" was their guards.

A low chuckle spilled from the man's lips. "The lot o' ya. You in particular though, Keegan; I know ya can be a right pain in the arse and do not like t' listen."

"I see my reputation precedes me."

"Same rules as Edreba; 'ave at least one guard with ya at all times. Until the rest o' your tutors arrive, you only need t' deal with Raelin and me."

"What are you teaching her?" Kade questioned. "And who even are you?"

Ravliean

The man patted the sword belted around his waist in answer to Kade's first question. "Hernando Barnsed," he introduced himself, "the next best thing after Bernot. Mornings with me, Keegan, afternoons with Raelin. You will each have your own tents, 'cept for Jared and Carter. Figured there wouldn't be an issue with you sharing with your brothers."

A stunted silence fell over them. By the plural, Jared assumed Lucas had somehow made it to the Lazado; but he dared not voice the wish. It seemed every time he hoped a little too much, catastrophe struck.

Hernando returned his full attention to the map. "Go see 'im. Men outside can point you in the right direction."

Before Hernando finished speaking, Carter was barreling over the rest of them. Once pointed in the right direction, he ran the short distance and burst into the tent. There was a startled yelp, then nothing more.

"Think that was the right one?" Keegan asked casually as they followed.

"I think we'd hear more cursing if it wasn't," Jared countered. He paused outside the tent. There was so much to explain—from both sides—and he knew Lucas would want to go after Nico.

Keegan placed a reassuring hand on his shoulder, sensing his apprehension.

Taking a deep breath and swallowing his fears, Jared pushed inside.

He found Lucas sitting on a cot, a hand over his eye. "You're not going to punch me, too, are you?"

"Not today." Jared grinned, going to hug his brother. "Maybe tomorrow."

Lucas gave a hearty laugh, which soured when he noticed Keegan.

"I see I'm not wanted," she tutted, slipping away.

"Who are you?" Lucas snapped.

Jared turned to see Zavier hovering.

"Zavier Tribianto," the guard answered. "Sorry, but one guard at all times."

"Since when did you become important?" Lucas jibbed to Jared.

"Since we learned he's a Child of Prophecy," Zavier said. "I can stand outside if you want, but cloth doesn't do much in the way of privacy."

"Still gives the sense of privacy," Carter refuted.

There was a tense moment of silence as they waited for Zavier to retreat before Jared pulled Lucas into another hug. "I'm glad you're here."

"Where's Nico?" Lucas asked Jared curtly, never one to beat around the barn.

Jared blinked slowly. He had completely forgotten that Lucas didn't know what had happened to their youngest brother.

"The Vosjnik took him," Carter said quietly.

The blood drained from Lucas's face.

"We have to win this war," Jared said. "That's the only way to get him back."

"If he's alive," Lucas muttered macabrely.

"Don't say that," Carter snapped. "Nico's alive. He's stronger than all of us."

"And he has his uses," Jared said quietly. Both as an elemental and leverage against him. It might not be much in the way of keeping Nico alive, but anything was better than nothing.

Lucas was silent for a moment. "You said the Vosjnik took him?"

"Yes, when they… attacked Keegan and I."

Lucas cursed. "If he's alive, he's in Agrielha. Reven and I just came from there."

"Wait, why were you in Agrielha? And how do you know Reven?"

"How do *you* know Reven?" Lucas parroted.

"He's a friend of Kade's. We met him in Suttan," Jared clarified.

"Who's Kade?"

"Long story and you can meet him later. Tell me about Reven."

"He was the one who convinced me to run off and kill the king."

Carter laughed. "You? Kill the king? You're joking, right?"

"No, I actually killed the king."

Dangerous ideas began to form in Jared's mind. "Have you told Hernando?"

"No," Lucas answered.

"Good. Don't."

《《《《 》》》》

Braxton watched as the sun continued to draw nearer to the horizon and knew it was now or never. Only a handful people compared to the crowds that usually gathered for public whippings had bothered to make an appearance—mostly the cruel and sadistic and those they forced along with them. Nico was tied to a post before him, his shirt having been cut away only moments before. Braxton felt his heart beating furiously while guilt hovered over him.

"Your time is almost up," Kolt goaded from the edge of the crowd, arms crossed loosely over his chest. His crown was a ring of red atop his blond hair.

Braxton tightened his grip and, taking a final breath to calm his nerves, let the whip lash across Nico's back. The boy gave no cry—not to his surprise.

It had not been his idea, but Nico's, and he had nothing but praise for the boy's ingenuity. Nico had noted that while Braxton had been ordered to inflict punishment, he had not been ordered to feel pain. Then it had been a matter of finding a spellcaster who would help—a problem they had not been expecting to overcome. Thaddeus, likely at Alyck's insistence, had sought them out, divulging his secret and volunteering his services.

Braxton let the lash fall across Nico's back four more times. The punishment complete, he dropped the whip like a hot coal and finally dared to look at his brother.

Kolt's face was taut with fury. "What did you do?" he hissed through clenched teeth.

Clearly, this whole thing was not only supposed to serve as a reminder that Braxton existed at his whim but to show his subjects their new king did not tolerate even the smallest infraction. This was going to end worse than Braxton had prepared for.

"Outsmarted you." He would pay for the comment, but it was worth it.

A few people—the smarter ones—began slipping away. Once no longer contained in the crowd, their steps quickened until they reached the castle.

"How is he not screaming in pain?" Kolt seethed.

"Because he feels no pain."

A mix of emotions ran across Kolt's features. Slowly, the king bent and picked up the whip, weighed it in his hands like one might a slab of meat at market. There was a crack and Braxton felt a line of force across his body. But the whip never touched his skin, never drew blood.

There was a collective murmur from those remaining in the yard. If he were not the one under scrutiny, Braxton would have partaken in the murmurs of confusion and amazement as well.

Kolt cracked the whip again with the same result. Scanning the crowd, he spotted one of the few women present, and yelled, "You."

The woman shook her head fearfully, understanding what she was being ordered to do.

Kolt held the whip toward her, snarling, "Do it."

Not daring to disobey, she stepped forward, accepting the weapon like a curse.

"Do it!" Kolt screamed, impatiently.

Panic contorted the woman's face, and Braxton gave her a small nod of reassurance.

There was a crack before he felt the sting across his neck and shoulder. The pain was nothing like he had ever felt before and stole his breath like a winter wind.

"Again," Kolt ordered.

The whip snapped and Braxton felt pain across the front of his torso.

He fell to his knees, excruciating, burning agony radiating from his wounds. Looking into his brother's eyes, all he saw was murderous intent. This could easily be how he died.

The woman did not move and when Kolt did not order her to strike again, slowly lowered her arm.

The world was deathly still, as if afraid any noise would turn Kolt's wrath into a bloody rage. When the king came and squatted before him, the woman dropped the whip and ran into the castle as fast as her legs would allow.

In a whisper that raised the hair on his arms, his brother said, "Do something like that again and you will wish the next punishment were a lashing." As Kolt stalked away, the remaining crowd parted around him.

Untied from the post, Nico offered him a hand up. Blood drenched the boy's back and Braxton was glad he could not feel the pain—at least not yet.

"We should get to the infirmary before the moon rises and I'm crying in a pool of my own blood," Nico said.

Braxton wanted to make a crude joke about the boy sounding like a woman but was not sure he was old enough to have had *that* talk with his parents—and he did not want the honor. He groaned as he got to his feet, feeling blood trickling down his stomach. He did not dare look at the wounds.

They had only just reached the infirmary when the moon's silky head began to peak over the horizon. Nico's face instantly drained of color, and he leaned heavily against Braxton as if his legs had become jelly. His own lashes protested, and Braxton was not sure how long he could support the boy.

"Vitt," Braxton muttered, stumbling into the wall. "Rohan!"

"Surprised you made it this far," the doctor said, materializing from an off-shooting chamber. He wrapped Nico's arm around his shoulder and all but carried him to the preemptively prepared table. Then he took a wet rag to Nico's back, causing the boy to hiss each time it touched his skin.

"Royik, this hurts!"

"I know," Braxton replied. "And watch your language. You are too young for that."

Nico just howled in pain as expert hands continued dabbing at his lacerations.

"What happened to you?" Rohan questioned, noticing the red staining Braxton's shirt and neck.

"Kolt did not like that we outsmarted him," he answered.

Rohan dipped the rag in a bowl of water beside the table, tinting it a deeper shade of red. "Brave and stupid at the same time. One for the books."

Braxton sat patiently while Rohan tended to Nico. There was a breeze coming from the open window and as air brushed against his wounds, they stung as if salt had been applied. By the time Rohan was done with the boy, fatigue had closed Nico's eyes.

Turning his ministrations to Braxton, Rohan used a pair of scissors to cut his shirt off.

Blood coated the fabric, making it stick to his skin. Together he and the doctor worked to carefully pull it from his body. In places his wounds reopened, oozing more blood that dribbled down his chest.

"Doesn't look too bad," Rohan said, beginning to mop up the blood.

"Still hurts like a yana."

"Be glad this is what you got away with."

Rather than use his own reserves, Rohan pulled the energy necessary for healing from Braxton. Slowly the gashes scabbed over but that was as far as the doctor dared go without facing Kolt's ire himself.

"Put a salve on the scabs as often as you can," Rohan instructed. "And both of you are on light duty. Too much movement will cause those to reopen. If Kolt orders otherwise, tell him to see me."

Braxton roused Nico and together they made their way back to their room. Without shirts, they both felt exposed, but speaking for himself, Braxton was not sure he could handle wearing one presently. His entire chest felt like it contained the heat of the sun and the lines that gouged his body were sensitive to everything.

Nico gingerly climbed into bed and promptly returned to sleep's grasp.

Braxton ruffled the boy's hair, quietly saying, "We will persist."

Chapter 5

Nico's back was painful and stiff, but Rohan had healed it enough that he could greet the Vosjnik with Braxton—not that he had any desire to.

The doors to the throne room slammed open to reveal a haggard, travel-weary group. A few people sported bloodstains here or there, but for the most part, tiredness was their biggest concern.

"I'd rather be two members short than have you," Vitia opened.

"We would prefer that too," Braxton said calmly. "But sadly, that is not an option."

"Besides, what use do I have for two earth elementals?" Vitia huffed.

"I will be acting as the archer."

Nico immediately focused on the young girl in the group—mostly because he didn't know her. And because she seemed so out of place. Her eyes hardly left the ground and there was no air of arrogance about her—this was someone simply trying to survive. Someone who had survived.

"Everyone, get some sleep, see Rohan if needed," Braxton said.

"What do you think you're doing?" Vitia barked.

"Taking command."

"*I* am Commander," Vitia hissed.

"Not anymore."

Quick as a hare, Vitia marched up to Braxton, grabbed him by the neck, and slammed him into the wall.

"I don't think so." She whispered something into Braxton's ear, turning him pale. With a malicious smile, the Alvor pulled away and addressed the tired members of the Vosjnik, "Clean your sorry arses up. Be on the training field at sunrise."

"Come to the gr—" Braxton started, but an invisible force hit him, and he hunched over coughing.

Nico stepped in his direction to help, but Braxton gave him a subtle shake of the head.

"We need to—" Braxton tried again as another blow had him falling to his knees. "We—" Lines of red began dripping from his mouth.

"Remember your place," Vitia said coolly, walking from the room.

The rest of the Vosjnik followed—all except the girl. She timidly approached Braxton, gently placing a hand in the crook of his arm to help him to his feet. "You should know better."

Braxton wiped the blood from his lips, breathing heavily. "I was trying to tell her we have been ordered to ride the griffins into battle—which entails training with them."

"You should've started with that instead of trying to supersede her."

"I had to try," Braxton groaned, feeling his stomach. His fingers came away red though he didn't seem overly concerned by it.

Mara noticed the blood coating his hands, "Are you… okay? Do I need to get Rohan?"

"I am fine. Less so than normal, but I will live." He sighed. "Kolt will have to give her the news." Then shrugged and walked from the throne room.

Nico chased after him. "What did Vitia threaten you with?"

"Nothing you need concern yourself with. Take Mara to see the griffins; I think she will be a good fit for Ima."

Nico wasn't sure how he felt about Mara, but if Braxton trusted her, she had to be a *halfway* decent person. And from what he'd just seen, he didn't believe she could be all bad. Returning to the throne room, he found Mara eyeing the chamber like it was some intricate marvel.

When she noticed him, she quickly diverted her gaze back to the floor.

"Uh…" he mumbled, "Braxton says you can meet them."

She cautiously glanced up. "Who?" Her blue eyes were beautiful and somehow… scarred.

"The… the griffins," he stuttered.

When she didn't answer, he took her silence as indecision and walked away. If she followed, they'd go see the griffins, if not—well, he still planned to go see them.

Mara's footsteps were light as they trailed behind him, indicative of someone who'd learned to tread carefully; something he was still working on.

"Your brother, Jared, is alive."

He stopped dead. "How do you know I have a brother? How do you know he's alive?"

By the way she wavered, weighing how to answer, he assumed the interaction had not been pleasant. And she could easily be playing him, he realized. "You're in the Vosjnik for a reason, I don't think it's kindness."

"I'm a telepath, and unfortunately, I'm strong." There was shame in the statement. "I never wanted this."

He wanted to believe her, but trust hadn't been built yet. If she was being honest, they could get there. "How old are you?" he asked, starting forward again.

Mara tucked a strand of her flame-colored hair behind her ears. "Fifteen. You?"

"Fourteen."

"I'm sorry," she muttered.

There was so much genuine pity and remorse in the words Nico wasn't unsure how to respond. So, he didn't. And he wasn't sure what to do—no one had shown him pity since his mother died.

There was something about Mara, something he couldn't express in words—but he knew she saw everything with those sharp blue eyes. There would be little he could hide from her—especially if she invaded his mind. He was going to have to get better about keeping up his telepathy lessons.

"Try to not make any sudden movements," he warned as they reached the stables.

Inside, the adults lifted their heads to scrutinize Mara. Harker and Ima came bounding from one of the stalls and all but tackled Nico. Once they realized he wasn't alone, they ducked into Crowlin's stall to hide behind her legs like frightened children.

Ima was the first to step forward from Crowlin's protection, curiosity overpowering her sense of fear.

This one has suffered but not lost her kindness, Crowlin told him.

Her words were another point in Mara's favor, but she still had a long way to go.

Mara squatted, holding her hand out toward the hatchling. It took Ima a long time to decide how she felt. Slowly, the griffin shifted so Mara's hand laid on her head.

Nico stated the obvious, "She likes you." He cringed at the words, realizing that's how he'd describe a dog's reaction to a stranger.

Ima nestled into Mara and let the girl wrap her arms around her. Mara buried her face into the hatchling's shoulder and after a moment Nico realized she was crying.

He stood frozen. What was he supposed to do? No one had prepared him for this! From the look Harker was giving him, he was equally flummoxed.

There is nothing for you to do, Crowlin said softly, *but offer an ear, a hand, and a shoulder when needed. And you will both need it in the coming times.*

«««« »»»»

Walking into the command tent, Bernot found Hernando staring at the war map.

His second glanced up, a tight look on his face. "This 's not going t' be an easy war."

Bernot came to study the map as well. "Tell me something new. I intend to make this a fall war. If we push, it can be done."

Hernando gave him a calculated, albeit skeptical look. "At what expenditure o' life?"

"Minimal," Bernot said, his mind seeing the many possibilities.

"What are you thinking 's the best way t' get t' the capital?"

He moved one of their white ram's head figurines. "First, we need to secure Grenadone."

"Why? Place 'as been abandoned since, what, the last war?"

"Because it still stands. *Should* this fail to be a short war, our army can be housed there. And we have to take one of the line cities; why not the one no one occupies? Save a few lives and quite a bit of time."

Hernando did not respond, though Bernot got the feeling he was making a silent prayer to the old gods. If Sola and Lunos were listening, he hoped they answered.

"Tell me, what has happened since we made camp?"

"Nothing too much out o' the ordinary," Hernando began. "A few skirmishes, the dragons are still their usual reclusive selves, a few refugees came in, too." He was silent for a moment, as if going through a mental list. "Oh, the third Sieme brother showed up with some kid named Broyker."

That got Bernot's attention. "Broyker? Are you sure? It could easily have been Brooker. I know your hearing is not what it used to be."

Hernando shrugged. "That 's what the kid said. See no reason for 'im to lie." The man did not add, "Or me."

Changing the subject, he asked, "How is Keegan's fire training going?"

"Nonexistent; Raelin was on a scouting mission. Just got back last night. I 'ave been working on the art o' the sword with her—she 's surprisingly adept."

Bernot gave a light chuckle. "The fact that she always surprises seems to be the consensus. And it helps that her brothers were her first teachers for a time." There was a pregnant pause. "Can I trust you to keep things running for a bit longer?"

Hernando laughed. "What 's a few more minutes going to hurt?"

Stepping outside, Bernot glanced toward the tent he and Lyerlly would occupy and saw his wife working tirelessly to move their belongings inside. He turned to the two men guarding the command tent and ordered them to help.

"I do not need help," Lyerlly insisted when the men began taking bags straight from her hands despite her protests. When her words did nothing to stop the men, she turned to look at Bernot, scowl on her face, hands akimbo.

He just smiled, saying telepathically to her, *No, but it is nice to have it regardless.*

Her expression softened and she began directing the soldiers who looked relieved to have something to do.

Satisfied Lyerlly would not overexert herself, Bernot took a stroll through camp. As he walked, he observed the state of the men. He heard no grumbling, which was an excellent sign. The more willing these men were to fight, the more likely they were to win—and survive. The only thing concerning him was that they were still few in numbers; but that would change.

Most of the Lazado and Alvor forces were close on their heels, while the Merfolk had begun trekking across the eastern skirts of the Alvor realm. And the Torrpeki were tramping through their mountains and could be expected before the next turn of the moon. He hoped. Moving armies through mountains had stymied many a timeline in the past. As far as the Buluo went, he would be glad if they joined them at all; they were nomadic tribes and getting them to do anything as a nation was near impossible.

Finding the tent he was looking for, Bernot entered unannounced.

A young man lounged on a cot but seeing him, sat up. "Finally. Took you long enough."

"You clearly know who I am," Bernot said, pretending to be at a disadvantage. He knew exactly who this was even without a name; Reven was the spitting image of Thaddeus and Rosh.

"Reven Broyker," Reven said, shaking his hand.

"How did you end up here of all places? Last I heard you and Thaddeus were quite happy running that bookshop in Suttan."

Reven's face darkened.

Bernot could only imagine what tragedy had befallen them—likely in the wake of Keegan. "Here may not be the best place to talk. Come."

Back at the command tent, he placed a spell to prevent eavesdropping. He easily could have placed a spell on the boy's tent, but he had the feeling he was going to calling on several more people throughout the day; better to make them come to a respected place than a random tent. Then he listened to Reven's tale.

When it was done, he ordered the soldiers outside, "Get Lucas Sieme."

«««« »»»»

Keegan cleared her mind and focused, bringing the fire paika into view. Its blue glow was like the ocean's siren call that intended to drown her in a riptide, then bash her against a cliff... except, with fire. She lent warmth to the paika, and power came forth, willing to be coaxed to do her bidding.

Hold it, Raelin commanded, patience engrained in every syllable.

But the burning sensation was overwhelming almost instantly, and she let the flame dissipate, giving a yelp. Dropping to her knees, she cradled her hand, the skin on her palm blistered and red.

Condensing water from the air, she wrapped it around the affected area. The pain dulled but the stinging bite persisted, throbbing at the same tempo as her pulse. Taking a deep breath, she sat properly on the ground, cross-legged. "Why is it burning?" she questioned, reaching for her life magic to attempt healing. She still struggled to heal herself... even after all the practice it felt like she'd gotten recently.

Raelin was careful in his response, *I am not sure. You should have control over the fire you create. Like every other fire elemental. There is no case I can recall of a wielder having this… problem.*

"Jesus girl," Nikita called.

She clenched her jaw, taking a sharp breath through her nose. "Keegan. My name is Keegan," she said staccato. "It's two, fucking, syllables."

"Jesus girl," Nikita said, ignoring her complaint flippantly, "make flame again."

She parodied, "You make fire again!"

Keegan… Raelin said, *if he has a helpful idea, humor him.*

Scowling and muttering under her breath about what she thought of humoring the Russian, she made a fireball and shot it at Nikita.

The Pexatose let it explode against his chest without so much as blinking. It was lucky he was fire retardant. "Make fire, Jesus girl!"

Glowering, she did as asked. A small fire popped into existence in her palm, and she held it for a mere second. Her already singed skin couldn't take much more. Nor could her patience.

"I see problem," Nikita said. "You fire intolerant. Opposite of me."

"What?"

"You… vhat, vhat the vord? Ah," he said excitedly, "allergic! You allergic to fire. Fire no good for you."

"Fire isn't good for anyone," she said sarcastically.

Nikita ignored her comment. "Vhen you make fire, it touch skin. Vhen… other human make fire, no touch skin."

Keegan thought for a moment, working out the ramifications of Nikita's discovery. "It's less like an allergy and more like an autoimmune disease." She could sense the confusion radiating from Raelin. "An autoimmune disease is where your immune system—that thing that keeps you from getting sick—doesn't realize that your cells aren't a foreign body and attacks them. So, the fire is acting like I'm the *target*, rather than the source."

Nikita muttered something in Russian and broken English. The only thing she caught was Jesus girl and allergies.

If it will only burn you, then there is no point in training you. I do not see the use in hurting yourself for something that will never work.

Keegan breathed a sigh of relief that Raelin wasn't one to beat a dead horse. But she was inclined to prove the universe wrong too. "Hold on, there might be an abstract way to use fire."

Raelin studied her with his dark yellow eyes, a scaled eyebrow raised.

"We don't know exactly how long it takes before the fire starts to burn me. If we figure that out, then we know how long a window I have. Also, can I control fire from other sources without getting burnt? Could I make a shield around myself with other elements to protect myself? Would lightning be something I can use, 'cause I kinda see a connection between fire and lightning." She had plenty more questions and theories, but the blank stares from Raelin and Nikita halted her train of thought.

"Chertova Jesus girl, chertova *smart* Jesus girl," Nikita mumbled.

Keegan couldn't help but smile.

Questions for another day, Raelin said. He clearly wasn't sure of the implications of her questions—and certainly not their answers—but they were going to explore them.

《《《《 》》》》

Quin's sword clanged against Jared's, nearly knocking it from his hands. They'd been sparring since midday and not *once* had he beaten her—or ever actually. Quin was an impressive swordswoman—better than most of the men practicing alongside them. Better than even Kade potentially. Watching Quin and Kade spar was… extraordinary. They were so evenly matched and capable of trickery that it was easier to predict rain than who would be victorious.

Jared swung and Quin dodged. Before he could make another move, she had her blade against his chest. He was honestly surprised the point hadn't worn a hole in his shirt for how many times it had rested in that exact spot that day alone.

"Why can't I beat you?" He knew he wouldn't become a master anytime soon… but still. He held his own against Kade, so what made Quin different? The thought that Kade might be taking it easy on him crossed his mind. It was possible, but Jared had never known Kade to pull a punch—or sword for that matter. Except for once on their way to the Lazado with Keegan.

Quin let her weapon fall with a laugh and pulled close to him, their bodies almost touching. "You think too much. About everything. Nothing should be in that head of yours. Not worries or cares, not your next move, not who your next sugore will be. Live in the moment and react."

Jared resisted the urge to back away. "Easier said than done. And I haven't…"

Her hand grazed his hip. "That's an easy fix."

Since the night in the forest, she hadn't pulled him into seclusion again but was always hinting that's what she wanted—and that she expected more than kisses next time. Part of him wanted to give that to her, but another part was… afraid?

Ravliean

Without warning, Quin pushed away and brought her sword up. Jared only just managed to block.

They settled into a routine, and it was easy to be in the moment—though it was the wrong one. Quin was beautiful, but he shouldn't be focusing on that. Not with a sword being swung at him. Even if it was blunted.

He snapped back to attention and realized there was nothing he could do to avoid Quin's attack. The sword ran painfully across his stomach, and he stumbled back, clutching his gut—and thanking the old gods it was just a sparring sword. A bruise for his foolishness was a fair price to pay.

"Vitt," Quin barked, "you're supposed to block!"

He just lay on the ground and groaned.

Once sure he was fine, Quin said. "It's a good thing you're pretty. But that isn't going to keep you alive in battle."

Chapter 6

From the corner of his eye, Kade watched Quin spar... Jared inevitably losing. Again. He was then forced to watch them flirt. If one could hurt themselves while rolling their eyes, he was about to do it.

"Focus," Elhyas chastised, "you can fantasize about Quin later."

Kade growled, "*Me*, fantasize about *her*? She wishes!"

"That ego of yours is going to be your downfall."

"No, it won't."

Elhyas laughed. "By the old gods, it's sheer luck you kept yourself alive in the Vosjnik."

"It wasn't luck."

"Oh really? You, more or less, had the position handed to you. I call it luck no one stronger came along. Or that someone didn't get tired of your attitude."

"It's not luck. I was... *am* the best."

"If you have to call yourself the best—"

"Then you're not the best," Kade finished angrily. Elhyas had said that more times than he cared to count.

"How was it you killed Noriss then, if not luck?"

Kade wasn't sure what Elhyas knew, but there was no hiding the fact he didn't believe he'd truly earned the position in the Vosjnik. He kept quiet, feeling that if he tried to justify himself, he'd only end up looking more the fool.

Elhyas slammed his shoulder into Kade. "I want an answer."

Barely holding his ground, Kade snarled, "He was drunk."

The guard swung at him. "Full story! You and I both know there's more to it." The strikes were ferocious; Elhyas had been holding back—not just today, but always.

"I was told by Caius," Kade started, pushing back, "I needed to kill Noriss if I wanted to be a part of the Vosjnik. So, I gathered information, but he was untouchable; he was never alone, never took the same path to his chambers, was cautious."

Elhyas parried lithely. "Then how'd you kill him?"

"Someone else was trying to kill him, too. They slipped him an ether and migun infused drink." Ether alone stole an elemental's powers temporarily. But mixed with migun, it became a mild hallucinogenic and sedative. Kade danced around Elhyas, taking advantage of the man's age and almost imperceptible loss of nimbleness. "When I followed Noriss, he assumed I was the one who'd drugged him and pulled a dagger. I drew my sword and slew him; wasn't much of a fight."

"Liar!"

"How would you know?" Kade swung his sword, the point raking across Elhyas's shirt, tearing a fresh seam.

Blocking his backhanded strike, Elhyas kicked Kade's legs from under him.

His head hit the ground, sending colored clouds scattering across his vision. By the time he remembered he was sparring, it was too late, and a sword was at his throat.

"You didn't slay Noriss; he fell on his own knife."

His heart froze. "How could you possibly know that?"

Elhyas pulled away. "Because I was there. *I* drugged Norris. He was my brother-in-law. Treated my sister kindly enough until she gave birth to a non-elemental. Soon after, he gave her a venereal disease that left her infertile and slowly dying. Noriss had no remorse and took every opportunity to beat her and the child. Slipping him the migun and ether was easy; he was a heavy drinker.

"I'll give you credit for recognizing an opportunity, but you take too much praise for the works of others. You are not the best, the strongest, or the brightest. You are *lucky*. You need to realize that and realize everyone here has worked for what they have."

"Keegan hasn't worked for anything," Kade spat. "Everyone hands her whatever she wants."

Elhyas stabbed his sword into the earth and leaned against it. "Your sister may not physically work for most things, but she uses that brain of hers. You're told no and continue to attack the problem in the same manner. Keegan is told no and thinks of a way to go around the set parameters. We give her what she wants because at least that way we know she's safe." His next words stung. "You're no better than anyone else, Kade."

He pushed himself up and grabbed his sword, ready for another round of sparring with all the anger boiling his blood.

"We're done for today," Elhyas said. "And you owe me a new shirt."

He had one chance to prove he wasn't what Elhyas said. "What happened to your sister's child?"

"You met Auckii."

Kade recalled the deaf boy Elhyas had introduced him to a few nights ago. The boy had seemed stunted, haunted somehow—yet had been lively beyond compare. That was why Elhyas had done it; love certainly was a powerful thing.

《《《《 》》》》

The sound of the hammer on the anvil was harsh, making Lucas cringe. It was his first day back in the forge and already he was finding it taxing—mostly on his hearing. By pure happenstance he'd come across Waylan in the mess tent. He hadn't needed to ask for his job back—though he had suffered through a long, loud, and public lecture first.

Lucas pounded away at the sword on his anvil. Back in Tratoleck, he would've been at the part of his apprenticeship that Waylan would be teaching him the finer points of the trade. But soldiers didn't need fancy swords with decorative hilts inlaid with gold and gems. And provided Lunos didn't have his name in mind, there'd be plenty of time for that later.

Satisfied with his work, Lucas quenched the blade and set to sharpening it. After a few minutes, he realized the forge was silent. Well, aside from the sound of the whet stone. Not seeing Waylan, he poked his head outside and found a soldier talking to the smith. From the way Waylan stood, arms crossed over his broad chest, he wasn't happy.

"Quit spying and have the balls to join the conversation," Waylan barked.

Feeling like a scolded child, Lucas did as instructed.

"I will not," Waylan said, resuming his conversation with the soldier.

"But—" the man remonstrated, red beginning to flush his face.

"But nothing. I'm a smith, not a tutor."

"Who do they want you to tutor?" Lucas questioned.

"Some Child of Prophecy."

"Keegan?" he guessed. "They want you to teach her blacksmithing?"

"No, metal magic." Given the smith never used his powers, it was easy to forget he had them.

"Why did they send you to ask this?" Lucas asked the soldier.

The man looked at him at a loss. "I... I'm not..."

"'Cause they know I'd cut my nose off to spite my face in regard to Bernot."

"What have you got against Bernot?"

"Now ain't the time for that story."

"This isn't for Bernot," the soldier said. "This is for all of us. For the Child of Prophecy."

"Why would she need my help anyway?" Waylan questioned. "From what I understand, she does just fine on her own. Besides, you can only have one element; last I heard she was working on fire with the dragons."

"She wields all five," Lucas told him. "Though I've only seen her do earth."

The smith gave a bewildered look. "What?" There was an awkward silence. "You mean to tell me the stories are true?"

Lucas shrugged. "Yeah."

The blacksmith silently weighed his options. "I want to meet her. Then I'll decide."

"Why not just agree?" the soldier whined.

"Ask me again and I'll say no just to spite you. I'll send for her in the next few days." Waylan walked away before the soldier could get another word in.

Back in the forge, sweat instantly beaded across Lucas's skin. A crash caused him to cringe. Looking toward Waylan, he saw the smith had kicked over a bin of scrap metal.

"Not a word," Waylan snapped, pointing a finger in his direction. "And get back to work. We need to be ahead of tomorrow's work since I have to pretend to give the *goddamn fucking* Child of Prophecy a chance."

"You might be surprised. Keegan has this tendency…" The look Waylan gave stopped him mid-sentence.

He'd seen Waylan donpox before but was more inclined to call this rage. Whatever he had against Bernot—whoever that was—was monumental.

Lucas continued working in silence, with Waylan muttering insults and curses not so quietly under his breath until another soldier interrupted. "Bernot needs to talk with you."

"Who you talking to?" Waylan snapped, without stopping his hammering.

"Lucas."

"We're busy."

"This isn't optional."

Waylan stopped. "*Does it look like I give a damn?*"

"I was told you can be obstinate. Lucas, be at the command tent in half an hour." The soldier exited, leaving Waylan glaring after him.

"Do I go?" Lucas questioned cautiously.

"Yes," Waylan growled, banging away at a sword with what might've been all his fury. "We live by Bernot's whims; that's the deal when you join the Lazado."

«««« »»»»

As Keegan marched through camp, she scanned the alleyways created by the tents. She was about to continue on when she found who she was looking for; thank God for Kade's auburn hair. And where there was Kade, she was likely to find Reven.

Getting closer, she was able to overhear their conversation. Tucking herself into a shadow, she listened in. Keegan didn't care to eavesdrop, but it was that or spend several hours trying to track Reven down again later. And she did not have the time or freedom for that.

"You know me," Reven chuckled, "not a whole lot that can hurt me."

Kade began listing things that had harmed Reven over the years, "Your own mind, my fist, my foot, Dunkirk's sword—"

"All right, all right, I 'm not as infallible as I like t' believe."

"Still royiken tough though," Kade laughed. "So, where's Thaddeus?"

Even though she couldn't see him, Keegan could feel the gloom and anger that settled over Reven.

"Likely dead."

Kade's voice was strained. "What happened?"

"Taite betrayed us."

"Seems we weren't the only ones."

Reven then went into the finer points of Taite's betrayal. The picture he painted made Keegan furious and she hoped that wherever the Kojote was it was hell.

"…He was captured just outside Suttan," Reven concluded.

"And you didn't go back to help?"

"I would 'ave but he put a barrier up."

"His magic came back?"

"Seems so."

"Then I'm sure he's fine. He's probably hunkered down somewhere. We'll find him. Alive," Kade promised.

It wasn't the most opportune time to interrupt, but knowing Reven, it was better than letting him go down a dark rabbit hole.

"Oh my god, Reven!" Keegan said happily, cringing as she realized she sounded like a Valley Girl, coming from the shadows and pretending to not notice the dark mood.

Kade and Reven shared a glance before putting on masks. If she hadn't overheard their conversation, she would've hardly known anything was amiss.

"So, Reven, can I ask you a favor?" Keegan said.

"Not even a hello!" he joked, playfully shaking a finger at her.

Keegan pursed her lips, which was hard to do with a smile. "Hello, Reven. It's good to see you. I like this much better than waking up to the threat of being handed to Caius."

Reven laughed and pulled her into a hug. "So, that favor?"

"I need a life tutor. Would you mind?"

"Wouldn't an Alvor be better?" Kade asked.

"I don't want to add another thing to Mahogen's plate," Keegan commented. "And I can't say I particularly trust any of them after the whole... Okleiy thing."

"I'll explain later," Kade headed Reven off.

"I 'm sure I can manage," Reven said.

"Keegan, where's your guard?" Kade snapped, suddenly realizing she was alone.

"Where's yours?" she bit back.

Reven raised an eyebrow. "Why do the two of you need guards?"

"Bernot's rule since trouble likes to find me," Keegan explained.

Kade countered, "I'm certain you go looking for it."

Keegan gave him a childish face that told him to shove it—though he was right. "I'm not sure where Quin got off to... after I accidentally ditched her."

"Accidentally? Right." Kade grumbled. "Though, she's probably used the time to try get into it with Jared."

Keegan grimaced. "Yeah... that's actually why I'm looking for her next." It crossed her mind that maybe she should have dealt with Quin first. Oh well; hindsight was 20/20.

Reven gave a look that encouraged her to continue.

It was her turn to point a finger. "No, it's none of your business. Well, I guess I'll keep looking for her. Reven, I'm glad you're here and thanks for agreeing to help me with life magic."

Keegan continued to run in circles for most of the afternoon. By the time she realized she was going to have to let Quin come to her, she was sweaty and irritable. It was only maybe an hour before sunset when Quin, just as tired and grumpy, decided to look for her in her tent.

"Take a seat," Keegan instructed, surprising Quin. "Let's talk about Jared." She almost laughed realizing she was getting to enact the whole parent surprising a child sneaking in trope.

The guard looked like she had been about to go all Mrs. Weasley "Where have you been", but Keegan's mention of Jared stopped her from doing so. Quin tensed defensively. "What about Jared?"

"I know what you're doing. And I don't like it."

Leaning back in the chair with a huff, Quin asked, "And what is it you think I'm doing?"

"You're using Jared to make Kade jealous. Well, attempting to."

Quin's grey eyes widened by a fraction.

"Honey, it's the *oldest* trick in the book," Keegan tittered.

"You can't prove anything."

"No, I can't." Keegan leaned forward, chin on hands. "But lemme put it this way, you hurt Jared, I hurt you."

Quin's mouth turned into a hard line and Keegan knew she wasn't going to relent. There was nothing she could actually do to stop her, but she meant what she said. If Jared got hurt, Quin was going to feel it, too. Tenfold.

"You can leave," Keegan said dismissively.

"You know I can't do that."

"You're right," Keegan admitted. "You can still go outside though. Might even spot Kade if you're lucky."

Quin's eyes narrowed as she stood sharply, the anger in her steps hardly concealed.

Chapter 7

One of two things was going to happen, neither of them good in Braxton's opinion. The Vosjnik needed to meet the griffins—aside from Mara. But, before that happened, he still had to talk to Kolt.

Walking through the halls, it seemed he was the late riser as servants and pages bustled about, sleep a long-forgotten wish. He could not help but notice that the staff, especially the women, walked by the king's door as quickly as possible without looking suspicious.

Reaching Kolt's door, he considered barging in out of spite, but refrained; he needed to try to get in his brother's good graces. After knocking and no response, he wondered if Kolt had risen early, then laughed; early for his brother was midday.

Finally, after several minutes of polite yet insistent knocking, the door was yanked open to reveal the king bleary-eyed and bedraggled.

Kolt gave him a confused look before slouching into his desk chair, rubbing his eyes, "What do you want?"

"I am here for the conversation you promised me yesterday," Braxton said, stepping into the room. "And the day before that. And the day before that. We have a problem with the griffins."

"Fix it," Kolt growled. "Or you know what happens."

"It is not that kind of problem. At least not the first one. I need to be made Commander of the Vosjnik."

"No. How big a fool do you take me for?" Kolt paused for a long while, his sleepy brain not up to the task of thought. "But things pertaining to the griffins I will give you authority over—including battles."

About to ask why, Braxton stopped himself. *Never* question a gift from Kolt. "You may want to inform Vitia of this."

"I will get to it eventually."

"*Before* they take their first flight this morning."

Kolt took an aggravated breath through his nose, but clearly understood the need for urgency. "Your second problem?"

"There are seven griffins and eight members of the Vosjnik."

Kolt's face fell. "Nico stays behind."

"I need someone small to ride the hatchlings; Mara and Nico are the only options."

"Who would you leave behind?"

"Vitia," Braxton said unabashedly.

Kolt laughed.

"It makes the most sense. Vitia can do the most... damage from the ground." He hated pointing the fact out, but if it meant she never touched the griffins, so be it.

"No. What about the earth elemental?"

"That is Nico."

He quickly realized Kolt did not know much about the Vosjnik, except that they did his bidding without question. Wondering how to use that to his advantage, Braxton thought about Kolt's proposal. He considered grounding Brennian Thandov, the swordsman, but he would prefer to keep him from doing any fighting on the ground, and his personality would hopefully mesh with Oxren.

"Fire elemental?" Kolt blurted, likely hoping to speed the process.

"Nicandro Quolt?" The fire elemental was past his prime and flying would not be comfortable for him. And he was not sure how the griffins would react to fireballs. "Potentially."

His brother waved him away and crawled back into bed. "There you go."

"Vitia," he reminded his brother.

Groaning and grumbling, Kolt grabbed a shirt and stomped from the room like a child.

««« »»»

When do they come? Phynex questioned.

"Soon. Please don't *try* to kill them," Nico implored.

The Vosjnik would be going on their first flight, and he was honestly hoping a few of them—all of them, except Mara—fell off. But he knew if such were to occur, Kolt's punishment would be brutal to say the least. He resisted the urge to scratch at the scabs covering his back: a harsh reminder of what Kolt could do.

Have we been assigned riders? Crowlin asked.

"Yes."

Myrish clicked his beak unhappily.

Nico took a seat on the ledge, watching Ima and Harker playfully tumble through the air, and realized how much they'd grown. They were now the size of ponies and well into the process of getting their adult feathers. Ima's were coming in as a true teal that often captured rainbows on their vanes, while Harker was becoming a dusky gold that glinted darkly.

Guthrie, appearing from seemingly nowhere, came and took a seat beside him. "What's it like to fly?" There were hints of fear and excitement in his voice.

"Freeing," Nico answered honestly.

A sudden gust tossed Ima and Harker high into the sky. The hatchlings happily glided on its breath, giving caws of delight as they continued their antics and acrobatics even higher above the ground.

"Which one is mine?" Guthrie asked.

"None of them are *yours*," Nico growled, loathing that the Vosjnik saw the griffins as nothing but untamed sky horses. "But we paired you with Crowlin."

"Which one is that?"

I am Crowlin, she answered, speaking so that Nico and Guthrie could hear her.

Guthrie went to her stall and bowed like a gentleman asking for a dance. Crowlin, pleasantly surprised by the token of respect, slowly lowered her dark gray head, returning the gesture.

When Braxton arrived, he recalled Ima and Harker. "I hope the rest of the meetings go similarly," he said, noting the civility with which Guthrie and Crowlin interacted. Approaching Myrish, he gently stroked his feathers. "Do not worry, you are with me."

The griffin playfully nipped at him in response.

The rest of the Vosjnik were slow to arrive, but it made introductions easier, giving the griffins time to feel out their riders.

Brennian and Oxren were both equally wary of each other. Nico barely contained a laugh as the swordsman hesitated to get anywhere near the black and white mottled griffin. From the way Brennian muttered, "It's not a bird," repeatedly under his breath, Nico wouldn't be surprised if he had a fear of feathered creatures.

The introduction between Phynex and Dax could've gone better. All things considered… Their relationship would be tenuous, but the Vosjnik water elemental at least now had a healthy fear and understanding of what the griffins could do—to him. Thankfully the bite wouldn't need stitches and could be passed off as a normal training injury.

Vitia, the last to arrive, growled, "Which one is mine?"

"They will never be *yours*. But I paired you with Niyth," Braxton explained, giving the griffin an apologetic look.

The metal-colored griffin gave an angry hiss, feeding off Vitia's foul mood.

The Alvor crossed her arms. "I want the bronze one."

"No," Braxton said, heading to where the saddles were kept.

"I want the bronze one!"

"And I said no."

"I am Commander; *I get what I want*."

"Did Kolt not talk with you?"

Vitia huffed, eyebrows in a flat line.

Nico wasn't sure what Kolt had discussed with her, but it clearly put more power in Braxton's hands.

Settling the saddle over Myrish's back, Braxton said, "This time, you do not get what you want. When it comes to the griffins, *I* am Commander."

Infuriated, Vitia shoved Braxton against the wall.

Myrish's feathers stood on end, making him seem twice as large as he let out a screeching yowl.

The Alvor glanced over her shoulder and released a spine-chilling growl in return.

Refusing to back down, Myrish lashed out with a taloned paw. Four wounds opened across Vitia's back, blood instantly soaking her shirt.

Grinning wickedly, Vitia set to healing the gashes. Blood still dripping down her back, the Alvor turned to face Myrish, raising her hand as if to strike. Her nails weren't as fierce as the griffin's, but with her magic, she'd likely do as much damage.

Braxton snatched Vitia's wrist and dragged her to the open wall, forcing her to the edge. Her heels rocked over the precipice and the only thing stopping her from falling was the prince.

Leaning close, Braxton said calmly, "If you ever hurt one of the griffins, I will throw you from here without a second thought."

Vitia let herself dangle on the edge of death. "Go ahead."

Nico wondered if the rest of the Vosjnik were also praying Braxton lived up to his threat.

It was hard to tell who backed down first, but eventually Vitia slid past Braxton, mumbling under her breath; whether it was a curse or a promise of pain later, Nico couldn't tell.

The Alvor went to stand in front of Niyth, hands on hips.

The feeling is mutual, you stupid, horned opida, Niyth said to everyone.

«««« »»»»

Keegan's heart slowed. Then its pace jumped like she'd been mildly electrocuted. Be it excitement, anticipation, or fear, Keegan wasn't sure, though it was likely a combination of all three. "Two days…"

"Yes," Kade answered, "we leave in two days."

Keegan knew the day was coming but so far had been able to delude herself. With the camp quiet and small, it was easy to forget the larger picture. Aron slipped his hand into hers and she relaxed as their fingers intertwined, finding herself grounded.

Kade glanced at their hands and Keegan's heart sank; this wasn't how he was supposed to find out.

"Aron," Kade said in a tone that raised the hairs on her arms, "outside. Now."

While Keegan wanted Aron to stay and act as a buffer, she had the feeling if he did, there was a good chance Kade would turn him into a kebab... or maybe a pincushion. She gave Aron a subtle nod.

There was a tense moment of silence while they waited for him to depart.

"You're sleeping with him," Kade stated.

"By your standards or mine?" she asked, attempting to soften the truth.

Her twin crossed his arms.

"Yeah," she admitted.

Kade was too calm, and she preemptively reached for her magic.

"How long has this been... happening?" he finally asked, grinding out the words like grit.

"Maybe a month." She made an effort to look anywhere but his eyes. She knew she'd find disappointment, betrayal, and anger there. He would be furious—about being kept out of the loop, and the fact that it was, well Aron—someone he'd never been inclined to trust or call friend.

"Why didn't you tell me?"

"Uhh... 'cause I was a hundred and ten percent sure you'd kill him." She scratched an ear. "I'm still not sure you're not gonna take a stab at him."

"I might." Kade sighed. "Depending on if he ever hurts you. I'm not particularly... *fond* of Aron, but I can think of worse people for you to..."

Keegan wasn't new to the overprotective brother scene, but this felt different. Maybe it was the fact Kade was actually blood. Maybe it was the fact she actually wanted someone looking out for her. Or maybe it was because Kade wasn't expected to be this way for her but chose to be. "Thanks... And trust me, if Aron hurts me, I can handle him myself. But I'll let you have round two."

Kade nodded. "I don't think he will though." And with nothing further to add, he walked past her toward the tent flap.

Keegan was flabbergasted. "Wait, where are you going?"

"To pack," Kade answered, taking his leave. "If you're happy, then... I'm okay with it."

This was not how she'd imagined that conversation going.

Chapter 8

The Merfolk had been trickling in since mid-morning, though Bernot still had not heard from the Merqueen. Okleiy waited with him in the command tent, an annoyed air about him.

"I take it your journey was not too harsh," Bernot said, hardly glancing up from the war map when Atlia finally pushed into the tent.

The Merqueen was covered in dust, and shadows were beginning to show under her eyes. It seemed she suffered as her people did—something he found to be the mark of a good leader.

"I would prefer to not be headed to war, but, given the circumstances…" Atlia answered.

"Explains why you took so long," Okleiy muttered.

"I apologize for my delay," she sniped. Coming to stand next to Bernot, she asked, "Trying to plan out the rest of the war?"

"'Try' being the operative word."

"There are many paths a river may take, but only time will tell over which it flows. What have you come up with?"

"I was thinking that going after Revod or Grevasia would be our best option—after Grenadone. Going north and dropping down on Agrielha will give us a better geographic advantage and use of the Nuewba's current but will take time. And attacking the capital head-on is not one of the better options as we will have nothing to fall back to."

"Take Ubëmble on the Lower River Fork."

"That is further south than we need go and offers no strategic advantage."

Atlia stood back. "Are you sure? You are protected on two sides by the river and there is no one to the south who could or would attack us. We can work up the river, taking cities along the way. We will never be without water, hunting grounds, or building materials."

"But if we lose and have our backs to the river, there is nothing we can do to flee," Okleiy said. "Plus, getting all of our forces across the river multiple times will be a tiresome, unnecessary exercise."

Atlia leaned against the table, "Merfolk operate best in aquatic environs. Help us help you."

"It is not our best move. We will be along the river at some point but going to the Lower River Fort is out of the question," Bernot said, using the human name for the area. Some time ago, a single letter had been changed on a map—and humans now called the forts guarding the three forks of the Nueweba River, well, forts. The other races still called them The Forks.

"War is not always about the most direct route; you must make detours and be prepared for delays. Patience is key," Atlia argued. "We both know this will not be a fall war; stop planning like it will be so. Especially with a child on the way."

Okleiy glanced up with a surprised look.

Atlia gauged their reactions. "She is beginning to show. Did you not…?"

"No, I knew," Bernot said quietly.

"You just did not know she was that far along."

"No." This had to be a fall war, or his child would be born in the midst of it all. "The journey must have been tiring and I am sure your tent has been set up by now. I would rest while you can. We leave for Grenadone in the morning."

The Merqueen seemed to debate pushing for her idea further but settled on a different topic, "I would like some of my soldiers to be added into the Children of Prophecy's guard."

"I have no problem with that."

Okleiy perked up. "Can the same be expected for the Alvor?"

Bernot had no doubt that plans to use any guards assigned to Keegan for his gain, were already going through the Alvor's head. He might have been worried if he could not count on Keegan to stymie them.

"Of course," he answered. "But it is Keegan who has final say. Should she decide none of your men are acceptable, I will not intercede."

Atlia nodded in assent. "Shall we call upon her then?"

"I supposed it would be best," Bernot said, pushing away from the table. His instructions to the soldiers outside were simple.

When Keegan arrived, the tent flap snapped open, irritation proceeding her like a wave—one that had the power to drown. "What the hell do you want this time?" she barked. "It's the fourth fucking time I've been ordered here today."

"Start by watching your mouth," Okleiy snarled. Though unfamiliar with the words she used to curse, they had come to understand the connotations behind them.

"Go fuck yourself."

The tension in the room was astounding.

"Keegan, you are ordered here as many times as is necessary," Bernot told her.

"Necessary by your standards or mine?"

"Mine. And should you choose to ignore me when I request your presence, you may find the consequences unfavorable."

"Are you my mother?"

Bernot gave her a confused look. "No…"

"Then don't act like it."

"I am your Commander—"

"No, *I* am my Commander, you just think you're mine," Keegan retorted.

Bernot prided himself in that few people ever got a rise out of him. If Keegan kept up though, he could not guarantee he would not have her flogged. He took a breath; getting bent out of shape was not going to win favors. But she needed to learn a lesson. "Restricted rations for a week."

Keegan cared for little, and he could do no harm to her or her brothers without backlash.

"Bread and soup for a week," he continued.

"*Excuse me?*"

"Everyone, settle down," Atlia said. "Bernot, have you considered she may speak truth. If this is indeed the fourth time you have called upon her today, I am inclined to agree you do call too often. They are but children, and children need their freedom."

The scarlet that shot up Keegan's neck said she was likely to have some choice words for the Merqueen next.

"Keegan," Atlia continued, "however, you must understand he calls you here as often as needed, whether convenient or not."

"He has no right—" Keegan started.

"He has every right. And you would do well to show us the respect we deserve."

Keegan gritted her teeth but did not push further. "What do you want?" she asked Bernot, her voice low and full of masked rage.

"Okleiy and Atlia would like you to consider their people for additional positions in your guard," Bernot explained.

Without missing a beat, she blurted, "Mahogen."

"And..." Okleiy prodded.

Keegan stared the king dead in the eyes. "No other Alvor."

When Okleiy started to protest, Bernot reminded him, "You know the deal."

"And what about my people?" Atlia asked.

"I haven't met your people," Keegan said. "Tell me who you think is best suited, introduce them, and I'll decide if I like 'em or not."

The Merqueen gave a conniving smile and called, "Enter." Four women clad in varying degrees of steel and leather armor silently streamed in. "I trust these women with my life, in fact, I do. They make up my own guard."

"I don't know about four more. I've already got four—five with Mahogen. I'll consider one."

"Then one of us will be honored," the Mermaid on the far right said.

"Fair warning, I'm not the easiest to deal with."

The Merwomen smiled deviously and answered unanimously, "You sound like our queen."

Keegan gave a little smile in return. "Uh... Look, I really don't know who to pick. Y'all seem like wonderful people."

Bernot barely concealed the annoyed look that crossed his face. When Keegan had chosen her guards back in Edreba, the process had been torture. He had run through almost three score of guards and soldiers before she found four she liked.

"Might I place Icella Bravano on the job then?" Atlia said, motioning for one of the women to step forward.

Icella was a wily-looking Mermaid, her short hair and cunning blue eyes giving her face the appearance of a young man up to no good. She was tall by Merfolk standards, matching the Alvor in height.

Keegan shrugged. "Sure."

"Icella, you will report to me each morning for assignment to one of the Children of Prophecy," Bernot said. "You are not obligated to do their bidding. Their safety is your only concern. Enjoy your last night of freedom."

«««< »»»»

Kade blocked an attack from Reven and parried. They knew each other well and were so evenly matched this wasn't about who would win, but who could show off the most. And it was the first time in a long time Kade could call a sparring match fun.

Reven itched to end the fight, dropping a hand from the pommel of his sword to reach for the dagger at his hip. Kade mimicked his movements and simultaneously they placed their knives against the other's chest. They remained frozen for a moment before pulling away, peals of laughter dripping from their lips.

"It seems you need a new partner," a refreshing voice said from the sidelines.

Kade turned to see a group of Merfolk, their blue skin making them obvious. Looking closely, he could make out silver-sheened scales glittering across their bodies like gemstones. The fins on their forearms and calves were held flush against their bodies with leather bands.

"I would offer t' spar," Reven started, "but I 'ould feel ashamed if I hurt you."

The Merwomen smirked.

Accustomed to fighting in more restricting environments, Kade knew being on land made them lighting fast—not that they were any less lethal in the water.

"I do not think it will be *I* who winds up injured," one of the Merwomen said. Her thick brown hair was cut short like a man's and a ring of scars marred her right shoulder; something—very large, with many rows of teeth—had bitten her. A small strip of cloth across her breasts was the only clothing on her torso and her skirt was made of rough pteruges. He was tempted to find out if there was anything underneath, but had the feeling that asking, or even worse, trying to get a look, would cause him to wind up without one appendage or another—likely his favorite one.

Reven grinned tauntingly. "Best me if you can."

The Merwoman drew an elegant and thin sword made of a blueish metal that seemed to ripple like water. She turned to Kade. "Are you not joining?"

"I wasn't intending to."

"Please, do; I need a challenge."

Not one to be cowed by a cocksure woman, Kade hefted his weapon.

The Mermaid was totally at ease—a warrior accustomed to being outnumbered. Flashing a smile, she attacked with a kind of feral intensity he'd only seen from cornered people and animals.

Reven barely managed to block, a perturbed expression gracing his face.

"Are you going to help your friend or sit there like a barnacle?" she asked.

The words prompted Kade into action and he lunged. The Mermaid stepped to the side, making it appear he and Reven were sparring again.

Kade raised an eyebrow and he and Reven turned to face her. They'd taken on the world together; she would be no different.

Ravliean

He attacked first, Reven following like a wayward shadow. There was hardly a second where the Mermaid wasn't being pressed and it showed as her self-assured smile faded to an expression of concentration.

When they'd first started fighting, Kade had used telepathy to synchronize with Reven. Now, even after half a decade apart, it was like they were the same person. He was impressed the Merwoman had evaded defeat so far—it wasn't something many people got to boast about when he and Reven finished with them.

Reven was getting overconfident and Kade knew it; they needed to end this, or his friend's ego would spell defeat. He slashed toward the Merwoman's shin and let his blade sail up toward her shoulder.

She hissed as the blade darted across her skin, bringing forth a trickle of red. Rage welled in her eyes the anger of an ocean storm and a spike of fear shot through him.

Reven lunged and Kade mimicked the movement. They weren't aiming to skewer the Merwoman like they would in proper battle, but their blades would trace along her sides and make the point. Hopefully without drawing more blood—which was only likely to infuriate her further.

As they moved, time slowed, and he watched the Mermaid launch into the air, twisting and tumbling to land behind them.

Turning to face her, they were each met with a sword at their throats; her blade had been pulled into identical, paper-thin weapons.

Smiling, the Mermaid pulled away.

Reven's brows furrowed, showing his unhappiness with the way they'd been defeated. "Do we get the name of the swordsman—swords*woman*—who defeated us?"

"You fought well, and I suppose you deserve some prize. I am Icella Bravano."

"Where'd you learn to fight like that?" Kade asked as Icella rejoined her swords with a magnetic click.

"We all fight like that," she answered with a sultry glance. "And you are?"

Reven sheathed his sword. "Reven Broyker."

"Kade Tavin."

Icella scrutinized Kade specifically. "So, you are one of the bastards who has been causing chaos."

"In which sense?" Reven muttered.

"He is a Child of Prophecy—and one of the Vosjnik. The latter explains why you are well-versed in the art of the sword—considering you are human. And the former explains why you still have your head."

"What am I, chopped liver?" Reven pouted.

"You would be a better swordsman if you stopped fishing for compliments," Icella hummed.

Red flushed to Reven's cheeks.

"Well, Kade Tavin, Reven Broyker, it was a pleasure. I hope to do this again."

"Anytime," Elhyas said, idling toward them. "Though, I'd be careful, there will come a day they beat you."

Icella grinned. "I look forward to it. Until then, happy training. And maybe I will see you in the morning." She walked away, the others of her kind following. A few looked back over their shoulders, giving coquettish glances.

"Don't get too enamored," Elhyas warned. "Merwomen can be devious."

"So can I," Kade muttered, already imaging the kind of conquest it would be.

«««« »»»»

Ravliean

Keegan made her way through camp, palms no longer on fire thanks to Lyerlly's healing touch. Hopefully this would be her last trip to the hospital tent today. Surveying the camp, it was obvious they'd be leaving in the morning; the thought clenched her stomach with fear.

When she returned to where Raelin lounged, she noticed Thoren—the one and only lightning dragon in existence—in the background, watching like a cat ready to pounce. His slitted eyes tracked her movements and the tip of his tail lazily flicked. She desperately wanted to approach the dragon, beg him to help her see if she could harness lightning. But something always stayed her, made her wary.

Keegan stopped in front of Raelin. "All set."

"Try air, Jesus girl," Nikita ordered, not moving from his reclined position against Raelin's leg.

She barked, "It's Keegan! Come on, it's not that hard."

Nikita rolled his eyes. "Maybe you no do fire 'cause it all gone to hair."

Her eyes narrowed. "Ha ha ha, very funny, Putin."

"No insult great Vladimir Putin by calling me him," Nikita fumed.

Focus, Raelin growled.

Taking a deep breath, Keegan reached for the green paika in her throat. Easily, compared to fire magic at least, she wrapped a layer of dense, dry air around her hands. She paused before pulling the magic from the cobalt blue paika, fearing the trick wouldn't work. *Knowing* the trick wouldn't work. Just like water hadn't. Repeatedly.

Letting the magic loose, a flame danced above her upturned hand. There was no pain at first but slowly the air protecting her began to heat. She released the magic, shaking her head. "No use." Thankfully Raelin didn't insist she keep trying until her skin was scalded.

Try an earth shield, Raelin said calmly.

Keegan pushed aside disappointment and frustration and created earthen gloves. As she released the magic from the fire paika, she struggled to keep a proper hold over the two energies. A dull pain split her body as she fought for control. Panic rose in her throat as she watched the fire meld with the earth shrouding her hands. She was about to release the magic when she realized something unexpected—the magics had fused, creating lava. And it didn't burn.

Studying the strange occurrence wrapped around her hands, she flexed her fingers, amazed the earth responded normally, yet the fire didn't burn. She removed the lava from around her hands, pleased with how it behaved.

Over his initial surprise, Raelin stood, dropping Nikita onto the ground with a thump. *Which element are you using?*

In the background, Thoren strained his neck trying to get a better look.

"Both," Keegan answered, using air magic to turn the magma to obsidian. "And I just used air magic to make it stone," she added.

Are you sure? There was an accusatory tone.

"Yes." Keegan worked on pulling the obsidian gloves off her hands. Which proved to be a hassle. "Lava's another one of those rare elements, ain't it?"

Yes and no, Raelin began, *there are several dragons who wield lava, but most humanoid earth elementals, even the Torrpeki, never master it.*

What is your true power, Pexatose? Thoren asked, creeping toward them. *You smell... odd.*

"I'm not technically a Pexatose," Keegan started. "I was born in this world but only returned a few months ago."

Thoren's scaled brows furrowed together. *You are the strange human everyone is up in wings about.*

Keegan gave him a mild grimace that stood as her answer.

Why the sudden interest? Raelin questioned.

The yellow dragon was quiet, *She is... different.*

"Obviously," Nikita laughed.

"Can I try lightning?" Keegan asked, seeing her chance.

Thoren roared in laughter. *What makes you think you can master what only the gods and I can do?*

"I can do everything else y'all say I can't," she said haughtily.

That seemed to stump the dragon and static began to crackle around him. *What makes you think you can master the impossible?*

The hair on Keegan's arms rose, making her want to be anywhere but in his shadow. She gulped, "Well... I've kind of already proved I can. I mean, I've got all five elements—and I can use them." She didn't add that that was at varying stages of success.

I did not ask what proves you can do the impossible; I asked what makes you think *you can.*

"Uh-h... well..." she stuttered, "things are only impossible until someone makes them possible. And I don't know I'm not that person until I at least try. And... I've got a pretty good track record so far."

Leaning forward, Thoren jabbed her with his nose.

Electricity coursed through her, seizing every muscle painfully, tracing down her spine and sucking the air from her lungs. Through the pain, Keegan reached for a paika, though she couldn't have said which one. And, in the moment, it didn't matter. Static jumped through the air, singeing the grass behind Thoren, leaving the smell of ozone and smoke in the air.

Nikita let out a low whistle.

As Thoren pulled away, Keegan dropped to her knees, muscles spasming. She sucked in deep breaths, lungs and heart working out of sync.

At least you can do something with lightning, the yellow dragon said. *What element did you use?*

Hell if I know, Keegan responded, words slightly slurred, her body not ready to work at full capacity yet. Random muscles twitched every few seconds.

Thoren began to near her again.

Keegan held up a hand. *Don't you fucking shock me again unless you wanna send me into cardiac arrest.*

The dragon pulled away, giving a confused look.

She took her time recuperating. Finally, getting to her feet, she asked, "Any chance you tone it down a notch?"

No, Thoren said, touching her again.

«««« »»»»

The night was cool on Jared's skin while apprehension hung in the air like dying leaves. Tomorrow they would move out—head to war. Or at least, closer to it. And all the horrible things that came with it. There were many ways Jared had seen people deal with that fact. Some had taken to friendly fistfights, others sulked, and there were those that hynakox themselves.

As he and Quin walked past yet another brawl, her eyes lingered on the bloodied men, a desire to join them in her cool gray eyes.

"They'll never hit you," Jared told her.

"Who said anything about them hitting me," Quin retorted, linking her arm with his.

The gesture was so nonchalant that he wasn't sure what to make of it. He let his mind wander and when he finally pulled himself from his musings, they were nowhere close to where he should've been. He should be in his tent, attempting to sleep—this was the other side of camp. "What are we doing here?"

"Getting those pre-war worries out," Quin answered, pulling him into a tent.

The inside was sparse, a cot and a trunk the only furnishings. Quin spun him around and he knew exactly what she had in mind.

He fumbled for words. "I'm not sure the occupant will appreciate…"

"You're talking to the occupant," Quin said breathily. Before he could protest further, she pulled him into a kiss.

Something stirred inside him; he wanted this. He pushed aside the voice in his head that said he shouldn't be doing this and focused on the current battle.

Pulling her close, he felt Quin smile.

She started taking small steps toward the bed and he followed obediently.

Quin kissed the side of his neck, drawing forth a kind of carnal bliss that had him forgetting to breathe. She moved his hands to her hips. "I can only help you so much."

He tried to work out what she meant but wasn't thinking with that head at the moment. Though, giving into his own desires was likely what Quin was edging him toward anyway.

Slowly, he untucked Quin's shirt; it felt wrong, but she didn't stop him—so, maybe it was right? He placed his hands on her waist. Her skin was warm and silken soft.

"Take it off," Quin encouraged, kissing his neck again.

He would've ripped her shirt off if she asked.

Slowly, he pushed her shirt up, his fingers trailing along her skin like reverse rivulets, bringing forth chills across Quin's body. And his.

He knew he shouldn't stare... but couldn't help himself. Everything about Quin's body was beautiful—even the bruises dotting her skin.

Grinning, he pulled her close, a feral hunger overtaking him. As they kissed, his hands roamed the contours of her body, exploring every inch. When his hands cupped her breasts, Quin took a sharp breath of pleasure.

With nimble fingers, she began to undo the lacing of his trousers. As his pants were worked off his hips, Jared's member stood proud and aching... longing.

Quin forced him onto the cot, then knelt between his legs.

"I may not have sugoreox before, but I know this isn't how you do it," he commented.

With a mischievous grin, Quin said, "This is just the lead up."

She started slowly and from the moment her mouth touched him, it was a wonderful kind of strange. Her movements sent a wave of warm pleasure through his body, and he leaned back on his hands, letting her do as she pleased until he thought he was going to explode.

"Now, for the real fun," she announced, pulling off her own trousers.

Jared was having trouble imagining anything felt better than what she'd just done, but if she could prove him wrong, so be it.

When she pushed him back onto the cot, he started, "I don't think this is the proper—"

"There's more than one way to kill a man," Quin said, leaning down to lock lips with him. She sat just forward of his member, and he could feel a slickness on his hips. "This is your last chance to say no."

Heart thumping wildly, he looked her in the eyes and nodded; he wanted this. He did, but... that little voice. He shoved it aside and let her take him on a wild ride. Every man wanted this, craved this, *begged* for this.

After Quin had situated herself on top of him, she grabbed his hands and held them to her chest. As she began to move up and down, she gave soft moans that he began to mimic. As the rhythm of her movements increased, Jared felt something stir within him. The world changed in seconds, and he let himself go. Colors danced in his brain, and he was barely aware Quin had come to lie beside him.

"Was that… was that… good for you?" he asked sheepishly.

Quin was reluctant to answer. "Not the worst encounter I've had."

"But not the best."

She laughed, though it was not mean spirited. "No. And certainly not the longest. But that was your first time; it's normal."

His cheeks colored. "I'm sorry. I'll get better."

She smiled, then kissed him. "Exactly what I wanted to hear. Get going, we both need sleep."

At the mention of sleep, he suddenly realized how tired he was—like he'd just been in a fistfight. "I could always just… sleep here."

Quin tossed him his pants. "Only if you want to sleep on the ground."

Not wanting to push, he pulled on his clothes, a sense of shame settling on his shoulders during the awkward silence.

Walking through camp, his mind was too preoccupied with his strange conquest to pay attention to his surroundings. He crashed into someone and stumbled back, finding himself faced with Mahogen.

"I know that look," the Alvor chuckled, placing a hand on his shoulder. "You have finally been bedded."

All he could do was stare and stutter, "H-how- what-how-?"

"That cocksure grin, for starters. And I can smell a woman's musk on you."

His face must be as red as a dragon—that's certainly how it felt.

The Alvor prince steered him into a nearby tent. "No need to be ashamed, every man in this camp has been with a woman. Most of them more than one." Once he had secured the tent flap, Mahogen asked, "How was it?"

Jared rubbed the back of his neck. "How do I describe it? A rush... a rush of pure ecstasy." As he said the words, they tasted like ash for a moment before turning into a pleasant wind.

Mahogen nodded at his answer, a laugh concealed.

"Have you ever..." Jared blurted, "been with a woman?"

"A few," Mahogen answered calmly.

"A few?"

He could only assume women threw themselves at Mahogen. Not only was he a prince, but even Jared had to admit he was the epitome of elegance.

"Yes, a few. But I do not particularly care for women."

He knew what Mahogen was insinuating but couldn't make his mouth utter the truth.

"You can say it, it is no secret. I prefer men," he said easily. His pure green irises asked for a response, clearly unsure of what his reaction would be.

"How did you know?"

"That I like men?" Mahogen frowned in contemplation. "Something within me just knew. Though, I admit, it took some time to listen to myself."

"And your father?"

The prince shrugged. "Love of all kinds is accepted by the Alvor."

Jared nodded, glad Mahogen belonged to a society where he could be himself. "I should go."

"Yes, we have a long day ahead of us," Mahogen agreed quietly.

Chapter 9

Lucas brought the hammer down, drowning out… nothing in particular, just the world, and the new apprentice. He had the feeling the apprentice wouldn't last past the day.

"Will you shut up?" Waylan roared. And there they had it; the smithy would be back down to two before the day was out.

The new apprentice must have started to stutter because Waylan quickly barked, "You're not going to save the world. And you're not going to kill anyone either."

"I could—"

"You can't even make a decent sword! If you could hit the broadside of a barn, it'd be a damn miracle. Get out! And don't come back."

"Geez, cut the kid some slack," Keegan's voice came.

Waylan stared at her, dumbstruck. "Who the fuck are you?"

"Keegan. I'm looking for Waylan… um…"

"Piscol?" the apprentice suggested as he left.

"Yeah. He's supposed to be training me in some special magic, but I haven't heard from him… and I got tired of waiting."

"I'm Waylan," the smith answered, "and while I was asked to teach you metal magic, I've chosen to decline."

"Why?"

"'Cause I have no desire to train an entitled bitch."

"I'm not a—" Keegan paused. "Hold on, no one in this world uses bitch. Also, you said metal magic, which is a specialization. You're a Pexatose! Where are you from? In the other world, I mean."

Waylan looked overwhelmed. "Yes... I'm... How do you know about... the other world?"

"I'm a Pexatose, too. Well, not *technically*, but I spent most of my life there."

"I'm from Cornelius. It's a town outside of—"

"Charlotte. I know. I'm from Cornelius, too. Piscol," she muttered. "Piscol. Wait... you're Ilene's husband?"

Waylan gulped. Finding a stool, he practically fell onto it. "How do you know Ilene?"

Sensing something important was about to happen, Lucas stopped hammering the metal and set it back into the fire. Then he sat in a corner, ready to learn more about Waylan's past.

A kind of pride appeared in Keegan's hazel eyes. "She was my foster mom."

It became hard to tell what emotion Waylan was feeling. Finally, he seemed to settle on a distraction. "Aren't you supposed to have guards?"

"Yeah." Keegan admitted. "But it's easier to get stuff done without them."

Waylan's face pulled into a disappointed fatherly expression. "I would've thought Ilene taught you better."

Keegan bit her lip. "She did... I'm just so tired of everyone babying me."

Waylan sighed. "I got the same treatment when I first arrived. The first few months in this world made me want to rip my hair out. But that ain't an excuse for what you're doing."

"Unh uh. You don't get to lecture me," Keegan argued. "Pot calling the kettle black."

The expression wasn't something Lucas had ever heard, but given Waylan's skin tone, had to wonder if it had something to do with that.

"Then don't be a bitch. Now, tell me about Ilene. How is she? Did she ever... remarry?"

Keegan sat on a stool across from Waylan. "She's really good. I mean, at least she was the last time I saw her. It'd been a bit since I last saw her since I started college... and since I've been here. And she never remarried. Said you were the only one for her."

A glossy sheen appeared into Waylan's eyes. "You said she was your foster mother, but I don't understand. After Arthur, she said she'd never foster a kid again."

"Who's Arthur?"

Waylan pulled out what Lucas now knew was a photo from his pocket and begrudgingly handed it to her. "Our first and only foster child."

Keegan gave the photo back. "She never talked about Arthur. I'm sorry, but I don't know what changed her mind."

The smith just nodded, longingly staring at the photograph. "Why do they want me to teach you metal magic?"

"'Cause I can do everything they say I can't." She held out an arm to show the markings on her wrist.

"I don't know if you'll be able to do it. Few can. And I'm not inclined to teach bitchy little girls; neither I nor anyone else owes you anything."

Keegan looked like she was about to argue but stopped. "Look, I'm just trying to survive, trying to not be made into a chess piece."

"Not even the damn king can avoid that," Waylan said calmly.

Lucas didn't know what chess was. But it sounded complicated.

"How about we see if I can do metal magic and move forward from there?" Keegan proffered.

Waylan offered a semblance of a smile. "I can agree to that."

"Okay, so how do I do it?"

"Are you versed in earth magic?"

"I'd like to think so. Process should the same theoretically then, right?"

"Yes. From what I understand, earth elementals have a hard time manipulating pure substances. For whatever reason, they do best with mixed substrate."

"Kinda the opposite of Merfolk," Keegan noted. "So, got some metal for me to work with?"

Waylan reached into his boot and handed her a knife. "Bend it but don't break it."

Lucas was surprised the smith was willing to sacrifice his dagger; piles of scrap metal littered the shop.

Keegan closed her eyes, apparently studying the knife. After several minutes, she took the tip of the blade and began to slowly pull it back. When she was done, the knife was folded neatly in two.

When she looked up, Waylan was scowling. "You used another element."

"No... just knew I had to take into account tensile strength and shift material to make up for it." She paused for a moment. "But you gave me this knife as a test because it isn't steel and it's easier to break." Standing, Keegan unfolded the knife, snapping it in half. "You never intended to teach me in the first place. And, at this point, I think I can manage on my own."

Waylan's calm expression didn't change, and he simply accepted the now broken knife. "I'm glad Ilene's fine, but my perception of you hasn't changed—nor will it. If you or Bernot need something, please hesitate to ask."

Lucas almost burst out laughing.

««« »»»

Bernot was accustomed to being shorter than many of the people he dealt with, as the Alvor were usually half a head taller than he, but being surrounded by the Torrpeki, who were usually twice his height, made him want to crawl somewhere and hide.

Noticing Garne, Bernot greeted the Torrpeki, "Glad you made it."

Garne was one of the shorter of the Torrpeki present, and he felt safer beside him somehow.

"Glad to have made it," was Garne's response. "Please, let me introduce you to Eoghan Rubel, our Reintablou."

The Torrpeki who stepped forward was the most unassuming of the group, standing at only eight feet tall. Bernot wondered what made him more adept at leading than his brethren.

Seemingly reading Bernot's mind, Eoghan said, "We value intelligence over brawn. And no, I am not a telepath, but I am accustomed to this being most peoples' first reaction to me."

Bernot cleared his throat. "Yes, well, I am glad to make your acquaintance."

"And glad for my troops."

Bernot wanted to correct him, but he was not wrong.

Eoghan turned to his men. "Settle yourselves in; the journey has been long, and you deserve the rest."

The other Torrpeki gave nods and filed from the tent—all except Garne. "Eoghan, you know better than to order me to leave," he said. "It is my sworn duty to be at your side, barring few exceptions."

"Does not mean I will not try, old friend." Eoghan turned back to Bernot. "I do not see *the* Child of Prophecy. I take it she is training or causing trouble."

"Wish I could say you were wrong," Aron answered, suddenly reminding Bernot he was there.

"Aron Alagard, I take it," the Reintablou said, shaking Aron's hand enthusiastically. "I have some questions for you later—if you are not opposed."

"Depends on the questions," Aron said cautiously.

Speaking to Bernot, Eoghan asked, "Is there any way to get Miss Digore here? Hmm… well, I suppose you already tried, and she proves yet again to have a mind of her own." There was hardly a moment's pause. "I should apologize, I tend to answer my own questions after I ask them. My mouth likes to spew words before my brain can pause to think of the likely answer." He gave a nervous laugh.

"How do you do that?" Aron asked with genuine curiosity.

"Simple really, I observe the world, apply previous knowledge, and draw conclusions. And yes, Okleiy, that means your word games will not stand with me."

The Alvor's face darkened into a scowl; it never did well to call him out.

"Bernot, I know we are headed to Grenadone, but I wonder if you have any ideas about afterwards."

"Atlia and I have discussed a few options," he answered, "but we would be appreciative of your input."

"Excellent!"

"Did your equipment arrive safely?" Atlia asked during the lull.

"I assume so," Eoghan said. "Oh, Bernot, I was wondering if you would consent to have Miss Digore assist me in some experiments."

Aron gave a groan. "You are only going to give her more arrows. My head hurts as is."

Eoghan's eyebrows raised. "Miss Digore is a scientist?"

Aron shrugged. "That is what she says. I could hardly get a moment's peace after that equipment showed up at the hospital tent."

Excitement changed Eoghan's features, and he darted from the tent.

Garne gave them an apologetic look before following. "Ever the inquisitive mind with him."

"Well… that was…" Bernot began.

"Strange," Okleiy finished.

Atlia chuckled. "You have hardly cracked the surface."

«««« »»»»

Braxton was surprised Kolt had agreed to their farce of a scouting mission—not that he was complaining. He had told his brother it was to gauge enemy forces, but really it was to get away from the rest of the Vosjnik. Really it was to see if they could change their fate.

As he released the chains around Myrish's neck, the other griffins eyed him, a single question likely tumbling through their thoughts: would he return? They knew he would, or the rest of them would face punishment, but still they longed to ask the question—for their answers would be the opposite of his.

After he had settled himself in the saddle on the griffin's back, Myrish shuffled to the opening in the wall. His wings raised until they were poised upwards, creating a bronze cocoon around Braxton.

Let us fly! Myrish called, propelling them into nothingness.

In that moment, while wind ran along Braxton's body, releasing the bindings on his soul, the world came to a standstill. He did not look back to see if Nico and Mara had made it to the skies; he could hear their laughs of joy. In that instant it was possible to forget and be content.

"Head east," he directed.

If they were alone, Myrish could cover the distance to the line cities in a day or so, but with the hatchlings tagging along it would be slow going. That was not a loss or even a worry; they could take the time to train and explore—better yet, it was time away from Kolt.

The city of Agrielha, pressed tightly against the banks of the Nueweba, passed quickly underneath, the river and city a fleeting blemish as the landscape transitioned into river plains and forest.

Once far enough from the city, Braxton and Myrish turned to face the hatchlings. Battle would be hard, and Nico and Mara had no idea what they were in for. He would never be able to adequately prepare them, but he could try—had to try; it could mean life or death.

Hold on, Myrish warned. *And do not feel so bad; they would have been doing this already had they been born free.*

"It is Mara and Nico I am worried about," he called.

The only way to survive is to learn and the only way to learn is to try.

Myrish turned abruptly and Braxton dug his fingers into the feathers at the griffin's shoulders. This was about to become a bumpy ride. Nico remained completely relaxed, not picking up on any of the aggressive cues Myrish gave. Mara, on the other hand, knew the warning signs and Ima readily rolled away from Myrish's attack.

As Myrish slammed into Harker, his talons latched onto the hatchling's wings.

Harker gave a wounded cry but had the sense to not rip away. Instead, he hung limply, acting as a dead weight. Nico clutched the saddle tightly, his knuckles ghastly white.

Unable to keep himself elevated with the added weight, Myrish let the hatchling go.

As soon as he was released, the younger griffin darted toward a meadow.

Looking for Ima and Mara, Braxton found them hovering high in the clouds, using the shadows to conceal themselves. They would not be tested today, for they had already learned this lesson.

Braxton crouched low on Myrish's back, the wind tearing across his body, as they chased after Harker. Blood dripped from the shallow gashes in the griffin's wing, splattering them with dots of purple. Folding his wings, Myrish plummeted below the hatchling.

As Harker caught an updraft, Nico turned to look at them, betrayal, confusion, and alarm plastered on his face. Harker was tiring—and an injured wing did not make things easier.

Reaching the cloud layer, Myrish gave a great flap of his wings and went to fly beside the hatchling. Without warning, he knocked into Harker, earning a pained shriek from the smaller griffin at the jostling of his injury. As they pushed away, Myrish's wing clipped Nico under the chin, sending him tumbling with a slightly dazed expression.

The boy fell as if in slow motion, mouth poised open to yell.

Myrish lazily chased after him; saving Nico was Harker's task, but they would be there should he fail.

Harker's form was like an arrow, his golden wings reminiscent of the tail of a comet. He quickly caught up to Nico and while the ground was still far below, stopping their descent would take almost all of that distance.

Desperately, Harker reached out for Nico, his talons locking around the boy's bicep, and jerked up; Braxton did not hear the telltale pop, but it was obvious Nico's shoulder was dislocated.

By the time the pair was a hundred feet from collision, Harker had things under control, though it would not be for long as he strained to keep aloft. He worked to gently deposit his rider onto the ground, but was spent, and Nico was dropped more than anything.

After Myrish landed, Braxton casually made his way over; before he could speak, Nico held up a hand and purged the contents of his stomach.

Nico wiped his mouth. "Royik you! You could've warned me."

Crouching down, Braxton said, "Then the exercise would have been moot."

Mara looked between the two of them. "I don't understand."

"This entire thing's a training exercise," Nico explained. "If we're going to survive the war, we have to be prepared."

It seems you failed one lesson but passed another, Myrish said. *Braxton, if you could tend to his shoulder, I would like to talk to them as a group.*

"Help me get my arm over my head," Nico said.

Braxton gently took his wrist and elbow and slowly raised his arm; Nico's face distorted in pain, and he grunted as his shoulder slipped back into place.

"Where did you learn to do that?" Mara asked softly.

Nico rose to his feet. "I have three older brothers; I've lost count of how many times I've dislocated my shoulders."

Come, Myrish commanded, making his way over to the hatchlings. He nudged one of Harker's wings, earning an angry hiss. *What did you do right?*

"Survived," Nico muttered coldly.

Myrish snorted. *Obviously! Now, be serious.* When the youngsters gave him blank looks, he rolled his eyes. *Harker, you were right to not rip your wings from my grasp. Mara and Ima, you were right to notice the warnings of my attack and to keep at a distance. But at what cost?*

"We weren't there to help them," Mara said, staring at the ground.

Self-preservation is important, but there comes a point where one is scared more than anything. During battle you will be nothing but scared, but you must fight. To my next point. Harker, you are a creature of air, why did you run to the ground?

I did not want Nico to fall, Harker answered, shuffling his feet.

A kind intention, Myrish began, *but you have more maneuverability in the air. A griffin may fight on the ground but will never be as strong as in the air. Height is your friend. And as you saw, the higher you are, the longer you have to catch your friend. Mara and Nico, what could you have done besides sitting there like ragdolls?*

They gave him confused looks.

Both of you have extraordinary powers; why not use them?

"There's no earth in the air," Nico argued.

What do you call that thing at your hip then?

"A knife?"

What is it made of?

"Metal?"

Which you find where? Myrish pried, exasperated by Nico's lack of understanding.

"Myrish, controlling metal is generally very difficult," Braxton said in Nico's defense. It was something he himself could *barely* do—without slajor manacles that was.

He will learn, was all Myrish said on the matter. *Mara, you are a telepath, you could have easily stopped me from attacking.*

"But it's wrong to do that," she said. "How can you ask me to… to invade your mind?"

"War is not pretty," Braxton said gently. "You are going to do some things that will keep you up at night. But if you want to survive…" A strangled silence enveloped them. "We will stop here for the day. Nico, attend to Harker."

Chapter 10

"I am looking for Miss Digore," said a deep voice that Keegan didn't recognize.

Turning, she was surprised to find it was a Torrpeki asking after her. His long black hair was pulled back in a braid. Combined with his small horns, it gave him very innocent air.

"Whatcha need?" she asked, slinging her pack over Bastille's back.

"Tell me, if I placed a glass of H_2O before you, would you drink it?"

It was a test, and this just the first question. She shrugged. "Yeah, it's just water."

"What about H_2O_2?"

"At this point I might. Ain't got a whole lot of good coming my way."

The Torrpeki chuckled. "They warned me about your sharp tongue."

Zavier's eyebrows furrowed, not grasping the nuances of the conversation. "I'm confused."

"H_2O is water," Keegan explained, "H_2O_2 is hydrogen peroxide and drinking it will kill you... in high enough concentrations." She turned back to the Torrpeki. "Who're you?"

The Torrpeki gave a slight bow. "Eoghan Rubel."

"I'm sorry, but am I supposed to know you?"

Eoghan thought for a moment. "Actually... no. And that was done both intentionally and unintentionally now that I think about it."

Zavier was doing the same mental gymnastics as she but seemed to be having more luck. His face dropped as he lowered into a bow. "Your... somethingness."

"I am the Reintablou, but I bear no title. Call me Eoghan."

Keegan grimaced, still out of the loop.

"I am in charge of all the giants running around," Eoghan finally told her.

"I thought Garne was in charge?" Then something clicked. "Wait! You're the Eoghan Rubel with all the equipment at the hospital tent. I get the science questions now."

Eoghan smiled, "Correct! I was wondering—"

"I'd love to," Keegan cut him off. "I can feel my brain turning to mush. That and I'd love to have an excuse to ask whatever questions I want."

"Don't you do that already?" Zavier teased.

She stuck her tongue out at him childishly.

"Excellent. Do you mind if I ask a few of my own?" Eoghan prompted.

Keegan shrugged. "Sure. Ask away."

"Can you do it while we ride?" Zavier asked, pointing out that the soldiers around them were mounting up.

"Of course," Eoghan responded.

Keegan pulled herself onto Bastille and was surprised when Eoghan began walking beside them. "You plannin' on walking all the way to Grenadone?"

"Of course; what horse could support me?"

"I dunno, I thought y'all might've had some weird mountain goats or something. So, how do you know about chemical formulas and element names?"

"A Pexatose by the name of Ernst Priesner," Eoghan answered. "He was a biologist studying pheromones and butterflies. Said he was from Austria. Are you familiar with that place. And what is it you study, Miss Digore?"

"Keegan. I know of Austria and where it is, but I've never been. And I was in school to become a marine biologist. Got less than halfway through the program before I wound up here though; so, I'm not exactly a proper scientist. By all the flasks and test tubes, I assume you're a chemist."

"Yes, though I dabble in everything. Do you know much about chemistry?"

"I know I'm shit at it," she laughed. "I've got a grasp of the basic principles, but that's about it. Same goes for physics and engineering. Too much math."

"Really? From what I understand you are always coming up with inventive ideas."

"I'm by no means inventive," she responded. "I just know how to apply random bits of knowledge to different problems. And it's usually solutions to things *not* involving numbers."

"Have any examples?"

"Uhhhh…" Keegan mumbled, wracking her brain. "Knowing that bones are made of minerals, there's iron in blood, humans are seventy-five percent water, there's dust particles in air and water."

Eoghan paused and had to take a few quick steps to catch up. "The implications of those… it does not always take a life… or any elemental to…"

She shrugged. "It's just simple biology and earth sciences."

"But it is not," Eoghan exclaimed. "How many thousands of elementals have walked this earth and come to the same conclusions?"

"How many had the schooling I did? I live… lived? in a day and age where most people go through thirteen years of primary school before going into college. Though, you probably call it university."

Eoghan tilted his head, conceding her point. "Do you know what element you started with?"

"What?"

"Before you left this world, do you know what element you possessed?"

"None. I didn't get my magic until I'd been here a few days."

"What element did you learn first?"

"Earth."

"And the one that comes easiest to you?"

"I dunno. All of them—except fire—have been easy… ish. Even specialties like blood and metal."

"Interesting. Along with assisting with my experimenting, would you possibly mind becoming one?"

"As long as needles and electrotherapy aren't involved. Just coordinate with everyone else who wants a piece of me."

"Excellent! I shall call upon you as soon as my equipment is set up in Grenadone."

《《《 》》》

From a distance, the city of Grenadone looked inhabitable. As they neared, it was easy to see the wilds had reclaimed it, forbidding man to keep his claim. Braxton wondered if it was the plants growing over the city that kept its crumbling buildings standing.

Near the abandoned line city, Myrish let himself glide toward the earth, lazily circling like a vulture. All three of the griffins were battered from their midflight sparring, Myrish worst of all. Braxton noticed he winced when the wind caught his wings wrong.

The hatchlings darted between the buildings like butterflies, chasing and nipping at each other, their injuries forgotten. Braxton would have preferred them to not chance crashing into a building, but as there was no one there to hurt but themselves, he let them go. And who knew where their battlegrounds might be—these could be potentially lifesaving antics.

Looking for a place to land, Braxton studied the ruined city. The streets were narrow and most of the courtyards too overgrown or debris covered for Myrish to land comfortably. A few squares on the outskirts were clear but hiking back to the castle would be arduous. The castle courtyard looked like their best option, as while it was overgrown, it looked safe enough from debris to land in.

Dropping into the courtyard, dust and grass flew into the air, creating a storm.

Braxton shielded his eyes until all the griffins had landed. "Mara, is anyone here?" he asked, brushing himself off.

There was a long moment of silence. "No."

"Stay here," he commanded, urging Myrish back into the sky.

He had told Kolt their mission was scouting, and Nico and Mara that it was for practice—but neither was the real reason for this trip.

You are walking a hazardous bridge, Myrish warned. *Should Kolt find out...*

"He will not," Braxton said. "He is no telepath; the only way for him to know is if we tell him."

Continuing east from Grenadone, the grass and few clumps of trees growing near the city quickly gave way to a field of waving green. The meadows and plains beneath soon turned to barren earth, gray and deathlike. On the horizon, he could see a hazy blot with a plume of dust hovering overhead like a storm cloud. He took this to be the Lazado making their way across the borderlands and was so focused on the army, he almost missed the scouting group.

The handful of riders were moving at a mild pace and clearly none of them had bothered to look up yet.

"Should we say hello?" Braxton shouted above the wind.

Myrish dove toward the ground, giving a warning screech.

The reactions of horses and riders were exactly what Braxton expected. The horses became unruly and bucked while their riders attempted to keep them from fleeing—some having more success than others. Sunlight glinted off the swords of those who managed to stay their animals, but no one would get close enough to effectively use them—nor could they.

He was not sure when he had noticed, or by whom the spell had been placed—for that was the only logical explanation—but men specifically could not land weaponed attacks on him. He wanted to look at it like some kind of blessing... but his gut said it was a curse. When he had pressed Alyck for information about his condition, the Blind Prophet had been less than forthcoming.

As Myrish landed, Braxton held his hands up in a show of compliance. "I am not here to fight. I was hoping to talk."

"Who are you?" a soldier snapped.

"That is Braxton Alagard," another man answered, sliding from his horse. "If you mean no harm, dismount and lay your weapon on the ground."

"Who might you be?" Braxton asked. "And I will consent to that if you do the same."

The man drew his sword and stabbed it into the earth. "I am Bernot Bællar; I assume you have heard the name."

Braxton drove his sword into the earth likewise. "I have. I am hoping you can help us."

"Help you? How? If you want us to yield…"

"I would prefer you do not. Exterminate the vermin that sits upon the throne."

Bernot did not seem surprised. "No love lost between brothers."

"Kolt is a menace that needs to be put down."

"Does that mean you are defecting?" There was a glimmer of hope in the words.

"If I could. Unfortunately, Kolt has ways to keep me in line."

"Slajor manacles?" Bernot presumed, eyeing the gold bands on his wrists.

"If it were only that. No, Kolt has threatened death to many friends."

"Who are?" Bernot pressed.

"The griffins and Nico Sieme."

"Nico Sieme? Youngest brother of—"

"Jared Sieme," Braxton cut in. "Yes. Be warned, Kolt is aware of his use against me *and* the Children of Prophecy."

"How do you know Jared Sieme is a Child of Prophecy?"

"A long, complicated story I do not have time for. A few pieces of information though. The Vosjnik will be flying into battle upon griffins, plan accordingly. Most of my brother's generals are idiots and believe the same of you; though you should worry about Branshaw Appen—I doubt he will underestimate you twice. Thaddeus Broyker is alive. I do not know if he is important to you, but I thought the return of the Keeper of Prophecy might signify something. He is well cared after and in no danger whatsoever." Grabbing his sword, he clambered back onto Myrish. "Best of luck."

Bernot gave him an appreciative nod before shielding his eyes from the dirt that was about to be raised into the air.

Myrish sprung into the sky, and as he was carried away, Braxton's heart grew heavier. The meeting had only set the future further into stone. He just hoped it was the right one.

««« »»»

Pushing into the night, Aron was surprised to find dinner with Eoghan and his wife had not been the torture he imagined it would be. Yes, Keegan had droned on and on about science—Eoghan often egging her on—but he had still been included in the conversation; and had not been made to feel like an idiot.

Elhyas was waiting for them outside Eoghan's, a bored expression on his face. When Keegan started off without him, he said, "You're never to be left alone."

"I'm not alone," Keegan huffed, "I'm with Aron."

"No."

Keegan sighed and there was a change in the atmosphere. Suddenly, Elhyas turned on his heels and walked off.

"What did—" Aron started.

Keegan pulled him down the rows of tents, whispering, "I implanted an idea."

He was tempted to scold her, but she felt no remorse. She did however feel like a prisoner, which he understood, and no true trespasses had been made—he hoped. By implanting the idea, Elhyas still had the ability to reject her intention… if his will was strong enough. They had discussed this many times already, so he skipped to the end of the argument. "It is because we care about you," he sighed, gently kissing her.

It was supposed to be a quick kiss, but he lingered.

Keegan bit her lip. "How about we take this elsewhere?"

Just those words were enough to have Aron aching.

Reaching Keegan's tent, though it was closer to *their* tent, they all but stumbled in, already removing clothing. Keegan staggered as she worked to kick off her boots while Aron used that time to pull his shirt over his head.

Kissing again, their mouths worked against each other, begging for more. He led her toward the cot, never giving ground in their battle, and pulled her onto the taut canvas.

Keegan settled in his lap, her body moving in time with her mouth, creating a rhythm. Aron gently lifted her shirt, his fingers trailing along her sides, passion surging through their connection. His hands ran along her back, pulling her close so he could soak up her warmth. Her fingers were twined in his hair.

His hands moved to her breasts, thumbs resting on her nipples. Keegan's breath caught for half a second and he smiled. Flipping her onto the cot, he earned a squeal of surprise. He kissed her lips, then her neck, then her breast, his tongue gently going in lazy circles of pleasure.

She did not stop him as he worked to remove her trousers, even helping him. He then kissed down her stomach and she let him push between her legs. He set his mouth to work again, drowning in her lust.

Her back arched and a moan escaped her lips as her fingers pulled at his hair. Aron rode on the feelings coming from their link that crashed over him like the sea. It was not long before Keegan was begging for all of him—and he was happy to oblige.

Aron had no doubt the entire camp knew what they were up to—Keegan was not good at being quiet in any capacity—but could not have cared less. Each thrust drove them closer to the brink and it was not long before ecstasy washed over them.

Keegan's arched back slowly lowered onto the cot as she gave a heaving sigh of contentment.

Carefully, he lay beside her, draping his arm over her stomach. "I love you," he managed. His tongue felt heavy with the words, as if they did not belong to her. But… they did. Shiloh had passed.

"I love you, too," Keegan whispered.

Chapter 11

While she hadn't been conscious for her first trip across the borderlands, Keegan knew twenty-three days was longer than it should've taken to cross the bleak wasteland. The war camp moved at a snail's pace, and it took all her self-control to not ride ahead. Her time spent training helped lessen that itch, but it was always there, always telling her to be efficient.

Grenadone was a looming city of ruins before them now, covered in lush greenery. Already she was imagining the long-forgotten corridors that had secrets to shed. She had the sinking suspicion she'd be ordered to do nothing of the sort—which, of course, she would ignore.

Closer to the city, she saw soldiers beginning to set up camp just outside the walls, many even making use of the crumbling wall as half their shelters.

"You've gotta be fucking kidding me," Keegan groaned to Ezekhial. "The city's right there!"

"What are you getting on about?" the guard questioned.

"Why the hell are we stopping outside the city?"

"Keegan, it's a ruin, there's no way for an *entire* army to reside within Grenadone. And quit your whining, Bernot *requires* you within the walls."

"Oh."

At the collapsed gate, a soldier took their horses, leading them away to a makeshift stable.

Turning her attention to the pile of rubble, Keegan felt her eyebrows rising into her hairline. The jumble of stones and boulders was easily four stories tall. And they were expected to get up and over it.

Keegan was tempted to try simply going through the rubble but figured there was a reason why no one had done that. Looking at the partially crumpled walls that filled in the gate's void, she figured it was because no one wanted to risk bringing down the rest of the walls.

To get through the rubble, Keegan and Ezekhial had to climb and crawl through the rocks. Keegan had a grand time, enjoying the change in routine, the challenge, and the adventure of it all. The same couldn't be said for Ezekhial who found rocks with his head more often than not.

"If Bernot wants to use this as a staging ground, he's gonna need to clear it out," Keegan panted, clambering over a boulder at the peak of the mound. Looking down, the city was like an apocalyptic wasteland. It was a weird dichotomy to find an archaeologist's wet dream in a world that felt like an ancient civilization to her.

"This isn't exactly easy to clear with just a handful of men," Ezekhial answered. "Once the Torrpeki get to it though, they should make short work of it."

Reaching the bottom of the wreckage, the debris drastically diminished, and it was more than possible to stroll through the streets like many once had—provided Keegan watched her step. The silence was poignant and unsettling after there never being a moment of quiet in camp. There were some signs—windows devoid of dust, cut vines, footprints—that people had recently passed through. The castle, looming like the Lonely Mountain, looked like someone had been working to clean it up but hadn't met the deadline.

"Bernot's work, I take it," Keegan said, referring to the castle.

"Yes. He wanted it habitable, the most… important people inside," Ezekhial said. "He reckons Kolt will eventually send people after us."

She noticed a feather on the ground and picked it up. There was a bronze tint to it, and it was large, almost as long as her forearm, the vanes stiff and coarse. This was from no bird she'd ever seen. And if the size of the feather was any indication of the size of the bird, then there was potentially another threat they needed to worry about.

Keegan was about to ask about the feather, when Ezekhial stopped her. "Not here. Bernot has some things to discuss with you—that's one of them."

Climbing the steps of the castle, her mind was already on other things—like what she would find within the monument of stone.

The days were no longer sweltering, as fall began to rear her tawny head, and the inside of the castle was cool enough to make Keegan shiver as she acclimated. Several halls converged at the entrance, each one shrouded in a menacing gloom. Taking one of several lanterns lined up along the wall, something across the room caught the light and Keegan's attention.

The source of the reflection was a beautiful mosaic depicting a sword, red as blood. Running her fingers over the tiles, she was surprised to find it felt like she was touching the actual blade. She was almost tempted to see if she could cut herself on its edge. Etched into the wall above the mosaic was an inscription.

"To learn, one must first know nothing. To die, one must first live. To love, one must lose. To be made whole, something must first be broken," Keegan read aloud.

"A bit macabre, do you not think?" a voice behind her said, making her jump out of her skin.

"Jesus, Bernot," Keegan gasped, holding a hand over her chest. "Didn't your mama ever warn you about sneaking up on people?"

"I see you found the riddle of the Queen Killer," Bernot said casually.

"The what?"

"The riddle—"

"I- I got what it is," Keegan stopped him with a chuckle. "I'm looking for further explanation."

"Ah. The Queen Killer was the infamous sword of the Dragon King," Bernot started.

"I read about him. He killed his wife because her dragon died."

"There was more to it than that, but yes."

"What's the riddle about?"

Bernot smiled. "After he killed Suki, the Dragon King was a shattered mess and swore to never pick up his bloody sword again, so he hid it."

She ran her fingers over the colorful tiles surrounding the effigy. "Why not just destroy it? What's the point in hiding it?"

"His sword could not be destroyed. It was made of starlight which not even dragon flame could melt. He did not want it falling into the wrong hands but knew someday someone would need it to vanquish evil, so he left a clue as to where it was."

"The riddle of the Queen Killer," Keegan murmured. "Why put the riddle in a ruined city? Why put the sword in a ruined city?"

"Because only someone who really needs it, or wants it, will come looking. And there is no guarantee the sword is even in Grenadone."

"A veritable sword in the stone," Keegan mumbled.

"Pardon?"

"An old tale from my world. There was a sword imbedded in this stone and only the true king of Britain could pull it out."

"A very interesting parallelism."

"You're the first one in this city in probably centuries," Keegan said, something not sitting well with her. "How do you know so much about the riddle?"

Bernot grinned. "I forget how astute you can be. My mother was Esen."

"The name's familiar, but…"

"If you read about the Dragon King, you read her name. Esen was his youngest daughter and obsessed with finding his sword when Caius came to power. That quest killed her. She went looking for it beyond the southern lands when I was small and never returned."

"I'm sorry," Keegan mumbled.

Bernot placed a gentle hand on her shoulder. "Nothing to apologize for. She left me with mostly vague memories, and some days it is like she was never really there."

Sensing this was a topic she shouldn't press, Keegan read the riddle again. "The first line talks about learning. Where's the library?"

"I am not sure, but likely buried in rubble."

"Why is nothing easy?"

"If it were easy, nothing would be secret or sacred." Bernot began walking away. "Though with you around, *nothing* is secret or sacred."

《《《 》》》

Gathering the Children of Prophecy, the Sieme boys, and Reven Broyker was more of a task than Bernot had anticipated as they had been allowed to scatter throughout the camp. Though that protected them, as anyone trying to attack them could only harm one at a time, it did mean waiting for them to congregate.

Keegan had been the first to arrive, and after finding the riddle of the Queen Killer, had begun scouring the castle for the library. He did not have the heart to tell her his mother had moved all the surviving books to Edreba as soon as Caius had taken power; the only thing she would find would be empty shelves and cobwebs.

The others had slowly trickled in covered in varying layers of dust. They now sat in what was once the servants' kitchen, as it was the only place that could currently accommodate them all and afford privacy.

"You 'ave us all here for a reason," Reven started. "Pro'lly nothing good."

"I have had word from Agrielha," Bernot said.

"Thought you didn't have spies there," Jared said, crossing his arms. "You made a point about it being too dangerous."

"Braxton and I ran into each other a few weeks back and he has no more love for Kolt than the rest of us." Bernot had chosen to be part of the vanguard to the city. If they could not shelter here for a time, he needed to know about it. Sooner rather than later.

"Braxton is alive? And well?" Aron said after a moment of disbelief.

"Alive, yes. Well is easily debatable. He wears a set of slajor manacles and Kolt has something to hold over him."

"Could be worse," Keegan said, quietly taking Aron's hand.

"Nico is also alive," Bernot told the Sieme brothers.

A palpable kind of tension dropped from their shoulders at the news.

Carter's heart was practically in his throat. "You saw him?"

"Unfortunately, no; we must take Braxton's word on his safety."

"That bastard could easily be lying," Lucas snarled.

"Why would he?" Keegan argued. "Lying about Nico does nothing for him. If he wanted to hurt us, he'd've told us Nico was dead *and* had proof."

The Sieme boys paled at the thought, though none argued her logic.

"Reven, Thaddeus is also alive," Bernot said.

Reven paled and his mouth hung agape. "That- that 's not possible. I… I watched…"

"You watched him get captured. I was not given details, so you must be content with knowing he is alive."

"I have to go back," the boy said more to himself than anyone else.

"I cannot let you do that. You will have to be patient, just like the Siemes."

Reven placed a hand on the pommel of his sword. "I can n't do that."

"Raven," Kade said warningly, "as much as I hate it, Bernot's right. If Thaddeus has made it this far without Kolt killing him, he'll make it through the war."

"He 's an old man," Reven snarled. "Do you think he 'ill survive in a dungeon for long?"

"I doubt he is in a dungeon," Aron spoke up. "If Braxton knows about him and figured it was important enough to tell us he is alive, then he is well cared after."

"He could 'ave been delivering a message," argued Reven.

"If that were the case, do you not think I would have gotten an actual message?" Bernot said calmly.

"You can n't stop me from going to rescue him," Reven challenged.

"Raven, I'm almost certain he can. And will," Kade said. "And should you fail or make it known Thaddeus is valuable to us, that'll guarantee his death. Kolt's a petty twyt."

"Do you really expect me t' just sit here and wait?" Reven snapped.

"Yes," Bernot answered. "It is the only thing to do."

Reven tensed and Kade grabbed his arm to stay him.

"We are going to attempt a formal dinner tonight with a few of my Commanders and the other leaders," Bernot told them. "By now, or at least I hope, rooms should be cleared out for you."

Seeing the myriad of emotions floating on all their faces, he decided to make his exit. Reven was dangerously close to attempting to clout him about the ears; and he was not sure that anyone, aside from Kade, could stop him.

He had intended to let them know about the griffins, but after the heaviness of the news he had already delivered, did not see how it would benefit them. And they would eventually be told or see the beasts for themselves.

«««« »»»»

Kade ate slowly, observing the people around him, but particularly keeping a close watch on Reven. Knowing Thaddeus was alive, there was no telling how his friend might proceed or blame himself. But Kade knew the signs to look for—and he wasn't the only one looking. Keegan was going to make sure he didn't do anything stupid either.

Though most of his attention was devoted to Reven, Kade's time in the Vosjnik reminded him to be aware of everything else as well. Having seen what a formal dinner was in the king's court, he'd expected this to be extravagant. It was simple, if anything. No one had bothered to dress in finery and weapons were slung across the backs of chairs carelessly, but also within easy reach—no coincidence. For some reason it felt like they were waiting for an attack.

There was no division amongst the races, and it was an interesting sight. The humans were dwarfed by the Torrpeki while the Merfolk stood out like sapphires. And the Alvor, with their easy grace, were akin to gods in comparison to everyone else.

Icella sat casually on his right while Quin, who was stabbing at her food so hard he was sure she was going to break either the fork or plate, sat on his left. Across the table was Okleiy and a massive Torrpeki, whom he was surprised was eating with cutlery; from the stories, at least the ones he'd heard, the Torrpeki were heathens.

"You need something?" the Torrpeki asked.

"Auhhh…" Kade droned.

"You are Kade Tavin."

He suddenly felt self-conscious. "Yeah."

"I am going to spar you tomorrow."

"You'll have to—" Kade started to protest.

"An excellent idea," Bernot said from down the table.

"I can only imagine how exciting a match it will be," Eoghan piped up.

Kade cursed under his breath; there was no way he could beat a Torrpeki. He might've been considered the best—one of the best—elementals in the human kingdom, but even the weakest Torrpeki had him beat blindfolded and both hands tied behind their back.

"Do I get your name?" Kade asked. "Since you know mine."

"Breccan Schun."

Even if he hadn't intended to keep up the conversation with Breccan, he still welcomed the diversion provided by the note that appeared before

Bernot. It materialized with a loud pop that made Keegan yelp in surprise.

A needle drop could've been heard, and everyone suddenly had a weapon ready—be it sword or whatever cutlery was in hand. The guards stationed around the hall had their heads on swivels and their shoulders hunched, ready for a fight.

Kade was just able to make out the sigil in the wax; it was from Kolt.

"What does it say?" Keegan dared ask.

"He is tired of waiting for me to bow," Bernot mumbled as he read, face stringent. "He has declared war."

Kegan leaned over Aron, who sat between her and Bernot, to read the letter herself.

Bernot continued, "And he has warned us to be on the lookout for assassins."

As Keegan, face pale, went to retake her seat, a knife sailed across the room and raked across the top of her shoulder before burying itself in the chairback.

Aron hissed and a hand shot up to hold his own shoulder like he'd been the one to get cut. Had Kade missed a second knife? Over the initial shock, the prince pushed Keegan under the table, their chairs toppling over with mighty clatters.

His twin out of sight, Kade scanned the room, knuckles white from the intensified grip on his blade. Time was paramount and he extended his consciousness; in the shadows of the hall, he found a ball of malice and shot stone forward to encase the source. He calmly walked toward the now entrapped attacker, most of the room following.

"Aron, take Keegan to the hospital," Bernot said in a voice so calm that Kade knew he was panicking.

Cautiously, Aron pulled Keegan from under the table. Keegan held a hand over her shoulder, though it hardly staunched the flow of blood. Eoghan ushered them out, acting as a living shield, Lyerlly hurrying after them.

Taking a torch from the wall, Bernot shed light upon the attacker. "Who are you?"

"Does it matter?" the man snarled.

"Not particularly. Kolt sent you?"

"Not as dumb as he makes you out to be," the would-be assassin said. "Though definitely just as slow. The little opida's lucky she moved."

"She's lucky you have bad aim," Elhyas said. "You know what comes next."

"I certainly do."

Kade wasn't sure if anyone else heard it, but there was a crunch—the bone-breaking kind.

The man began laughing maniacally. "Long live the king." Foam formed at the corners of his mouth and his head slumped forward.

Walking away from the dead assassin, Bernot said loudly, "If I find Keegan alone ever again, I will string up whatever guard let her run off. And tell Keegan I will tie her to her guards if she even dares to *think* about doing something asinine!"

Kade might have laughed at Bernot's audacity if he hadn't been completely serious.

«««« »»»»

Aron was on high alert on their way to the infirmary. He could not imagine a second assassin had infiltrated the castle, but stranger things had occurred—and often did with Keegan involved.

He breathed a sigh of relief when the double doors were closed and barred. The infirmary was still in the process of being unpacked and set up, but for what they needed was perfectly fine.

Keegan found a chair and slumped into it, blood sliding down her arm and dripping onto the floor from her fingers in faint *tap, tap, taps*.

From the strange link he had with her, he knew the cut was not life-threateningly deep; but that did not stop it from hurting in the slightest.

Already setting to work, Lyerlly had bandages, needle, and thread in hand. "I can heal it magically if you—"

"I can't imagine healing got any easier when you became pregnant," Keegan cut in. "If it's not bad, the old-fashioned way is fine."

Lyerlly was clearly not pleased at Keegan's assertion, yet the relief at her understanding was clear. "I am going to have to remove at least the sleeve," the doctor said, motioning for Keegan to remove her hand from the wound.

"Aron, a word," Eoghan said gently, leading him to the other side of the room.

He thought the Torrpeki meant to give Keegan privacy—then realized it had nothing to do with her at all. Aron gave an involuntary hiss as the sensation of water over his shoulder made him shudder.

"How long have you had an empathy link with Keegan?" Eoghan asked bluntly.

Aron rolled his shoulder in discomfort. "A what?"

"How long have you been able to feel the mental and physical things Keegan does?"

"I am not sure, but the earliest I can remember... is a couple of months ago."

"Did you experience any life-threatening situations about that time?"

Aron was about to say no when he remembered something. "I was shot. Arrow to the heart."

"I was afraid of this," Eoghan muttered, shaking his head. "What exactly happened?"

Aron explained the nature of Wexsley and Halcyon's betrayal ending with, "Thahan shot me. Next thing I knew, I was awake, and Keegan was all but hanging onto life."

"And you do not bear a scar?"

He shook his head. He started to reach for his collar to show Eoghan, but the Torrpeki motioned that it was not necessary. "How did this… empathy link happen?"

"When Keegan pulled you from the fingers of Lunos, she unintentionally sacrificed her life source, her soul—well, a part of it—for you. Now your life is tied to hers. Her body has been searching for the part of her soul she gave you. Since you cannot relinquish it, a tie has been created: an empathy link. Because you have within you a small part of Keegan's soul, you feel the hurts she does."

He resisted the urge to look at Keegan. "There are worse things to live with."

"An empathy link can be dangerous," Eoghan pressed. "Should you not be able to handle a pain Keegan experiences, it could kill you. Should she ever die, the chances of you passing into the void with her are extremely high."

"I can handle whatever she goes through." And he would not let Keegan die anytime soon. His anxiety, stemming from the revelation of the empathy link, and amplified by Keegan's own feelings of pain, formed a lump in his throat.

Eoghan grabbed a chair and bid him to sit. "I would not be so sure."

A sudden sense of exhaustion overcame him as he dropped into the chair. Keegan had talked about this before, the come down after an adrenaline rush. A burning liquid coursed down Keegan's throat, staving the tiredness. He choked on the taste, and it was not long before the world felt as if it was muted.

"When was the first time specifically you were aware of what she was feeling?" Eoghan asked, providing a distraction while Keegan was stitched up.

"Back in Edreba," he mumbled, tensing as the needle pushed through Keegan's skin. "A few weeks after…" he casually waved his hand to signify the whole inciting incident.

"Is this the first time that what Keegan feels has affected you greatly?"

"I… Maybe? I have used the link to find her. And when she was trying to learn fire, I knew when she had burnt herself. And when we—" He choked off the last words, unwilling to share the moments of passion.

"So, you can use the link for your own devices," Eoghan said, more to himself than Aron. "Have you ever been able to block her out completely?"

Aron did not generally spend his days around Keegan and, for the most part, did not usually notice their connection. "I am not sure. There are times when I feel like it is just myself I am aware of…"

Eoghan scratched at the base of one of his small horns. "Good. Whether it is your own body trying to preserve itself, or Keegan's desire to remain independent, or your own unknowing ability to block out her hurts, you are on a good track."

"How do you know so much about empathy links?"

The Torrpeki gave a small smile. "Because I have been there and lost that part of myself."

"I—"

"A story for another time. I suspect Keegan will be sleeping here tonight and I fear I must return to the scene of the crime. We will begin working to control your empathy link tomorrow—and it is not optional.

Chapter 12

Jared was surprised the sparring match between Kade and Breccan had been allowed, if not *encouraged* to happen. Though, he did consider it was being done as a front to pretend last night hadn't happened.

Keegan stood nearby, five of her guards present, all on high alert; for once she wasn't complaining. She had recently picked up a ring from somewhere—it was a simple onyx gemstone on a silver band—and she was fiddling with it furiously, constantly twisting it around her finger or sliding it from her middle digit to her thumb.

"How are you doing?" Mahogen asked Keegan, finally returning from a private conversation with his father and Bernot.

Keegan began with a sigh. "Not too bad. Self-healing isn't going well." She rolled her shoulder, the fabric of her shirt clearly irritating her wound.

Jared looked away from them, finding Bernot and the other humanoid leaders across the courtyard on another first-floor patio. He caught the glint of something in Bernot's hand and thought it might be a mirror. Then, Bernot and Eoghan shook hands eagerly, schemes shimmering in both of their black eyes.

"Probably betting on who is going to win," Mahogen said quietly. "Care to place your own bet? I say Breccan will win. The Torrpeki simply has the size and skill on Kade."

"You haven't left me much of a choice but to wager on Kade," Jared said, earning a conniving grin from the Alvor. "But he's skilled; he could win."

Mahogen placed an elbow on his shoulder, leaning against him. "And what is it we are betting?" There was a strange nature to the words, like he hoped something other than coin would be wagered.

"I don't have much to offer."

"How about we venture a drink? I think both of us can manage that."

Jared held out a hand and they shook.

"It's gonna be a tie," Keegan commented.

Mahogen turned to her. "What makes you say that?"

"Breccan might be bigger, smarter, and better with earth magic," Keegan began, "but Kade's stubborn."

"How does being stubborn equate to winning a fight?" Quin snapped.

Keegan raised an eyebrow connivingly. "How do you think I get anything done?"

A roar erupted from the Torrpeki around the courtyard and Jared turned to find Breccan sauntering in. He was wearing only a koilk—something Keegan compared to a loincloth. Even without armor and weapons he looked formidable. The humans in the crowd began shouting and stomping their feet as Kade cautiously entered the yard. He seemed as surprised by his warm welcome as the people giving it were.

"The little man may wear armor if he pleases," Breccan said belittlingly.

Surprisingly, Kade nodded in thanks and headed to the weapons rack to slip on armor. He chose to wear only a chest plate and greaves. There were some hisses from the crowd as the men noticed the Alagard's griffin emblem.

"Remind me to fix that later," Keegan said quietly. "I get the feeling someone might try to kill him in battle not knowing he's on our side." She tilted her head to the side. "Though, they're just as likely to do it on purpose."

"His choice in armor is smart," Mahogen commented. "Agility will be important, but so is protection."

"What's your weapon?" Kade asked.

"Sword," Breccan answered, pulling the longest sword Jared had ever seen off the rack. It was easily the size of Kade. "To make it fair."

"A six-foot sword is hardly fair," Keegan muttered.

Kade seemed to have the same sentiments, though didn't voice them. He grabbed his sword and came to the center of the courtyard, the cheering slowly quieting to an anxious whisper.

"Let me know when you have had enough," Breccan told him.

"Same goes for you," Kade returned, rousing the spectators to cheer and taunt the Torrpeki once more.

Bernot and Eoghan shared a look before yelling, "Begin!"

Breccan wasted no time.

Kade anticipated this and was long gone before the Torrpeki had even begun to move.

"Why didn't he slip past his guard and try and cut him?" Keegan asked.

"Torrpeki skin is armor in and of itself," Mahogen answered. "Trying to cut one of them is like trying to cut a diamond with a butter knife."

Kade continued to dodge and avoid Breccan, which only seemed to infuriate the Torrpeki. Each of Breccan's failed attacks landed against the cobblestones with a clang that sent nervous tremors through the earth. If this was all in good fun sparring, Jared never wanted to face a Torrpeki in battle.

Kade wasn't the kind of person to dodge in a fight—there had to be some kind of plan. Jared just didn't know what it was. The game of cat and dragon continued for several minutes.

"It is me, or is Breccan's sword turning into earth?" Elhyas said.

Jared stared in shock; Elhyas was right. And Breccan had noticeably worn down, his arms dragging the sword like he was pulling it through something viscous.

Mahogen smiled. "Seems you may win, Jared. Kade has slowly been making earth coat Breccan's sword, increasing its weight."

"That's not fair," Quin growled. "He's cheating."

"No one asked him what weapon he was fighting with," Keegan said. "He never claimed to be fighting with sword, he just simply picked one up. And if you notice, he hasn't used."

Breccan made to swing his sword and couldn't lift it. The Torrpeki looked at his weapon, then at Kade. "Smart twyt; I like you."

The ruse up, both fighters tossed their weapons aside.

Kade pulled several rocks from the ground, sending them toward the Torrpeki, who lunged with a delighted smile. Breccan didn't bother to dodge the projectiles—and they didn't slow him down.

With more agility than Jared had realized he possessed, Kade clambered up the ivy-covered wall to perch on a windowsill outside Breccan's range.

"Coward," Breccan taunted.

"I'm only a coward if I flee," Kade returned. "Assessing my options on the other hand…"

Breccan stepped back and crossed his arms.

Jared looked at Keegan, hoping to discuss Kade's tactic but found her frowning and shaking her head, clearly in conversation with Kade.

"If this holds up, Keegan, you will be right," Mahogen said, eyes never leaving the stalemate.

"Don't hold your breath," she responded.

As she spoke, Kade jumped from the windowsill, a ferocious yell leaving his mouth. He landed on Breccan's head, then maneuvered himself to sit on his shoulders, legs around his neck and a hold on his stubby horns. Clinging on, Kade wasn't going to be dislodged easily—at least that had been the goal.

Breccan reached back and grabbed Kade by the shirt, flinging him across the courtyard; he landed in a puff of dust with a winded groan.

By the time Kade caught his breath and pulled himself to his feet, Breccan was upon him. Without many options, he caused the earth to pull itself out from underneath the Torrpeki.

Jared watched as Breccan sailed through the air, still on target to collide with Kade. As he landed, Kade caused earthen spikes to present themselves at the Torrpeki's exposed throat.

With it all said and done, both Breccan and Kade were left in compromising situations. The only thing they could see of Kade was his boots, and if Breccan were to move, he'd be impaled.

Stepping into the courtyard, Keegan glanced back at Jared and Mahogen with a devilish grin. "Looks like y'all owe me a drink." She then asked Breccan, "Would y'all like some help?"

"Yes, please," the Torrpeki answered, unabashedly.

With a quick movement of her fingers, Keegan returned the spikes to the ground.

Breccan carefully lifted himself and walked over to Eoghan, the Reintablou smiling and clapping him on the back jovially.

Kade was still in shock from being sat on.

"Shall we go see what has scared the voice out of him?" Mahogen asked.

"What does the backside of a Torrpeki look like?" Elhyas asked heartily, offering a hand to Kade.

"Heavy," he muttered.

"You had help," Breccan said, coming to tower above them.

Kade gulped. "Can you prove that?"

"Bernot can feel guilt coming off Keegan."

Kade hung his head. "Yes, my sister gave me ideas. You win."

"I most certainly do not," Breccan laughed. "You were the one to implement them. A good warrior must know when to listen to the council of others. And now I would very much like to fight Keegan."

"One day," Keegan grinned. "I am sorry about tag-teaming with him though."

"Battle is about innovation; do not apologize," Breccan said, casually giving Keegan a little shove, causing her to stumble. "I expect both of you to share a drink with me tonight."

"My pleasure," Keegan said mischievously.

«««« »»»»

The dining hall was stuffed to capacity with humans, Torrpeki, Alvor, and Merfolk. The comradery made Aron feel out of place—being Caius's son and all.

He sat at a table with Breccan, Eoghan, Kade, Jared, and Mahogen. Though they had all finished eating, they were enjoying each other's company and a drink—in some cases drinks.

Breccan waved at someone, and he glanced up to see Keegan and the rest of her entourage finally coming to join them. With Mahogen there, the rest of her guards could take some time to relax and fill their bellies.

"Eoghan, what're you doing down here with the common folk?" Keegan teased, taking a seat between the two Torrpeki.

"I am not too high and mighty to share a meal and a drink with my people," Eoghan laughed, taking a swig from his tankard.

When he set it down, Keegan got a good whiff of what was inside: liquor. Even from across the table, Aron could smell the cloying scent.

"I do believe I owe you a drink. What would you like?" Mahogen said.

"I wanna say tequila, but I don't think that exists here, so I'll take a cider or mead," Keegan answered. As soon as the words were out of her mouth, she realized what bag of snakes she had opened.

"Alcohol from your world?" Eoghan assumed.

She nodded.

"So, Keegan, was it your idea to help Kade?" Breccan asked.

"Actually, he asked me. I was shocked!"

Jared jokingly jabbed Kade in the ribs, making his drink slosh and drip. Thankfully, the laughter of the table diffused the situation.

"I really did pick the wrong Tavin," Breccan sulked.

Keegan laughed. "I'm actually a Digore. And, hey, Kade did give you a run for your money."

"Only because I had help." To Breccan, Kade said, "I apologize again for not playing fair."

"No worries," Breccan replied. "Like *I* said, one should use everything they can."

A tankard was placed before Keegan and beside her Eoghan downed the rest of his drink in a single gulp.

"So..." Keegan said to the Reintablou, "I'm gonna assume you've got a hella high tolerance for alcohol."

"Sadly," Eoghan said. "Human liquor will only get us as drunk as you on ale."

"But thank the old gods for enishnom!" Breccan noted.

"I'd love to try some," she said casually.

Breccan and Eoghan shared a look before bursting into bellyaching laughter.

"What's so funny?" Keegan demanded.

"Well," Eoghan said slowly, "the only human I have seen not make a complete fool of themselves after drinking enishnom was Nikita."

"Vhat you vant?" the Russian called from a nearby table.

"I'll be fine," Keegan pressed. Boasting, she added, "I have been known to drink a few guys under the table."

Breccan raised an eyebrow, giving Eoghan a questioning look that asked for permission to make Keegan eat her words.

"Royik it," Eoghan said, pulling out a flask that looked like it held a few liters from his pocket. He poured some liquor into his empty cup and handed it to Keegan.

Keegan swirled the liquid around the cup, seeming to steel herself, before throwing her head back. Given that she barely grimaced, enishnom could not be that bad.

Breccan, Eoghan, and Mahogen looked at her incredulously.

"What?" she asked.

"Not even Nikita took it that well," Eoghan said.

She shrugged. "It tastes like moonshine." Then she grimaced. "Oof. There's the kicker."

"You have this in your world?"

"Something similar."

With a devious smile, Eoghan poured more enishnom into Keegan's cup. Aron did not have to rely on their empathy link to know she was drunk soon following. Between the mead she was now sipping and portions of enishnom, Aron would have been flabbergasted if she was not.

Elhyas must have been keeping an eye on her from afar as he came to give her a warning piece of advice with the intent to keep her from indulging further. "Don't think being hungover will get you out of training tomorrow."

Keegan laughed. "I'll be fine; I don't get hangovers."

Elhyas did not seem inclined to believe her but walked away leaving her to her own foolishness and folly.

Through their link, Aron could feel the alcohol's effects intensifying; she might have severely underestimated the enishnom. "Keegan, let us head to bed."

He was glad when she readily agreed, and Ezekhial trailed them from the dining hall.

Halfway across the entrance hall, Keegan stopped, gaze fixated on the riddle of the Queen Killer.

"It will be here in the morning," Aron promised, trying to pull her away.

"There's something about…" Keegan hiccupped, walking toward the mosaic, "it. I just can't get my mind around… *hiccup*… it."

"Come on," Ezekhial said, lightly taking her arm.

Keegan pulled away violently. "No." Hiccup.

As she reached out to touch the tiles, confusion and anger dappled her consciousness.

Impatiently, Ezekhial grabbed her arm again, setting her off balance. Keegan threw a hand against the wall and Aron felt something slice into her palm.

Grabbing her hand, he was shocked to find blood spilling from a deep gash. How sharp were the shards of the mosaic?

"Sola and Lunos," Ezekhial muttered both in apology and frustration.

Keegan was not paying attention, focusing on her hand. Slowly the blood stopped, and her skin knitted together, good as new. She wiped the blood on her trousers, though that did little aside from ruin a laundress's day.

"Keegan," Aron said quietly, "did you just heal yourself? Easily?"

She pushed past them. "Yeah."

Finally reaching their room, Keegan barreled in and flopped onto the bed.

At the doorway, Aron whispered to Ezekhial, "Maybe, do not tell Bernot about…"

"Too late."

Sighing, Aron wished the guard a good watch and locked the door.

"Come 'ere," Keegan said, rolling onto her back and opening her arms to him.

Before climbing into bed, he pulled off her boots. She normally slept in just a shirt, but it was not his place to undress her. He let her wrap her arms around him and was surprised when she began kissing his neck.

"Keegan," he said calmly.

"What?"

"Not tonight."

She pulled away, pouting. "Why not?"

"You are drunk."

He felt a spike of annoyance, but it faded to understanding. She kissed his lips before rolling over and falling into sleep's grasp.

«««« »»»»

It was not going to be a fall war and Bernot hated admitting it. It was now October, and they were not even past planning what to do after Grenadone.

There was a knock, and he looked up to find Jared standing in the doorway.

"You wanted to see me?"

"Yes," Bernot said, returning to the map. Planning what came next had almost become an obsession. "I heard a few interesting stories about Keegan last night."

Jared muttered, "I *saw* a few interesting stories about Keegan."

"Is it true she *walked* away after having three bits of enishnom?"

"Plus a glass of mead."

"Sola and Lunos, that girl should have been carried out! Have you heard anything of her this morning?"

"Last I saw, she was in the courtyard with Elhyas."

Bernot went to the window and looked down to see Keegan training with Elhyas like she had never drunk a drop of alcohol in her life.

"She should be in a bad state."

"She mentioned she doesn't get hangovers," Jared offered. "Honestly, hard to not envy her."

Bernot shook his head, muttering, "As if she was not powerful enough before."

"How long are we going to stay in Grenadone?" Jared asked after a long silence.

"Not too much longer, I hope."

Jared crept forward to look at the map. "Where are we going next?"

Bernot smiled. "Can you keep a secret?"

He shrugged. "Sure."

"I have no idea."

Jared was silent for a tense moment. Then, "The rivers are going to be their biggest defense."

Bernot gave him a puzzled look, hoping that would be enough to prompt him to continue.

"Agrielha is surrounded by rivers, so, no matter what, we're going to have to cross at least once. They'll see us coming. Unless you're strong enough to make the entire army invisible with a spell."

"What would you propose?"

"Confine them to the Land Between Rivers, unideally. Let them cross and then engage, ideally."

"Why let them cross?"

"Once across, they have a river at their backs and no easy way to retreat. Also, that leaves the Merfolk open to attack from the river. And saves us from needing to cross."

Bernot began to feel more confident about his decision. "Any other suggestions?"

Jared studied the pieces on the board representing the different races. "Split the army." He moved the blue Merfolk pieces to Revod, the red dragon pieces to Lake Romann, and small portions of the green Alvor, white human, and brown Torrpeki pieces to Grevasia.

Bernot was well aware of what the boy was thinking but wanted to hear it from his mouth. "Explain."

"The dragons should go to Lake Romann and cut Agrielha off from men and resources from the west. The hardest things to kill will keep them quite busy while the rest of us work on getting there. The Merfolk are most effective in water. After Revod, they can march to the Middle River Fort, capturing boats and supplies along the way. It also means fleeing down river isn't an option. Sending some of the remaining forces to Grevasia sets them up to take the Upper River Fort and work their way down. The rest then attack head on and there's nowhere Kolt isn't being pressed, spreading him thin. And there's nowhere for him to run either."

"This is assuming his army does not make it far past the river before we head them off."

"Even if they do, forces will still have to be reallocated to deal with the other sides of the attack, making them easier to push back."

"Not bad, boy," Bernot said. "Not bad at all."

The commendation perplexed Jared.

"Not everyone can plan a war," Bernot said. "It is a blessing and a curse."

Jared gave an awkward smile and when he did not say more, took that as his cue to leave.

Bernot could tell he was wondering what plans might now be hinging or centering around him, for this had clearly been a test.

When Jared finally left, furtive glances cast over his shoulder, Lyerlly put her book down and pushed herself from the armchair in the corner. Standing next to Bernot, she ran her fingers through his thick hair. "What was that all about?"

"I wanted to see if he was suitable to replace me."

Lyerlly's hand froze.

"Do not worry, I do not plan on going anywhere anytime soon but… this is war. I have to be prepared for the worst."

"Why not name Hernando your successor? He has much more experience and the men know and respect him."

"That is true, but Jared is a Child of Prophecy. And he, more than anyone, has something to lose; he will do whatever he needs to make sure we win. Hernando will not hesitate to sacrifice himself, but I need someone who is not afraid to sacrifice his men." He knew before Lyerlly opened her mouth that she did not like the way he was talking. "No, I do not want to sacrifice people either, but sometimes it must be done. I am going to formally announce Jared as my successor to the other leaders later and formalize his plan."

Chapter 13

"Hey, Eoghan," Keegan called loudly, entering the lab.

A haze smothered the air and clogged her nose with the smell of sulfur. The room might've been small, but Eoghan made it seem like a mansion. To get from one side to the other could take hours depending on how lost and distracted one got.

Eoghan poked his head from around a corner. "Good afternoon, my dear."

"What're you working on today?"

"Not working on, perfecting," the Torrpeki corrected, swirling a clear liquid in a flask. "And, if you will consent, I will have you quell one of the many questions bouncing around my skull."

Keegan crossed her arms loosely. "You've got my attention."

Eoghan pipetted the liquid from the flask into eight petri dishes. "I have created a compound that—I hope—can predict elemental abilities in newborns." He reached for a rack of test tubes containing blood, taking a sample from the first one. "The compound reacts differently with each type of magic—even before someone has gone through their changing."

He pipetted a drop of blood into a dish and Keegan watched the reagent turn to stone. "An earth elemental?"

Eoghan nodded and began working his way through the rest of the samples. The reactions for the elements were fairly straightforward; the blood from the water elemental turned into ice, the fire elemental burst into flame, the air elemental evaporated, and the life elemental caused a sprout to grow. The telepath's blood caused the solution to turn a vibrant shade of pink while the spellcaster's turned into a tar-like substance. And of course, the blood of someone born without magic had no reaction at all.

"Interesting," Keegan said, ideas already flying through her mind. "How does it react with Pexatoses?"

"That is precisely what I was hoping you would help me find out," Eoghan said. "I wanted to ask Waylan for a sample but did not think it would go over well. Nikita and Felix were happy to oblige; both reacted normally. But a sample size of two really does me no good."

"I'm not technically a Pexatose," Keegan reminded him.

"I always forget that," Eoghan said, scratching his chin and handing her a scalpel. "Any which way, let us see what happens."

Digging the scalpel into the pad of her thumb, blood beaded at the seam, and she let it fall into the petri dish. As soon as the blood touched the reagent, there was a violent reaction and the petri dish exploded.

"Interesting," Eoghan said, dusting glass fragments from his shoulders. A small trickle of blood ran down his forehead from a nick and he casually wiped it away.

Keegan picked up a shard of the petri dish from the floor. "Wasn't expecting that. What's that rule about elementals? The one where you get your powers."

"They come to fruition at thirty-five days of age," Eoghan answered.

"Right," Keegan said, working a curl of hair around a finger, mulling things over. "Explains why I got my powers a few days after I arrived—'cause I left at like a month old. Wait, is it thirty-five days of age, or thirty-five days of *presence* in this world?"

"We thought it was thirty-five days of age," Eoghan answered, "though you proved it might be thirty-five days of existence in this world."

"Does your reagent only work with blood?"

"I have only tried it with blood, but I do not see why it would not work with any biological tissue."

Keegan pulled a strand of hair from her head and stretched it out on the table.

"Care to explain?" the Torrpeki asked.

"So, the rule is thirty-five days after birth… or maybe existence in this world, right?" she started, taking the scalpel, and cutting the hair. "I don't know the replacement rate of blood cells, but with all the different components, something in there is likely older than thirty-five days. Hair, on the other hand, is constantly growing. And we know that you grow about a half inch to an inch a month. Thus, if we take the top portion closest to the root, erring on the side of caution and taking about a quarter inch, we have a sample less than thirty-five days of age to test."

Holding the small portion of hair, she waited while Eoghan prepared another petri dish. As she dropped the hair into the reagent, he flinched. The reaction wasn't volatile, simply turning to ice.

"I see we have our answer," Eoghan said. "And a curious one at that."

"Curious how?"

"In that water is not the element you find easiest."

"They're all relatively easy. Well, except fire."

"Water can be considered an opposite of all other elements, but that does not stop you from being highly adept in them."

"Except for fire." Keegan paused for a moment. "Wow, that actually explains a lot."

Eoghan gave her an inquiring look. "Proceed."

"You can argue that all the elements are complete opposites of each other, but some relate and interact with each other more than others. Water and fire are like, legit, polar opposites, which is maybe why for the life of me I can't do it."

"What do you mean they interact?" Eoghan questioned, as if she were an expert rather than just voicing theories.

"No element is purely that element. Fire needs air to thrive, air contains dust and water particles, water has dust particles and dissolved gases, earth usually has a portion of water and air and is largely organic matter, and life is a culmination of everything but fire."

The Torrpeki was silent as he mulled things over. "Do you think you will ever learn to control fire?"

"I think it'll be like trying to shove your right foot in your left shoe." When Eoghan gave her a perplexed look, she explained, "Entirely possible if you try hard enough, but difficult and uncomfortable. Also, mind if I ask another question?"

Eoghan perked up. "Of course!"

"With your test, we know that I was supposed to be a water elemental. So, how did I end up with… all five? And why doesn't Kade have the same abilities? You'd think with us being twins and all."

"An excellent question. And one that will not keep me up at night, for I know the answer. Well, I have a very good theory at least. And it was actually you who gave me the answer.

"It is all about genetics. We know that you should have been a water elemental. Yet, that is not the case. Why? What makes you different than any other elemental?" He paused, waiting for her to blurt an answer.

When she said nothing, he continued, "Your Nanagin. Or to be more precise, *Nanagins*; you experienced four."

"Okay…?"

"My theory is that Nanagins alter your genetics. So, you started with one element and telepathic abilities—likely from being a twin with abilities—and you then experienced four Nanagins, which altered your genetics four times, giving you the use of four additional elements."

Keegan raised her eyebrows in shock. The answer was so simple, yet still completely inconceivable. "Will you ever be able to prove any of this?"

"I think so. I have another project going, looking at what genes make an elemental. So far, I have found there are three. But I have a long way to go before I fully understand them."

"Wait… if my DNA's been altered by the Nanagins, why did the hair sample only show as a water elemental? Regardless of age, I would still have all the genes for every element."

Eoghan stopped to consider the question and slowly his face fell. "You are right, that is not possible." Lost in thought, the Torrpeki plucked another strand of her hair and cut it to length.

When he dropped it into the reagent, a sprout grew.

Heading him off, Keegan was already pulling more hair.

Several minutes later, they had petri dishes with various reactions.

"I do not know how to explain this," Eoghan finally said, shaking his head, bewilderment controlling his features.

"I do! It's genetic mosaicism. Or… some weird form of it. Not all of my cells have the same elemental magic expression."

A bell chimed from somewhere within the lab. "As always you seem to answer one question and raise five more," Eoghan griped. "Go get yourself ready for dinner."

She didn't need to be told twice.

《《《《 》》》》

Quin continued pulling Jared up the stairs, ignoring his questions and protests.

The spiral stairwell was making him dizzy, but if he just focused on her, he was able to see straight... er.

Suddenly, the walls dropped away, and the ceiling was replaced by the boundless night sky. A brisk breeze pulled over the battlements, raising gooseflesh, reminding them it was autumn.

Tremors racing across her body from the chill, Quin pulled him into a kiss, gentle and yearning. "No one is going to bother us here."

Taking that as permission, Jared began to pull at her clothes, and she gladly helped him; his soon followed.

Grabbing her hips, he hoisted Quin into the air. She was quick to wrap her legs around him and settle against his waist.

Wanting more, needing more, Jared laid her on one of the smooth stone tables bizarrely cemented to the roof; Quin's back arched underneath the cold touch.

He fumbled between Quin's legs before sliding into place, letting out a soft moan. She was truly the most beautiful when all she wore was a seductive smile and he leaned forward to kiss her.

As Quin began to nip and kiss at his neck while gently dragging her nails down his back, Jared let out a moan. The muscles in his back tensed, and unable to contain himself, pulled away, wanting to have no chance of Quin becoming in a family sort of way.

When he turned back to Quin, she had propped herself up on her elbows.

"Don't look so disappointed," he said kneeling before her.

Before Quin had the chance to say anything, he grabbed her legs and pulled her toward him and the edge of the table. She had explained this act to him before and he desperately wanted to make her experience the same kind of euphoria he had.

Realizing what he was doing, Quin didn't resist and lay back, arms reaching above her head to grip the edge of the stone. Already laden with lust, it was only seconds before moans of pleasure escaped her lips. Her back arched as she twined her fingers through his hair, her grip tightening as he pushed her closer to the edge.

Jared felt the tension and desire seeping from her every pore. And he knew the moment it all fell away, replaced by sweet feelings of release.

《《《《 》》》》

"Think you're up for it?" Zavier asked.

"Why wouldn't I be?" Keegan quipped. "I'm decent in everything."

"Except fire," Zavier blurted.

She shoved his shoulder playfully, causing him to stumble away in an exaggerated manner. "Don't need it." Raising her sword, she began to press him. While she was becoming a master at magic, her swordsmanship was still lacking.

As they sparred, Keegan felt eyes on her back. Scanning the field, she found a group of men and women blatantly staring. The group was ragged, as if they'd been traveling for some time. Only a few of the women had hair past their shoulders and she fumbled when she noticed the massive wolves amongst the group.

"Buluo," Bernot said, approaching from their left.

Keegan spun, surprised. "When'd they get here?"

"This morning. And they are only a very small portion of what I hope will be many." From the way he spoke, Keegan got the feeling there were bigger politics at play than just "defeat the evil king by any means necessary".

"I take it they're the reason for the skill test."

"Correct."

Keegan handed her training sword to Zavier and took a gulp of water. The other leaders weren't long in arriving.

Bernot began to give introductions, "Ne'Khole Sharp Tooth, this is—"

"I do not care who she is, only what she can do," Ne'Khole cut him off.

"You'd better give a damn about who I am," Keegan snapped, "'cause I ain't here for my own fucking benefit."

"No one asked you to speak," Ne'Khole snarled. "When you are wanted, you will know."

"*Oh, will I now?*"

Keegan, Bernot warned telepathically. "Why do we not begin the skills test?"

"Start with—" Ne'Khole began.

"I'll start with earth. And if you don't like it, tough shit." Keegan gave a petty smile to drive the point home.

Ne'Khole's blue eyes darkened.

"What would you like me to do?" Keegan asked the other leaders.

"See if you can make diamonds from dust," Eoghan said.

The impossible task was meant to challenge her— and impress the Buluo... if she could pull it off.

Keegan concentrated on the ground beneath her feet and searched for any unlikely pockets of coal. It quickly became apparent she wasn't going to be that lucky. So, she turned her search toward graphite. There were trace amounts, forcing her to pull the mineral from across the city.

Taking her block of graphite, she began to pressurize it. After minutes of straining, she knew she'd never be able to create enough pressure. But the carbon bonds were becoming unstable, and she attempted to shift a few. After the first bond shifted to jut out from its sheet-like layer, the rest followed. Unfurling her fingers, she displayed the rough diamond before tossing it to Eoghan.

He held it up to the light checking its clarity. "A few flaws," he muttered. "But truly astounding. Care to explain your methodology?"

"I started by looking for coal—" Keegan said, as the diamond was passed around.

"Coal is not diamond," Ne'Khole retorted.

Keegan forced herself to retain a pleasant tone. "With enough pressure coal turns into diamonds. As I was saying, with no coal, I looked for graphite, which has the same atomic composition minus one carbon-carbon bond. I tried to pressure it into a diamond but couldn't create enough force. But the pressure I did manage allowed me to shift the carbon bonds and create a tetrahedral shape rather than the sheets that exist in graphite. And, voilà, dust to diamond—kinda."

"Not what he asked for," Ne'Khole said. "What use are you—"

"I'm not a goddamn miracle worker; take what you get," Keegan barked. To move things forward, she said, "Life is next."

"Kill someone, then bring them back," Okleiy said.

Keegan closed her eyes and groaned. "Do I have a volunteer?"

"I will do it," Mahogen said, pushing forward.

His father grabbed his arm. "I will not allow that!"

"I have faith in her."

There was the hidden implication that Okleiy hoped she'd fail, using her as a pawn to remove a less than liked individual. Realizing the predicament he'd put himself in, the Alvor king let his son step forward.

"Do please try to bring me back," Mahogen whispered.

"Oh, don't worry, this one's easy." Keegan forewarned, "Sorry for any pain."

Mahogen's expression immediately turned to worry, but he gave a minute nod to proceed anyway.

Placing a hand on the Alvor prince's chest, Keegan felt his heart beating, pumping blood. Closing her fist, she stopped it.

Mahogen began gasping like a fish out of water. When he stumbled back, Keegan created a chair and helped him sit. It took longer than she'd anticipated for him to slip away and by the time it was over, her nerves were frayed.

Taking a deep breath, she placed her hand on his chest again. Feeling his now cold heart, she gently curled her fingers. Mahogen's heart responded as if it were being moved by her hand, and slowly she worked the muscle back to life.

"Welcome back," she said when Mahogen at last took a ragged breath. "I'd chill here for a while."

"I have no intention of going anywhere," Mahogen groaned.

"That was not bringing someone back to life," Ne'Khole argued.

"Depends on how you define death," Keegan said. "I caused a clinical death, which is reversible. What you're asking for is biological death and I don't think *anyone* can reverse that."

"Whoever your life tutor is, they are doing an excellent job," Eoghan said.

Keegan gave him a puzzled look. "I haven't been given a life tutor. I just work with Reven whenever we get the chance."

The leaders shared a few concerned looks while Okleiy's eyes widened in horror.

"By Okleiy's expression I'm gonna assume that was an accidental oversight," Keegan said.

You seem to be doing well with Reven, Tahrin said. *Might I suggest just making this Reven officially her tutor.*

"Fine by me," Bernot said, to be quickly agreed with by everyone but Okleiy, who was too busy cursing at himself.

"Moving along," Atlia said, "water next."

"Please don't ask me to do blood manipulation," Keegan cut in. "I told Bernot no and I'll tell you the same thing."

"I was going to ask you to make a cloud," Atlia said sympathetically.

"Oh, easy." She curled her fingers while twisting her wrist and a small cloud floated above her hand. "Just cool the water vapor, and, presto, cloud." She opened her hand and let it dissipate.

Dare we try fire next? Tahrin asked.

Keegan grimaced. "Probably not one of our better ideas." But, just to prove it could be done, she created a little flame that sputtered for all but a second. "That leaves us with air."

Without warning, someone from the group of Buluo shot a blast of air at her—at least she assumed it was one of them—sending her tumbling backwards. As she fought to get to her feet, the force increased, making her body feel heavy as stone.

Keegan let them think she was beaten before easily rising to her feet. "It's gonna take more than that to keep me down."

"I was told she had no training in air magic," Ne'Khole said.

"That is true," Bernot said, a smile playing on his lips. "But she tends to work things out on her own."

"Impossible."

Keegan laughed. "You clearly don't know me very well."

Ne'Khole tensed and Keegan prepared herself for what the woman thought was going to be a surprise attack. The gale was hurricane strength and she lazily flicked it aside, sending a rack of weapons flying, earning her dead silence.

"That went well," Keegan said sarcastically as Ne'Khole stormed away.

Chapter 14

"You finally going to pay attention?" Ezekhial asked as Keegan and the entourage of leaders finally left the training field.

Instead of answering, Kade smiled and disarmed the guard with a deft flick of the wrist.

"How about a challenge?" a woman called.

Kade looked over to find Icella leaning provocatively against a sword rack, arms crossed loosely over her chest. She still hardly wore any clothing by human standards, a Merfolk trend he and every other man found quite distracting.

"Sure," he said. "But no doubling your weapon!"

Icella playfully rolled her eyes. "Not man enough?"

"Two weapons, two opponents," he told her, "and I don't know where Raven is."

"A shame, but anyhow." The Mermaid came forward, the sun shining off her thin blade as she pulled it from its sheath. She rushed at him and had her sword to his neck before he could even move.

Pushing her blade aside, Kade began an attack of his own. Icella danced around him as he blocked each of her strikes. Out of tune with each other, he hiccuped at her attacks until he slowly settled into her rhythm.

Together they moved, their weapons hardly touching for a heartbeat whenever they met. This was easy and... pure, and not even Icella's acrobatics could throw him off. Soon, sweat began to slide down his back while Icella looked like she was growing bored.

"Not enough of a challenge for you?" he grunted, dodging an attack that would've sliced his throat.

"Very few things are challenges for me," she answered calmly.

Kade smiled wickedly before pulling something Keegan would do. He bid his time and when Icella's sword was momentarily focused elsewhere, rushed in, and placed his shoulder on her hip, grabbed her legs, and dropped her to the ground.

To her credit, the Mermaid didn't squeal in surprise. As she landed, she released her grip on her sword, letting it fly. Here, Kade had the advantage, or so he hoped.

They grappled, each trying to pin the other, neither succeeding. At one point, he found Icella's chest pressed against his face, suffocating him. Then, somehow, Kade managed to get a hold of Icella's wrists and pin her down. The Mermaid squirmed, bucking to throw him off, but he had the weight advantage. Eventually, she settled and Kade took that as a sign of submission.

Pulling away and rising to his feet, Kade watched as Icella lay on the grass, sucking in deep mouthfuls of air like a fish out of water. "You all right?"

It was a moment before she managed to wheeze, "Yes. I am just not used to weights on top of me. We are so much lighter underwater."

"Sounds like you're calling me fat." he joked.

Icella lightly tapped her own stomach breathlessly. "Maybe I am."

Rolling his eyes, he offered her a hand up. Icella didn't get far before the ground shook terribly while from the air came a fearsome cry. The tremor set Kade off balance and he fell forward, just managing to brace himself on his forearms to keep from crushing Icella again.

Watching the sky, he saw hundreds of dragons taking to the air. He braced for the slamming wind he knew was coming, but still wasn't strong enough to withstand it. When the downdraft abated, he flung himself off Icella who'd been trapped beneath him.

"Where do you think the dragons are going?" Icella asked, helping dust him off.

He watched the cloud of dragons meld with the horizon. "Not a clue."

《《《《 》》》》

It was hard for Braxton to fathom how Kolt had raised an army in less than a month, but the proof stood before him. The men did not glitter in steel armor like he would have preferred, instead sporting dull and dented armor or leather armor. It was better than nothing, but it would not ensure they saw the other side of this war. Granted, nothing but benevolence from the old gods could guarantee that. There was a chaotic nervousness filling the air and it was beginning to put Braxton on edge.

Busy mulling over the not-so-distant future, he almost failed to notice Kolt approaching. Slung across his back were two bows and quivers of arrows.

The king leaned on the windowsill beside him. "Ready?" he asked easily. Not headed to war himself, Kolt could be nonchalant.

"Do I have a choice?" Braxton asked sourly.

"No."

He had no desire to be around Kolt, to be reminded of every horrible thing he was going to do and started to push away.

"Not so fast. Firstly, you are, hence forth, Commander of the Vosjnik."

Braxton would have questioned the decision if Kolt stopped talking.

"Vitia rules with an iron fist, which I quite like, but the griffins will not listen to her, and too many cooks spoil the soup. Mind you, I expect the results I want."

"I shall do my best," Braxton stammered obediently to his own shock and dismay.

"I am sure you will," Kolt said lazily. "Now, on matters concerning the Children of Prophecy; I want Keegan brought back alive—in pieces if you must, but alive. Aron is to be brought back alive and as whole as possible—*I* want the joy of destroying him. As for Jared and Kade—kill them."

"Why do you want Keegan alive?"

"In case you decide to lie."

He gave a heavy sigh through his nose, pretending there was no merit to the reasoning. "Will you remove the slajor manacles?"

Kolt gave him a bemused look. "Why should I do that?"

"If you want to win this war, would it not make sense to give me every capability to do so?"

"You are an archer and do not need magic to be one."

"But why limit me?"

"Because, if I were to remove the manacles, with the griffins and Nico away from me, what is stopping you from defecting?"

"What if I swore to return?" The words were soot in his mouth.

"You and every other member of the Vosjnik and the griffins," Kolt specified.

Braxton was ready to balk when he remembered he and Nico were only part of the Vosjnik in a ceremonial sense; neither of them bore the brand. "Deal," Braxton said, putting on a show of defeat. "Though, should anyone fall in battle, I do not relish the thought of dragging their bodies across the continent." So many doors were opening at once it was hard to know which would lead to liberation.

"Should someone die, leave them," Kolt growled. "What use do I have for a sack of meat and bones?" He held out a hand.

Braxton shook it.

While they solidified their deal, Kolt pulled at a slajor manacle.

As it was removed, magic washed over Braxton like a cool summer wind.

When he held out his other hand for Kolt to remove the second manacle, his brother refused. "Cannot make it too easy for you. Oh, almost forgot." He unslung a bow and quiver.

"I already have a bow…"

"But is it a magic one?" Kolt forced the weapon into his hands. "These arrows can punch through just about anything aside from diamond and a protection spell. Do not say I never gave you anything."

"Who is the second set for?" Braxton called as Kolt ambled away.

"Never you mind. Oh, I am placing a spell on Nico so that should he touch his brother, he will die. I will remove it once he returns."

Braxton would have responded had there not been a sudden shooting pain in his head, blinding him with hues of blues and oranges. He felt himself falling.

He could hardly feel the stones of the castle underneath him, as too many voices to count echoed off the walls, making them indecipherable. Images flashed and raced before his eyes in a sickening blur.

When the world finally slowed and returned to normal, he rolled over and vomited.

«««« »»»»

Ravliean

Alyck called frantically, "Thad. Thad!"

"I am right here," Thaddeus said, crossing the room and gently taking ahold of Alyck's arm, realizing he was having a vision. His usually milky eyes had become like white obsidian.

"Listen closely," Alyck started, face pale and clammy. His hands scrabbled to latch onto Thaddeus's shirt. "I see Keegan dying two deaths. Each a possibility. In the first, she is young and bloodied, defeated before my brother. In the second, she is old."

"Focus on the second," Thaddeus prompted, gently prying Alyck's fingers from his shirt. "How does she get there?"

"By kneeling before Kolt and—" he hiccupped, "a sword at her throat."

Thaddeus tried to work out how being killed by Kolt meant the girl lived to die of old age but could think of no explanation. Unless it would only appear she had been defeated by Kolt. "How does she die the first death?"

"A sword to the gut from my brother."

But Caius was dead. So little of this prophecy made sense.

"Ravliean. Ravliean…" Alyck mumbled.

"Return? Who is returning?" Thaddeus asked recognizing the Old Language word.

"It has to happen," Alyck pleaded. "*King* Kolt must kill her. Braxton must bring her here to face that fate."

"The Lazado will never just hand her over."

Alyck tried out the words, "Hand her over… hand her over… They must. They must! Ravliean."

Thaddeus tried to reason with the Blind Prophet, but there was no use.

"Paper," Alyck barked, cutting him off.

He had seen Alyck get this stubborn only a handful of times. All with due cause. The Blind Prophet had seen an impossible future and only he knew how to make it come to be.

Carefully, Thaddeus placed the quill in Alyck's grasp and guided his hand until the nib touched the parchment. "Write, my friend."

Alyck scribbled furiously before calling for an envelope. Dripping wax onto the envelope, he embossed it with the Alagard sigil, using a ring he pulled from his vest. "Get this to Braxton and tell him it is life or death."

Thaddeus hesitated.

"Go!" Alyck barked, "Now! And spell it so no one but the recipient may open it."

Knowing Alyck did not get impatient or angry without reason—with him at least—Thaddeus rushed to find Braxton.

Hurrying through the halls, he nearly collided with many a servant. By some luck, he stumbled upon Kolt. "Where is your brother?" he said breathlessly.

"Why does it matter?" Kolt sneered.

He gave a partial truth, "Alyck has information on how to capture Keegan."

"In his room," Kolt said, "hurry before he leaves."

Tearing through the halls once more, he worked on the sealing spell. Reaching Braxton's room, he was out of breath and a stitch had him clutching at his side; he was certainly feeling his age. Pushing past his limitations, he barged into the room, startling the prince.

"Are you all right?" Braxton asked, gently placing a hand on Thaddeus's back as he hunched over, wheezing and sucking in deep breaths.

He waved the letter in the prince's face until he took it.

"Bernot Bællar?" Braxton questioned, going to open the letter.

"No," Thaddeus puffed, "deliver it to him. If you do not, Keegan will die."

Swallowing a lump in his throat, Braxton nodded and tucked the letter into his sketchbook before packing both in a satchel he slung over his shoulder. "I will make sure he gets it. Stay as long as you need to recover." In the doorway, he lingered, perhaps realizing this might be the last he saw of his home. Perhaps wishing it were so.

Chapter 15

Quin parried Jared's attack. "Soon, you'll be able to beat Kade," she crowed in that seductive way of hers.

"I don't know about that," Jared countered, though, he had to admit that he had come a long way. Mere weeks ago, maintaining a conversation while sparring would've been impossible. He slashed at her and was going to grab his dagger when she spun and walked off. Once past his surprise, he called, "Where are you going?"

"My shift's over; I'm going to sleep. You should join me if you can beat your next guard." She winked and by the way she smiled, he was never going to win.

He turned to find Mahogen waiting patiently, his layered hair bristling easily in the light October wind. "I am sure we can have me defeated by the end of an hour."

Jared could muster no response as his face flushed. It was still a mystery how anyone could be so casual about sex.

Gracefully, Mahogen pulled his sword from its sheath. The cut and detailing of the blade matched its owner and could practically have been an accessory.

Jared raised his own weapon, suddenly hating how bullish it appeared; the metal was dull, and the blade could use honing. It honestly looked no better than one of the sparring swords, though would still cut rather than bruise.

"Do you have a sword of your own?" Mahogen asked, striking out.

Jared blocked, grimacing as he realized the Alvor thought this was a training sword. "This is it. Kade bought it for me in Suttan and I never really thought I needed anything more."

The Alvor clanged his sword against Jared's and twisted, wrenching the weapon from his grip. "No sword is useless, only improperly used." With a flick of the wrist, he had the tip of his sword at Jared's chin.

"I'll never beat you," he snapped, pushing the sword away and going to retrieve his own.

"I would not say never," Mahogen teased, poking Jared's arse with the weapon.

Jared yelped, causing the Alvor to laugh, tears in the corner of his eyes.

"That's not funny!" he yelled. "How would you like it if someone stuck a sword up your arse?"

Mahogen paused. "You would not see me complaining."

Jared immediately knew he was missing something… he just didn't know what; he would have to ask Keegan later.

Pushing past the moment, sword in hand, Jared turned on Mahogen and they settled into a rhythm. Unable to just react and think of nothing, he took in the details of the world around him.

The leaves on the few surviving trees were no longer green, instead colored in pale yellows and bright reds. He felt a sudden pang, realizing the green-tinged streaks in Mahogen's hair no longer reflected the state of the world. Yet, the forest greens dancing around his pupils promised rebirth if the world was patient—which it always was.

Jared watched as the corners of Mahogen's thin lips twitched and realized the Alvor was enjoying the exercise. No, he was enjoying playing with Jared—for he could not say this was truly training or sparring with Mahogen's skills so far outmatching his own.

Yet he didn't mind. Jared liked spending time with the Alvor. Around him he felt… free of duty. His own lips pulled into a reciprocating expression. Though he disliked finding himself at the end of a sword, the physical exertion was something he enjoyed—something that kept him from drowning in worry at night.

Figuring he was going to lose, Jared decided to try a move Quin had taught him. With Mahogen's next attack, he let his sword fly. Hands free, he reached for the dagger belted at his waist and the one in his boot. He used one to block Mahogen's next attack and the other to counter. His dagger found the inside of Mahogen's thigh and the Alvor froze.

"Seems I am beaten if I would like to keep my manhood."

Realizing he'd done the seemingly impossible, Jared slowly withdrew.

"An interesting thing to do while sparring or against one opponent, but in battle that will get you killed," Mahogen warned, lithely sheathing his sword. "Go see Quin; you have earned it."

Jared's mind was abuzz and knowing he wouldn't be told twice, scooped up his sword and all but raced toward the castle. In what felt like seconds, he was outside Quin's door. He knocked once and, courtesy aside, barged in.

At his intrusion, Quin bolted upright, a dagger in hand—although seconds ago it appeared she'd been sound asleep. Realizing it was him, she relaxed.

Quin rose from the bed, stretching her arms above her head. "Wasn't expecting you."

He was pleased to find she'd been sleeping without clothes. A smile rose to his lips as he stalked forward to kiss her.

Quin had no qualms with what he wanted, and her fingers were already working to undo the lacing on his trousers.

««« »»»

"What I would 've given t' see the looks on their faces," Reven exclaimed through bouts of laughter as Keegan recounted the events of her skills test. "Well, I guess since I 'm officially your tutor, we 're goin' t' have t' make things a little more difficult for ya."

"Bring, it, on," she said with a smirk.

Reven crossed his arms and put a hand on his chin while he thought out loud, "We know you can heal—eh, well, not yourself, but that 's pretty standard."

"I did heal my hand that night I got a tad trashy," Keegan interjected.

"A kyfa." When Keegan gave him a confused look, he stumbled, "A… what 's that word you use for things that happen… weirdly?"

"A fluke?"

"Yes! It was a fluke," Reven said. "We call that a kyfa. You have n't been able to do it again. You 're not half bad at manipulation. Can even do blood manipulation… though, that 's with water." There was a moment of silence. "Have we tried transformations yet?"

"Nope," she answered, excited to see what this new aspect of life magic had in store. "By the name I'm assuming it's turning one thing into another."

"Correct."

"Any limitations?"

"Mostly that you can n't take a plant and expect a human," Reven said.

"So, like can become like. Got it. What should we try first?"

Reven never got the chance to respond, stopping short as he noticed Eoghan approaching, a stern and concerned look on his face.

"Hey, Eoghan," Keegan said, brows creasing in unease, "everything okay?"

"Things could be better," the Torrpeki told her. "With the autumn comes the sickness."

"Ah, flu season," Keegan said, pretending to reminisce about simpler times.

Brushing her statement aside with a confused look, Eoghan said, "Yes, well, this time of year can present some challenges for Pexatoses."

"If you're worried about me getting sick, don't be. I rarely get sick."

"That might have been true in the other world, but here it could mean death for you. For whatever reason, Pexatoses seem to be greatly affected by pesky diseases and easily killed by anything more."

Keegan muttered, "Smallpox blankets."

"What?" Reven said.

"Smallpox blankets," she repeated. "Uh, bear with me. So, smallpox was a really nasty disease in my world. People in Europe had a bit of a higher tolerance for it because they were exposed to it so often. When the Europeans went exploring and found 'the new world', one of the ways they conquered the natives was with smallpox blankets. They gave the natives blankets infected with smallpox and it essentially wiped them out. This happened because the natives had never encountered the disease, so their immune systems were completely inept at fighting it off, leading to a whole lot of death. So here, your diseases are the smallpox blankets and Pexatoses are the natives."

"I see," Eoghan said.

Keegan had a thought. "Hey, maybe we should look into vaccines."

"What is a vaccine?"

"A vaccine is… it's medicine, generally given as an injection. It contains dead or weakened cells of a disease; and since the cells are dead or weak, your immune system fights them off with no problem. And when or if you encounter the full-strength strain, your body is already familiar with the virus and knows what antigens to make and it makes it way less likely that you'll even show symptoms of the disease and suffer from it… or die."

"Astonishing," Eoghan mumbled. "I must create this."

A small part of her wanted to burst his bubble and let him know it wasn't such an easy thing to do; but if the diseases of this world were so deadly to her, she needed him to believe he could—and then do it.

"Well," Reven said, thinking Eoghan's reason for coming over was taken care of, "Keegan, back to training."

"Oh, I was not here for information," Eoghan answered. "I need Keegan to go into quarantine."

"I don't think that'll be necessary," she contested. "Hardly anyone is sick."

"I have seen many Pexatoses fall quickly. Several who have said the same thing as you."

Keegan tried to blow him off.

"Keegan, please," Eoghan said, stooping to look her in the eyes. "I thought I would ask nicely before I got the other leaders involved. One way or another, you will go into quarantine."

Realizing he'd live up to the threat, she decided to save some time and concede.

《《《《 》》》》

"You will be fine," Lyerlly told the man, wondering why the smallest ailments turned men into children. "Bed rest and tea will knock it right out."

"But it feels as if my chest's burdened," the man complained.

"Completely normal with an autumn ail," she contested, sending him on his way.

Noticing Eoghan, which was not hard to do when he towered above everyone, she let one of the nurses take over. She realized the Torrpeki was with someone. "Surprised to see you here, Waylan; I heard you have a mind of your own. Well, the quarantine ward is over here. You are the last to arrive."

"There's others?" Waylan said.

"Yes, the other Pexatoses are also being quarantined," Eoghan explained.

Waylan groaned. "Who am I going to be stuck with—besides Keegan?"

Lyerlly opened the door to the ward to reveal Nikita Sokolov, Felix Isaacs, and of course, Keegan Digore.

Keegan glanced up to offer a smile, which soured when she saw Waylan.

Waylan made to flee. "Oh, fuck this."

Eoghan deftly moved to stand in his path. "Come friend, this will not kill you."

"Can't fucking prove that," Waylan grumbled.

There was only one bed left unclaimed which Waylan took cautiously, eyeing the others like a wounded animal.

"We are going to minimize contact with anyone outside this room, so try to need us as little as possible," Lyerlly said.

"How long we gonna be here?" Keegan asked.

"At least a few days, likely longer. Eoghan mentioned something about a vaccine, but I am not sure what that entails or how long that will take."

"Ughh," Keegan groaned, flopping backwards onto her cot dramatically. "What are we supposed to do until then?"

"You can train on a small scale," Eoghan suggested.

"Gonna have to," she groused.

Lyerlly felt for her, but it was better Keegan be bored and frustrated than on the brink of death or dead. She motioned for Eoghan to leave and closed the door securely.

"I do not think it will take me long to isolate the illness," Eoghan claimed.

"Let us hope not, or we may find none of them are sane," she noted. "I do wonder though what makes you believe illnesses here are potentially deadly to Pexatoses."

Eoghan said, "What is hardly an inconvenience to us, I have seen kill a Pexatose in a matter of days. And though Felix and Waylan should be fine having been in this world so long, Nikita and Keegan are extremely vulnerable."

She subconsciously placed a hand on her ever-growing belly. "If you do not think Felix and Waylan are in danger, why include them in the quarantine?"

"Felix's powers relate to healing, and it never hurts to have him on hand. As for Waylan, I am hoping forced proximity with Keegan will convince him to train her in metal magic. Not that she has not already mostly figured it out on her own; but I am sure there is something more he can teach her."

"Well, let us hope Felix's services are not needed. In the meantime, you should start working on that... what was it?"

"Vaccine."

"I doubt Keegan will stay complacent for long."

"Lyerlly, are you sure I cannot convince *you* to partake in the quarantine?"

She snapped, "I am not incapable due to this baby."

"I know, I know," Eoghan said, raising his hands in manner meant to reassure her that he believed her. "But expecting mothers tend to be susceptible to sickness."

Lyerlly waved him off. "I will be fine—and if not, you can be the first to tell me I told you so."

"I will have to be the first one to make an attempt to make you better or your husband will have my head," Eoghan returned.

«««« »»»»

Kade opened his mind to Reven. Icella was on the other side of the Mermaids, working to fight her way back to them.

He'd originally been wary of Icella, but somehow, she seemed to round out he and Reven. And he couldn't admit he was sad their duo had become a trio. Icella was an accomplished swordswoman who had much to teach them—and to learn from them.

Quickly realizing it was no challenge for Kade or Reven to spar each other, and that they could hold their own against her, Icella had invented a game. It was by no means easy to win, but Kade enjoyed it—and the challenge it gave.

Even though she was sparring her own kind, Icella was like light as she danced between their opponents, making Kade feel like he was moving through molasses. But what he lacked in speed and aerobatics, he made up for in stubbornness and strength. Well, stubbornness, as the Mermaids equaled, if not exceeded, his strength.

Kade blocked an attack and found his back pressed against Reven's as they each dueled a Mermaid. A familiar situation. When the moment was right, they ducked under the Mermaids' guards and reversed their positions. They quickly tapped the women with their swords rendering them "dead". Both dropped to the ground, giggles slipping past their lips.

There were only three opponents left compared to the six they'd started with. They'd never made it this far.

Let 's get wild, Reven suggested.

Casually, Kade let Icella know the plan. There was some grumbling from her end, but she'd learned when they presented a plan to her, it was going to happen, regardless of if she wanted it to or not.

Giving Reven a nod, Kade raised his sword and released a wild yell, charging at the smallest Mermaid. She was taken aback, but quickly regained her composure. At the last second, he and Reven peeled away, attacking the two women trailing them.

Somehow, the Mermaids were prepared, and Kade found a sword against his chest. True to the rules of the game, he dropped. Reven was similarly dispatched.

Left against three opponents, Icella was unperturbed, her movements fluid and never faltering as she parried and countered. She felled another attacker before being taken down.

There was a moment of silence before all those who had fallen rose again, laughs and compliments spilling forth. Many of the Mermaids came and ran their fingers along Reven's arms and chest, ridiculous accolades of his prowess coming like honey from their mouths. None of them approached him though.

Icella grinned, coming to lean against Kade. "Much better," she whispered into his ear.

Had it been almost anyone else leaning on him like that, they would've found a knife in their gut. Multiple times. And had it been anyone else, he might have believed the words to be a kind of seduction.

"I 'ould hope so," Reven snapped. "We 've been doing this day in, day out."

"What was our downfall this time?" Kade asked.

"You got cocksure," Icella answered. "Nothing is over until it is over."

"We'll keep that in mind."

"Ready to go again?"

Reven cracked his knuckles. "Always!"

Chapter 16

The army had not moved from outside the castle of Agrielha. Braxton could easily sleep in his own bed, but he felt better—*freer*—amongst the soldiers. Though a prince, and now Commander, deserving of lavish accommodations, he had declined such comforts, happy to share his tent with Nico. He felt safer that way… further away from Kolt. And better yet, he knew they were near untouchable with the griffins just outside. When the time came, not even Bernot's spies and assassins would dare to try to touch him inside this tent.

Braxton could not help but smile into the darkness, recalling how the griffins had become their sentinels.

Harker had wanted to sleep inside the tent with them, excited to be free of the stone that normally separated him from Nico. But the hatchling did not exactly *fit* inside. And, unfortunately, Harker only discovered that after getting caught in the canvas and destroying the tent.

Myrish had chuckled in his odd way the entire time, bemused as the hatchling thrashed in the canvas. Thankfully, the hatchling had gotten the tent free of its pegs and set off blindly through camp, leaving Braxton and Nico in a heap, only able to stare in utter shock after him. It was a wonder the hatchling had not done more damage blundering around, blinded as he was.

The soldiers nearest them had understandably not been happy. But it worked in Braxton's favor; the other men had shied away, physically moving to other parts of the camp to give them as wide a berth as possible. It had left them with a clearing that all seven griffins were able to settle into. And from the wary glances their newest neighbors gave them, it would not be long before they were afforded even more space.

Across the tent, Nico snored in his usual deafening way, as he had been for several hours. It was why Braxton was still awake. Through the noise though, tiredness eventually found him, as it always did.

In his dream, night was still upon him, but he was not in his tent, as the stars twinkled clearly above. He stood alongside a road, though it was like nothing he had ever seen before. It was neatly paved in a thick, black substance with yellow lines demarcating the edges and white dashes running through the middle. What those lines meant, he could only guess. The road was fringed by what was seemingly a vast nothingness in the low light of the mostly waned moon.

Hearing something tramping across the terrain, Braxton ducked into a ditch and lay on the dusty ground, hoping the darkness would give adequate cover.

Two men stumbled from the dark, headed toward a metal contraption sitting along the roadside, silver in color, that he had previously overlooked. It had four wheels, but not made of a substance he recognized.

Distracted as he was by the contraption, he almost did not pay attention to the men. He only caught a glance at them before they yanked open the doors of the thing and sat inside. Braxton's mouth dropped open when he recognized his father. What was this? Caius was dead. Was he seeing into the afterlife?

The machine gave a roar and began moving forward. Braxton rose and chased after it but with a lurch, abruptly found he was back in the tent, Nico's snores filling the night.

Sitting up, he rubbed his eyes, trying to figure out what he had seen. Could it have been a vision? No, he told himself, he still wore a slajor manacle. That was impossible. But... much of what was once thought impossible had recently been proven otherwise.

So... maybe. Maybe.

"Just a dream," he muttered, forcing himself to believe the words.

《《《《 》》》》

Keegan took a deep breath and held it. It hadn't even been twenty-four hours and she was losing her mind. There was nothing to do, and everyone had quickly declined to practice magic with her... for various good reasons.

Felix and Waylan were only just managing to not kill each other—which sadly offered the most in the way of entertainment. Waylan couldn't help but call the Irishman "Lucky Charms" and Felix's response was always... well, not nice—even if justified.

At the knock on the door, they all shot to attention like startled rabbits.

"How is everyone doing?" Lyerlly called through a crack in the door.

"Get me out of here." Keegan said dramatically, "Or kill me, please!"

"Eoghan thinks he has found a vaccine," Lyerlly said, "so hopefully, you can leave soon."

The door opened fully and the Torrpeki slipped in, a few vials in hand. Each was the color of tar and from the looks it, had the same consistency.

"That was fast," Felix commented, going to meet him.

Eoghan handed the vials to Felix, who stared at them for hardly a moment before giving them back with a shake of the head. "Won't do. This one's close though."

"So much for getting out of here," Keegan muttered, flopping back onto the bed. "There's *literally* nothing to do."

"What about practicing magic?" Eoghan asked innocently.

"No," the other Pexatoses yelled in unison.

Eoghan gave them worried and confused looks.

"Trust us," Nikita said, "Jesus girl is perfect at using magic. Except for fire."

"I have some books in my laboratory, if that will help."

"Please," Keegan said. "Have anything on the Dragon King?"

Eoghan shook his head. "Most of everything on the Dragon King is oral."

She sighed. "Wanna get to tellin' then?"

Eoghan seemed to debate whether that was a good idea or not before taking a seat on the floor. Unfortunately, he didn't bring much to light that she hadn't read.

"Anything else?" she asked once he was done. "I knew most of that already."

"How?"

"*The Peoples of Arciol*," she told him.

Eoghan looked genuinely surprised, even a little disturbed. "Where did you find that book?"

"Thaddeus's shop... Is it rare or something?"

"Incredibly," Eoghan answered. "There is only one in existence. It was handwritten by the Dragon King himself."

There was the sound of breaking glass and a curse from Felix. The vials were now shattered on the floor and the Pexatose was sucking the pad of his thumb.

Waylan started to call for Lyerlly to ask for a broom and dustpan, but Keegan stopped him. "I got it."

Reaching for the earth paika, she encouraged the glass to rejoin. The vials mended, and she handed them back to the Torrpeki; though there was no magic that was going to clean the goo from the floor.

By Eoghan's incredulous expression, Keegan assumed glass was one of those difficult subtypes. "Glass is made of superheated silica, a mineral. What breaks, I can fix."

The statement struck a chord like a phantom music note and there was a shadow of pain in her hand, as if someone had cut it. A hazy memory on the edge of her mind crept forward. She remembered her hand resting on the mosaic of the Queen Killer. Then Ezekhial knocked into her, and she sliced her palm on the tiles. No, not the tiles, the *sword*.

Keegan didn't bother pleading to be released and rushed for the door. Causing a great gust of wind, she was satisfied to hear the heavy wooden bar on the other side smash into the ground.

"Jesus girl, vhat the fuck!" Nikita yelled.

With the commotion behind her, she knew at least two people were giving chase. She could only hope she'd reach the mosaic before anyone managed to haul her back to quarantine.

Calling over her shoulder, she recited the first line of the riddle, "To be made whole, something must first be broken!" No one would understand, but she didn't have time to explain. Not if she wanted to test her idea.

Her Converse protested against the stone floor, nearly tripping her as she skidded to a stop in the entrance hall. She placed a hand against the mosaic where the hilt of the sword was depicted. At first it felt like a flat surface, but as she concentrated, her hand sank into the wall. Smiling, she pulled the sword from the artwork.

It was a long weapon, entirely red as a rose. Set in the pommel was a large ruby that reflected flecks of light across the hall like flower petals. There were murmurs from those behind her and a cracking sound as a stone protruded from the wall in the shape of a handle; inside was a scabbard the same shade as the sword.

"Okay, back to quarantine," Keegan said, uniting sword and sheath.

She couldn't help but be gleeful in the fact that everyone's jaw was on the floor.

《《《《 》》》》

"Apologies. Keegan always seems to keep us on our toes," Eoghan said, slightly out of breath as he arrived. Pulling a key from his pocket, he unlocked the laboratory's door and ushered Aron inside.

"What could she have possibly done?" Aron asked. "Last I heard she was in quarantine." And he felt it, too. Keegan was bored out of her mind—though *something* had changed in the last hour. He could feel… pride… and excitement through their link.

"She escaped." Eoghan shook his head. "And then pulled the Queen Killer from the mosaic. She pulled a royiken sword from the wall!"

Muttering under his breath, Eoghan led Aron to the back of the laboratory. There was a small section of a table cleared for them to lean against and the Torrpeki offered him a stool. "She is a little too smart for her own good. But enough about Keegan, our focus today is you. And your empathy link. To start, do you have any questions?"

"You mentioned you lost the other half of your empathy link," Aron recalled. "Which end were you?"

"The one who was saved. Stalia… saved my life after a sword went through my stomach. She was a dear friend, but it was not until the empathy link that I realized her love for me was more than friendship.

"My heart belonged to Amathya, and we were set to be married. Stalia of course wanted me to be happy, even if not with her. I had known for a while that something between Stalia and I had changed, as I could read her emotions better than before. Yet, I did not know why. And as the wedding drew nearer, Stalia hurt more and more. Not that she told anyone, but I knew. On the day of the wedding, Stalia was not present.

"From her, all I got was a sense of peace, and I thought she was fine. Oh, how horribly wrong I was. Just after Amathya and I said our vows, I felt myself falling. Stalia… had taken a short flight off a cliff. I remember when she hit the rocks below. Sola and Lunos, it hurt.

"After that, I do not recall much. I am told I floated between life and death for a long time. The little bit of Stalia's soul inside me was dead, and it tried to pull me to the other side, so it could become whole.

"Afterwards, I realized Stalia and I had an empathy link. At that time, I was only one of roughly two score in the entire history of any race to have an empathy link.

"So, do not take yours lightly, it can kill you. Very few have survived the death of their Giver. I count myself amongst only three others."

Given Keegan's destined path, a sense of dread lodged in Aron's heart. But he reminded himself that he and so many others would not be letting death befall Keegan anytime soon. Still, he knew Sola and Lunos often had their own plans and were not easily swayed.

"Can I… can I stop myself feeling what she does?" Aron asked.

"You will always feel what your Giver does, but you can dampen it," Eoghan explained. "Some have said being able to do this helps a Receiver survive the death of their Giver. But as so few have managed the feat, nothing conclusive can be said. I want you to concentrate on her now. What is she feeling?"

"Boredom, wonder, smugness," he answered quickly.

"Now, block it out. Create a wall, much like you would to keep someone from your mind, around your heart."

Taking a breath, Aron created a wall, but there Keegan was, bursting through it like paper. He made another, but she took down bricks as he put them up. Then another, but there she was behind it, with him. "She always gets in," he said.

"It is going to take time, so keep trying."

Chapter 17

Bernot and Atlia walked to where the remaining dragons were camped outside Grenadone. The awkward silence with Tahrin on the other side of the Looking Glass was stifling.

"What does she look like?" he asked Tahrin's speaker.

Before the speaker could answer, Tahrin released a magnificent roar that the Looking Glass did nothing to dampen. Beside him, Atlia pulled at her ear—as if that would do anything to stop the ringing.

A dragon across the field popped its head up and began bounding toward them. Each time it landed, a tremor raced through the earth. It was nearly enough to have Bernot tumbling onto his knees.

Bernot had been cautious to let Tahrin lead the Western front, but she was right in that they needed a leader there—where they were closest to Kolt, and decisions might need to be made quickly. And, due to her size, she was rarely personally present for important meetings anyway.

Within a hundred feet of them, the dragon stopped her bounding and let her paws rake through the grass and ground to slow her down. Ezadeen was sea-green and smaller than most dragons, only about as big as a horse. Bernot wondered about her age and if she was fit to lead in Tahrin's stead.

Do not think less of me because of my stature, the dragon snapped, seemingly reading his mind. *I am just as old at Tahrin. I suffer from what you humans call dwarfism.*

"What do you have to report, Tahrin?" Bernot asked, brushing aside Ezadeen's rightful distaste of his judgmental thoughts. He held the glass so they could all see Tahrin's... side? leg? part of her head? and her speaker's face.

"We sit on the western shore of Lake Romann," Tahrin's speaker said. "We faced no opposition. There is an army heading toward you, but they have not crossed the river yet. The two-legs are settled in and doing well under Hernando and Garne."

"Were you able to get an estimate of Kolt's forces?" Atlia asked.

"I suspect we possess more elementals, and the other races are much like having two for each human, but our numbers seem evenly matched." The speaker added quickly, "Not to detract from the value of humans. Just repeating what I'm told."

"Did any of the troops come back to deal with you?"

"No. We hid in the clouds."

"Excellent. Do not attack the castle yet," Bernot reminded Tahrin. "Just make a nuisance of yourself around Lake Romann."

"I remember the plan, Bernot." Tahrin's speaker conveyed none of the annoyance he assumed had been in her voice.

"Mind if I talk to Hernando?"

The image on the Looking Glass shifted until it settled on Hernando's face.

"Was not aware you were there the whole time," Bernot said.

"Tahrin tends t' shadow out others," was Hernando's answer.

There was a growl behind him.

Hernando looked back at her. "It 's true! You are so royiken big, when any human stands next t' ya we look like a scale!"

The sound coming from the dragon changed to what Bernot had learned was their approximation of a chuckle.

Satisfied everyone was playing nicely, they talked about the finer points of capturing the cities along Lake Romann.

"I want an update every two days," Bernot concluded.

"Can do," Hernando said, handing the Looking Glass back to Tahrin's speaker.

"The rest is in your hands," the speaker said, ending the connection.

We need to start moving soon, Ezadeen told him.

"I know," Bernot noted. "But we need to give the Southern and Northern forces time to get in place."

The dragon cocked her head. It was hard to tell what was going through her mind. *That could be some time. Move forward if you do not want to be stuck here come winter.*

«««« »»»»

Quarantine wasn't ideal, but with the Queen Killer it'd been manageable for the past three days. The red sword was like nothing Keegan had seen before. It was light as a feather, sharper than anything, and not even Waylan's magic could put a scratch on it—which seemed to irk the smith more than she did.

Eoghan entered, four vials in hand. "Vaccines," he said plainly.

Felix had confirmed the Torrpeki had gotten it right the day before. Unfortunately, Eoghan had only made one dose. It had been a brutal realization that they'd have to remain quarantined while he manufactured enough for all of them.

The others grabbed vials first and the faces they made as they swallowed it told Keegan it wasn't pleasant. She drank her dose before she could think too much about it. It tasted like someone had managed to combine the taste of dirt with the smell of rotten fish. Personally, she thought it was worse than the crappy Bertie Botts beans.

Choking past the flavor, she said, "I take it we're free to go."

"Yes," Eoghan said. "Though, maybe not you. Your air tutor is waiting for you in the courtyard."

This was the first she was hearing about having an air tutor and Keegan mulled over who it might be as she ambled through the castle. Stepping into the crisp autumn day, Keegan took a moment to soak in the sunshine, letting the rays sink into her soul. Pulling herself back to reality, she noticed a woman across the courtyard and a massive wolf lounging beside her. The beast was a rich brown with mild shocks of darker coloration interwoven around its face and paws. The woman standing next to it had richly colored skin and lustrous black hair pulled into a braid falling to the small of her back.

Figuring, and praying, she wouldn't need her sword, Keegan leaned the Queen Killer against the steps. The second her feet hit the flagstones a roaring wind pushed her to the ground. Cautiously rising, the wind picked up and pinned her again. It didn't take a genius to figure out who was causing it.

Keegan reached for the green air paika in her throat. Just simply being in proximity to the paika gave her access to the magic—and she let it rip. Exploding outwards, Keegan let her own blast cancel out the one pinning her. She'd hardly gotten to her knees when she went down again, pebbles digging into her shoulders and face.

"Seems she was a kyfa, Ne'Khole," the woman said to the wolf with a false air of disappointment.

The wolf rose and transformed. "Seems so."

In her human form, Ne'Khole's legs were as proportionally long as when she'd been a wolf. Her hair was the same rich brown, but now strands of gray could be found. Ne'Khole's eyes hadn't changed though; they were still that same wolfish blue that made Keegan feel like prey.

Keegan had intended to retaliate, but… well, seeing the transformation was a bit unexpected—and intriguing.

The women came to stand above her much like bullies on the playground.

Smiling, Keegan rose to her feet, continuing to let the wind push against her. "Keegan Digore," she said, holding out a hand to the woman she was unfamiliar with.

The woman didn't return the gesture, though did give her name. "Cataline Wind Breaker."

Keegan let her hand hang for a moment before withdrawing and creating a draft of her own, throwing Ne'Khole to the ground.

"Who taught you the power of wind?" Cataline demanded. Her demeanor was cool, as if Keegan were completely beneath her.

Keegan shrugged, the motion difficult as she fought the Buluo's continuing attack. "I did."

The force increased and she found her face acquainting itself with the courtyard. Again.

Into the dirt she growled, "I taught myself," then slowly picked herself up, expecting another draft. Prepared, the gust parted around her, flinging dirt and loose stones into the air to clang against the castle wall.

One stone must have struck a window for there was the telltale sound of fracturing glass.

"How?"

"Dunno, just kinda gave it a whirl," Keegan said, enjoying the unintentional play on words.

Wind slammed into her again, forcing her to increase her buffer. Tired of the antics, Keegan created a dense, hollow, cylindrical barrier around Cataline and the now pouting Ne'Khole who sat cross-legged beside her. Taking Cataline's wind, she directed it into the cylinder, letting it rotate. Satisfied with her work, she dropped the inner wall and let the cyclonic air steal their breath.

It wasn't long before Cataline's wind abated. Keegan let her magic dissipate as the Buluo sunk to her knees, sucking in breaths like a fish out of water.

She sneered, "How's that for a fluke!"

A furry mass slammed into her. Instantly Keegan found herself on the ground, a very angry wolf standing on her chest—the message from Ne'Khole was painfully clear. Afraid of upsetting her more, Keegan didn't bother to mention she was struggling to breathe under the weight of the wolf.

"Relax," Cataline said, getting to her feet and dusting herself off easily.

Ne'Khole snapped at Keegan for good measure, her teeth closing a fraction of an inch above her face, before retreating and returning to her human form.

"You should not attack your instructors," Cataline chided.

Sitting up, Keegan crossed her arms, letting her legs bow outwards. "The same could be said in reverse!"

"Truly, who instructed you in air magic?"

"I taught myself," Keegan repeated with a scowl. Her shoulders tensed, preparing for attack. "Why does no one believe me the first fucking time?"

Cataline took a seat on the castle steps, apparently done trying to bully her way into the answer. "Because it is so unlikely. Of course, many humans need to discover and teach themselves magic. But what makes you different is that compared to a survival-based ability, you seem to have formal training. Your skills are not that of a farmer's daughter or the like."

Keegan came and took a seat beside the Buluo, rubbing her face to remove the stones and dirt lodged on her skin. A few of the larger bits of rock came away painfully.

"How often do you practice air magic, Keegan Breath Thief?"

"Not often. And it's Digore, Keegan Digore."

"Then how is this magic so easy for you?"

Keegan took a moment to think. "Air reminds me of water magic. There's a flow and force that have to be in balance. And water magic has always been… comforting to me. Like it's just part of who I am."

"You have much control of your magic for disregarding it so much. And amongst my people, we make our own names."

Keegan cocked her head, momentarily confused. "Huh?"

"Breath Thief. Since it seems you enjoy taking our breath away, you shall be known as Breath Thief."

She shrugged. "Whatever. So why isn't Ne'Khole teaching me air?"

I cannot use magic. No wolf can, Ne'Khole said, now lounging in the sun in her wolf form. In the light her fur took on a warm chocolatey tone that had Keegan's sweet tooth aching.

"Then who… at the—"

"Me." Cataline studied her. "There are many questions in your eyes."

"You ready for them to come spoutin' out my mouth?"

The Buluo gave a light chuckle. "I have a feeling what some of them might be, so let me see if I can answer the obvious. Wolves cannot use magic and Buluo cannot transform. We work together and form pairs for life called Paranaths. Our pairing is not for mating, but mutual survival.

"There are wolves who cannot transform, as there are Buluo who cannot use magic. The pairings of these people are called Harangs."

"How are pairs decided?"

"Sola and Lunos guide us. Yes, there have been bad pairings. And Ne'Khole and I have been a Paranath since we were both hardly off the breast."

"Do wolves grow and mature at the same rate as humans?"

"Yes… and no. A pup is helpless after birth. To be stuck in this state for the same amount of time it would take a humanoid child to lose helplessness would place a heavy burden on the mother. Wolves grow like a wolf until they are about ten weeks of age where their growth idles until they reach an equivalent age in human years. From there, their growth matches that of their pairing."

"Do wolves have a preference for human or wolf form?" Keegan asked, directing the question at Ne'Khole.

Yes, she answered. *I am one of the few without a true preference, so do not take me as the standard.*

They continued to talk and by the time they stopped, Keegan's stomach was roaring with hunger.

Bidding Ne'Khole and Cataline goodbye, she went to pull the castle door open; a wind pushed it shut. "What, am I forbidden from eating?" she said haughtily.

"No," Cataline said calmly, "but first tell me something you learned."

"Is this gonna happen every meal?"
"Yes."
Rolling her eyes indignantly, Keegan said, "I learned your name."

««« »»»

Jared accepted the bundle from Mahogen warily. From the length and weight, he knew it was a sword. His only question as he carefully pulled back the cloth was why. The weapon inside was stunning, and he couldn't imagine ever using it for death and destruction.

"Why?" he managed to ask finally.

"Can I not give a friend a gift?" Mahogen returned.

The word friend sounded melodic, and Jared swam in the timbre of it. "You know what I mean."

The sheath was made of paper-thin hardened leather; he could only assume it was enchanted. Running down the center were studs of gems. Most appeared to be emeralds, rubies, and sapphires, but there were a few diamonds mixed in, sparkling like stars.

"The cost," he muttered. He could only imagine it cost more money than he'd ever see in his whole life... and probably more than he was worth.

Mahogen placed a hand on his shoulder. "Is nothing to me; I am a prince and the Torrpeki toss these aside like common rocks."

He must have given the Alvor a bewildered look because Mahogen laughed.

"These gems are too small for much use by the Torrpeki. And they value star metal over anything else. Which we Alvor have in abundance. The trade makes everyone happy. Including you."

"I- I can't accept this," Jared said quietly. "It's too much." He would've loved to look at the blade but feared if he did, he wouldn't be able to refuse the costly item.

"No," Mahogen insisted. "It is a gift. And, besides, you need a better sword."

"What's wrong with mine?" he asked, miffed.

"To start, it is dull. Plus, with the nicks in the blade, it is not something you can fix; I am not sure even a master smith could rehone it. And it is a little too short for you."

Mahogen was right, but he'd come to like the sword and learned to work past its flaws.

"You have to let me pay you for this," he persisted.

"I will not hear of it. This is a gift! Do not insult me."

Jared wanted the sword, more than he'd wanted a lot of things.

"Jared, I like you," Mahogen said, placing a hand on his shoulder, "and I want to make sure you make it through this war. Just accept the royiken sword and put it to good use. Manage to kill Kolt or one of the Vosjnik and we will call it even."

"I'll try…"

"Good." Smiling, Mahogen steered him toward a corner of the training field. "Now, let us see how it feels in the hand."

Jared nodded. Off the gem studs, the sunlight cast a rainbow of colors that waxed and waned like his resolve. Finally, he gave in and pulled the sword from the scabbard. The sunlight off the metal was blinding… and magical. Intricate gold lines traced almost the entire surface of the blade, creating a delicate pattern of knots. The cross-guard looked as if it was made of braided metal, yet under his touch, was soft as silk. The pommel contained a large emerald and the metal around it contained more of the line work.

"Sola and Lunos," he muttered. It felt as if the sword had been made specifically for his body and preferences; judging the look Mahogen was giving him, it had.

"Ready to try it out?" the prince asked, brandishing his own weapon.

Jared nodded and the Alvor swung. Rather than block, he backed away, afraid of damaging the sword.

"It will not break," Mahogen promised. "I did not have it made to sit above a mantle."

Before he could think too much, Jared gulped and lunged. With a sword built for him, he felt like the embodiment of grace—though he was sure he didn't look the part. Every movement came so easily it might have been choreographed.

Losing himself in the beauty of how the sword handled, he faltered and came back to reality with Mahogen's sword at his breast. The Alvor was only inches away, his face so near, Jared could feel his breath. The smile playing on Mahogen's mouth was conniving and he wished to remove it.

One idea came to mind; he started to act, then quickly pulled away. "Thank you for the sword," Jared said, grabbing the sheath and making an expedited departure.

Chapter 18

It felt like ages since Keegan had trained with Thoren, and it was more than just a feeling. After weeks of being caught up in other things, the lightning dragon was finally making demands—not that she minded. It was currently saving her from an hour in the theory and practice of air magic with Cataline. She figured no one dared to argue that the other aspects of her training were more important mostly because no one was willing to go head-to-head with a peeved off dragon. Keegan wouldn't have been surprised if Ne'Khole hadn't at least tried, but the wolf had seemingly decided fighting a dragon wasn't on the day's agenda.

Though there were noticeably fewer dragons in the encampment, finding Thoren wasn't any easier in the rippling sea of color. Her only advantage was that once she saw a bit of yellow, that was it.

Approaching the lightning dragon, Keegan tensed in preparation for the shock she was likely to get. Thoren had taken a liking to trying to catch her off guard. He'd managed it more than once, but thankfully it hadn't resulted in her becoming a fried afterthought.

You can relax, Thoren thrummed, enjoying her paranoid state. *Today I want to see if you can create your own lightning.* He settled onto the ground, his taloned paws crossed over each other expectantly.

Taking a breath, Keegan set to thinking about how she could create her own lightning. She assumed creating an electrical current would be similar to manipulating it—

find a source and command it. Reaching for her magic, the green air paika in her throat was ready to do her bidding, though the blue fire paika pulsing alongside her heart was a little more stubborn.

Combining the magics, a ripping force settled into her chest as the air and fire magics fought each other. Feeling the latent static in her body racing toward her fingertips, she reached out a hand to discharge the energy. The result was more than a bit lackluster; instead of an impressive booming bolt, she got a slight fizzle like a sparkler.

She couldn't keep her shoulders from sagging in disappointment. Pushing aside the dismay, she straightened her back and tried again. The second attempt was even more pathetic, nothing more than a tiny flash and pop. At least she could be a walking snap pop. Actually, depending on who she managed to scare the bejeebers out of, that could be quite fun.

Keegan was preparing to try again when Thoren stopped her. *It will not come in a day... I think.* Rising, the dragon slowly snaked his head forward and touched her fingertips.

Instantly, she felt a drastic change. Funneling the energy through her body, she discharged a powerful bolt that singed the grass and released a pressure wave that made her stumble.

Tell me, were you creating your own electricity or pulling it from the atmosphere? Thoren asked, settling onto the ground again. He was referring to her pathetic attempts not what they'd just done.

"Uh, creating my own," she answered, her body still feeling like a livewire. "Should I not be?"

Thoren gave an approximation of a shrug. *Remember, this is a learning experience for us both. But try pulling static from the air, if you will.*

Pulling at her magics, Keegan searched for the miniscule traces of electricity in the air and gathered them into a singular mass. Thinking she had enough, she discharged the energy and was pleased to find she got a substantial bolt, though it still wasn't as powerful as when Thoren gave input.

Interesting, the dragon mused. *Let us hope an electrical storm forms before we leave Grenadone.*

"Why would you want a thunderstorm?" she asked, not liking where the dragon was headed.

To harness its lightning, of course!

Keegan glanced toward Zavier, hoping the guard would have something to say—something along the lines of "Are you nuts?!"

"Is that the best idea?" Zavier proffered, finally heeding the frantic look Keegan was throwing him. Or maybe it was Zavier's desire not to be in the middle of a thunderstorm.

Thoren pulled his lips back in what Keegan had learned was a smile. *Probably not, but we are going to do it anyway.*

«««« »»»»

Though sweat dripped off his body and soaked his clothes, Braxton did not feel like he had done much training. His limits had not been pushed and he was exhausted simply by the sheer amount of time he had hacked at dummies and fired at targets. Given that men could no longer harm him, it was pointless to even ask them to spar; there were no consequences for a misstep or laziness. There was no way to learn from pain.

Also, he worried his newfound apparent invincibility would make people fear him... or despise him—more than they already did because of his family name. And the only women in camp he knew were Vitia—whom he was inclined to deal with as little as possible—and Mara—who had no idea how to use a sword. So that left him with straw men as opponents—and they never put up much of a fight. Though, they were always happy to take a relentless beating.

While the army had been raised and prepared for war, they had yet to march forward. If he did not know better, Braxton might have thought this was all an elaborate training exercise. Part of him wanted to know what the holdup was, but another part did not care and was thankful to put off the inevitable.

Reaching his tent, Braxton stripped from his sweaty clothes, leaving them strewn haphazardly about, and fell onto his cot.

Sleep came easily and, for a long while, nothing but darkness and his consciousness existed. Then, he was awake, standing in an unfamiliar room. It was devoid of furnishings but for a few chairs, a desk, and a table with a raised relief map like the one in the command tent. Bernot slowly materialized, sitting at the desk, shuffling through papers.

Slowly, Braxton approached the map, amazed to find Bernot did not notice him. He even waved a hand wildly to draw his attention. Nothing. He wondered if this was one of his dreams, as unlikely as that was given he still wore a slajor manacle.

Yet, it was possible to use magic with one manacle. Difficult to impossible at times and there were limitations, but it could be done. Maybe this really was one of his prophetic dreams.

Looking at the map, it took him a moment to make sense of it.

There were red pieces representing the dragons sitting next to Lake Romann—which corresponded with a report they had gotten a few days past. The black griffin pieces stationed near Agrielha certainly represented Kolt's forces. And the mass of white rams' skulls and green trees signified the Lazado and Alvor respectively in Grenadone. But he had to question the blue fish pieces denoting the Merfolk sitting at Revod and the brown drinking horns representing the Torrpeki in Grevasia. When and how had the Lazado managed to split their forces without them knowing?

Before he could take anything more in, Braxton found himself looking up at the canvas of his tent. Folding his hands on his chest, he thought about what he had seen. The placements on the war map did not make sense to him... but it did not have to make sense to him, it only had to make sense to Bernot and his Commanders.

Think like Bernot, he told himself.

Shifting his thought pattern was not easy, but slowly he came to understand. Or at least he thought he did. What Bernot was doing could spell defeat if something went awry but was ingenious if it panned out.

He put his hands behind his head. Oh, Kolt's Commanders would kill for this information. And if only they knew he knew. But they did not. And he was not about to change that.

《《《 》》》

The sun was midway through its descent, and it seemed word for the army to stop had been given. Behind Jared, Grenadone was hardly visible on the horizon, a raised smudge in the undulating grass. They'd made considerable progress given how long it'd taken to get to the abandoned line city, and yet, it didn't feel like it was enough. He supposed their newfound speed came from the fact over half the army had headed toward Revod and Grevasia.

Jared watched as the Buluo dismounted their wolves and many of the beasts shifted. Of the wolves that now stood on two feet, a few playfully knocked over their counterparts while others simply stretched. All the wolves, on two or four legs, settled onto the ground in relaxed positions, watching their partners and friends pitch tents and light fires. Give and take.

Finding an area he deemed big enough for the cluster of people that would be making use of it, Jared dropped his gear and set to finding the others. He wasn't surprised it took a considerable amount of time and mental communication with Keegan and Kade. They all had their own duties and friends that scattered them throughout camp. It would be easier to remain apart at night, but it somehow made them feel better to be together. Well, it made him feel better; he couldn't speak for anyone else.

Hearing the tell-tale clop of hooves, he glanced up to see Keegan and Icella riding over.

As Keegan dismounted, he asked, "Can you let Lucas and Carter know where we are?" More than once his brothers had been left to fend for themselves due to oversight. Then again, almost everyone had been forgotten at one point or another.

After a moment, Keegan said, "Lucas is staying with Waylan tonight; Carter's on his way."

Satisfied, Jared continued with his efforts to pitch his tent. Keegan and Icella were quick to disappear, presumably to get their rations. By the time they returned, everyone else had arrived and even Keegan's and Icella's tents had been raised. Give and take.

Setting the copious amounts of food on the cloth spread on the ground, Keegan began preparing the meal. This was something from her world and she was excited to share it with them. Seeing that the meat and vegetables were uncooked, he could only assume the camp's cooks had been happy to have a few less mouths to feed for the night. Jared watched as Keegan cut onions and potatoes into chunks, leaving the meat to be diced in Icella's capable hands.

The chopping done, Keegan began to look around, as if missing something. She gave a grumbled curse and closed her eyes. Without warning, thin spikes of metal began to rise from the ground. Jared thankfully wasn't the only one to jump to his feet like a fire had been lit under his arse.

Taking the spikes, Keegan slid bits of meat, potato, and onion onto the rods. "Okay, kebabs are ready," she said. "Take what you want and cook them in the fire."

Jared was the last to take a kebab and there almost wasn't room for his in the fire. As the meal cooked, the smell of roasting meat and the sound of growling bellies filled the space.

Everyone waited patiently for Keegan to deem the kebabs cooked. Once she did, they all quickly pulled their skewers from the flames. Carter was the first to take a bite, which he instantly regretted; the food was, understandably, piping hot.

The kebabs were by no means gourmet, but they were filling, and something different. And likely something that would become a staple for they were simple, variable, and could be made by the rich and poor alike. He didn't doubt that somehow the camp's cooks would catch wind of this and demand a lesson in making them.

Stomach full, Jared leaned back on his hands, surveying his companions.

Keegan was still loudly berating Icella for upholding Cataline's rule. If he remembered correctly, it was Keegan had to say something she'd learned that day before she could eat. Today's kernel of knowledge was just how far Cataline's reach could be. He didn't understand why Keegan seemed to make a joke of this rule, but it was exactly the kind of thing he expected from her.

Kade was talking with Elhyas's nephew, Auckii, using hand signals. Auckii didn't generally join them, but Jared enjoyed his presence—even if they had a hard time communicating. Thankfully, Auckii could read lips and Kade had picked up some of the sign language that he used when lip reading was not possible. From the look on Auckii's face, Kade had said something degradingly humorous.

Ezekhial, Zavier, Elhyas, and Carter talked amongst themselves. From the crease in Carter's brows, he was being given royit for inexperience. Be it women or the sword, Jared wasn't sure—likely both. Sadly, both of those would likely be remedied before long and his heart panged upon realizing that Carter was no longer the child he remembered him as.

Continuing to look around their circle of friends, he found Mahogen lazily staring into the fire across from him. The reflection of the flame dancing around the prince's pupils was mesmerizing. After a moment, Jared realized the Alvor wasn't starting into the fire, but at him. No, not him, that was ridiculous—it was more likely he just happened to be *directly* across the fire from the Mahogen.

A light growl from the inky darkness had them all reaching for weapons and jumping out of their skins. His own heart was apt to leap out of his mouth from the way the hairs on his arm rose.

Silence returned, heavy and ominous, and they carefully stared into the darkness between their tents, ready for foe to emerge and demand blood.

The growl came again, and Jared watched as a massive wolf pushed from the shadows. It was a friend by expectation, but reality might prove otherwise. Between its jaws something hung limply—likely its dinner.

Ignoring their uneasiness, the wolf padded over to Jared.

He was about to begin backing away when Mahogen said, *Put your knife away. She is a friend. And kneel.*

He glanced at the Alvor and Mahogen gave him a subtle nod.

Fighting against the apprehension in his belly, Jared tucked his knife into his boot and knelt.

As the wolf got closer, he could see what hung between its teeth; not dinner, but a pup, held by the scruff of its neck.

The wolf sniffed Jared, her breath warm over his face, carrying the scent of decay. Seemingly satisfied, the wolf dropped the pup at his feet and slunk back into the night.

As he began to fret, a feminine voice pushed into his thoughts, *He is yours for now, but ultimately belongs to another. You will know when he finds his pairing.* It took him a moment to realize it was the wolf speaking. *His name is Jarshua.*

As the world released its pent-up breath, slowly their group began to move, first warily looking at each other, then coming to see the pup. Only Icella and Mahogen seemed unperturbed.

"He's mine," Jared said quietly. "For now…"

"What?" Keegan questioned, cradling the wolf. The pup was sleepy and snuggled into her arms, his feet kicking into the air wildly.

"Jarshua… I'm supposed to look after him… until he finds his pairing."

"Why?" Kade bit.

"Because he is a one-being," Mahogen said, gentling stroking the pup's belly. "Not all wolves are born with the ability to shift. Those that can are paired with Buluo who possess magic, and their pairings are called Paranaths. Those that cannot are paired with the magically ungifted and the pairings are called Harangs."

"Why me?" Jared said quietly.

"Who knows," Mahogen said. "The wolves are guided by mysterious forces but are rarely wrong. You should feel honored she trusted you to look after him."

Jared certainly didn't feel honored, but maybe that would come with time. Carefully he took the pup from Keegan and headed into his tent. He left the flap open so he wouldn't need to light a candle.

With one hand he pulled the extra blanket from his trunk and created a nest from it on the ground. It would have to do for Jarshua for tonight.

Pulling his boots off, Jared let the tent flap close and crawled into his cot. The temperature in the tent was comfortable and he was soon on the verge of sleep. Then his cot shook as something jumped onto it.

A ball of fur pushed against Jared's side and a wet nose found the crook of his armpit. He could only imagine the pup was missing his mother. Taking a deep breath, he moved over to give the pup a little more room.

Jared couldn't put what he was feeling into words. But he did know one thing, Jarshua was here to stay.

«««« »»»»

Once darkness fell, Keegan was usually left to her own devices and devious means. That was not currently the case; though not in Grenadone, the thunderstorm Thoren had hoped for had materialized.

Walking through camp, Keegan and Quin were just about the only ones still outside. Everyone with a lick of sense was inside their tents—or stuck on guard duty. And even those on guard duty tucked themselves under whatever meager cover they could find. On the edge of camp, Thoren was waiting for them, visible static jumping across his body expressing his excitement. If he were ten times smaller, she might've compared him to a very famous Pokémon.

"If I die, I'm blaming you," Keegan told the dragon deadpan. In the distance, lightning flashed, and thunder rumbled, the noise tangible in her body, a laugh at her unease.

Thoren declined to respond, and bounded off, leading them a half mile away—in case things went awry. Which they were often wont to do.

In the distance, a wall of rain inched toward them. The storm seemed to run for miles—a blot in the night promising no dawn.

It will be just as if I am providing the electricity, Thoren promised, gouging the earth with his talons, creating a ditch. *Quin, you may want to wait in here.*

"Why would I do that?" the guard snapped above the low whistling of the wind that steadily rose with each second. She was already unhappy to be dragged into a storm in the middle of the night and being asked to lie in the dirt was apparently pushing things too far.

"Lighting strikes the tallest object," Keegan explained. "And even if you don't take a direct hit, being in the vicinity of me, or any strikes… let's just say you'll wind up a little crispy."

Eyes widening, Quin quickly clambered into the ditch without further argument.

As the storm drew nearer, the static in the air made Keegan's nerves stand on edge while the soundwaves made her teeth rattle in her skull like little maracas.

Carefully, Thoren let his tail touch the back of her leg; a precaution in case this went south. *Whenever you are ready.*

Keegan took a deep breath, calming her racing heart, extended an arm, and waited. Whatever gods ruled this world were having a good laugh, as the next bolt of lightning was ages in coming. She had a millisecond of warning, the clouds glowing an ominous gray white before releasing their fury.

As the bolt descended, Keegan willed the lightning to come to her, to obey her command. And it did just that. The energy raced down her arm, did a circuit in her chest, circling yet avoiding her heart, then lashed out from her fingertips like a whip. The boom as the electricity struck the ground mere yards away was beyond deafening.

A small fire burst into existence that Keegan quickly extinguished. If Thoren had them out here long enough, the rain would eventually do it for her. But she hoped that wouldn't be the case; she had no desire to trudge back to camp soaked and chafed.

Thoren hummed proudly. *Excellent. Again.*

The excitement in her blood overriding her apprehension, Keegan waited. Each strike the storm threw at her was harnessed and unleashed with spectacular force. The surge of power she felt each time was death-defying, liberating. She was starting to see why the storm had made Thoren so… ecstatic.

When heavy raindrops started to pound on their skin, promising welts if they didn't heed the warning, Thoren stopped her. The dragon touched the top of her head with his nose to pull away any remnants of electricity. *Well done.*

Chapter 19

Bernot gently kissed Lyerlly's head before slipping from the tent. Sleep did not find her easily these days, the baby's constant kicking and the distortion of her body made it difficult to get comfortable. The world was still in the moments before dawn—and it did not sit right with him. It never had. Lunos reigned here if one was not careful.

A few miles away, he could see the outline of Vercase waiting to bask in the pale light of the rising sun. The city slept, seemingly unaware of her doom, while his camp of preparing invaders sat about, joking over breakfasts that were being greedily shoved down throats or still sizzling over fires.

When they had sighted Vercase's walls yesterday, no alarm had been sounded. No soldiers had come to greet them, to defend the city. The only noticeable response was the closure of the gates. Even now, no one manned the wall.

Bernot had sent a messenger, asking for parley, but the man had not returned. Though he was worried, he knew better than to make a rash decision; he would wait until the man's head came back on a spike or the sun set today.

But he still had another play at hand. Icella, Kade, Reven, and Lucas had been sent into the city under the cover of darkness. Between the four of them, they could no doubt coerce the city lord into their favor.

Bernot had just entered the command tent when a soldier came to inform him a rider was approaching. The man left with the instructions to bring the rider to him immediately and it was not long before he glanced up to see the messenger he had sent to Vercase.

He released a sigh of relief. "Glad to see you are alive. What did the city lord have to say?"

"Nothing much; he's dead," the messenger shrugged. "The new lord however, had quite a lot to say. Mostly good. He wants to join our cause."

"Did he seem trustworthy?"

"I trust him more than Kolt."

Bernot chuckled. "Not a hard feat. Fetch Miss Digore and meet me on the front line."

The man bit his tongue in compliance, though it was impossible to ignore his sour look. Some humans were still set in the old ways when it came to the roles men and women played. And Keegan was particularly good at getting into people's blood.

Strapping on his sword and putting an extra dagger on the small of his back, Bernot prepared to ride to Vercase. As he made his way through the tents and soldiers, he called upon a few trusted men. By the time the growing group made it to where the dragons sat as their line of first defense, he had an entourage of twenty good men. Should the new lord of Vercase turn out to be out for blood rather than an ally, he would soon be reunited with the previous city lord.

"The hell do you want?" Keegan asked grumpily, pulling her black mount to a stop when she arrived. Her hair stood at odd angles and crust graced the corners of her eyes.

"You. To meet the lord of Vercase with me."

"Why? Y'all never let me go anywhere." She was silent for a moment as she began braiding back her snarl of red locks. "Ohhh, you're showing me off. Next time, wait till a reasonable time of day, let's say AFTER THE SUN IS UP!"

The sun was up, but Bernot did not deign to comment.

The ride to Vercase was not long and there was not much chatter amongst the men, most realizing there were limited outcomes ahead. He got the sense the men assumed they were headed toward a skirmish by the way hands were near weapons. If he could do anything to quell their hesitation, he would—but he was not entirely sure their fears were unfounded.

Coming upon the gate, a pole sat before the open portcullis with a head atop it. He had the feeling it belonged to the previous city lord.

There was no fanfare when they passed through the gate; instead, they were greeted by Vercaseans lining the streets. While he had not expected cheers, he was put off by the fact the townsfolk appeared to have come from battle, many covered in splashes of blood, others nursing minor injuries, most doing little to conceal the makeshift weapons held in hand. With the crowd lining the street, they only had one path—forward.

Taking a breath to steady himself, Bernot gently spurred his horse on. As they progressed, the only sounds came from the flapping of crows' wings overhead and the clop of their horses' hooves. All at once the city felt ghastly, empty, suffocating, and ominous.

None of Vercase's inhabitants made any move to harm them, yet the hard stares they gave had him questioning their intentions. When they passed through the gate into the castle courtyard, they were met with a mass of people.

He whispered to the messenger, "What is going on?"

"Easier for the new lord to explain. But don't worry, they mean us no harm." The man was completely at ease as he dismounted and let a woman with a club take his horse.

Bernot had to pray they were not being led to slaughter.

The inside of the castle was in a state of disarray, with blood splattered across walls and floors like decorations. He could only be thankful glassy eyes and flies were not there to also greet them.

Outside the dining hall, they were stopped by two men with clubs that looked to have once been legs of a table. "Only three may pass," one said, "and not with weapons."

"I, the girl, and him," Bernot announced, pointing to the messenger, who already had a rapport with the new lord and could smooth over any misunderstandings. Keegan was a weapon in and of herself. Not that she looked it—which worked to their benefit.

Though Keegan claimed to be no good with a sword, she still shot him a nervous glance as she handed over the Queen Killer. Good hard steel was more than just a weapon, it was a deterrent, too.

At the sight of the red sword, both men hastily kneeled, dropping their clubs like hot coals.

Bernot cursed to himself, remembering the people of Vercase worshiped the person who wielded the Queen Killer. This was going to go to Keegan's head, get them killed, or work in their favor. Only time would tell which.

Keegan's eyes darted between the kneeling men and Bernot. "Uhh…"

"You are destined to save us," a man said.

She brushed the statement off, assuming her reputation preceded her as usual.

Not wanting to keep the lord waiting, Bernot pushed inside. The guards trailed after them, one man holding the Queen Killer out like a relic.

Instead of finding the new lord sitting on a lesser throne, he sat at one of the long tables. He turned to look at them, face still spattered with blood; his brown eyes were tired, but there was a hint of pride in them, too.

The messenger began to introduce the lord, "Bernot, this is Caius Niranda."

"Please, it's just Niranda."

"Wow, either your parents really loved Caius or hated you," Keegan blurted rudely.

"Bit of both," Niranda answered, not minding her crassness. He noticed the Queen Killer and looked toward Keegan. Gracefully he rose from the table and bowed. "My Lady."

"Not a lady," Keegan said coolly.

"How do you know that is Miss Digore's sword?" Bernot asked. He knew the answer but wondered if the man did.

Niranda walked toward the dais where the lesser throne sat, beckoning for them to follow.

Upon coming closer, Bernot was able to see the mural painted along the baseboards of the chair.

Keegan knelt to inspect it. "What is this?" There was a hint of marvel in her voice.

"One of Angela Alga's last prophecies," Niranda answered.

"Her last days were spent by Seleena's side; how could you possibly know of it?" Bernot countered, baiting the new lord.

"Esen Bællar. Though, *she* always thought she was the woman the prophecy spoke of."

Bernot was about to rebuke the man for speaking ill of his mother, but Niranda was not wrong. His mother had always wanted to be a great hero like her father; but no amount of trying had ever made that dream come to pass. And chasing it had led her to abandon him.

Bernot stooped to observe the pictorial. It began with a woman whose hair was made of flames. She pulled a red sword from a wall, then turned to face opponents from the other races. Except, she never fought them. Together they faced a wild monster—it was a fearsome creature with death-colored eyes, wings, and a lashing tail. It was a rudimentary depiction of a griffin. The pictorials ended with the flame-haired woman sitting upon a throne beside a crown, but if one looked carefully, the Queen Killer was no longer in her possession.

The prophecy would always be up to interpretation for, to his knowledge, the words had long since been lost. And there were those who claimed this was not a prophecy at all, but an ancient fable about the first human.

Keegan's hair alone made it seem obvious she was the woman in the graphics. With the Queen Killer, it was almost impossible to deny it might be her.

"Well, I'll be damned," Keegan said straightening up, "there's more than one prophecy saying I save the world!" Her face fell and her shoulders sagged, realizing how much more responsibility and expectation would be burdened upon her. Just audibly, he heard her mutter, "Ah, fuck."

"You say this was one of her last prophecies," Bernot said, "what makes you sure it was not *the* last?"

"I was the lord's librarian; Vercase has the only other copy of the Prophet's predictions."

"But how? It's not like y'all can email back and forth," Keegan chimed in.

Bernot was glad he was not the only one to look at her perplexed.

"Uh… uhm…" Niranda stuttered, "The Dragon King made twin books; what's written in one, appears in the other. He feared one day the Blind Prophet would be hidden away for the use of one man's gain; this was his way of trying to thwart that.

"The prophecy read: When it seems all but hope is lost, a child, a girl with fire gracing heart and hair shall remove the Queen Killer from its untimely resting place. She will face threats never seen before, one cruel beyond measure and one misguided beyond measure. By kingdom come, the Queen Killer will be used once again to sever life from royalty."

Bernot was shocked, he had never heard this prophecy. This must have been a secret hoarded for centuries, maybe even from Thaddeus. One somehow kept even from the Dragon King's own children. Had Caius even marginally believed that a woman with red hair would defeat him, all such women would not be alive currently.

"I've got no interest in becoming Queen," Keegan said, motioning toward the woman sitting next to the crown. "Hell, I've got no interest in fighting a war."

"But you will do both regardless," Niranda said calmly.

"How did you take the city?" Bernot asked. "From what I can tell, it was a citizens' rising."

"It was. We have long regarded she who bears the Queen Killer to be our leader. The lord knew this but kept us down with taxes and harsh punishments for those who spoke against him."

"Clearly, that did jack shit," Keegan mumbled with a minute quirk of an eyebrow.

"We have never supported Caius either," Niranda continued. "With you on our doorstep, we knew we had to act. And did. Both sides lost many, but most of the guards were once commoners and aided us. Every man and woman of Vercase would like to join your cause."

"Of course," Bernot said.

"However, we will only answer to our saving lady."

Keegan rolled her eyes before giving Niranda a hard stare. "Fine, I order y'all to listen to Bernot."

"As My Lady wishes," Niranda said, bowing.

"Not a lady," Keegan protested, walking away.

"Tend to your wounded," Bernot said. "Then prepare as many of your people as you can to move forward with the campaign."

««« »»»

The sun had long ago crept over the horizon—Kade assumed—though that did little for them behind the city walls where they couldn't see it. He could only accept the sun had risen because the sky wasn't pitch. He gave a small, aggravated sigh and shook his head; this mission was supposed to have been over before sunrise and they were nowhere close to done.

If anyone in the Lazado learned how they'd managed to muck this up, they'd surely be a laughingstock.

Creeping up to the city walls had been what Keegan might call a walk in the park. But from there, things had started going sideways. Quickly.

The plan had been to use magic to tunnel through the wall. And all would have gone according to plan had he not overlooked the clumsiness factor of *certain* people. Lucas had managed to knock a stone loose, which was followed by many, partially burying Icella.

Once out of the tunnel, the Mermaid was forced to ditch her crushed armor.

Kade offered her his, but she shrugged him off, saying no human was going to land a blow on her anyway. He was tempted to prove her wrong out of spite, but that could wait till later.

As they began to creep through the seemingly empty streets, Lucas complained about an iron tang in the air.

The rest of them not noticing the tang or anything out of the ordinary, pushed on.

Reven claimed to have memorized the city's blueprints, but his mental map of Agrielha's secret passages and Vercase's streets ran together; it wasn't long before they were hopelessly lost. In the dark, they couldn't even look up to find the castle and be guided by its hulking mass. Reven suggested waking some poor bastard up and making them lead them to the castle. Kade and Icella immediately shot down that idea in case said poor bastard managed to raise an alarm—or kill them. Stranger things had happened.

Having no choice but to wait until dawn, they hunkered down in an alley, doing their best to look like innocent beggars. Reven was the only one to find sleep; originally, Kade had been annoyed that he left the rest of them on watch—now he envied him.

Sunrise didn't come quickly and when it did, left them with more concerns and questions; it would've taken a blind man to not see the blood splatter and gore covering the city. At first, they thought the lord of the city was a brutal bastard, but as people limped from their homes, clubs, shovels, daggers, and what looked like stolen swords in hand, they were forced to consider there might have been an uprising.

Lucas wanted to return to the Lazado until they figured out what was happening, Kade insisted they go forward. He won.

Able to see the castle, they were able to progress through the city with ease. Reaching the castle wall, Kade created a tunnel through—and made sure no one *could* or *would* knock stones loose this time.

The courtyard itself was littered with more signs of an uprising and seemed to be an epicenter. The castle had yet to wake itself—possibly because there was no one left to wake. He was about to lead them through the giant front doors when a horse whinnied, and they ducked behind whatever shelter they could find, scattering.

"I'll bring him back as soon as I can," a man promised, mounting a bay mare. The sound of hooves against cobblestone resounded through the courtyard shortly thereafter.

"When he comes back, bring him to the dining hall," another man instructed what appeared to be citizens turned sentinels.

Kade waited until they could hear nothing more, human and horse alike, before peering from behind the bush he was hiding in. The courtyard was empty, aside from the two men standing at the portcullis. If he was quiet, they'd never look back.

He was halfway from behind the bush when Icella said, *Wait. I do not think coming in the front door will earn us anything more than gravestones.*

Then what would you suggest? he snapped.

Icella drew his attention to a door tucked away in the corner of the courtyard. *Servants' entrance.*

We'll stick out like donc in snow, he retorted.

Icella began creeping toward the door, snapping back, *Then how about we look like servants.*

Going to be mighty hard with your scales—and the fact you're blue!

The Mermaid huffed at his rebuke but didn't alter her course.

Remaining hidden in the courtyard left them with their thumbs up their arses, so he quickly told Lucas and Reven about the door. Some—Lucas—were less stealthy and it was a wonder they weren't heard or seen.

Inside, they resorted to whispered yelling as they all fought to make what they thought was the best plan become reality. Icella won.

Reven worked his magic and when done, Kade had to admit she wasn't particularly beautiful as a human—not that he'd *ever* tell her that. The rest of them doffed their armor and any weapons they couldn't conceal—which was most of them for everyone but Icella. Kade had watched her strap on weapon after weapon for the mission and still had no idea where she was hiding most of them.

With Reven's mental map of the castle a waste of time, they were forced to blindly tramp through. By a stroke of luck—or as Icella called it, misfortune—they found their way to the entrance hall. A few armed citizens loitered, and thankfully looked exhausted and unlikely to discern human from shadow in their current states.

Kade considered intimidating someone into telling them where the lord of Vercase was when the doors opened, sending the four of them scattering—again—like rats in candlelight.

He opened his mind to the others, instructing them not to go far. Lucas and Reven listened well. Icella… he might throttle her later. Kade was inclined to chase after her, to ring her neck now, but to do so meant crossing the entranceway where twenty soldiers now milled about.

Where are you going? Kade demanded of the Mermaid.

Dining hall, was her answer.

The soldiers in the entrance hall would likely be heading there soon to give a report. If they could beat them there, they might accomplish something today.

Kade eyed the men in the hall and wondered if they'd notice him. Without his armor, he looked like anyone. Without much else to do, he took a chance and bowed his head, praying to the old gods no one called attention to him.

Thankfully, Reven scurried after him without so much a "What the nastor 're you doing?" and they joined Lucas on the other side.

They set off after Icella. Her head start and their lack of familiarity with the castle made it difficult to follow her.

Kade did his best to track the strength of her thoughts, but time and time again they found themselves not where they needed to be.

Have the soldiers left the entrance hall? the Mermaid asked.

How should I know, I'm chasing you. Why?
Those soldiers do not belong to the city.
How do you know that?
Remember who holds this city now.

Kade cursed to himself. Those men were likely Kolt's scouts, terrified and trying to not get killed or ready to put down the insurrection. The four of them were in for a world of hurt if caught—and then likely the world of Lunos. The only thing that might save them if discovered by Kolt's men was that they both would be fighting for their lives against the Vercasians—and could deal with each other later.

Kade quickened his steps, Reven and Lucas echoing his haste.

Miraculously, they found Icella—un-miraculously, she was just as lost as they. Knowing they could keep running about like cockroaches or make an attempt at logic, Kade let Reven lead their wanderings. His mental map wasn't as far off as they thought, for soon they found themselves outside the dining hall.

The doors were closed, and no guards stood outside. The lack of security likely meant the lord was elsewhere. But a part of him had to check, just to be sure—he'd seen people do far more foolish things.

Kade was halfway to the doors when they began to open from the inside. Scuttling behind a tapestry, he just managed to not be discovered.

"I'm not a lady," someone called, her footsteps signaling she was leaving the hall. The voice was familiar, sounding like Keegan. But that was impossible—his sister was back at camp.

As the woman's footsteps faded, Kade drew his dagger. *On the count of three,* he told the others.

On his count, they launched from their hiding spots and stormed the hall. He wasn't sure who started the yell, but they all picked it up. Inside, two men were talking, and both turned to look at them in surprise.

Seeing who they were and recognizing them—well, recognizing one of them—he grabbed the collar of Lucas's shirt to halt his charge. "Bernot?"

Bernot gave him a confused look before realization sank across his features.

"You had best ex—" Icella started.

Pain radiated across the back of Kade's head and suddenly he was on the floor. When he was finally able to straighten out the world again, Keegan was staring down at him, eyebrows cinched together.

"What the royik?" he muttered dazedly, blinking madly.

"Sorry, heard the yelling and… ya know," Keegan said, offering him a hand.

He groggily accepted her help. "Since when can you knock me out with a punch?" The world lurched, and he leaned against his twin until everything became steady once more.

"She 's not," Reven groaned. "She shot rocks at the back o' our heads." Where his friend rubbed his scalp, blood flowed. "Sola and Lunos, was that really necessary."

Keegan grimaced. "I didn't know y'all were friends. You come barging in here like freakin' barbarians; what'd you expect?"

"Care to explain what is going on here?" Icella managed to demand.

"Ah, yes," Bernot said. "The citizens of Vercase rose against the city lord and defeated him—easily it seems. Niranda has agreed to join our cause."

"Wait," Lucas said, "what about Kolt's men?"

The man Kade didn't know, Niranda, asked, "What are you talking about?"

"We saw a group of soldiers in the entry hall."

"Ah," Bernot said, in understanding. "Those are our men. No need to worry." Walking from the hall, he ordered, "Get some sleep."

If his head wasn't throbbing, Kade would've demanded a better explanation.

Chapter 20

"Please," Kolt begged, all but dropping onto his knees, "tell me what I need to do. The men are dying in droves against the dragons. I have no other council!"

"I wonder why?" Alyck said snidely. No doubt Kolt had no council because he did not believe in asking for help… or listening to others.

Thaddeus held his head in his hands quietly staring at the floor; now was not the time to provoke Kolt. Anyone could see he was like a cornered dog—terrified and willing to bite.

"How are we supposed to keep the dragons at bay?" Kolt roared. "Do you even know how to fight a dragon?"

"Well, if you want to keep a dragon at bay, I suggest you have it encamped on a bay," Alyck started, turning a vibrant shade of red as he did his best to not laugh.

Thaddeus did his best to melt into the shadows, feeling the conversation might turn deadly if Alyck did not start giving reasonable answers.

Surprising both him and Kolt, Alyck then gave a half valuable response, "But I do believe your skirmishes are one sided."

"This is war! There is nothing one-sided about it."

"Are you so sure about that?" Alyck probed. "What have the dragons done to you?"

"They… they…" Kolt paused. "Are you saying all I have to do to stop the losses is do nothing?"

That was what Alyck had meant by one sided; so far, the dragons had simply sat on the shore of Lake Romann and defended. While he understood Kolt's first inclination that an attack was coming, a small part of him could only hope the boy was mentally calling himself an idiot.

"Unprovoked, most people are happy to let you make a fool of yourself on your own. I know I am."

Kolt went from angry to embarrassed. "And what do I do to replace the men I have lost?"

"You have plenty of soldiers running around the castle. Why not them?" Alyck had proposed the idea before—and would continue to do so unashamedly.

"And leave *myself* unprotected?"

"Do you mean to tell me all those boasts about your power were a façade? My, how we overestimated you! Poor little Kolt, he truly is poor little Kolt."

The king gave a low growl that only made him look more like the bratty child he was.

Alyck crossed his arms dismissively. "Either protect your empire or protect yourself. You can only choose one. And to choosing wrong will see you toppled by winter's first tantrum."

Kolt stared down his uncle, the anger in his eyes communicating the wish to strike him, but Alyck had told him what he wanted and needed to know. Storming from the room, it was clear the choices were putting the boy king between a dragon and a hard place—literally.

"How much of what you just told him was true?" Thaddeus asked, pulling himself from the shadows.

"All of it. If he leaves the dragons alone, they will leave him alone." Then, quietly, "And he will be toppled by first snowfall."

《《《《 》》》》

If he really wanted to, Braxton could fly to Agrielha for lunch and be back at camp in time for dinner. He had truly underestimated how slowly armies moved—and how willing to rip his hair out over it he was.

The soldiers set the pace. A group ready for vengeance could move rapidly. But looking at their men, Braxton knew many had been plucked from the streets, fields, and mother's arms and had swords thrust into their hands. He imagined they were not keen to reach their destination, in this life or the next. And the men from Agrielha proper were dawdling as they spent time with families instead of soldiers.

Though, maybe there was an upside to all this. He could nary espy a man who looked underfed. He could tell some had signed up to simply die without hunger and perhaps to leave a penny behind for family. Even so, they were not about to make Lunos's job easy, and most sported cuts and bruises, tokens of training, signs of their desire to live.

When he reached the command tent at the eastern edge of camp, he could hear shouting from inside. A man stormed out, almost barreling into Braxton.

"Braxton," Branshaw barked when he cautiously pushed into the tent, "where do you think the Lazado will strike next?"

His heartrate spiked, knowing the answer. Though his vision had been nearly a month ago, he could still picture the war map clearly. Slowly, he made his way to the map the men were gathered around. From the way pieces were scattered across the board, someone had taken their anger out on it. He studied the map, pretending to think, using the time to debate what he would divulge.

Taking the white rams' head figures used to denote the Lazado, Braxton placed four pieces. "They will attack from Lake Romann—eventually. For now, it is more of a distraction."

"Obviously," someone muttered sharply.

"Shut it," Branshaw snapped quickly.

"Here, at the Middle River Fort," Braxton continued, placing another piece. "The Merfolk do best in water. They would be fools to not use their strengths against us."

There was some muttering. It seemed a few others had had the same idea.

"Here, at Upper River Fort," he added.

There was more muttering from others that thought this was more likely than his previous statement.

"And here." He moved the final piece to Vercase. From the last report, they had been nearing the city, probably with the intent of taking it.

Knowing what the Lazado had planned would ruin any element of surprise, but it might help guarantee Branshaw spread their forces thin. If his "assumptions" proved true, he might be able to divert Branshaw's attention later as well.

"They took it," Branshaw said referencing Vercase. "News came this morning."

Braxton realized why they were so tense; the Lazado were going to be that much harder to defeat. Vercase was another notch in their belt, one more thing making them believe they could win. And it gave them one more place to fall back to as well.

"Of these three," Branshaw said, motioning to the pieces at the Upper and Middle River Forts and Vercase, "where are they most likely to attack from?"

"This is not an *or*," Braxton said. "They will attack from all three."

The silence he was met with told him no one had considered that possibility.

"Why?" Branshaw asked calmly.

"Spread us thin, keep us on our toes," Braxton shrugged. "It is probably a play to keep us in the land between rivers."

Branshaw tugged on his short beard. "Do you think they will split their forces equally?"

There was an uproar as the rest of the Commanders called him a number of harsh, brazen, and crass things.

"Shut it," Branshaw roared. "We cannot afford to not consider *all* possibilities—no matter how unlikely."

"No," Braxton answered, after thinking for a moment. "The force at Lake Romann is small and I do not foresee them increasing their numbers there. I think they will send a few thousand soldiers toward the River Forts. But the main part of the army will attack from Vercase. And it will be where the Children of Prophecy are."

"Why would they keep the Children of Prophecy in the main section?" a Commander snapped. "If you are right, that section will see the most fighting."

"Use your strengths," Branshaw muttered.

"And that is where they are the most protected, too," Braxton added. "Besides, imagine what just catching a glimpse of Keegan could do. The common folk are easily rallied."

Realization sank in for a few of the Commanders. But some were still unwilling to listen.

"Their next stop will be the river," Branshaw said.

"No, there is one more *decently* sized town between the river and Vercase. Jims." Braxton had to point out the city on the map because it was so small, so insignificant, there was not even a label for it.

The town had, at best, a thousand inhabitants. Regardless, the castle had survived countless wars, invasions, and rulers. After Jims, the forest dropped away and became the river plains.

"Send two thousand men each to the Middle and Upper River Forts," Branshaw ordered with balking from the other Commanders. "Then we march toward Jims. With any luck, we will not reach the city before they take it."

Braxton gave Branshaw a confused look.

"Kolt wants Keegan alive. If we have to fight, it might as well be on our terms. The Merfolk do best in water, so we keep them from it. The dragons fight best from the sky. But we have trebuchets."

««« »»»

Though it was November, the night didn't feel overly cold, and not only because Nico was sitting practically on top of the fire; winter was late this year.

"Sit any closer and you'll be on fire," Mara laughed.

"It's cold," he responded. Shifting back slightly from the flames, he immediately felt the chill of the night creeping in, winter's promise of near arrival.

Mara shook her head and opened her arm to him.

Smiling, Nico moved into her embrace, letting her welcome him into the confines of a blanket.

Across the fire, Harker and Ima fought over the thigh bone of a cow. Eventually there was a shattering crack as the bone split in two. Ima gave Harker a playful head-butt for good measure before plopping down to suck the marrow from her portion.

"Look at the lovers," Vitia sneered behind them.

Nico quickly freed himself from the blanket, the knife in his boot ready and in hand. Realizing it was only Vitia, he put it away but did not relax.

Ima and Harker were both on their feet, the bone forgotten, feathers on end. Vitia raised her lip, revealing pointed canines. The griffins returned in kind, hisses spilling from their beaks like mist—they were a lot more terrifying.

"What do you want?" Mara asked coolly, refusing to turn her attention from the fire.

"For starters, you can stop cavorting. It's disgusting," Vitia snarled.

Nico rolled his eyes. There was nothing but friendship between him and Mara.

"Didn't your mother ever tell you if you roll your eyes they'll get stuck like that?" Vitia gibed.

He smartly refrained from repeating the action, knowing she would make them get stuck.

"What do you want?" Mara repeated.

"You're on duty tonight," Vitia said with a malicious grin.

"We were on duty last night," Nico said. "As I recall, it's your turn."

"And I don't feel like it. So, as your superior, you'll do as I say."

"Superior opida," he muttered under his breath.

He clearly hadn't been quiet enough because Vitia grabbed the front of his shirt and punched him in the jaw. As she struck, she released him, launching him back toward the fire; he landed mere inches from the flames. His hair might look like a blaze, but he by no means wanted it to *become* one.

Before either of them could move, a voice from the shadows called out, "What is going on here?"

Squinting against the brightness of the fire, they searched the darkness for life. It wasn't until the man stepped from the chasm of night that they found him. Nico had seen him before but couldn't remember who he was. His short blond beard was riddled with gray, and he'd be lucky if it wasn't entirely so before the war was over. The man's pale blue eyes took in everything and gave orders without his lips moving.

"The boy tripped," Vitia answered, offering him a hand to help him up.

"He is on his back, looks more like he was pushed," the man countered.

Vitia shrugged, as if to imply he was exceedingly clumsy. When Nico didn't take her extended hand, malice flashed in her brown eyes, and he wondered if this would get him killed.

"I do not appreciate liars," the man said. "Braxton, what do you think a fitting punishment will be?"

From the gloom, Braxton came forward to stand beside the man, hands clasped behind his back like a disappointed father. Nico caught the glint of a smile in the prince's eyes and prayed no one else realized he was taking pleasure from this.

Vitia paled; she might finally be getting some of what she deserved.

"Well, Branshaw," Braxton started, "for trying to pawn her duties off, she will get a week of night watches. For hitting the boy, she will get a week on half rations. For lying, she forfeits a week's pay."

Branshaw raised an eyebrow, seemingly pleased with the doled punishment and reasons behind them.

Seething, Vitia roared, "You can't do that! What right do you have?"

"I am Commander of the Vosjnik," Braxton reminded her. "I have every right. Return to your duty. And should you try or succeed to pawn, bribe, threaten, steal, or coerce your way out of your punishment, I will march you through camp before whipping you. Understood?"

"Understood," Vitia growled.

Braxton gave her a lingering glare before melting back into the darkness with Branshaw, hushed words passing between them.

Vitia waited a moment before grabbing Nico's shirt and hoisting him to his feet. "So help me—"

"Put him down," Mara said, standing, flames dancing in her eyes, and it wasn't a mere reflection of the fire.

"Make me."

Nico was surprised when Mara did just that. Vitia's arms shook as she was forced to release him.

"Did you know elemental abilities are all mental?" Mara said offhandedly. "I'll bet you didn't. You do now. Leave us alone, or I'll take your powers. Permanently."

"Liar," Vitia started. The Alvor moved her fingers and was surprised when nothing happened.

"I don't lie," Mara claimed. "Now leave us alone."

The women stared each other down, but ultimately it was Vitia who blinked.

Once they could no longer hear the Alvor destroying whatever was in arm's reach as she stormed away, Nico relaxed, letting out a heavy breath. Mara opened her arms, welcoming him into the folds of the blanket once more.

"Can you really take her powers?" Nico asked quietly, slightly terrified of the answer.

"Sola and Lunos, no." Mara smirked. "But I can make her believe that—which makes it true… temporarily."

"Remind me to never make you mad."

Mara laid her head on his shoulder. "You could never do that."

Chapter 21

Aron's nerves simultaneously froze and erupted underneath Keegan's touch. Her lips pressed against his neck softly, occasionally giving a gentle bite—sometimes a not so gentle one. All through dinner, she had found ways to make him want… no, *need* so much more than what was given—and publicly appropriate.

At some point on the way back to their room, his mind cracked, and lust shamelessly took over. He did not care that Elhyas was mere paces behind them, nor that anyone was free to stumble upon them. He pushed Keegan against a wall and kissed her deeply. Deeper than he had ever kissed her before, deeper than he thought was possible.

And though he had her trapped, seemingly at his command, it did not mean he was the one in power. She was leading the dance, and set her own pace, regardless of how it tortured him so.

He would have her in the hall if she allowed it. He would beg if she asked. He would do whatever she wanted, as long as he could have her.

She kissed him and his body ground against hers, begging, while her fingers coiled in the fabric of his shirt, pulling him closer still.

They must have been moving slowly, tiny steps at a time, for suddenly they were tipping backwards through a doorway. The sudden drop wrenched them apart and he had the foresight to close the door.

Although no candle lit the room Aron could see Keegan's form clear as day with the light provided by the moon through the open window. All of it. She stood before him, dress in hands, asking for so much more. Though her body was the most beautiful thing he had ever seen, he could not stand the sight of it if it meant he must be so far away.

Keegan smiled, raising an eyebrow in that devious way of hers—he was hers for the night. Closing the distance between them, Aron pulled her lips to his.

She pulled at his hips, undoing the buckle of his belt. Aron could feel blood rushing from his head and begged for her to undo the laces of his trousers too.

Instead, she traced her fingers up his ribs, forcing his shirt to rise. For the barest of moments, Aron broke away, lazily throwing his shirt on the floor as he returned to her.

She bit at his lip and his heart felt like it was going to explode. Her hands roamed his back, tracing his skin, while his pulled at her hips, molded her breasts, tugged at her hair, pulling her as close as he could. He needed her.

Grabbing Keegan's legs, he hoisted her up, settling her on his hips. Unable to resist any longer, he moved toward the bed, roughly depositing her. Faster than he thought possible, he removed his trousers. Then he was there with her, telling her how he felt with gentle kisses that trailed up her stomach and between her breasts.

Where their bodies touched might as well be pure flame and his temperature rose with each second. Keegan's hand was between his legs, captivating him. If she kept up, he would not last long—and she knew it.

With the empathy link, Aron felt as if drugged. All the wonderful things he was experiencing were added to and multiplied by Keegan's own experience. Some moments, everything was so euphoric he swore he entered another realm where the only thing that existed were random shadows of bright colors. Other moments it was too much to handle, and he had to close the link—though it was more like dampening it; the proximity to Keegan made it nigh impossible to completely block her out.

Carefully, he pushed between Keegan's legs. When she did not resist, he knew he had been granted the key to his heart's desire. He wanted her, desperately so, but he also wanted her to feel the same desperation. Aron needed her to feel that same desperation.

He started by kissing her inner thigh, lightly, so lightly he could see the gooseflesh rising across her body as a whimper escaped her lips. He worked his way up her leg, pausing in the crook of her hip. He kissed up her stomach, stopping at her breasts, earning a shallow moan. Meanwhile, his fingers touched her tenderly, eliciting moans from her lips. Such a passionate heat came from her it was a wonder they had the barest of holds upon their baser desires.

"Don't make me beg," Keegan whispered, forcefully pulling his lips to hers.

And no more could he deny her or himself.

For him alone, there was no way to describe it. Each movement sent rapture across his body, taking his breath. Sola and Lunos, if he never had to leave this moment, he would give everything and more.

Finding himself unable to breathe as they kissed, he broke away and turned to her neck. He meant to bite and kiss but found himself unable to do anything but breathe. Electricity coursed through her body, originating where his lips caressed her skin. His fingers rolled and pinched her nipples, slowly bringing her to a precipice.

Then, time broke, and they began to move in a passionate frenzy. Keegan's nails glided down his back, bringing pain and pleasure. He sank his teeth into her shoulder and was rewarded with a moan of desire. They were so close.

He plied her breasts, feeling the pressure building within her like a storm. One that matched his own tempest. Then thunder struck, blinding Aron, and setting a ringing in his ears. His muscles turned to jelly, and it was all he could do to not become a dead weight.

Lying beside Keegan, control of his body was slow to return, color clouding his vision in a symphony.

Keegan nestled in the crook of his arm, fingers tracing imaginary lines across his stomach. Where she touched, ice burned, pleasant and warm.

Aron placed a hand over hers, the beating of their hearts slowly climbing down from their mountains. They were happy to lie in silence. But it was not silence; something… was not right. He could easily imagine the sounds of clanging metal—as if there was a battle. He pushed it aside, telling himself it was nothing—how could it be anything?

A knock on the door pulled them from their not so quiet silence.

"Hold on," Keegan called, rising from the bed. She quickly slipped on her clothes while Aron pulled the covers over his hips.

Opening the door, they were faced with Kade.

"Whatcha want?" Keegan demanded.

Though she blocked her twin from his line of sight, Aron caught the glint of armor and sat up slowly. Maybe there was a battle going on.

"Stay here," Kade ordered.

Before Keegan could respond, her brother shoved her back and threw something into the chamber after her. The door slammed shut and the room filled with a cloying smoke. Keegan began to cough, and he could feel the burning in her throat. And he could feel… something slipping away.

Closing the empathy link as much as he could, he rushed to help her from the floor where she was gasping and wheezing. "What is going on?"

Keegan panted, "Bitch used an ether bomb."

Her breath returning, she rose and stormed to the door, flinging it open. Aron did not have to see her face to know she was donpox. Where the doorway had once opened into the hall was now a solid stone wall.

Looking out the window, all Aron could see was darkness and hints of shadowy shapes amongst the light given off by the chaos of torches. Battle *was* happening.

"Can you get us out of here?" he asked.

"No," she answered, going to look out the window with him. "But I'm gonna kill him when we do."

«««   »»»

Braxton might have tried to leave the unfamiliar bedroom if two people had not barreled in, lust oozing from every pore. Instinctively he knew he was having one of his dreams. He watched as the woman removed her clothes and waited patiently for her lover.

The woman's face was blurred, but her hair danced with fire that was quenched to an ember by the brown beside it. The door closed and Braxton looked toward the second person. His mouth dropped as he recognized Aron. Looking back toward the woman, he realized it was Keegan.

Not a match he would have guessed, but if they were happy, what did it matter to him. But it did matter because it was his job to rip Keegan away from Aron—from this life. He was set upon a path to bring his brother pain and sadness. And there was very little he could do to alter that course.

But as much as his mind wanted to linger on that worry, it was pushed aside as his brother and Keegan further succumbed to passion.

He did not want to see this, so he turned away. Aron was a child... that was all he could think of his brother as, even if he was twenty.

Against his will, his attention was refocused on the two as they truly united in love. He tried to look elsewhere, but some force prevented him from doing so. Thankfully, he was able to shut his eyes, though that did nothing to dampen the sounds.

He could not say how long they were together, but it was much too long for his liking. Hearing a knock at the door, he thanked Sola and Lunos. Opening his eyes just enough to see shadows and shapes, he saw Keegan rise from the bed and quickly slip on clothes.

Opening the door, she was faced with Kade Tavin. The fled Vosjnik soldier seemed perturbed, and Braxton could only wonder what was happening.

Keegan stumbled back, and the sounds of coughing filled the room while smoke clogged the air.

Blinking the smoke from his eyes, he was no longer in the chamber with Aron and Keegan. Now, battle raged around him. A blade passed through his gut, and while he felt nothing, bile longed to rise in his throat. It was only once his stomach settled that Braxton realized he was not a corporeal form. He must be dreaming. No, he was seeing the future.

When he spied the sigil of the ruling family of Vercase on a door, understanding dawned on him; he was seeing the present. Whatever magic allowed him to glean the future was still at work but, dampened due to the remaining slajor manacle, limiting him to the now. He thought back to his previous dream about Caius. It raised questions he was not ready to ask, so he stuffed them away as an ache to sort out later.

Taking in his surroundings, he could tell he was near the entrance hall of the castle. The way was packed with people, weapons in hand reflecting the low light.

The living who rushed by were warped blurs, their cries and yells punctuating his vision with sharp colors. A few bodies scattered along the hallway were the only people he could see clearly as he walked along. Most of the bodies belonged to humans, but he did spot a Mermaid, eyes glazed and open, her blue skin a dead giveaway.

A movement caught his attention and he focused on it. The man was nothing out of the ordinary, likely a farmer scooped up by fate based upon the commoner's clothing he wore. However long he had been training—likely not long enough to see the end of the war—it was enough to give him a chance to see sunrise. Be that blessing or curse, only time would tell.

As Braxton watched the man make his way through opponents, there was something familiar about him. But what was it?

His body suddenly began to shake, and the world shifted.

Above him stood Nico, his red hair sticking out as if his pillow had licked it during his sleep.

"You're talking in your sleep. Something about a man?"

It all became clear. How had he not seen it immediately? The man from his dream was related to Nico. If he had to guess, it was Jared Sieme.

Urging Nico back to bed, he said a small prayer to the old gods for Jared.

《《《《 》》》》

It didn't feel like he'd trained particularly hard, but it appeared Jared was wrong. As soon as he sat down to dinner, exhaustion settled over him, shrouding him in a deep fog; it took every bit of willpower to not fall asleep then and there. As soon as he finished eating, he headed to the room he, Carter, and Lucas shared, Jarshua following along, pouncing on shadows much like a cat might a mouse.

He promptly fell into bed and was asleep before his head hit the pillow.

The next thing he knew, a bright light was blinding him. Jarshua gave an annoyed yip and dug his head underneath the blankets. Covering his head with the pillow, Jared effectively blocked out the light and fell into another dreamless sleep.

Sometime later, he assumed it was morning because there was no other reason to be woken up, someone was shaking his shoulder in a violent and desperate manner. Though groggy, he was painfully aware the room was like pitch, meaning it was still night. Angrily, he gave whoever had woken him an obscene gesture and rolled over.

He bolted upright when he felt the slap to the back of his head. "What the royik?" Blinking the vestiges of sleep from his eyes, he realized Lucas was standing over him.

"Vercase is being attacked," his brother said in greeting.

Cursing, Jared pulled himself from bed. Jarshua was unceremoniously knocked to the ground, and he stared up at Jared with a confused and annoyed look that only a pup can manage. Luckily—though only in hindsight—Jared had been too tired to undress or even remove his boots before bed. His gifted sword sat by the bedside, and he grabbed it, buckling it around his waist as he headed for the door.

His brothers were hot on his heels and Carter made sure to push Jarshua back into the room before shutting the door. Jared felt bad for the pup, but this was no place to have him running wild. When he was older and bigger though… the wolf would be a near unstoppable force. And needed in skirmishes. But for now, it was safer if he was left behind.

Now paying attention, Jared could hear the horns sounding the alarm and the clashing of metal, signifying the battle had already started.

On the upper levels of the castle, they were able to move freely, but as they neared the ground floor, the halls became congested.

Jared pushed through the crowd, trying to get to the armory. When he made it there, he was dismayed to find he'd lost Lucas and Carter—it was Revod all over again. Cursing, he grabbed a chest plate and darted from the room.

He raced down the corridors toward the entrance hall and found himself faced with two soldiers bearing unfamiliar sigils. Around them lay dead men, most of them Lazado.

"One more for good luck," one of the soldiers said with a bloodthirsty smile.

"I call the kill," the other said, rushing at Jared.

He knew he stood a chance with one opponent, but two… it might not end well for him. He needed to change the odds.

Jared didn't know the castle well, but assumed he knew it better than these men. He turned back the way he'd come and, as he ran, prayed they'd follow. His plan relied on it, even if his survival did not.

"Coward," voices called mockingly.

The sound of their shoes slapping against the floor told Jared they were doing exactly what he wanted. If he remembered correctly, there was a small alcove just ahead. Finding it, he ducked inside, using the shadows to cloak himself.

The two soldiers passed by then slowed as they reached the next junction, heads turning as if he might materialize from one of the walls.

"Where'd he go?" one asked.

Jared pushed from the shadows and plunged his sword into the chest of the nearest man. "I'm right here."

The cracking and squelching as he pulled his sword free was sickening, but he didn't have time to dwell on it. The man fell, blood bubbling between his lips, his final moments fleeting. Jared focused on the other soldier, attacking immediately and without hesitation.

They fought back and forth, their swords occasionally clashing against the wall, breaking free a chip or two of stone. The world became silent, and the only thing Jared heard was his heart and the clanking of swords.

The trance was broken as his opponent's sword raked across his thigh. The cut wasn't deep and didn't hurt—yet—but blood spilled forth in a fluid sheet. Knowing he wasn't in a good position, Jared lunged at the man, twisting the pommel of his sword to pull out a hidden dagger.

The soldier wasn't prepared, and Jared slammed the knife into the underside of his jaw. The man gurgled and gasped, his fingers losing their grip on his sword. As Jared pulled the blade free, he watched the life slip from the man's eyes. He might have felt pity or remorse if there weren't a long night still ahead of him.

«««« »»»»

"Over there," Lyerlly said, directing a man who was holding up his companion.

With so much blood on them, it was hard to tell where the injury was, or even who was injured—though it was likely both and a matter of who was worse off. She turned back to her original patient, setting to working again with needle and thread. Tonight, she would not be using magic but for the most grievous wounds. While she hated to leave people in pain, there were too many for her to worry about and not enough magic—certainly not this late into her pregnancy.

The stream of injured and dying never ceased, trickling steadily into the hospital in twos and threes. As she flitted between patients, she lost track of time, doing what she could and offering kind words to those who would have to survive without their friends.

Mostly, it was humans who made their way through the hospital doors. From what she knew, only a handful of Buluo and one Mermaid were there.

As dawn's light began to peer through the windows like a naughty child, the stream of injured slowed and she was able to take a breath—what felt like the first one all night. Exhaustion washed over her like the tide, making heavy threats, but now was not the time to sleep.

Looking around the room, every bed and cot was filled, as was much of the floor space. Many were already dead and outside the hospital she knew she would find more deceased littering the hallways. But the dead were Lunos's problem, she only had to worry about the living. *She* had to make sure they remained in the hands of Sola.

Lyerlly ran her hands over her face and tasted iron as her fingers pulled over her lips. Looking down at herself, her entire person was splattered and drenched in blood. She laughed morbidly, realizing she must look like one of the injured.

Hearing footsteps coming down the hallway, Lyerlly prepared herself for a second wave. Instead, she was surprised to find the people, mainly Alvor, marching through the doors were in fine fettle.

An Alvor woman came to her. "We are here to help."

Normally, Lyerlly might have said their help was needed elsewhere. She directed the healers and soon everyone had someone assisting them… or holding their hand if it was a little too late.

As relief washed over her, she was vaguely conscious of someone placing a hand on her shoulder and asking something. She was aware of responding, but not of what she said. Someone asked for a chair and guided her into it. Sola and Lunos, it felt good to sit.

"Ma'am," the person said, snapping their fingers to get her attention, "how many months along are you?"

"Eight," she answered, lightly shaking her head to clear her mind.

"You should not have given—" the Alvor started.

"I give as much as needed," Lyerlly said, forcing herself out of the chair, despite her growing weariness. "Tend to those who need it; I can handle myself."

The Alvor looked like she wanted to argue, but a steely look from Lyerlly sent her loping off to attend to the wounded.

As she drove back into her work, a thought lingered. This was the outcome of war, and so much more was coming. "Sola and Lunos…" she muttered.

Chapter 22

Though they had been caught unawares, the Lazado's numbers had been superior and by dawn the battle was over. Blood still dripped down Kade's armor in dwindling and drying rivulets. He hadn't made it far outside the castle, but it was still far enough that he had to trudge back, weary and in need of sleep.

Bodies littered the streets, and he stepped over them delicately.

The castle hadn't been spared bloodshed, surprise allowing the enemy to get further than they should have. It was a mistake Bernot would not let them repeat. Kade might have searched the living minds for Keegan, but, with any luck, she was still holed up in her room with Aron, surrounded by stone; reaching or sensing her would be difficult and he wasn't up to the challenge. Nor did he feel like dealing with a donpox off Keegan. That was a storm he wouldn't be able to hide from when it came.

Stepping into the chilled interior of the castle, it looked much like the outside, not good. But for all the evidence of violence, it could've been worse.

The doors to the dining hall were open wide. From inside, Kade could hear several voices clamoring, steadily rising in volume as each one fought to be heard first. Peeking in, he found all the leaders and a few other people. Everyone was covered in varying amounts of blood, even Bernot. He spotted the Sieme brothers sitting at a table, Jared looking like he wanted to fall asleep, a no-longer white bandage around his thigh. The other two seemed like they had escaped without significant injury. Keegan and Aron were nowhere to be seen and he took that to mean they were still locked away. Maybe Sola and Lunos would grace him with luck today after all.

Bernot noticed him and gave a subtle nod. *Have you seen Keegan?*

Yeah. I locked her and Aron— He wasn't given time to finish the thought as a force sent him stumbling. Exhausted as he was, he was knocked to his knees.

Found her, Bernot drawled.

Rising, Kade turned and was met with a fist. He didn't need to step back to see who his attacker was.

Keegan was worked into a lather the likes of which he'd never seen. And prayed to never see again.

"Pull something like that again and I will *fucking* kill you!" his sister seethed, pulling her fist back to strike again. She was halfway through the motion when Aron grabbed her around the waist and pulled her back.

For once, he was glad the exiled prince was around.

Keegan raged and screamed but Aron never put her down, taking the mild abuses she was able to give him in stride.

"Keegan," Atlia said, seemingly unperturbed by her anger, "why do you not calm down and tell us what is going on?"

His twin by no means calmed, but she did gladly elucidate them. "He threw a fucking ether bomb in our room and sealed us in!"

"How did you do that? The ether bomb I mean," Eoghan asked.

Keegan stared in stunned silence at the Reintablou.

"Saltpeter, sugar, potassium, water, a small vase, and some ether," Kade answered, rubbing his jaw. "Or something like that. Throw it and some kind of reaction causes it to catch fire. As the saltpeter and sugar burn, the ether vaporizes and mixes with the smoke."

"Where did you learn this?" Cataline asked. "From what I understood, you were not the intellectual one."

Kade bit the inside of his cheek to prevent himself from giving a snide retort. And the blatant insult hurt more than he cared to admit.

"We were working together on it," Keegan answered, finally calming enough to not be yelling.

Aron tentatively unwrapped his arms from around her waist and when she didn't immediately rush at Kade, relaxed. As soon as he did, Keegan flew at Kade and landed another hit. She was quickly pulled back by Aron, who this time had the sense to pin her arms to her side in a hug.

Kade walked across the hall, not wanting to take another chance with his sister. She could try again, but at least he would see her coming.

"Keegan, do you know the mechanics behind this bomb of yours?" Eoghan asked.

"Yeah," she said, pushing Aron off. "Small glass phial with water, wrap potassium around it. Put that in the center of a vase with saltpeter, sugar, and ether. When you throw the vase, the phial breaks and the potassium reacts with the water in an exothermic reaction, igniting, which sets the saltpeter and sugar on fire. With the ether mixed in, as that burns, it turns to smoke—and, voilà, ether smoke bomb."

"Why were you working on this?" Bernot asked.

"Figured we could put a whole lot of people out of commission without actually doing any permanent damage."

The leaders shared some sideway glances, but none pressed the matter further. Kade knew this was a conversation involving him and Keegan that would happen later—and in depth.

"Who attacked us, and how?" Bernot said, looking to the few lieutenants and Commanders standing about the room.

"Lord of Hamrick," Niranda answered. "Seems someone got a raven out before he lost his head."

"We should have known to watch our backs," Atlia said. "How bad are our losses?"

"Not as bad as it could have been," one of Atlia's Commanders answered. "I would say a few hundred dead, a few hundred wounded. Most of both human."

Atlia sighed. "You are right, it could have been worse. But it also could be better."

Bernot scanned the room and his face softened. "Everyone, get some sleep. You all deserve it."

No one said a word and people began shuffling out, the sudden weight of exhaustion pressing down on them.

"Kade, Keegan," Bernot called, halting them.

Aron also remained, an arm preemptively around Keegan's shoulders.

"Kade, thank you for looking after your sister," Bernot started. He raised a hand to waylay Keegan when she opened her mouth to argue. "However, she is going to end up in the fray no matter what we do."

"Doesn't mean I can't limit the number of battles she has to fight," Kade answered placidly. He had no remorse for doing what it took to protect his family.

Bernot dipped his head in agreement. "True, but a better way of protecting her will be to get her a good set of armor. I will talk to Waylan and Eoghan about putting something together."

Keegan should've been given armor long ago. But with bigger dragons to fight, Kade could understand how they'd all believed they'd have plenty of time to get it done. Until time had run out unexpectedly.

Bernot continued, "And while they are at it, maybe they can do something for you."

Kade looked down at the griffin sigil on his chest plate. Here, it was one of a kind—as well as an insult and invitation for death. Though the armor had served him well, he knew the time had come to part with it.

"Now, both of you, get some sleep."

Keegan turned to look at him, the traces of a scowl still there, but it had softened significantly. "Bring me that rust bucket tomorrow; I'll see what I can do about the sigil."

««« »»»

The forge was atrociously hot, and Keegan didn't understand how the smiths worked in those conditions—especially while wearing heavy leather aprons and gloves. That, and the noise.

In her lap sat Kade's chest plate. She was working to change the sigil—well, not really, not yet anyway. She still needed to figure out what to change it *to*.

Kade, she tested.

What?

Does our family have a crest or sigil?

There was a moment of silence. *We come from peasants, not lords.*

Still, wouldn't we have a crest?

No. That's reserved for people who have money and matter.

Keegan cut the connection and thought to herself, *We matter now.*

With complete creative freedom, the best question to ask was: what best represented their family?

Niranda had found her a book about the crests and sigils of Arciol. As she flipped through, there were plenty of symbols that represented Kade or her well, but none that worked for *both* of them.

Growing frustrated and about to give up, she decided to flip one more page. She was glad she did. This was perfect.

Reaching for her earth magic, she directed it toward the chest plate. Then she paused; she hadn't thought about how she was going to do this. The new sigil would be similar to the Alagards' in a sense, and she wondered if she could simply move the etched elements around. There was only one way to find out.

She found it surprisingly easy to move the engraved lines about the metal's face as if they were nothing more than magnets. The wings of the griffin were kept with a few adjustments to their shape. The body she had to completely redo, flattening out lines she wished to erase by pulling the needed metal from the lines she wished to deepen to give the image depth. Done, she held the armor at arm's length. It had turned out better than she'd hoped, given she was no artist.

"It's not bad," Lucas yelled over the noise of his hammer against the rod of metal he was currently working.

Looking over her shoulder, she gave him a proud smile. "Thanks." She wasn't sure if he heard her or not.

"You done?" Eoghan called across the forge, pausing in his work. Sweat dripped down the Torrpeki's forehead in fat globules. "Let us see." He wiped his face, quickly becoming the leader he usually was.

Keegan turned the armor to show him.

"You chose a hawk," Eoghan said, quickly returning to hammering. "Why?"

"Well," Keegan started, speaking loudly to be heard over the din, "the book says a hawk or falcon in heraldry represents someone who doesn't rest until they've achieved their goal. AKA someone who's stubborn as fuck. I'd say that's Kade and I to a damn T."

"You both are quite stubborn," Eoghan admitted with a chuckle, sounding like tinkling between the strikes of the hammer.

"Ready for us to take measurements?" Waylan grunted, pushing on the bellows. The fire roared with the added breath in its belly, sending heat across the smithy.

"Sure," she said, sliding off the counter she'd been sitting on instead of a chair.

"Lucas," Waylan called, "think you can do it without strangling her?"

Though it sounded like a joke, Keegan was well aware the blacksmith likely dreamed about doing just that. And some days, she didn't doubt the same held true for the oldest Sieme brother.

Lucas was quick about his business and in minutes was waving her off.

Scooping up Kade's chest plate, she left the smithy, welcoming the cool kiss of the autumn air outside. The sweat that beaded across her body made her cold and she quickly wicked the moisture away. Knowing Kade, he was likely training, and her assumption was correct; she found him in the courtyard sparring against Elhyas.

She paused in the wall's shadow to watch them. It was amazing how far Kade had come from his first anger-filled match against the guard. He'd always been a good swordsman, but now... hell, even Elhyas was having to resort to trickery.

Finally noticing her, Elhyas pulled away, causing Kade to run into the stairs.

Once he finished cursing what was a now bruised shin, he dusted himself off. From the look on his face, he was nervous; this would define their family for generations to come—granted, they had to survive first.

Keegan turned the chest plate to face him, and his anxiety dropped away, confusion and... dare she say it, pride, muddling his face.

"A hawk," he said, scratching his head. "Why?"

"Cause neither of us give up."

"That we do not," Kade admitted, taking the armor. His hands traced the etching tenderly. "You... it looks like Waylan crafted it himself."

"Thank you. Now," she said with a smirk and a dip of the head, "get back to work."

"Wait," Kade said, fumbling to pull a pale blue stone of larimar from his pocket.

"This was Cassidy's," she said, taking the stone.

Her brother rubbed the back of his neck. "I- I was hoping you could put it in the armor."

She gently placed a hand on Kade's forearm. This was as close as her brother was ever going to get to... she struggled to describe it. Grieve? Regret? Though she couldn't put it into words, she knew it made him human. Vulnerable. That was it. "Not a problem."

Setting the armor on the ground, she squatted beside it, studying the metal to find the best place for the pendant. She decided on the base of the throat, mimicking how the stone would've sat around Cassidy's neck, and created a small pit in the metal. Once she was sure the stone wouldn't come loose, she stood and handed the armor to Kade. "*Now*, back to work."

At her words, Elhyas attacked. Kade barely had a second to block and he brought the chest plate up like a shield.

Frantically, Keegan yelled, "Hey! Don't go destroying it now."

Her words fell on deaf ears and, shaking her head with a sigh, she walked away. When Kade brought it back to her scuffed and dented, she had a right mind to make him fix it himself.

««« »»»

His heart hammered away in his chest and Jared was certain it was going to explode. Ahead, he saw a door and prayed it led to an empty room. Throwing it open, he was relieved to find cobwebs and dust. Slamming the door, he hastily did the lock. He tried to take several deep breaths to calm himself, but his heart was too busy pounding against his lungs, refusing to allow a full breath.

His mind and body quickly plummeted into darkness, a safe space, as he sank into a corner, the world swirling and crumbling around him. There was one thing he wanted to think about, but doing so wouldn't make the situation any better.

Eventually his heart calmed enough for his heavy breathing to cease, and his brain forced him to reflect upon the events that had led him to here, to this moment, this... *crisis*.

It had been a normal day. Well... the day had started normal. He'd woken and breakfasted with his brothers, bantering the entire time, pretending to not see the evidence of the attack on the walls, mostly in the form of wayward splatters of blood. Two days was not enough time to entirely erase the reminders of Lunos's reach.

Afterwards, Lucas went to the forge, Keegan following quietly behind him. Her not so newfound aptitude with metal magic had her mending armor. Carter had taken to training with Elhyas's nephew, Auckii, and was quick on Elhyas's heels when he pulled Kade and his nephew from the hall.

Left alone, Jared began to relive the battle. The wound to his thigh, deemed not life threatening, had been left to heal on its own. Keegan had offered to heal it, but he refused; he needed the reminder of what was at stake.

His leg was sore, and the wound caused him to have a temporary limp. But while he had walked away, he'd caused several men to not. He couldn't afford to forget the costs of a mistake.

"Best to not think about it," Mahogen said, pulling him from his spiraling thoughts.

Jared looked around the room; they were alone. His hand absentmindedly moved to the pommel of his sword, exploring its details, the action calming. This gift from the Alvor prince had allowed him to survive.

He and Mahogen would train today, even if he was injured; his skills needed honing and sharpening if he wanted to survive to see peace again. The next person he fought would likely be better trained than the men of Hamrick. And if injured in battle, no one would pity or spare him. As a Child of Prophecy, he was expected to fight in any condition—and live.

"Do you ever forget their faces?" he finally asked.

"Of the men you kill?" Mahogen replied.

Jared nodded.

"No."

"How… how do you deal with knowing… you killed them?"

Mahogen was slow to answer, chewing on a way to make sense of the destruction. "Everyone has their own method. I remember they were trying to kill me, and their death is for a greater good… if we win. Though, even if we lose, they still went toward someone's greater good."

A man's face flashed before his eyes. He was neither young nor old—young enough to have experienced the joy of living but not old enough to know it. And Jared's sword had pierced his gut, stealing any chance of his hair graying. His body must have tensed because Mahogen put a hand on his shoulder.

They were silent for a time and Jared closed his eyes, finding it strange that his mind was suddenly calm, as if

Mahogen's touch kept him grounded. If it was grounding him, he was thankful for the friendship, for knowing family was not just blood.

When Jared finally opened his eyes with a sigh, he found Mahogen staring at him with a look of concern, though a hidden longing danced behind the green shards of his eyes.

The Alvor scooted to the edge of his seat and placed his hands on either side of Jared's face. "I promise, their lives will have been for something."

Jared just nodded. The words were true, but they wouldn't stop the wailing of a man's wife or the tears of his children or the anguish of his parents. He was a thousand miles away again, wondering over the fate of those the dead left behind, because he was only pulled back to reality by Mahogen's lips brushing against his.

At first, he was too shocked to do anything besides sit there as Mahogen begged for a retort. Then, he slowly began to relish the contact. There was just something right about the moment—about the person.

When realization came crashing down on him like a waterfall, his breath was sucked away, and his body reeled as if in pain. This could never be—*should* never be. Jared pulled away and muttered something unintelligible before abruptly standing, sending his chair crashing backwards.

He was hardly a step toward the door when Mahogen grabbed his arm. "When you decide what you want, I will be here. Whether it be as friend or more, teacher or guard. When you decide, let me know. And know I will respect your decision. Whatever it may be."

Jared wasn't sure if he responded before yanking his arm away and sprinting from the hall. His breakneck run through the castle had led him to this empty room and impossible choice.

Deep down, he knew what he wanted. The problem was, he wasn't sure the rest of the world would allow it—at least the humans wouldn't.

He wasn't sure how long he sat in that corner, knees pulled to chest, lump in his throat. When he did become aware of time again, the room seemed darker, suggesting the sun was beginning her descent.

There was a knock on the door, and he about jumped out of his skin, smacking the back of his head into the wall.

"Jared," Keegan called softly. When he didn't respond, the door opened slowly. Worry was written on her face.

A small shape pushed past her legs, darting into the room. Jarshua jumped onto his chest, fervently licking his face. Jared pushed the wolf away, bile rising in his throat. He'd been tasked with protecting the pup… and he'd certainly failed today.

"How did you know I was here?" he asked quietly. "How did you get in, I…" Magic.

"You're a bundle of nerves," Keegan said, taking a seat beside him. She pulled Jarshua off him, and playfully rubbed the pup's belly while he nipped at her fingers. "You've been driving Kade and I nuts all day."

"Sorry."

She gently nudged him with her elbow. "Is everything okay?"

"I… yes." Burdening Keegan with his problems would help neither of them. If he pretended— "No. Sola and Lunos, no," he muttered, putting his head between his knees.

Keegan didn't say anything and rubbed his back.

The slow circles her hand made were comforting and helped to keep him from spiraling into a bottomless pit—again. When he finally raised his head, Keegan bore a knowing kind of look. His heart sank; if even she didn't approve...

"Whoa there, don't get your britches in a bunch."

"What?"

"I don't disapprove."

"You know what's going on?"

"Yeah..."

"How dare you force yourself into my mind!"

"Didn't have to. You're broadcasting."

He felt the blood drain from his face.

"Don't worry," Keegan sighed, leaning back against the wall, "I'm shielding you."

Relief loosened the lump in his throat. "I, I..."

"Don't know how to feel?" Keegan finished.

He nodded.

"I can't answer that one for you," she started, "buttt... I can offer some advice. Fuck whatever homophobic societal norms that've been drilled into your head. It's okay to love another man. You don't have to admit that you like Mah— men, today, tomorrow, or even a year from now. When you do decide to let yourself admit that though, good. Those who love you for who you are won't care."

"Promise?" he hiccupped, not sure when he'd started crying.

"Promise," she said, taking his hand and giving it a gentle squeeze.

Chapter 23

Keegan drummed her fingers against the table as Eoghan and Waylan made the finishing touches on her armor.

"Ready?" Eoghan asked, finally setting down his hammer.

"I was ready a week ago," Keegan said, sliding down from the table she had chosen over a chair.

Eoghan made a big show of revealing the armor and his face fell upon seeing her lackluster reaction. To her it was plain, like anyone else's armor—it didn't even have the Tavin's new sigil. She began stumbling over her words in an attempt to not hurt the Torrpeki's feelings.

"Quit your blubbering," Waylan barked, "and let us explain its features. Firstly, this is probably the strongest armor in the world. There's a thin layer of diamond on the inside. As long as it doesn't shatter, just about nothing's gonna get through."

"Well, provided the attacking object is not spelled," Eoghan amended.

Keegan felt along the inside. It was cold, but definitely not metal. Looking inside, she saw a crystal-clear layer of diamond at least a quarter of an inch thick. "Jesus, fuck," she muttered. "This must've cost a fortune."

"Not to this bastard," Waylan mumbled, jerking a thumb in the Reintablou's direction.

"Continuing," Eoghan said. "We have also hidden lots of tricks up your sleeves. Here in the cuisse," he picked up a piece that would protect her upper leg, "if you press this little circle here on the side." He did so and a thin knife popped out. "There are five of these on each leg."

"That looks too thin to actually stab anyone with," Keegan said.

Waylan snatched the dagger from Eoghan and threw it at a wooden post across the smithy. It struck true and her doubts evaporated.

Next, they showed her the gauntlet where they'd hidden spikes in the fingertips—much like the claws of a cat. In the ribcage of her cuirass two metal rods with sharpened tips were embedded—presumably also for stabbing. There was a small whip she could pull from the metal around her waist, though she had doubts on how accessible it'd be in battle. All in all, she'd never be left defenseless.

Once every facet of the armor had been explained, Eoghan asked, "Are you ready for another skills test?"

Keegan groaned, knowing there was no choice. She considered putting the armor on in the forge but didn't feel like tramping through camp in a tin can; even if there was no chance of being boiled alive now that the days were no longer stifling. Plus, she could only imagine the racket she'd make when she inevitably tripped.

Gathering the armor together, she packed it into a bag and headed toward the training field.

The air had a brisk chill about it and there was no doubting winter was on its way. She'd been warned winter was brutal in this world, but it hadn't lived up to expectation—yet. With winter's arrival, Bernot's hope of a fall war had to wait until next year. She wasn't sure if they'd be wintering in Vercase, but she wouldn't mind—there was a quaint charm about the city, and the library was a daydream.

The training field was littered with men, though not as many as there had been in previous weeks. The chill saw that many found other things to do in warmer places. And many had left for other battlefronts.

The leaders stood at the edge of the field in a solemn line. Tahrin had gone to the Western front and in her stead was Ezadeen. Poor Atlia looked miserable and was covered head to toe in furs; though used to freezing waters, the wind dried her skin like a hot sun did a lake in a summer drought.

"Alright, let's get this over with," Keegan said, stopping before the leaders and putting on her armor.

"Where is your sword?" Okleiy asked.

"In my room," she answered, struggling to put the greaves and cuisses on.

"Why?" Cataline asked.

"'Cause I don't generally need it. Most of the time I'm working on magic."

The leaders shared a worried look.

"I would like you to start carrying it at all times," Bernot said, "as well as a few daggers."

Armor donned, Keegan glanced toward the leaders. Before anyone said a word, she was attacked. Thankfully, the sword thrust at her chest was deflected by her near infallible armor.

Working to get her bearings, she realized the world had shifted. Blood and death had laid waste to the area and screams of anger and pain saturated the air. This was battle and she was in the midst of it—without a weapon.

She attempted to run when she saw her attacker acting to strike again. The ground pulled itself up, sending her sprawling, dirt lodging between her lips. Desperately, she searched for a means to defend herself and found nothing.

«««« »»»»

As soon as Keegan had her armor on, Bernot sent her into a nightmare. They had to test her, see how she would handle battle—it could mean life or death for her, and by association, the rest of them. Eoghan raised walls around them to conceal them from the rest of the world. They could not predict what might come from Keegan's mouth, nor how she might physically react to the simulation.

Bernot expanded his consciousness to overlap with the other leaders' minds and took them to Keegan's battle.

She lay on the ground, a petrified expression plastered on her face.

A soldier had his sword poised to stab her in the gut.

Keegan had no time to react as the man slammed the sword into her stomach. As soon as the blade hit her, it shattered, sending sharp shards sailing sideways.

"Not my work," Eoghan said referring to the armor. "That sword should have just gotten stuck in the metal or deflected."

Then it was Keegan's doing. Bernot was about to question how when he remembered magic was born of fear, instinct, and the desire to live. Clearly, she had quite a bit of all three at the moment.

Confusion and fear clouded Keegan's features, before realization settled over her. Had she forgotten she possessed magic?

Bernot let the soldier look confused at first, but the mirage hardly missed a second beat before pulling a dagger from his hip.

Determination lit Keegan's eyes. "Not today, motherfucker." She jerked her head to the side and there was a crack as the man's neck snapped.

Here, in the moment of life or death, guilt had no home, but sooner or later it would appear, and Bernot hoped Keegan had the fortitude to deal with it.

After taking a quick glance at her surroundings, Keegan sprinted across the field. He could hear her calling for her brothers mentally. His shield was strong, and they would not hear her. Eventually, she found a sword and grabbed it, hardly stopping long enough to lose momentum.

Again, Ezadeen said.

Bernot willed soldiers to materialize and they chased after Keegan with a bloodthirsty zeal. She stopped to look at them and the men flew together like magnets. When they tried to pull apart, they found their chest plates had fused together.

"Keep them coming," Atlia said.

And that he did. Keegan rarely had more than a few seconds to think. He did find it interesting she chose to incapacitate her opponents—aside from the first man.

"Take her magic," Cataline instructed. "She may not always have use of it."

He gave a soldier an ether-soaked rag and watched as the man snuck up behind Keegan. The man grabbed her around the shoulders and pressed the rag over her nose and mouth. The effect was near instantaneous. Keegan's knees buckled and it was only after the man pulled the rag away that she seemed able to stand on her own again.

Though she coughed and wheezed, the discomfort only made her angrier and did not seem to hinder her magic in any capacity. Ether had always had a different effect on her; sometimes it worked, sometimes it did not, sometimes it dampened her abilities, sometimes its effects only lasted a short time. In this simulated battle it should have had its normal debilitating effect.

Able to breathe again, Keegan grabbed the arm of the man and flipped him over her shoulder. He landed on the ground with a heavy thump. Then she darted away.

They could think of little that would stop her, so Bernot let her continue to fight her way across the battlefield. With each opponent she felled, she became more and more cocksure—and less aware.

She finally came upon an opponent whom she was not able to bend to her will and was a very good actor. Thinking she had defeated him, Keegan sauntered away, hardly making it five paces before he attacked.

The soldier rose to his knees and drove his blade behind the lip of her cuirass. As he pulled the sword out violently, Keegan toppled onto her stomach, gasping.

"End it," Atlia demanded. Back under the winter sunlight, the Merqueen hurriedly made her way to Keegan.

As soon as Bernot let the scene drop away, Keegan was able to regain her breath. Surprisingly, the first thing she did was rip her chest plate off and begin to feel her torso, searching for a wound. When she found herself unscathed, she rolled onto her side and divulged the contents of her stomach.

Atlia crouched beside her, rubbing her back gently, saying soothing words.

Keegan did not respond and was compliant as Atlia helped her to her feet and steered her off the field, face pale as snow.

"That was unexpected," Eoghan said.

That girl will never survive battle, Ezadeen said. *She is not strong enough to kill her enemy.*

"I am not sure I would call that a weakness in its entirety," Cataline said in Keegan's defense. "But I do see it leading to her downfall in the end—as it did here."

"What are we going to do about it?" Okleiy asked.

"I do not know," Bernot answered. "Her powers and abilities are too great to not put them to use, but her compassion will leave her vulnerable."

"I might have an idea," Eoghan said, finally speaking. "But it will take quite a bit of resources."

"We will at least hear it," Okleiy said.

"Let us use her kindness to our advantage. No doubt Kolt has painted us as bloodthirsty. If we can disprove that, how many men might join our cause? As she disarms men, have people ready to take them into custody. Plus, imagine what seeing her on the battlefield will do to bolster our own forces."

"Something to consider, for sure," Bernot muttered.

«««« »»»»

"You up to spar?" Guthrie asked. "Or are you too high and mighty for that?"

Braxton bit back a response, knowing Guthrie wanted to rile him up. Though he had seldom sparred with the Vosjnik before, now that he was Commander, it was even less likely. He typically trained with Mara and Nico and rarely where people could see him struggle against the remaining slajor manacle. Or that he sometimes seemed infallible. He considered giving an excuse, but maybe it was high time he gave himself a challenge—not that Guthrie could harm him thanks to Kolt's spell.

"Sure," he answered. "I could use a good warm up."

"Let's make it a real challenge then," Brennian spoke up. "You against us."

Braxton cursed to himself. To refuse showed he was afraid, but to agree meant one of them might figure out men could not hurt him. Might.

"Magic or sword?" he asked. This way only one of them would be in their element.

Brennian and Guthrie shared a vicious smile. "Both," they called, rushing at him.

With no time to draw his sword, Braxton reached for his magic—as finicky as it was. He raised a small wall, large enough to trip them up, and was thankful when the slajor manacle did not make it difficult. Brennian and Guthrie slid on their faces, their momentum not hindered by the fall.

Taking his time, Braxton drew his sword, and a smile crossed his face. Maybe this would be fun. His muscles ached to give it everything they had. How long had it been since he had not held himself back?

Then, it was not Brennian and Guthrie he was facing, but Keegan. And the world around him was painted in blood. The sky itself seemed to drip red and the air carried the whispers of Lunos. The sword in her hand showed him a reflection of himself. But it was not his reflection; the man looking back was brown-eyed and blond-haired. A crooked smile revealed a long-gone tooth.

Keegan's finger twitched and there was a blinding pain in the back of his head. His vision darkened and when light resurfaced, he lay face down on the ground.

As Keegan sauntered away, his fingers reached for the sword lying beside him. Stealthily, he rose to his feet and rammed the blade up underneath her armor. He removed it violently, his lips turning into a feral smile as she fell forward.

"Braxton," Guthrie called, giving his cheek a slap.

He blinked and tried to bolt upright. Something… hands on his shoulders, kept him pressed to the ground. His vision cleared and he was staring up at Brennian and Guthrie who both wore remarkably worried expressions.

Braxton reached up to touch his head lightly. Where Keegan's stone had hit was tender, but no blood or knot had surfaced. The tenderness was more akin to having hit his head in a fall. "What happened?" he asked groggily.

"We have no idea," Brennian said. "When we got to our feet after you tripped us, you were lying on the ground. No convulsions, but it's been about five minutes. Are you sick?"

Braxton groaned, lurching to his feet. "Keep training."

"Against you?" Guthrie questioned with raised brows.

He gave no answer, already stumbling away into the maze of tents, flashes of scenes he did not recognize racing across his vision.

Chapter 24

This last group—*finally*—leaving Vercase was small compared to the horde that had departed two weeks before. Most of the men at the Eastern Front had been sent ahead, leaving behind mostly key personnel and wounded.

Once, Kade would have pleaded to be on the forefront of battle. Now… he had no thoughts on the matter. He would find battle sooner or later. But the bloodlust of a vengeful boy was gone.

The word to move out rippled through the castle courtyard and streets packed with the Lazado. At the rear, a few people watched them forlornly; some were still healing from grievous injuries and needed continued care and rest. Like a wave, people and horses began slowly marching forward, the sounds of life clacking off the stone streets and buildings.

Kade hadn't seen his sister amongst the crowd but could feel her nervous energy—just as he had for the past two weeks; a state that was becoming annoyingly common. Few others had the brass to complain to her face. And when he did complain, her apology was always sincere. But whatever was worrying her was not easily contained behind her mental walls.

While his twin had been kept busy training, making finding her for answers impossible, Aron had been much simpler to find—and cajole. Keegan was worried about having to kill. But more so, having to kill on other people's terms. *He* didn't understand the difference... but, of course, he'd been killing people for a long time—sometimes for good reasons, sometimes not. There was a time when he'd felt the same hesitation, but that was long ago.

With the battles to come, would he again? He certainly couldn't say he was the same person who had joined the Vosjnik five years ago. Or even the same person who had showed up on the Lazado's doorstep only several months prior.

The thought of fighting brought him no fear. The thought of killing brought him no remorse. The thought of dying brought him no anxiety. The thought of winning brought him no joy. But the thought of vengeance did bring him pain.

Not pain because he would kill an old comrade or because his conscience would be burdened, but because he should've done it years ago. Pain because he hadn't been able to save Cassidy. He reached up to the collar of his chest plate where the larimar pendant was now imbedded and drowned in its silken touch.

Someone gently intertwined their fingers with his free hand, and he looked over to find Icella. He expected to find pity in her eyes, but there was none.

"Who was she?" the Mermaid asked.

He snatched his hand away, doing his best to ignore the heat spreading up his throat. "Who was who?"

The Mermaid gave him a knowing look.

Kade considered blowing her off, but surprisingly, he wanted to talk about Cassidy—with someone who hadn't known her, who wouldn't judge her. He didn't want to let her go—he doubted he ever could, she was the only woman to have ever truly seen him—but she was dead, and he alive... and one couldn't hold a ghost.

I don't know how we defined ourselves, he started, reaching out telepathically. This wasn't something he wanted to be common knowledge, and it was easier to talk about Cassidy if he didn't have to physically say the words and hurts.

Icella let him talk, never interrupting and her face was a blank mask of impartiality.

But you loved her, Icella finished as they passed through Vercase's gate.

He nodded, shielding his eyes from the afternoon sun.

How did you lose her?

The name was like poison. *Vitia.*

Icella didn't say anything more, but the look on her face said she'd been through similar. The icy buildup in her eyes said the person who'd hurt her was also still alive.

Part of him wanted to reach out and take her hand, like she'd done for him, but her horse had drifted, placing her out of reach. Instead, he sent the thought of warmth, shrouding her in gratitude and understanding.

She returned in kind, and ice that Kade hadn't known was sheltering in his heart started to fracture.

《《《《 》》》》

His ears felt assaulted, and there was no room for Aron to contradict them. A ruckus came from inside the tent he shared with Keegan—and there was only one person who could be making this much noise all by themself. Pushing back the flap, he carefully stepped inside, wondering why Keegan was being so flippantly loud and obnoxious. He found her alone, aside from a bottle of what he assumed contained alcohol by the cloying scent in the air. From the way he could hear the drink sloshing in the bottle, Keegan likely had imbibed more than she ought have.

"Keegan, what is going on?" he asked.

Her face lit up with one of the most genuine smiles he had ever seen. "It's December first!"

"Uh… is that supposed to mean something?"

"It means I can start singing Christmas songs!"

"Christmas songs?"

Her face fell, but her self-induced elation was tenacious. Seconds later she was smiling again and belting out a line about clanging bells. When she was done with the song, he was still confused. She gave a heavy sigh from her nostrils and motioned for him to sit beside her on the cot. Keegan offered him the bottle and he politely declined—but she insisted.

The liquid left a lingering burn in his throat and mouth. He took another gulp to appease Keegan, choking past the burn, and she began explaining.

"Christmas is a religious holiday in my world. It's supposed to center around Christ and all, but for a lot of families its more about just being together. And then you have Christmas songs which are about, well, Christmas, and some are about winter. In my family we have a rule that you can't start singing Christmas songs until December first. And since it's December first…"

"You are singing Christmas songs," he finished.

She encouraged him to take another swig, knocking his elbow with hers. "Bingo!"

"All right, just… maybe not so loud."

Indignantly, Keegan protested, "I am not being loud!" She began to scream another song, this one about a winter paradise.

He slapped a hand over her mouth to stifle her. Keegan began giggling and he quickly found himself joining in her mirth. And if laughing kept her from singing, so be it.

"Why do you not teach me one of these Christmas songs?" he said. "Quietly," he added, the mischievous gleam in her eyes impossible to ignore.

Her face lit up and she belted, "Jingle bells, Batman smells, Robin laid an egg!"

His eyebrows knitted together as he gave a confused chuckle. "What is all that supposed to mean?"

"It's not supposed to mean anything. Jingle bells, Batman smells, Robin laid an egg."

"Shut up in there!" a man from outside yelled. By the tone of his voice, this was a long time coming.

Keegan just screamed the line again.

Instead of letting the matter go, the man shouted the line back and it became a yelling match. By the end, Keegan could hardly call back through bellyaching laughter. Once the man realized he had won—this round at least—the night became quiet.

Then Aron heard it again, but from far off. He poked his head outside and heard the line once more, followed by the clinking of flasks and laughter. What had Keegan started?

Chapter 25

Accepting Bernot's hand, Lyerlly carefully stepped down from the wagon. Internally, she wanted to be stubborn and insist she could do it on her own. But she could not—and had not been able to for several weeks now. Some days, it was enough to not be winded after a brisk walk or to be able to put her shoes on without help. As her feet touched the ground, she placed a hand on her distended belly, feeling a gentle kick from the being inside.

"Are you sure you want to go straight to the hospital?" Bernot asked. "Are you sure I cannot convince you to relax?" Mumbling, he added, "From now until well after the baby is born."

"No, you cannot," she insisted, her head held high and proud. As she began to walk away—though it was more a waddle… and not very fast—she added, "I am pregnant, not incapacitated." Though that was less and less true by the day.

Bernot had the sense to not press, though did send a guard tottering along after her. She might have been amused at his overprotectiveness if they had not just bullied Jims into submission; she could be an easy target for retribution if anyone was desperate enough.

Lyerlly had heard the battle of Jims had been an easy victory, but from the way the hospital looked, it might have been said otherwise. Even when Sola smiled upon them, Lunos still saw fit to darken their door. Men, mostly human, filled the cots. Thankfully the winding cries of pain had long since lapsed into only the occasional grunt of discomfort.

A sharp pain in her stomach made her wince. False contractions had been part of this pregnancy for a long time—no terrifying stranger now. Once the pain passed, she continued her assessment of the hospital. None of this would do.

Bustling toward the woman who appeared to be in charge, she said, "I have got it from here."

The woman looked her up and down, disbelief relayed in the gesture. "Who might you be?"

Another false contraction waylaid her answer. "Lyerlly Bællar."

"I heard you had been sent back to Edreba."

She gave a pursed smile. "Clearly not."

They stared at each other, in that the way only women could. And even when there was another contraction, Lyerlly did not falter.

It was Eoghan who ended the war. "Lyerlly, so glad to see you made it," he said cheerfully. "The nurses here have done an excellent job keeping everything in order."

"Yes, well, thank you. Now," she said, going to take an apron off a rack, "I have work to do." Mumbling, she added, "More than I should have." That was not true, but she was feeling snide.

As she tied the apron around her waist, there was another acute pain. Normally, she only ever had one or two false contractions before she was left in peace for a few days—at worst, a few hours. This was the fourth one… in how long? Maybe there was need for concern. She shook the thought off; eight months into pregnancy things were bound to become abnormal.

About to see to a patient, something dripped down her legs.

Her face must have showed her worry because Eoghan was quickly at her side, a reassuring hand on her back.

"I think I have gone into labor," she managed to whisper, fear clutching her heart.

Eoghan's eyes widened. "Oh… my. It is a good thing I prepared for this."

Lyerlly was not sure what to say to that. And she might have pondered on it more if another contraction had not interrupted.

She consented to let the Torrpeki steer her toward a private room—the only one—her heart fluttering in her chest. "It is too early," she told him. "I am only eight months."

"It is going to be fine," he told her soothingly. "This happens sometimes."

"But the baby will not survive! It is too early."

Normal babies were usually fat and healthy. Babies that were too eager had never been long for this world, sickly little things.

"The baby—and you—will be fine." Eoghan called for a nurse and gave her a list of people she should find.

Another contraction rippled pain across her body.

The Torrpeki held her hand, letting her crush his knuckles. "I am right here."

She was carefully helped into the bed, already stripped of linens with stacks of towels and bowls of water sitting on the table beside it. Bless Eoghan for having some modicum of foresight.

"Who should I be getting to deliver the babe?"

Lyerlly took a sharp breath of both pain and fear; she had not thought about this—Sola and Lunos, how had she forgotten a midwife? A part of her knew; in Edreba, *she* delivered most of the human children. But she had forgotten she could not deliver her own child.

Seeing her panic, Eoghan covered her hand in his massive ones. "Do you trust me?"

"Of course," she whispered.

"Will you give me the honor then?"

She barely managed to nod.

««« »»»

The battle of Jims had been more destructive than the one of Vercase. Ash and scorch marks denoted the use of fire—successfully or unsuccessfully, Jared could not tell. Gaping holes in the walls showed where catapults had done damage, and divots in the city's wooden gate bore the signs of a battering ram. But for all that, life went on.

He had been told that Jims was a city of battle. This little town, sitting by its lonesome in a field of grass had seen more attacks than anywhere else. Why? No one could say. But something about the place made it valuable.

Walking through the castle, he was pleased to find the original inhabitants were thankful for their presence. Though Jims's citizens had not risen to the occasion like those of Vercase, they still made their thanks known— often in small ways such as a smile or a small morsel of food that could be spared. Even the soldiers of the city had been quick to change their allegiances.

And while the Lazado had attacked and conquered the city, there was no animosity. Women did not need to fear for themselves or their daughters. Houses were not set to the torch in abandon. The Lazado were simply here... simply trying to complete a goal that did not require the citizens of Jims to anguish or perish.

He and Bernot didn't talk as they walked the corridor. Jared could not speak for the Lazado's leader, but he was taking stock—this would likely be as far as they made it before winter decided to truly arrive. While the city was too small to house all their men like Vercase or Grevasia, it left them in good standing coming the spring to set into motion once more.

Soon, they came to a room that Jared took would serve as Bernot's office the command center. Inside was Bernot's trusty map and a stack of reports… and nothing else, not even a chair.

When there is little to give, take as little as possible, Jared realized.

Bernot picked up the papers and shuffled through them quickly before looking at the map. On the table, the two armies looked so close together that they should be on top of each other. Thank Sola and Lunos that was not reality; he wasn't sure if he was ready for that… if he would ever be ready for that.

"They let us take Jims," Jared opened.

"I am aware. They," Bernot referred to Kolt's army, "are close enough to have done something. But did not. Why?"

"Probably because where they are is advantageous to them," Jared premised. "Though, I'm not sure what advantage they have sitting on the river plains. Or this is meant to be a trap."

"I do not think it is a trap—unless they hope the winter snows will force us to remain here until spring when they can muster larger numbers. And they hope we will run out of supplies. But truth be told, being on the river plains would be better for us, too; the space would let the dragons fly."

"Trebuchets," Jared muttered, having a sudden realization. "I'll bet they have trebuchets to take down the dragons mid-flight."

Bernot rubbed the stubble on his chin in contemplation. "An interesting thought. We will have to do some reconnaissance."

There was a knock at the door.

"Enter," Bernot called.

A woman stuck her head in the door. "Your wife has gone into labor," she said casually before disappearing.

As soon as the words sank in, Bernot barreled through the door and down the halls. Not knowing what else to do, Jared followed, struggling to keep up with the breakneck pace.

In the hospital, they found Keegan, Aron, Icella, and Mahogen sitting outside a room. From within came screaming—the kind that set his teeth on edge. He'd heard this kind of pain before—when his mother had delivered Carter and Nico. Fear was already rising in his stomach, remnants of a child's misunderstanding bubbling to the surface.

Bernot was ready to barge into the room, to do what… who knew, but Mahogen stopped him. No words were said, but some kind of understanding passed between them.

Bernot took the chair offered to him by Icella, his face white. And waited.

«««« »»»»

There was darkness—which was not surprising given it was night. What concerned Braxton was the world did not exist… but that could not be true. No, the world seemed to have shrunk beyond measure, confining him to a space so tight that movement was near impossible. He could move and kick, but never enough to break free. A boundary—not soft, or hard, or harsh—was tightly wrapped around him. He thought nothing of it until it contracted, mashing his bones together painfully.

There was no sound reason for this new reality. Except if it was a prophetic vision. Which, with the remaining slajor manacle, meant he was seeing something that was currently happening.

As the pressure released, he tried to make sense of his surroundings but seeing there was not much to it, or light to see by, he was forced to wait, exist, and hope. Every so often, the world constricted momentarily, but it did not bother him, and no sense of panic increased his heart rate. A little voice in the back of his mind told him he should be panicking, but he could not muster the fear. Somehow, this semblance of existence was normal.

Existing was… not relaxing, but something close, and after a time he realized he was upside-down.

Then, his head began to feel a tight pressure, one that did not dissipate. It started in his ears and traveled through his skull, enough that he worried his bones might shatter. He wanted to scream, but no sound came. And even if he had managed to make a noise, he knew it would be drowned by this new reality. The pressure on his head continued to increase and it was not long before his bones started to shift. All so he could fit through a small space. A chill glanced across the top of his head and after another contraction of the world, he was forced into another new reality, this one cold and bright.

Braxton took a moment before sucking in a breath. As he released it, along with it came a harsh cry. It had never felt so good to just… wail.

He might have taken in the world, save the mucus covering his eyes. Something warm was wrapped around him, and the pressure of hands along his body was comforting… reminiscent of the place he had just left. The filth on his face was wiped away and through weary eyes he saw for the first time.

He was in a small room, with people who were, at first, nothing but shapes. Slowly, as his eyes began to clear, and he neared the people, he was able to focus on them. One was a woman, her brown hair hanging in sweaty, limp strands. She looked beyond exhausted, yet a pure kind of joy radiated from her. Her arms reached out for him. His eyes flicked to the other person, a... he knew what he was looking at, yet could not put it into words. He, Braxton, knew what to call this thing, but the eyes he was seeing through had never encountered this and had no word for what they saw. The person was massive, as big as a stone, yet as gentle as the wind's kiss.

Braxton was handed to the woman and cradled. His eyes closed softly, and he was content.

«««« »»»»

Bernot was a mess. He had no capacity to sit still and if he wasn't wringing his hands, he was bouncing his leg or pacing—not that Keegan blamed him for being fidgety. Word of Lyerlly going into labor had spread like wildfire and it seemed everyone was gathered in the hospital. Waiting.

There weren't enough seats for them all, so some leaned against the walls. Smarter people had elected to return to the doldrums of daily life, promising to return when the baby was born. It was probably best; Keegan could only imagine how overwhelmed Lyerlly might feel to have the doors open on a crowd of people—even if they were well-wishers.

From what they'd been told, Eoghan was acting as midwife. With no prior experience to draw from, she couldn't ascertain if he was doing well or not, but by the unperturbed expressions of the nurses who scampered to and from the room, all was well.

Morning—when all this had begun—had long since passed, and even the sun had faded. Someone brought them food, though Bernot had hardly taken a bite before turning it away, his face a pale green. Honestly, it was hard to tell who was in more pain, him or Lyerlly.

Lyerlly's screams hadn't been hindered by the stone walls and wooden door, setting them all on edge in anticipation of the next one. Even Mahogen's normally cool demeanor was starting to chip away.

Keegan spent a long time on the edge of her seat before realizing something; the world had become deathly silent. Fear began to percolate in the shadows lining the walls and she didn't want to say anything, but others were starting to notice as well.

Before any of them were allowed to let their minds wander too far down dark and desolate roads, the door was yanked open.

Bernot was instantly on his feet.

"Come on in… father," Eoghan said with a wide smile.

Relief crossed Bernot's face, and he anxiously looked between all of them who had gathered.

"Go on," Mahogen coaxed him gently.

On tiptoe, Bernot headed toward the door, pausing in the shelter of the frame, gulping before embracing parenthood.

Keegan went to the doorway where Eoghan held up a hand. This first moment was precious, not to be taken away.

Lyerlly sat propped against several pillows, her forehead slick with sweat, hair plastered against her face and neck. A bundle of blankets was nestled in her arms. Weariness wore her features down, but joy welled in her eyes.

As Bernot reached her side, she looked up at him and smiled. "Meet Adjran."

A laugh spilled from Bernot's mouth as a tear fell from his eyes. He bent and kissed Lyerlly's head. "My girls."

Chapter 26

The last five days had been a whirl of emotions—and sleep deprivation. But Bernot would not trade a single moment of it. Adjran was a light that could bring him nothing but joy.

Bernot kissed his daughter's forehead before gently handing her back to Lyerlly. He hated to go, but it was his duty as a leader. He lingered as he kissed his wife. As he pulled away, she gave him a smile that said he would be in her arms again shortly.

He carefully closed the door to their rooms to avoid waking Adjran. The child was determined to never miss a thing while in sleep's grasp—she truly was his daughter.

Heading to his office, dread filled his heart. A messenger had arrived at Jims this morning with the request that he and the other leaders meet with one of Kolt's Commanders. In his office, he found Atlia ready for battle, clad head to toe in gleaming scaled armor. Her caution might save her life if things went badly.

Even Okleiy had the sense to wear a cuirass and had a helm tucked under his arm. The Alvor had proven time and time again that all but a select number of humans posed any threat to him; if even he was being cautious, Bernot would need to tread lightly. Eoghan, however, believed his skin was all he needed to protect himself—and it was likely true given just how durable Torrpeki hides were.

"Give me a moment to get some armor on and we can go," Bernot said. Thankfully, he faced no rebuke for being tardy; they understood how hard it was for a new parent to leave his child, even for a few minutes.

He elected to take only a cuirass, pauldrons, and vambraces. His choices showed caution in that his most exposed and vital parts were covered, but also that he was willing to talk. His choices were a double-edged sword though, one that could easily be his death.

Together he and the other leaders walked down the halls, the clacking of their armor ruining the silence and creating an aura of malice. Outside the castle, three horses waited for them.

Eoghan led them through the city, walking since no horse could bear his weight. At the gate they found Ezadeen waiting for them, her sharp teeth glaring against her light green scales. The horses eyed her nervously, shying away anytime she moved.

Huffing at the skittishness of the horses, Ezadeen led the way across the sparsely laid trees that almost immediately gave way to the lush grass of the river plains.

On the horizon, Bernot could see a figure riding toward them. It soon separated into two, then three, then four. He breathed a sigh of relief when there was not an entire army at the Commander's heels.

Their groups converged slowly, almost painfully so. He was surprised to spot Braxton. The man riding at the lead, whom he assumed to be Branshaw, showed no fear at the sight of Ezadeen; the two unknown men however did horrendous jobs of hiding their dread.

When their groups were within a hundred feet of each other, they stopped.

"Weapons on the saddle and we meet in the middle," Branshaw called. His tone conveyed a sense of ease.

You will need more than that to stop me setting you ablaze, Ezadeen said, gnashing her teeth audibly.

Branshaw calmly dismounted, sword hanging lazily from his saddle horn. "Doubtful, as you are a life dragon—plants to be specific, I believe."

Ezadeen roared and the grass beneath Branshaw's feet began to twist around his ankles. The commander stood calmly and let the dragon rage.

"Ezadeen," Atlia said, "this is to be a peaceful meeting."

The dragon huffed, her eyes closing to slits, but the grass unwound itself—though a few blades remained snagged around Branshaw's feet as a reminder of the threat she could be.

Hanging his sword over the saddle, Bernot slowly came to the halfway point. "I assume you are here to ask for our surrender."

"No, I simply ask you to turn around," Branshaw said. "Leave this fight for another day, another generation."

"Is this for your benefit or ours?"

"Both."

"I cannot," Bernot said after letting a heavy silence linger. "I cannot let the world suffer under a fate worse than Caius. I am sorry it must be this way."

"Then so be it. I too am sorry for what is to come," Branshaw said, genuine regret in his eyes. Walking back to his horse, he was quick to pull himself into the saddle.

As Branshaw and his men rode away, Bernot felt a voice on the outskirts of his mind pleading to be heard.

I hear you, he said.

The voice was faint, but the message was clear. *Meet me here at the height of the night.*

《《《《 》》》》

"Do you see anyone?" Braxton asked. Though he only bore a single slajor manacle, telepathic communication was still a challenge on the best of days. And for now, it was outside of his abilities. He was just thankful Bernot had been able to hear his plea earlier.

Yes, Myrish answered, drifting down from their high perch in the sky.

Braxton shivered against the wind that slapped his face. Winter, and not just the mockery that had been toying with them would be here soon. Yet not soon enough, for a fight was still brewing and not even the threat of snow could stop it.

Myrish landed with the grace of a cat, his wings pulling in against his sides with hardly a whisper. With no trees, Braxton could see the bubbles of lights marking Jims and where Kolt's army rested behind him. Soon, one of them would be extinguished. Though, as Braxton thought on it, he realized that was not true. Some of the lights making up the whole would sputter out, but those spheres of lights would always remain, ready to strike again when they had regained their brightness.

Myrish alerted him that a rider was approaching. He heard the clinking of metal on metal and the shuffle of hooves on the ground well before he could even see the shadow of the rider.

Bernot, he tested, hoping the slajor manacles would stop being so finicky. If this was not Bernot, then it was likely his death. But he had to take the risk.

Yes, the rider responded.

He breathed a sigh of relief and slid from Myrish's back, his sword left where it was no threat.

The horse came closer, enough so they could see more than just the shape of each other before Bernot dismounted. The Lazado leader kept his sword at hand, and Braxton could not blame him. He only hoped he did not plan to make use of it.

"I assume you have some important information for me," Bernot said, likely hoping for a rendezvous similar to their one near Grenadone.

"I… I am not sure," he admitted, pulling the letter from his pocket. "But Alyck wanted me to get this to you."

Bernot took the envelope warily, acting as if the paper might bite him. "You did not open it."

He climbed back onto Myrish. "It was not for me."

A stark silence settled between them as Bernot waited for something more and Braxton waited for him to dare to ask.

"How many men do you have?"

"I have not been given exact numbers, but it is likely we are equally matched." Before urging the griffin back to the star-studded sky, Braxton added, "Be wary of Branshaw. He is more dangerous than you think."

«««« »»»»

Quin trailed behind Jared dutifully as he walked back to the rooms he shared with his brothers. There had been a lustful gleam in her gray eyes all night and he prayed to Sola and Lunos one of his brothers would be in the room. He was positive it'd be the only thing stopping Quin from having her way with him.

A small part of him wanted to laugh; it was not so long ago he would've been happy to endure her machinations. But now, to continue pretending… Jared didn't think he could do it.

Nearing the room, all was quiet in the hallway. Which wasn't unusual if Lucas or Carter were alone… and he prayed was the case.

But he knew he would open the door and find no one inside. He didn't want to be right, but if he didn't go in,

Quin would. And then she might know something was afoot. That he had changed.

Bracing himself, he opened the door like it was going to explode and was greeted by darkness and quiet.

Quin wasted no time, pulling him into the murk by the collar of his shirt. As soon as he'd cleared the doorframe, she closed the door and did the lock. They'd learned being interrupted ruined everything. And the person doing the interrupting was never happy to do so.

Jared heard the clank of a metal object hitting the stone floor—likely Quin's belt buckle. Then her hands were on his body, roaming as her lips pressed hungrily against his.

He told himself he could do this—why would it be difficult? He'd done it before. But… it had been increasingly difficult to want to do it… with Quinn… with any woman—and not just within the past few days; the disinclination had been hovering for months now that he recognized it for what it was. It had always been there; it was just that now he was listening to it.

He reached for Quin's shoulders to push her away, and his palms met skin. And though he wanted to stop, he found he couldn't. What could he tell her that would be believable? What would Quin say? She was only going to accept excuses for so long. What choice did he have?

While indecision tumbled through his mind, Quin successfully undid the lacing of his trousers. She wasn't bothered that baring all didn't rouse him and was already working to coax him forward. If she knew what tortuous work this would turn out to be, she might be inclined to save herself the effort.

A small part of him was ignited by her touch and he did begin to rise to the occasion, but that spark wasn't enough to fully do the trick. Only one thing would satisfy him now. And it was the one thing he couldn't have.

Quin's efforts began to slow as she noticed something wasn't right, that he wasn't... excited. "Is everything all right?" she asked between the kisses she planted on his neck.

How to answer, Jared could not figure out. Being honest would be better in the long run. But lying might help him save face for at least a while. It might hold off the derision and ridicule he knew to expect if anyone found out.

Quin stopped completely and pulled away. "Jared?"

When he continued with his silence, he could sense her darkest fears beginning to form.

"Is there... someone else? Have you been sugoren someone else?"

"No, of course not," he said quickly, too quickly.

Quin gulped. "Liar! You.... noxþ royiken liar! Tell me who it is. Oh, is it one of those Mermaid hynaks?" Her hand lashed out, finding his cheek.

"No, it's not," he insisted, his face prickling. Quickly he made his way to the table and lit a candle. Its light wasn't much but it was better than battling whatever truths were about to be told in darkness.

Quin stood in the center of the room, face red with fury. She was naked, as expected, beautiful as ever. But only that, beautiful. The sight of her elicited nothing further.

"Who is it? Who have you been sugoren?" she screeched again.

Jared slammed his hand on the table. "There isn't anyone else!" He sank into a chair, feigning tiredness. "I'm just... exhausted." A subtle glance at Quin proved the lie had been believed.

And he believed she believed him right up until she stormed over and took his chin in her hands, forcing him to look her in the eyes. "Have you been sleeping with someone else?"

"No."

Quin's eyebrows furrowed. She didn't entirely believe him. "Is there another woman… you maybe… admire?"

"No."

He wasn't sure how she saw the truth, but he could tell.

Her eyes widened and she slipped back, lips trembling. "Who is he? The man you…" The fact she couldn't finish the sentence proved how bad *it* was.

Jared couldn't bring himself to answer. How could he? So, instead, he just stared guiltily. He wanted to lower his eyes, pretend to seek the course most men did. But doing so now would only further articulate his guilt and shame.

Slowly, Quin's hands moved to cover her body, embarrassment finally taking the reins from lust and fury.

Watching her dress was only going to make the situation worse, so Jared rose and handed her the quilt from his bed. Carefully he averted his eyes until Quin had the blanket wrapped around her body. Then he returned to the table, sagging into the chair.

Tears shining in her eyes, Quin stood wrapped in the quilt like it was the only thing tethering her to reality. "How long?" she managed to whisper.

"How long what?" he asked, laying his head on the table. He was tired. Tired of pretending and lying. Tired of being afraid. Just… tired.

Silver threads dripped from Quin's eyes. "How long have you known you like men?"

"Barely a turn of the moon," he managed to whisper. Somehow, finally saying it, admitting it, made it all the more concrete.

"I'm sorry. I'm so sorry."

His head shot up, puzzled by the turn of events. Why the nastor was *she* apologizing?

"I should've seen the signs sooner." Quin gave a hiccupped laugh as tears slid down her cheeks in a torrent. "Sad thing is, I was originally using you to get to Kade. And then I fell for my own dirty trick. I'm sorry to have used you. And I'm… just… sorry."

"You don't care that I like…" Jared gulped. He'd been prepared for so much worse. To have this reprieve was a feeling that couldn't be explained.

Quin shook her head, wiping her eyes. "I grew up in Edreba. The humans there are much more open to that kind of love. And my brother… he's very happy with his partner."

"I'm sorry, I didn't want to hurt you. I—"

"It's not your fault. I did this to myself."

For using him, then falling for him, yes, she had done this to herself. But she genuinely had come to care for him, and it was hard to fault her for that, to blame her for being upset. And he did care for her in turn—just not in the same way she did.

Carefully, Jared wrapped his arms around her. "I'm sure if you talk to Kade…"

"No, he's fallen for Icella. Maybe at first… he could've been swayed to love me, but not now." She didn't add that Kade was no longer who her heart sought.

They stayed together in their embrace for a long time, both needing it.

Finally, with another hiccup, Quin pulled away. "I'm sorry… for—"

"I'm not," Jared cut in, brushing a fresh tear from her cheek. "I did enjoy my time with you. I learned a lot. And I do care for you."

"Just not in the same way I care for you."

He nodded. "And you—"

"Won't tell anyone else. It's not my place. And love is love, whatever the form."

Jared gave a grimace of a smile. It wasn't what he'd been about to ask. But it did mean a lot to him.

An awkward silence developed and grew until finally Quin gathered her clothes.

With a light cough to clear his throat, Jared turned—even if he'd seen it all before, it was different now.

Feeling a hand on his shoulder he turned to find Quin still wrapped in the quilt. Standing on her toes, she gave him a lingering kiss. "I'm sorry," she said, and left.

Chapter 27

The afternoon air was cold, and Keegan was glad for her many layers. Unlike most days, they wouldn't be quickly shed as she sweated through them in training. She stood on the outskirts of camp next to Thoren, watching the world. Without warning, the lightning dragon, touched his nose to her shoulder. The static that coursed through her was no longer painful and she quickly shot it from her fingertips, lifting the smell of singed grass and ozone into the air.

The few sentries that bothered to patrol near the dragons passed by tensely, flinching at the booming noise of electricity meeting earth. Keegan couldn't blame them for jumping each time she released a lightning bolt.

Used to the sentries' presence, Keegan hardly noticed them until one began rubbing at his shoulder. She couldn't say what grabbed her attention, just that it felt off. Before she could voice concern, the man tumbled from his horse's back.

She didn't hesitate to rush toward the man, Thoren lumbering after her. The fallen guard's partner was completely unaware of the predicament until the dragon's thundering footsteps spooked his horse.

Keegan reached the downed man first. Aside from a growing knot on his head, there was nothing obviously wrong. But just because an ailment couldn't be seen didn't mean it didn't exist. Carefully, she checked for a pulse and found none. Well, that certainly explained the obvious about the man's condition.

Knowing that getting the man's heart beating and lungs pumping again was vital, Keegan knew what she needed to do. Not wanting to waste time asking Thoren for help, she pulled static from the air, feeling the energy crackling and sizzling between her fingers. She placed her fingertips over the man's left pectoral and released the energy. When she felt for a pulse again, she was dismayed to still find none.

She cursed, hating that she lost so much energy when she pulled rather than conducted electricity. "Thoren, I need some help," she said. "And tone it down, I don't need to be thrown a hundred feet back."

The yellow dragon gently touched the hand she held toward him, and she quickly released the energy into the man's body before checking again for a pulse. Still nothing. She gave the man another two shocks before she got a heartbeat. Though the pulse was weak, at least there was one. And that was what mattered at the moment.

One problem down, she thought to herself.

Now that she had a pulse, Keegan needed to figure out what had caused all of this in the first place. As she thought, she carefully worked his lungs, not wanting to undo what little progress had been made. Given the weather was chilly, the cause was unlikely to be heat exhaustion. The man seemed warm enough, so it wasn't hypothermia either—not that hypothermia caused such a sudden reaction.

The man gave a shuddering breath, and she instinctively flooded more magic into his body, truly focusing on heart and lungs. As his breathing evened to what could be considered normal, Keegan relaxed enough to notice something strange. As she monitored his heart, she became aware of a restriction. She focused on it and found the reason for the heart attack and subsequent cardiac arrest; his coronary artery was almost completely blocked.

Slowly, she began chipping the plaque away. When the restriction was widened enough for the man to be in little danger going forward, she pulled away and turned to his companion. "You might want to get him to the hospital."

Either in shock or confused, the man just nodded, picked his friend up, slung him over his horse, and began riding for the castle as fast as his unconscious companion's condition would allow.

Taking a deep breath, Keegan dropped onto the cold grass. The chill of the ground was calming, and she was able to push all thoughts out of her head. The clouds above were a dusky gray blue, fat and voluminous.

Thoren lay down beside her, so she was acutely aware of his gray eyes boring into her. *Care to explain what that was all about?*

"Dude had a heart attack and went into cardiac arrest," she started. "Needed electricity to get his heart going again and then I cleared the obstruction. He should be fine; he wasn't without oxygen and blood for very long. CPR can do some wonders. Not that it was actual CPR…"

What is CPR?

She opened her mouth to respond, then stopped. "I actually don't know what the acronym stands for. I just know it's what you do when hearts and lungs stop working."

You did a good thing today. Those men will not forget it… nor will I.

《《《 》》》

After experiencing two battles—proper battles, not skirmishes against poorly armed peasants or a few well-armed mercenaries—Kade was glad to hear they were marching toward a third; at least he would've been glad if he was seeking Lunos. The news had been spread through camp that morning and everyone was packing, some more slowly than others in a desperate bid to delay the inevitable. Most of the men outside the walls had been ready in what seemed minutes, likely from having few things to pack. Those inside the castle were taking a little longer, loathe to be giving up their luxuries.

They wouldn't be moving far and Kade was still unsure what the point of it all was. Why did it matter if they were a few miles closer to Agrielha? As much as he was inclined to grumble, his job was to do as told and keep his sister breathing. One was significantly easier than the other.

Entering the courtyard, he found Bernot helping Lyerlly into a wagon, Adjran nestled in her arms. By the looks of it, the baby was asleep. A good thing too as Kade had discovered he had very little tolerance for when the beastly thing decided to scream. Keegan had once compared Adjran's angry wailing to that of a banshee; he had no idea what a banshee was, but it seemed to fit the babe nicely.

Looking around, he spotted the Sieme brothers, Carter and Lucas, and Reven.

As Bernot walked by, Kade asked, "Where's Keegan?"

"Training with Atlia."

"She should be getting ready to go."

"Keegan is not leaving for a few more days."

"Why?"

"We wanted to give her as much time as possible to train."

"And what about Jared and Aron?"

"Their talents are also better put to use by staying here a bit longer. As are mine."

"You mean Jared is your little protégé and Aron keeps Keegan calm and in line. What am I to you, chopped liver?" he seethed. "And if you're staying, why are you sending your wife ahead?" Whispering, he added, "Is being a father really that horrible?"

He knew he shouldn't have made the last comment as soon as it was out of his mouth. Bernot flushed a dark shade of red and for a moment Kade wondered if he might actually be sent to the whipping post.

"No, you are a warrior," Icella said, butting into the conversation.

Bernot huffed and Kade was inwardly glad the Mermaid was there to temper the Lazado leader.

"Your sister's strengths lie elsewhere," Icella continued.

"And you are slightly more adept at keeping yourself out of trouble," Bernot said, his angry color beginning to fade. "I need you to rally the men. And my wife is going because she insists upon it. She would rather have the hospital ready for what is coming than be comfortable here. And I cannot fault her sentiments."

"Why do you want me to rally the men?"

"When they look at Keegan, they see a woman. A mystery they cannot solve and something to be wary of. They see a symbol they cannot hope to match. With Jared, they see themselves. A commoner, but nothing more. And with Aron, they see what we are fighting against and resent him just for his name. But you, they see a solider, a warrior, someone who has spat in the face of the beast—and lived to tell the tale. In you, they see who they want to be."

Kade tipped his head back and laughed loudly. "They cursed my name. For years!"

"True, but now they know why. You managed to defy the king," Icella said. "How many can say they have bested Caius's best men once, let alone multiple times? How many can say they survived the Vosjnik with nothing more than scars?"

Playing at his ego was a dangerous game, but one that was working in their favor—this time.

The call to move out drifted over his head and men and horses were urged forward.

"See you in a few days," he said to Icella and Bernot, swinging up into Aros's saddle.

"You are not getting rid of me that easily," Icella chided. With a wink, she said, "Who would keep you out of the trouble that always manages to find you?"

«««« »»»»

Picking up the letter he had hastily tossed onto the floor of his office in anger, Bernot read it for the umpteenth time since his midnight meeting with Braxton, cursing to himself all the while.

Dear Bernot Bællar,

What I am about to ask you to do will not be easy, but completely *necessary. You must relinquish Keegan Digore. You must let her face her death at the hands of Kolt.*

This is the only way she will live. The only way the world will live. To save her you must let her go.

But like any smart leader, you will think this is a ploy to convince you to give up your only key to winning. So, I will say this, it is either sacrifice Keegan now, or sacrifice your daughter, Adjran, later. She will grow up to be strong and beautiful if you let her.

You are about to make the hardest choice of your life Bær. Please make the right one.

Alyck Alagard
October 6th

P.S. You made the right decision in choosing Jared as your successor.

Bernot despised what he was about to do but it was the only choice if they wanted to win… if he wanted his daughter to live. And for her, he would do anything. He brushed aside the thought of anything ever happening to Adjran; to go down that path would ensure madness.

He called upon the other leaders telepathically and it wasn't long before they were all gather before him. Atlia already had Tahrin and her speaker on the other side of the Looking Glass.

"What is so important?" Eoghan asked, true concern in his voice.

Bernot tossed Alyck's letter on the desk and let them read.

"You have to be joking." Okleiy laughed, glancing nervously at the other leaders. "This is a ploy! You have never been stupid, Bernot. Now is not the time to start."

"Would anyone like to elucidate me?" the man speaking for Tahrin asked.

Atlia read the letter aloud, her voice clear and void of emotion. When she was done there was a loud growl from Tahrin that signified her aggravation.

"What makes you believe Alyck?" Eoghan questioned, as always, the voice of mediation.

"Bær," he answered, sucking on his cheek. "My mother used to call me that."

"And how many people know that?" Okleiy huffed.

"Just my mother. Not even my father knew she called me that."

A silence fell over them.

"And from the date…" Bernot added, "it was well before Adjran was born… before Lyerlly and I even discussed names. If this letter is not Alyck's, then whose? I see no other likely answer."

There were some mumblings about spies and deserters, but they were halfhearted at best. No spy could have been privy to such personal facts and conversations. The truth was staring them in the face, and it could not be chalked up to coincidence. Not since they came from the Blind Prophet.

"We know what we have to do then," Tahrin's speaker said. "It is not comfortable, but if it is the only way…"

"How do we know Alyck is telling the truth?" Okleiy demanded.

"How do we know he is not?" Atlia returned. "What reason does he have to lie? It gains him nothing but countless more decades, potentially centuries under Kolt's thumb if he has an elongated life like his father."

"Those in favor," Eoghan said quietly.

"Aye," Tahrin's man answered.

"Aye," Atlia said angrily.

"Aye," Bernot said, refusing to look anyone in the eye.

"Aye," Eoghan muttered.

"Nay," Okleiy said. "And you cannot call a vote without the Buluo."

"They have not chosen a leader and do not aid us as a nation yet," Atlia said. "They forfeit any right to an opinion in the matter until they elect a Henshren."

"This is the wrong choice," the Alvor insisted.

"If Keegan must endure pain so others may endure life, so be it," Atlia said. "It is better than death for us all."

Bernot could feel a headache forming. Were they really so willing to sacrifice Keegan so that they might see a new dawn? It seemed absurd, yet, here they were, agreeing to do just that.

"Her brothers cannot know," Tahrin's translator said.

"I agree," Bernot sighed. "Those boys would sooner kill us than let us hand her over."

There were nods and murmurs of agreement around the room.

"How do you propose we go about this?" Okleiy asked, angrily. "If we just send her off to Kolt, no man will fight for you anymore."

Silence enveloped them once again.

"We let her fail," Eoghan finally said. "She expects to go into battle with an army at her back. If we let her go alone, someone will do the deed for us."

"I cannot imagine anyone *not* giving their life to protect her," Atlia commented. "My own niece included. She has a way of endearing many toward herself, regardless of how infuriating she is."

"We order them not to," Tahrin's speaker said.

Bernot stood and poked his head out the door. "Call in all of Keegan's guards," he ordered the man standing outside.

Waiting for the men and women who were about to betray their charge was painful. Guilt sat heavily on his shoulders and Bernot loathed himself. But he kept reminding himself this was for Adjran… for the world. Alyck had promised this was how Keegan survived, too. How though, he had no clue.

Slowly the guards filed in, coming from various parts of the castle. Icella and Elhyas would have to be filled in later as they had left with Kade and two of the Sieme brothers.

"You all must swear to follow the orders I am about to give without question and without hesitation," Bernot stated.

The guards were slow to give their word, clearly aware they were not going to like what was about to happen.

"In the battle to come, you are not to aid Keegan aside from protecting her from imminent death. Should she be captured, you are to let it happen. You are to tell no one and never talk of this again."

Shock and hatred flooded the guards' features, but they had already given their word and were bound by it.

"You can't ask us to do that!" Zavier roared.

"Quiet," Ezekhial said. "There's a reason behind this heinous deed."

"I won't do it," Zavier argued.

Quin said, "We gave our word."

There was a moment of silence, then Zavier stormed from the room, "Lunos will not greet you kindly."

A shiver raced down Bernot's back, as if the words were prophetic.

Chapter 28

Keegan hated knowing Kolt's army was so near, hated being so close to the men she'd soon have to kill. But it was them or her. That's what she told herself in the hopes of convincing herself to cast someone down. Ultimately, she knew she'd never be able to do it. But a small part of her feared she'd find the strength.

She remembered some of Bernot's projected battles and how there she hadn't thought about what she was doing. If she could incapacitate someone without killing them, she did. But if not, then she did what she needed. And there was no time to think which option was better in the moment.

She'd been back in the main portion of camp for two days and nothing had happened. It was worse than being left behind in Jims. At least there she could pretend the largest clash they'd yet to see wasn't coming. At least there she could distract herself with books and exploring.

The anticipation of… anything, was like a burden upon everyone's shoulders. Fights broke out so often between the soldiers it was a wonder they hadn't started a war with themselves. No race was exempt from the anxiety and the need to keep their hands busy, even in a destructive manner.

Keegan jerked back to reality as she was knocked to the ground, the Queen Killer flying from her hand. It sat in a tuft of grass, contrasting with it exactly the way blood did.

"Pay attention," Atlia snapped, wiping a strand of hair from her forehead. "This is life or death!" The Merqueen pulled water from the air and a new battle began.

Feeling a lack of energy, Keegan fought from her position on the ground, which angered Atlia, making her attack harder. They ended in a stalemate, Atlia drenched in sweat—a rare sight.

Exasperated, the Merqueen stormed away, leaving Keegan alone with her thoughts. Well, not truly alone, Quin stood on the sidelines. She should've gotten up, gone to do some other form of training, but she had no desire to—couldn't muster the will. Staring at the sky blankly, she watched heavy clouds float overhead. She tried to see shapes in the billows, like she had as a child, but they were all morbid, reminding her of what lay ahead.

"Now isn't the time to give up," Elhyas said, standing over her. "The battle hasn't begun and Sola and Lunos have yet to cast their judgement."

Though he was talking to her, she sensed Elhyas was fortifying himself too. Something, whatever it was, was affecting the rest of her guards as well. Every one of them seemed... guilt-ridden. They laughed at the weirdest things and were jumpier than mice.

"What does it matter?" she snapped. "Sooner or later, it'll come. And I'll have to kill."

Elhyas sighed and squatted next to her. "Yes, men will die. So is the way of the world."

"But what if there was another way?"

"There isn't. No amount of ether bombs or manipulation will save everyone on a battlefield. Everyone greets Lunos at the time he decides."

She had no argument because he was right. They all died at some point—and no one had control over the how and when... except maybe in a few extreme cases.

The cold found its way into her bones, and she rose, walking away quietly, a biting wind nipping at her heels. The Arciolan winter had been mild, so far, but even she knew it was about to change any day. The signs were blatant in the smell of the air and the timbre of the wind.

By the time she reached the tent she shared with Aron, the short winter day had faded to dusk. Inside, a small fire crackled in the stove, staving off the chill, though fingers of cold wormed their way in where they could. Aron sat in a chair, a mug of steaming coffee in his hands.

Noticing her, he set the mug on the ground and came to greet her, wrapping his arms around her. For a while they just stood there.

As Aron leeched the cold from her body, her emotions began to thaw and eat at her. She did the only thing she knew to make them disperse, even if it would only be fleeting. Her fingers made quick work of Aron's belt buckle.

He was surprised but didn't complain and he brought his lips to hers.

The world slipped away, all her worries fled, and the future ceased to exist. Keegan was happy in that moment, happy as Aron's warm hands traced along her body, bringing back heat and hope the world had sucked away.

His hands pushed her shirt above her head, and she could feel the chill of the night against her skin, trying to dig its nails in and drag her away. But Aron was there, his hands on her hips, claiming her as his. He was stronger than darkness.

Aron pulled his own shirt off and backed toward the bed. She followed, desperate to remain connected—desperate to never be parted.

Aron kissed down her stomach, stopping in the crook of her hip as he worked her pants down her legs. She didn't have to tell him what she wanted, and he was more than happy to oblige. As he sank into her, the floodgates broke, and nothing would be held back. But that wouldn't stop her from trying to fix a dam with Band-Aids and duct tape—lots of duct tape.

She pulled Aron close, kissing his lips, then his neck. From the way his breath caught, this was enough for him. But not for her. Nothing was enough to stay the fear.

Tears spilled across her cheeks, and she couldn't hold back a sob that Aron's lips muffled. How she wished he could suck away the pain.

Aron pulled away, acutely aware all was not right, and Keegan covered her face with her hands. She didn't want to see his worry or disappointment. She couldn't bear it.

Lying beside her, Aron wrapped her in his arms and draped soothing words over her. He pulled the blanket high, cocooning her in his fortitude. This was what she needed; someone to be there, not debate if her fears were founded. She didn't need to say what was wrong. He always knew and always would thanks to their empathy link.

After a time, the tears subsided, and she lay in his warmth, tiredness offering another form of escape.

"Nothing is going to happen to you," Aron muttered, brushing away the tears gently with his thumb.

"Promise?" Keegan croaked.

Aron kissed her forehead. "I promise." Then he made a sloppy crossing motion above his heart.

Keegan couldn't help but give a halfhearted laugh.

Gently, Aron kissed her again, locking his promise in place.

A sharp cry caught Keegan's attention, and she turned her head to listen better, waiting patiently for the stillness of the night to be broken again.

Yelling, and lots of it drifted on the wind. Panic imbued the sound.

"What's going on?" she asked, pushing herself upright, fear jolting through her. *Please don't let it be happening now*, was all she could think.

Aron knew the question was rhetorical and they silently dressed before stepping into the night to investigate.

He had promised she would survive, and he held her hand with a ferocious tenderness and tightness, letting her know only his death would make him break that pledge.

«««« »»»»

The night was cold, and Braxton's fur-lined cloak hardly kept the icy tendrils that buffeted against him at bay. Until now, it had seemed winter would be mild, but there was no doubt now that snow would soon arrive and make warfare harder than it already was.

Myrish seemed unaffected by the cold, and Braxton guessed his feathers acted as an unfailing shield. What he would not give to have the same. His cheeks stung from the cold and his nose was running worse than a waterfall.

A blast of frozen air hit Braxton's face, making his teeth chatter with enough force to begin a small ache at the back of his head. He could not believe anyone would willingly be up to no good in these conditions.

"Turn back," he called above the wind.

As Myrish floated and glided toward the bulb of light demarking their camp, Braxton spotted a shadow through the darkness. It crept from the light of their camp, a horse in tow. It was hard to tell what happened from there, but he could guess. No doubt the man would mount and race over no man's land. One entered that swath of land between the armies at their own peril. Yet that peril very well might lead to sanctuary.

Do you see that? Myrish asked.

"Yes."

Should we do anything?

Braxton was aware men would defect, and had, but this was the first time seeing it with his own eyes. It made everything all the more harsh and real. Many of the men below had not willingly agreed to fight for his brother.

It was his duty to bring the man back—for his punishment of death—but he would not. The man had a right to cast his stones, as did they all. He would do the same if he could. But he could not, so tonight he would take pity on a man simply seeking a better future.

Putting the defector from his mind, Braxton urged Myrish back toward camp. They flew over spiked trenches and landed on the outskirts of the forest of tents in a clearing left specially for them.

Walking through camp, it was as if the men had forgotten they would soon be facing Lunos and were drinking mugs of ale or borzan around fires. Likely to stave off boredom or maybe to bring back a false sense of warmth.

He heard a call to cheers he had never heard before. "Jingle bells," one man started. "Batman smells," another followed. "And Robin laid an egg," the third finished. The three joined together in raucous laughter.

Braxton stopped in the shadows, desperately wanting to dash forward and berate them. How could they be merry when any moment could be their last? How could they not fear what they would have to do to their fellow humans?

Let them have their moments of happiness, Myrish said, nudging him in the back to start him walking again. *They will be far and few between soon.*

Begrudgingly, Braxton left behind the out-of-place merriment. As he stepped inside his tent, an insidious feeling dropped down on him like a spider. Instantly, he was snared within a web of emotion and felt a line of cold across his throat. Then a sticky warmth seeped down his neck and chest, making his head feel light.

Braxton struggled to catch a breath and pulled at the collar of his shirt before toppling over.

«««« »»»»

As the sound of the last note of her song melted into the night, Lyerlly sighed. The child in her arms did not cry for more—and for that she was thankful. Adjran was exactly like her father; she wanted to see as much of life as she could, even if it was to her own detriment. And the detriment of her mother who was forced to stay awake with her.

Exhaustion settled over Lyerlly as well, heavy like a comforting quilt, and she knew it would not be long before she followed her daughter into the realm of dreams. It might not be for long, but she would cherish it all the same.

Carefully rising from the rocking chair, Lyerlly made her way to the bassinet at the foot of the bed. It was a simple thing, as dictated by their current circumstances, yet it was still beautiful. She was not sure when Bernot had found the time, but he had, and his own hands had crafted it.

Adjran gave a soft and sleepy coo as she nestled into the copious furs and blankets but thankfully did not wake.

Lyerlly ran a finger over her soft cheek before leaning down to kiss her forehead.

Straightening up, she could not imagine there existed another being as wonderful as her daughter. Stifling a yawn, Lyerlly turned, ready to prepare herself for sleep.

She froze, her blood turning to ice as the shadows across the tent rippled and stepped forth, forming into a man dressed head to toe in the color of night. She caught the glint of a knife in his hand cautiously concealed behind a leg and knew it was poised to deliver heartache.

"You weren't supposed to be here," the man said solemnly, as if he actually felt some form of remorse. "I came for one man."

She knew he was talking about Bernot. "You will never deliver him to the old gods," she seethed.

"I will, as I will you. For you have seen too much."

Fury boiled in her belly like a wildfire and Lyerlly reached for her magic. She lashed out, seeking to rend flesh from bone of this would-be assassin. How dare he contrive to take her and her husband away from their daughter? How dare he believe she would be so easily discarded?

Slowly the wrath of her magic abated, and she was dismayed to find it had no effect upon the man. What sorcery was this?

The man gave a harsh and scraping laugh before dissipating like mist. Two more of him emerged from the shadows on either side of her. She looked between the two figures at a loss. Her heart hammered in her chest, panic snaking up her spine.

Glancing over her shoulder at Adjran asleep in her bassinet, Lyerlly fortified herself. She had to prevail. For Bernot. For Adjran. There was no other option. No harm would come to her daughter.

Her heart caught as four more shadow men materialized. It did not matter. Her daughter would not be left motherless. Her husband would not be left a widower. They would prevail.

There was no other option.

《《《 》》》

Bernot raced through camp, feeling Lyerlly's terror increase with each step he took. He ran faster, willing his body to ignore what it said was impossible. He could not begin to imagine what monster his wife was fighting, but he would be there by her side and together they would vanquish it.

Suddenly, the emotion exuding from his Lyerlly dropped away. In the wake of the sudden silence, a pit formed in his stomach. The void left behind was painful. Their tent was just ahead, and he could see the faint seam of light spilling from beneath the canvas. In any other instance, the sight would be a welcome one—now, it only promised the potential of unspeakable pain.

With caution long since thrown into the wind, Bernot burst into the tent. All that mattered was that Lyerlly and Adjran were unhurt. All that mattered was that he could save them.

Bernot stopped dead, scanning the spacious tent as his mind struggled to accept what his eyes saw. Blood. So much blood. It covered the ground in a sick sheen, creeping forward in deadly expansion. And Lyerlly lay on the floor, the source of the pool, her blood spilling in bubbling spurts from a gash in her neck.

If he had been in his right mind, he might have noticed the blood was still flowing steadily from the wound—relaying it was recent. That it was likely that who or what had done this was still there, still a danger. But all he could think was that there was still time—he could rip Lyerlly from Lunos's clutches if he was quick.

Bernot raced forward, scooping his wife up in his arms. He fought past the bile rising in his throat at the warmth of the blood that dripped onto his hands and soaked into his clothes, so volatile it might as well burn like acid. He placed a hand over the tear in Lyerlly's skin, willing the blood flowing from the laceration to cease. Demanding it.

A spell spilled from his lips, a quick and furious and passionate plea, a demand that Lunos spare his wife, but the magic had no effect—spells could do nothing for the dead.

Anguish ripped at his heart at the realization and a cry tore from his throat as he pulled Lyerlly close, clinging to her fleeting warmth. His heart felt like it was being rendered in two and it hurt to breathe.

"I'm sorry, truly I am," a voice said. "She wasn't supposed to be here."

Bernot jerked his head up and through tear-soaked eyes saw a man dressed in black standing across from him. In his hand was a knife slick with blood—*Lyerlly's* blood.

"She wasn't supposed to die," the man said. "But she saw me. I didn't have a choice. You need to understand that. Your daughter though, I will spare her. I can promise you that."

Shock and grief kept Bernot from responding—from attacking. A hand twined through his hair, pulling his head back, and a dagger was plunged into his chest. The pain was like ice, so cold it numbed his entire body.

"Gexanlim æayi granklos," he muttered, the words clear and deliberate, before the knife was removed.

The mirage before him disappeared and the man behind him gave a curdling scream.

Bernot took no pleasure in dragging this assassin to the realm of the old gods with him, but it would have to do. It would never be enough to avenge Lyerlly's senseless murder, but it would have to do.

He clasped a hand to the wound in his chest, a feeble attempt to staunch the blood flow. He knew he should rise and seek help, but already the world was fading. His body was no longer his own to command and he fell sideways.

Outside, he could hear people and knew they would be too late to do anything besides hear his last words and to lay him to rest alongside his wife.

Chapter 29

Jared was silent as Mahogen walked him back to his tent. He wished the human would make up his mind, but his fear of reproach from his own kind kept him at bay. Mahogen could see the longing in Jared's muddy eyes; but while Jared wanted to follow his heart, he was far from ready to take the arduous path it would require.

In his own time, Mahogen reminded himself. Even he had not been quick to accept his own nature. Even he had, at times, attempted to deny what was.

Jarshua followed at Jared's heels, occasionally nipping at them playfully. The cold had no effect on the pup, in fact, he reveled in it. He was a child of winter.

When they reached Jared's tent, strangely his brothers were nowhere in sight. Mahogen was hard pressed to recall an evening when the three of them were not laughing or arguing over some childhood incident. The thought of the easy comradery between the brothers brought a faint smile into existence.

"Would you like to come in out of the cold?" Jared asked shyly, looking him in the eye for only an instant before his gaze flitted to the ground.

Mahogen wanted to think something other than sympathy and sociable consideration hid in the question but knew better. Until Jared was willing and ready to admit what he felt in his heart, nothing more could be a possibility.

"Very much," he answered, pulling his fur-lined cloak closer.

As Mahogen made to step inside, an unsettling feeling burgeoned in his chest, blooming like a briar. It stabbed into his spine and gut and heart, threatening to never release its thorny grasp.

He must have stumbled under the force of emotion for Jared reached out to steady him. "What's wrong?"

There was no reason he could think of to feel this kind of fear. And until he knew what was causing it, he could only say who was feeling this dread. "I am not sure, but Lyerlly is… it is Lyerlly."

"Let's go," Jared said, giving a low whistle to pull Jarshua off the cot he had just settled onto.

Racing through camp, Lyerlly's alarm continued to grow, spreading like an unwelcome heat across Mahogen's body that centered in his gut. It was not long before the panic spread to Bernot as well and Mahogen picked up the pace, hoping Jared would be able to keep up.

As an Alvor, he could easily outpace Jared, but he had promised to protect this human—and if Lyerlly were in danger, there was a likely chance Jared would also need defending. No, he could not abandon his charge for the sake of a friend.

As they reached Bernot and Lyerlly's tent, everything looked pristine, at ease. That all changed when he caught a whiff of iron in the air. Mahogen did not want to enter the tent for fear of what might lie inside, what he knew lay inside, but he had to. And he had to pray to Sola and Lunos the damage was not irreversible.

Compared to the gore and blood he expected to find, the tent was hardly bathed in red. But that did not diminish the significance of the carnage. He spotted Lyerlly first and instantly knew she was dead; the gash in her neck was too deep to have spared her from Lunos for more than a few seconds. His eyes drifted to Bernot beside her.

Ragged breaths came from him and Mahogen rushed to his friend, placing a hand over the gouge in his chest.

He was vaguely aware of Jared turning back into the night and calling for help. It would not matter. Lunos would claim another life tonight. As soon as he touched Bernot, he began shoveling his magic into the wound for he had to try to fight the god of death. But too much blood had been lost, too much damage had been done to save his friend.

"I am here," he told Bernot, taking his hand.

Bernot tried to speak but only a gurgled sound, mingled with half understandable words came forth on rivulets of blood.

"Do not speak. I am here."

"Adjran," Bernot managed in hoarse defiance.

"I've got her," Jared said, walking quickly to the bassinet.

Mahogen could tell it was all Jared could do to not stare at Lyerlly's body and be sick.

Jarshua was distracted by something and Mahogen realized the assassin, lying mere yards away, was still alive. The shallow breaths he took were pathetic and raspy. The man was misshapen and from the look on his face, was in agony. He deserved it.

The wolf sniffed the man, then without warning sunk his teeth into his throat. There was a faint exhale from the man, declaring his pain and fear. Then his eyes glazed over, and his muscles relaxed in a way that only the dead could. The man did not deserve to die quickly and Mahogen cursed Jarshua for doing him the favor.

Sleep had a heavy claim on Adjran, and she did not wake as Jared knelt beside her father.

Bernot reached out weakly and placed a hand on his daughter's cheek, a tear sliding down his own. Left behind was a streak of blood that would become an invisible stain on the child, for he and Jared would always remember it, remember its cause.

"Look… after her," Bernot pleaded faintly.

Mahogen wanted to reply, offer some words of fortitude, promise that Bernot would be there to see her grow. All he could do was nod because any of those words would be a lie.

Both of you, Bernot told them telepathically, as speaking verbally was no longer possible.

Mahogen watched as Lunos slowly claimed Bernot. He had always known Bernot would die well before him, as was the way of humans, but this was too soon. Tears slid down his cheeks as he gently closed Bernot's eyes.

He felt a hand on his shoulder and looked toward Jared. The human did not need to speak for him to understand everything he wanted to say. Jared wrapped an arm around Mahogen. Pulled his head against his shoulder, wet trails down his own face, mirrored the ones on Mahogen's.

Mahogen made no effort to stop Jared from holding him close. He needed the support offered. They both did. They all would.

From his position and through the tears, he watched as Jarshua leaned on Jared's leg and sniffed at Adjran. Slowly, the wolf began to lick away the blood from Bernot's final touch. As he did, a kind of static surrounded the baby and the wolf—even in the presence of death, life flourished. Jarshua had found his Harang.

«««« »»»»

The world was a mess. People ran about, yelling, but no one really knew what was happening. No one but he and Mahogen. Jared wished he could plead ignorance like the rest of them. It would certainly burden the load on his heart.

Adjran gave a mumbled cry through her easy sleep in Mahogen's arms as he gently rocked her—maybe she was having a good dream in this living nightmare. He remembered Bernot's last plea; that he and Mahogen care for his daughter. Though he couldn't begin to fathom what it would mean to become Adjran's guardian, he would do it without complaint. He owed the girl that much for the kindness her father had shown him. And he owed Bernot for so much more.

Beside him, Jarshua's ears perked. The pup's head jerked up, looking for any signs that something might be coming to harm the baby. Though no evil presented itself, the wolf remained on alert, his ears twitching at every slight sound, aware that calamity had struck and could again if Lunos decreed it.

They'd been in the command tent for what felt like days, though it could've been minutes or hours—time had lost meaning. Bernot had tried to remain calm in his final moments, but Jared had seen the fear in his eyes. That look haunted him. He could see the same expression upon the face of everyone he met now—they all feared battle had come and so too had their time to meet the gods of life and death.

The tent flap flared open, and the leaders trudged in. There was a mixture of emotions ranging from weary to angry to somber.

A nurse followed them and approached Mahogen, reaching for the child.

"No," Mahogen growled, possessiveness already reigning in his heart. "Bernot designated me as her guardian. And Jared."

The leaders took their seats and turned their attention toward him and the Alvor prince.

"Jared," Eoghan started, "tonight has been trying, but I fear I must burden you with something more. It was Bernot's wish that you lead the Lazado in the event of his untimely death."

His jaw dropped. Him? Of all people? "There has to be some kind of mistake."

"I promise there is not," Okleiy said, tones of bitterness in the words. "Will you accept?"

"I- Is there really a choice?"

"There is always a choice," Eoghan said.

Looking around the tent, he could see already so much was expected—*demanded*—of him and he hadn't even agreed to take up the mantle; he hated it. But Bernot had chosen him for a reason. Jared only wished he knew what Bernot had seen in him.

Gulping, and knowing the weight of the words he was about to utter, he said, "I accept." Whatever the reason, Bernot would have chosen carefully.

Relief crossed the other leaders' faces to quickly be replaced by guilt.

"Before we can retire for a few restless hours," Atlia said with a sigh, "we must ask one more thing of you."

Jared surmised it would be nothing good.

The leaders looked amongst themselves as if arguing over who had to deliver the bad news. Eventually it seemed Eoghan drew the short straw.

"Keegan…" the Reintablou began slowly, reading his reaction, "you have to let her go."

What is that supposed to mean? was all Jared could think.

"If she gets captured… you have to let it happen."

Jared raised an eyebrow before bursting into laughter that made his belly ache. They had to be testing him. Let Keegan go? She was the only one keeping them from being obliterated. His laugh slowly dwindled into confusion when no one else responded in kind. Not even Mahogen. "Oh, you're serious? Absolutely not!"

"It has to be done," Okleiy said through his teeth. "Bernot would not have asked us to make that decision if it were not imperative. And, although I disagree, the decision has already been made. You just have to uphold it."

Out of the corner of his eye, he noticed Mahogen staring at the ground—guiltily. Jared turned toward the Alvor prince. "You knew?"

"Yes, as do all of her guards," Mahogen admitted. "We were sworn to secrecy."

Anger boiled in his stomach and bile raced up his throat. Turning back to the other leaders, he snarled, "No. I will not hand Keegan over to Kolt."

"It is the only way she survives," Atlia said. "It is the only way any of us survive."

"How can you know that?"

"Bernot received a letter from the Blind Prophet."

"Anyone could've written it," he argued.

Eoghan produced the letter and Jared took his time reading it, looking for any fallacy. When he came to the last line, he almost choked.

"Jared," Mahogen said, placing a hand on his shoulder, "this will be the hardest thing you ever do. But I trusted Bernot to lead us to the end of the earth and back. Trust his decision, regardless of how illogical it may seem. He wanted to keep Keegan alive more than anyone. He had more to *lose* than any of us."

Jared looked around the room, studying his new equals. A degree of remorse shaped each of their features, but behind that stood conviction. If they did not win this war, all of their efforts and the lives lost would be senseless. To sacrifice one to save the many… it was a hard path to ignore, especially when he had seen what was in store.

"All right," he said past the pressure in his throat, "Bernot's plan holds." Already he hated himself.

«««   »»»

Kade couldn't believe his ears. There was no way Jared had just agreed to let his sister be captured! What in the name of Sola and Lunos was he thinking?

Respect be noxþox, he stormed into the tent, howling, "You won't be handing my sister over to Kolt." There was no way for him to truly relay the anger coursing through him. "Over my dead body!"

Jared whipped around, startled. Remorse swam in his brown eyes, but so did conviction. Slowly, Kade's so-called friend turned back to face the leaders, head hung low. Kade realized he was serious; he was going to let Keegan be taken.

"It seems Bernot's anti-eavesdropping spell has broken," Okleiy said absentmindedly. "It is such a shame most spells die with the caster. Guards."

Alvor soldiers materialized from seemingly nowhere and latched onto Kade's arms with iron grips.

"Okleiy," Atlia said warningly.

"I am not going to hurt him," the Alvor king said flippantly, "much. I will just detain him until what needs to happen has."

"There is another way," Eoghan said, speaking to Kade. "We are going to need you in the battle to come. Please do not make us do something we will all regret."

Anger pulled at Kade's lips and brows, transforming his face into a furious scowl. He spat on the ground to show them what he thought of their other way. "You're already doing something you'll regret."

"Letting Keegan go is a *regrettable* decision," Eoghan corrected, "but I do not regret it. If her loss results in the salvation of the rest of us, it behooves me to make that choice. Thousands rely upon me to make the best decision as their Reintablou, regardless of how hard it might be."

"Let me talk to him," Jared said. When the leaders didn't move, he added, "Alone."

Atlia shared a look with Eoghan before both rose and strode silently from the tent, heads held high. Okleiy was more hesitant but eventually shadowed them, snapping his fingers for his men to follow.

Kade waited for Mahogen to leave as well, but when he made no motion to do so, resigned himself to the fact that the Alvor prince would be present. Jared clearly trusted him, and Kade liked to believe he did too. But maybe he had to rethink that after what he'd just learned.

"How can you agree to…" the act was so atrocious he hated to speak of it and give it substance.

"It may be the only way she lives. The only way *any of us* live," Jared started, handing him the letter.

Kade read slowly. The information made him more inclined to see the other side of the coin… but still, how could Jared have agreed—and so quickly?

"There's another way," he insisted. "There has to be. Even if Kolt doesn't kill her immediately, who knows what she'll be subjected to."

"Whatever it is, it will be better than death," Mahogen said. "I know you want to protect her, but we are trying to protect everyone else, too. And if Alyck speaks true… this is how she lives as well."

"Do you trust me?" Jared asked.

Kade grumbled, crossing his arms. "Unfortunately." He'd seen the lengths Jared would go for those he cared about. He'd experienced them.

"Then you know what we have to do. And this will happen whether you—or I—want it to. I have no doubt the other leaders have zero qualms about putting us down for a few hours."

Kade could think of nothing to say and simply nodded.

Chapter 30

The silence was numbing. Even if anyone had wanted to break it, Keegan wasn't sure they'd be able to. This was the kind of silence that demanded respect and took no prisoners. This was the kind of silence that followed calamity.

They were all reeling from the night's events, and it was a wonder half the army hadn't fled back to Edreba or decided to take their chances across no man's land. It showed the men's faith in the Lazado and whoever would take charge next—or it proved some words did travel slowly.

After the discovery of Bernot's and Lyerlly's assassination, she and Aron had quickly been ushered back to their tent, five out of six of her guards called to their posts. Not a single one of them was tolerating anything but meek obedience from her tonight. Keegan might've put up a fight had she not been positively terrified.

Her guards had been in and out like flies, four of them always guarding the tent, and by the time she managed to pull herself from the gruesome thoughts and possibilities racing through her mind to realize they were collecting people, only Jared, Kade, and Mahogen were missing. Even Waylan had been convinced to take advantage of safety in numbers—though a small part of her had to wonder if they weren't just sitting ducks all huddled together as such.

Ravliean

From the now orange-tinted light coming from underneath the edges of the tent, sunrise was imminent—and who knew what kind of fresh horror the day would bring. Lucas, Reven, and Nikita had taken to pacing, creating a never-ending stream of anxiety that was making her itchy. She wanted to snap at them to sit down, but everyone handled things differently.

The tent flap was pulled back, and Aron jumped to his feet without releasing his iron grip on her hand.

In slipped Jared, Kade, and Mahogen, all unscathed, the sunrise only accentuating their drained expressions. There was a bundle in Mahogen's arms, and she knew it was Adjran. Whatever gods reigned supreme in this world, there was some sense of kindness to them.

Rising from the cot, Keegan took the babe from the Alvor prince, holding onto her like she was the last piece of good in the world. Likely, she was. Adjran hardly stirred as Keegan headed back to the cot.

Jarshua followed and jumped up to sit beside her, leaning his head on her lap protectively. She got the feeling it wasn't intended for her, not with how the pup's eyes never left Adjran. When she looked up again, she found everyone staring at Jared fixedly. Waiting.

"Bernot and Lyerlly are dead," Jared reiterated, barely managing to say the words.

Their stares didn't waver as they waited for more.

"We send them to Sola and Lunos this morning."

Still, they stared.

"Get some sleep."

No one faltered.

"I am the new Commander of the Lazado."

Under different circumstances, Keegan would've congratulated him. Maybe one day she could, but not now while blood still lay on the ground.

And yet, they continued to stare.

Jared looked between all of them, his eyes begging them to stop demanding more information—begging for more from him in general. This was likely one of many reasons Bernot had chosen him as successor: those who did not seek power were often the best suited for it.

Slowly, realizing there was nothing more to be said, the others began to look away and slip from the tent, no words of parting mumbled haphazardly. But Keegan kept staring; there was one last thing Jared had to say, she could feel it in her gut.

When only she, Aron, and Mahogen were left, Jared approached her. He placed a hand on Adjran's forehead and whispered, "I'm sorry."

Keegan got the feeling it was intended for her.

«««« »»»»

The only sound in the world was the biting howl of the wind that tore and wormed its way through the gathered crowd, leaving no person untouched by its icy fingernails. The sky above was a perilous gray, one that threatened snow and misery—but misery had already visited them; surely they would be spared more. Before Aron sat two pyres, their offerings, their shrouds a color that foreshadowed what the clouds above had in store, laid upon them.

A dragon slowly picked its way to stand before the pyres. *By this light, be cast anew,* she said in a soft feminine voice that only increased the heartache. *Your legacy will live until Sola herself falls to the hands of Lunos. By this light, we shall defeat your enemies.* The dragon added before releasing a stream of fire, *I am honored to have fought for you, alongside you.*

The pyres were not slow to catch and smoke and the scent of burning cloth and flesh filled the air pungently. It made Aron want to gag.

Sniffles came from Keegan and silent tears dripped down Mahogen's face who stood beside her. There was no shame in showing grief today—not when ones with so much to do had been stolen in the night. Not when their already tenuous fates were cast further into uncertainty.

He reached behind Keegan and placed a hand on the Alvor's shoulder. The gesture would do little to soften his loss, but it was the only thing Aron could offer. It was the only thing anyone could offer.

The dragon released a roar before taking to the sky and returning to the back of the crowd with the rest of her kith and kin.

It was not long before Kade elbowed Jared in the ribs.

Reluctantly, Jared stepped forward and turned to face the crowd. Their new leader stared at the people gathered silently, his voice hesitant to give light to the words he wished to speak; that, or he did not know what to say.

Fumbling, Jared found his voice, "Uh… um, today is not an auspicious day."

Keegan groaned, shaking her head.

"But tomorrow is a new day. In the face of this travesty, I know Bernot would've wanted us to fight, to win, rather than shed tears. And Lyerlly, she would've wanted us to show Kolt not even the power of Lunos can stop us."

Someone behind them gave a halfhearted cheer. It was something; at least someone was willing to put some kind of faith in Jared.

"It is now for my own brothers, those of blood and those of heart, and for their daughter, Adjran, that I fight. And I fight for all the children that yet are to come. That they may live in a better world; one without fear. One with peace. I don't know about you," Jared said, his confidence bolstered by the singular unenthusiastic cheer, "but I don't plan on dying tomorrow, or the day after that, or the day after that, or the day after that. Lunos can have me when I'm old and ready!"

There were a few more cheers.

"I doubt I'll ever be able to equal Bernot, but I'll be noxþox if I don't try. And I, we, will defeat Kolt and any who follow him."

More cheers rose into the air, and these were heartfelt.

"Will you stand with me?" Jared yelled. "Will you follow me and place your trust in me?"

The roar from the crowd was deafening. And it only grew with each passing second, like gentle waves that lapped upon a shore and flourished in the approach of an imminent storm.

Eventually, Aron found even he was adding his voice to the din, truly believing they could be victorious.

With a fervor, the likes of which Aron had never seen before, Jared yelled, "Then we fight! And we win! Battle awaits us on the morrow's morn!"

«««« »»»»

Braxton pushed his way into the crowd, stopping when he was finally able to see Branshaw. Even though it was the wee hours of the day, the Commander looked invigorated, if not… satisfied. Smugly so.

Then, he was somewhere else, though it could not be far. The landscape looked much the same, flat and unburdened. Around him stood men, soldiers, but these did not belong to Kolt's army. The crowd was made up of the various races and each one of them wore the same solemn look.

Braxton snapped back to himself and from the men around him came whispers in a discord so that no word could be distinguished from another except by the intended recipient. Part of him wanted to know what rumors were running rampant, but if he knew Branshaw like he thought he did, they were about to be informed of the truth. The clamor slowly drifted to oblivion as the other men came to the same realization and all eyes snapped to Branshaw who had come to stand on a quickly erected podium.

Then, instead of the podium, Braxton saw two pyres, hastily constructed with care. Underneath the shrouds that covered the bodies it was impossible to tell who the people were. But they must have been important, and loved, for there was nary a dry eye in sight. Braxton feared who these people were.

"Today we have dealt a defeating blow," Branshaw announced, his voice ringing above the heads gathered before him.

Rumors started to mill again as the men tried to work out what blow they had dealt while sleeping or drinking. Certainly, whatever it was, it could not have been them.

"Bernot Bællar is dead!" Branshaw called.

Braxton recalled the feeling of a knife slicing into his throat and subconsciously reached to feel his neck. Had that been how Bernot died? Was Bernot one of the two people on the pyre?

At first, there was no reaction from the men, all seemingly stunned. Then one man gave a jubilant yell, and the others picked it up. Soon, he was surrounded in a deafening roar that made more than just his ears hurt.

It dawned on him. The deserter from last night was no deserter. His stomach churned in guilt. He could have—should have—stopped the man. *This* was his fault. Now, his only hope of ever being free was gone.

Over the yelling, Braxton was just able to hear Branshaw proclaiming they would attack at dawn the next day. Enough time to prepare, but also to fret. As the noise of the cheering men intensified, he pushed from the crowd, holding his stomach, the taste of bile slick in the back of his throat.

Before his eyes, the world became tinder beneath orange flame, raging and demanding vengeance. Heat seared across his body. Braxton might have sought to quench the inferno, but those in this part of the world deserved to burn. And he was no exception. But no, the flames were for Bernot.

And tomorrow the fire would only burn brighter as more souls were released to the old gods.

Braxton was not sure where he was going, the staccato visions from across no man's land making the world topsy turvy. At one point, he recalled the cool feel of the earth, a tuft of spared grass tickling his cheek. Cheering burned in his ears, and the chill of the air bit into his flesh.

Then he was floating through the world, yet he was very aware of the earth pressing against him.

Then he was looking at himself. Rage—pure, unadulterated rage marred the features of his face. No, that was not strictly true, pain blemished the mask of fury. Braxton hated seeing himself like this, but could do nothing to stop it, for he was simply an observer.

His gaze slid past his own hate-filled expression and took in the person he held against the wall. Their features were fuzzy and at first all he could see was the color of flame surrounding their head. Whatever this person had done must have been serious because he was willing to kill over it.

Slowly, the person came into focus and Braxton realized it was Keegan. Her hands—hand, her left arm hung limply at her side—scrabbled at him, trying to break his grip on her throat. But nothing could defeat his ire and he watched her slip into oblivion, gasping for air like a fish pulled from its dwelling.

Then, he was choking, struggling to take a breath.

Bolting upright, he gave a shuddering gasp, sucking in as much air as his lungs would allow. He was on a cot... his cot, judging by the snores surrounding him. His head throbbed, akin to the morning after too much drink, and his throat was dry, as if he had screamed himself hoarse.

The tent was dark, and he concluded it was night. So much time he had lost. And to what? He could recall nothing of his visions, nothing but an impenetrable fury directed toward Keegan.

Realizing his face felt wet, he reached up to investigate. The source of the water was his eyes.

The tent flap pushed open, allowing the chill of winter to gain a temporary hold over him. From the torchlight outside, he was just able to make out Myrish.

You are awake. Is everything all right? the griffin asked, his bronze feathers dully reflecting the torch light.

Yes, he lied. *What happened?*

I cannot say for sure, the griffin began, *but I think it was your visions.*

Besides Alyck and Thaddeus, Myrish was the only other being that knew he was haunted by glimpses of the future. And of the present with the slajor manacle in place.

You were found lying in the mud, eyes open. Except... they had turned white and milky with cataracts.

I... I think I can see just fine, Braxton said, fear coursing through him. The next time he saw the Blind Prophet, certain questions would be asked. Braxton's gut told him he knew what was happening, yet he did not want to jump to conclusions—for he did not want to be burdened with the truth he feared.

Are you sure everything is all right?

Yes. Nothing was all right, but to admit that was to lose everything.

Myrish clicked his beak, knowing he was lying, but did not push. As he retreated outside, leaving Braxton to whatever remained of the night, winter lost her hold.

Alone, aside from Nico's snores, Braxton carefully reached under his pillow. His hand easily found the hilt of the knife he kept there. He let his thumb trace along the razored edge of the blade. The steel was just not cold, it was freezing, every inch of it dipped in the poison of malice, hate, and death.

A scene flashed before his eyes, and he watched as a sword barreled toward Keegan's neck. The fear on her face brought acid to his throat. He would be the cause of this. Him—no one else—*him*.

Returning to the dark tent, his fingers found the knife's tip and he thought about what it could do. What it could steal from people. What people sometimes willingly gave it.

He slowly brought the knife from under his pillow. Winter welcomed the weapon with open arms, finding its ice-encrusted heart a kindred soul. He was seeing the future—a possible future; but it could also be nothing more than a dream of guilt. There was one thing he could do to prevent it if this was to be the future. But could he really do that? Would he?

Light filled his vision and any hold winter had over him was sucked away to be replaced with a loving warmth. Two people stood before him, clad in the colors of spring, in the colors of new beginnings. The two people leaned forward and kissed, claiming the other as theirs for life. When they pulled apart, he realized who they were.

Blinking, he was brought back to darkness, to winter, to death. The knife in his hand was heavy, as was the decision it held. Slowly, he returned the blade to its place under the pillow and lay down. To achieve good, bad needed to happen.

Chapter 31

Staring at the plains, Keegan searched for an army and could see nothing but the flat horizon. Part of her wanted to hope Kolt's men had overslept, run away in fear, anything besides the truth. Behind her, the soft creaks of saddles and clanks of armor followed any minute movement of the men and horses.

Looking to her left, Keegan could see nothing but a line of dragons, foreboding and formidable compared to the hardly lethal-looking Alvor, Merfolk, and humans milling behind and between them. The Torrpeki were a fearsome force all their own, fangs, horns, and size making them appear like mountains of unbreakable stone.

Ready? Sulle asked.

As I'll ever be, she told him.

Without a word, the orange dragon lowered himself to the ground so she could clamber onto his back.

The morning was peaceful, unaware of the horrors about to transpire—or maybe it did know and was offering them one last moment of peace. The lightly falling snow didn't help to dispel the stagnant atmosphere.

With Keegan situated in the crook of his shoulders, Sulle rose slowly.

She took a deep breath to stop herself from being sick. It wasn't the height that turned her stomach; she didn't want to think about how many lives she'd be ending today—directly or indirectly.

Sulle's wings rose, enshrining her in the color of a pure sunset, before dropping heavily. They lifted from the ground and the men nearby stumbled as they were buffeted by the wind and battered with chips of rock and blades of grass.

When they were well above the earth, Keegan began to see a haze on the horizon. Sulle lazily drifted toward it, and she was dismayed to see how many men made up Kolt's army. Looking behind them, she ascertained the Lazado had equal numbers. Not equal—the other races were so much stronger than humans.

Continuing to near Kolt's army, she espied trebuchets. The dragons were normally infallible, but even they couldn't survive being hit by a hurtling boulder. Even if it missed, the carnage a boulder flung into the fray might cause was unimaginable. This would change how the Lazado fought. Likely, someone—or several someones—would be sent on a suicide mission to destroy the war machines. She couldn't destroy them without causing Kolt's army to know they were ready. But until then, plans had to change, and she reached out to Jared so they could do just that.

Closing her eyes, Keegan crushed the earth paika, feeling its shards rip through her body guiltily. Quickly, she released the magic and there was a deafening sound as miles and miles of earth sank itself into trenches hundreds of feet wide, pointed spikes lining the bottom like nightmarish teeth. Earth elementals would find ways across, but any extra seconds to delay the inevitable…

Exhaustion that would be quickly expelled by her hyperactivity settled over her and Keegan made no complaints as Sulle turned and headed back to where their army waited. At moments it was all she could to do keep her eyes open. Some of it was tiredness—the rest of it was exhaustion with… everything.

You should have sunk those under the men, Sulle reprimanded.

It's not my job or desire to kill people, was all she said on the matter.

«««« »»»»

The leaders, his brother included, were idiots for thinking they could be ready for battle by sunrise. Even with a full day—much closer to less than though—to work, they were woefully unprepared. Though Lucas had the suspicion they would've been underprepared no matter the circumstances. So many had joined as the Lazado marched and liberated—mostly peasants without a lick of training—and it was not as if they'd brought their own weapons and armor either.

Lucas doubted even half of the surplus of newcomers had anything but the clothes on their backs. But desperation brought about invigorated ingenuity. In the last few hours, he and Waylan had hastily tied mildly sharpened pieces of metal to poles for makeshift spears. They had taken tent stakes and sharpened them into weapons. They had even helped one man fashion a rake into something that might keep him alive.

Lucas wasn't sure what the other smiths had taken to doing, but he'd bet it was something similar. Hopefully, people would be smart enough to pick up fallen swords the first chance they got. Though they might be better off with shoddy weapons that resembled the tools they were familiar with.

As Lucas continued to work, ignoring the tiredness brought on by only a half night's sleep, he finished another spear and tossed it into the pile.

"Go find your brothers," Waylan instructed without breaking from his work. "And take armor, a shield, and a sword." There was a pregnant pause. "I expect to see you tomorrow morning."

Part of Lucas wanted to keep working, keep doing what he could to make sure as many of the Lazado as possible would see the next sunrise. But he needed rest; and needed to find his brothers—if only to ensure there was nothing left unsaid… just in case.

"Same to you," he said.

Waylan snorted in response. "Boy, worse things than war have been trying to kill me for twenty years. Be safe."

Outside the smithy, the world seemed to be holding its breath, and he could only hope Lunos hadn't put a bounty on his head. Snow drifted lazily toward the ground, and he pulled his cloak tighter around his shoulders. He was still sticky and warm with sweat, but the cool, predawn air quickly pulled the warmth from his body. His cloak did little against the chill and disquiet blooming in his chest. Soon, the cloak would fall, like so many of the men in this camp, as the frenzy of battle warmed him.

Most of the men he walked past were headed west where they would face Kolt's army. He headed in the opposite direction, knowing Jared would invariably be in the command tent for a while longer.

Someone called his name and he turned to find Carter jogging to catch up, mismatched armor covering his body. Lucas hated to admit it, but Carter was made for the armor, regardless of whether it matched or not. The disparity from how he remembered his brother, the shy shepherd, was a rent in his heart.

"You seen Jared?" Carter asked, his heavy breaths steaming in the winter air.

"Was just looking for him myself," he answered, continuing to walk. "I'm betting he's in the command tent."

Carter fell in step with him.

They'd hardly made it a thousand yards before the sound of a horn filled the air... long, morose, intrepid. Snow swirled in the sound, creating eddies that offered different paths if they were willing to be cowards. Lucas was about to complain it was too soon when he realized the golden hair of the sun was lighting the world.

He could tell Carter was about to dart forward and see if he could make it to the command tent before pandemonium struck. Lucas grabbed his brother's arm. "No time now."

"But what if he dies in battle?" Carter said.

"He won't."

"What if we die?"

Lucas clouted his brother about the ear, hoping to knock some sense into him. "Don't ever, ever say that again!" Then he placed his hands on the sides of Carter's neck, thumbs resting just abreast of his ears. "We're Siemes. None of us are dying until we have Nico back—and even then, Lunos won't be meeting us for quite some time. Not if I have anything to say about it."

«««« »»»»

Alyck made another lap around the room, his grim expression never shifting as his feet beat along the familiar imaginary path. Today, history changed, for better or worse—worse for some, better for others. But only time could tell Thaddeus what the outcome would be for them.

"I do not like this," Alyck snapped. "I still see two fates for Keegan."

Thaddeus knew what they were: one, where she was brutally murdered by Caius; the other, where she was kindly killed by old age. As to why there were disparagingly different outcomes, he did not know. He could not even offer a thought as to how either came about. Nor how to swing fate so Lunos did not take Keegan in her youth.

Alyck continued pacing, the steps angry and frustrated, more akin to stomps.

"What can you see about the battle?" Thaddeus probed, hoping to take Alyck's mind off the fact that fate sat at a precipice and there was nothing he could do to dictate what would come.

"Blood. Agony. Death. The only person who wins today is Lunos."

"Lunos always wins, sooner or later."

The Blind Prophet conceded to his statement with a harumph. A moment later, fury contorted his features. He flipped over a table in anger, kicking its contents about the room like a child in the throes of a tantrum.

Thaddeus let him fume and destroy. There was no stopping his rage, and even he knew how cathartic destruction could be—when it was correctly channeled. Alyck might regret the outburst later as he had to clean up the mess, but for now, it was what he needed.

Finally, the anger passed and Alyck sank down against a wall, sobbing. "Why was I cursed with the ability to see the future, but not to change it?"

Thaddeus wished he had an answer, but all he could offer was a comforting touch. "What is it you see?"

"So much pain. So much pain," Alyck wept.

«««« »»»»

Aron watched Sulle glide across the sky, a tinged image of the sun herself in his orange scales, with Keegan hardly more than a glint of reflection on his back in her armor. He desperately wanted the dragon to just fly into the rising sun and not return until all of this was over. But that would never happen. Keegan was too stubborn and was needed too much. *He* needed her too much.

"She won't be the same after this," Kade said, ambling up to him, watching the dragon mingle with the sun's rays. His arms hung loosely at his side, betraying a kind of calm Aron knew he was not feeling.

Aron wished he could contradict Kade. Finally, he said quietly, "None of us will be the same after this."

The light clanking of metal behind Aron reminded him of the army at his back—of all the people who would die today, each of them believing it was for a better world. But would it truly be for a better world?

"You know it's you and me looking after her today?" Kade said.

"Always has been. You, me, Jared, and the old gods," Aron answered.

Kade seemed to grimace at the mention of Jared.

The ground trembled and he knew Keegan had done what she intended to. The trenches had not been her idea, but she was the only one strong enough to do it so quickly. What might have taken hours or days and countless hands, required only two and the blink of an eye with her.

The orange blot that was Sulle turned and began to head back, letting Aron breathe a sigh of relief. It would have been so easy for Kolt's men to assume they were attacking and engage in kind—and no one would have been able to do a thing about it.

"If she dies today, I'm holding you personally accountable," Kade said flatly.

Aron knew he could be held no more accountable for Keegan's fate than anyone else. "Would not have it any other way."

"I'll see you on the other side," Kade said, walking away.

"See you on the other side," Aron mumbled, his eyes never leaving Sulle.

Chapter 32

A pit sat in Braxton's stomach. He knew what was going to happen today: life or death. He had the power to choose but saving one life meant sacrificing another. He had to choose those he cared about or the world—there was no both.

Ready when you are, Myrish said, shuffling his wings.

Braxton took a deep breath, steadying himself. If he made the right choices, good would come. The only problem was he was not entirely sure what those choices were.

"Where do you want us?" Nico asked, climbing onto Harker, a kind of eagerness sparking in his blue eyes.

Braxton hated that. To see one so young eager to take life and endanger his own, it made Braxton want to be sick. It made him want to take Nico by the shoulders and shake him. "I want you and Mara away from the battle," he said.

Nico and Mara were aware of their roles—but now he had to justify it to them and the rest of the Vosjnik. Until they faced war, it was nothing but a possibility. What Nico did not know was that this was more than sparing his innocence; should the boy manage to find his family in battle, he would go to their aid and that would be just as deadly as a sword.

"How dare you—" Vitia started.

"The hatchlings are not experienced enough to survive against a dragon if it comes to that," Braxton said. "They can be useful picking off men who manage to break past the front lines."

Vitia looked ready to argue, but surprisingly kept her mouth shut. He did not want to think about what vile plans she might have or how she might seek retribution later. But her lack of argument ensured no one else spoke up.

"Are you sure?" Mara asked him quietly.

He placed an armored hand on her shoulder. "If I need you, I will call." Whispering, he added, "I have another job for you. Kolt has spelled Nico so that if he touches any of his brothers he will die. *Do not* let that happen."

Mara nodded grimly, steely resolve setting the features of her face. Nico could be in no better hands.

Once Braxton was settled on Myrish's back, the griffin unfurled his wings. The other adults followed suit, and together took to the sky.

All he had said about the hatchlings was true, as were his personal sentiments about protecting their riders. But it was also to protect himself. Should Nico fall today, he did not look forward to the Sieme brothers setting out for revenge—and something told him they would succeed, sooner rather than later.

There was no noise from the griffins besides the almost indiscernible whistling of the wind over their lithe bodies. He would have preferred they wear armor, but all had refused. Their reasoning was that agility was their shield. And while that was true, just like him, there was an underlying reason; they refused armor because if they fell, so be it, they never had to return to captivity. It was an honorable way to fight, for it both satisfied his need for them to battle and their desire to be free.

Looking down onto the plain that would fuel nightmares for years and lifetimes to come, he saw trenches running for miles in either direction. On the horizon a blot of orange descended toward a wall of soldiers—a scout no doubt. The Lazado army looked calm and organized; maybe the assassin had failed… at least he hoped so. But he knew that was not true, not after his visions. At least two had been felled by the assassin, so a better sentiment was that he hoped it was not Bernot who had fallen. But deep down he knew Bernot no longer led the Lazado.

You see that? Myrish asked, referencing the trenches.

Returning his attention to the troughs, the pit in his stomach deepened. The ditches had not been there yesterday and were too expansive to have been dug overnight. Which left magic. But by the sheer scale of it, no single elemental could have done this alone; they would have collapsed from exhaustion well before finishing even a significant portion of the project. And the many hands a project like this should have required would not have gone unnoticed. So, how had they not noticed the Lazado working on it?

"Hard to miss," he called after failing to reach Myrish telepathically. Today, or this moment, the slajor manacle would not let him communicate telepathically.

They have someone up their proverbial sleeve. Someone strong.

"Someone like Keegan."

I hope not. I hope she is far from here. I wish her no harm, but our hand has been forced if she is.

Braxton nodded, even though he knew Myrish couldn't see the motion. He wished no harm upon Keegan… but greater beings had other ideas.

And she was the only one who could have caused the trenches single handedly. Against the odds that the old gods would ignore him, Braxton released a prayer to them. With all his heart, he hoped he did not have to meet any of the Children of Prophecy on the field of battle today.

«««« »»»»

He wasn't sure what portion of the night it was, but sunrise couldn't be far off. Not from the way the barest hope of light was starting to peer through the cracks in the tent. Jared sat up and slowly pulled himself from the cot. The chill in the air was shocking, ordering him back beneath the blankets. Ignoring the command, he dressed and pulled on his armor, the cool metal giving no false hopes about the outcome of the day. A tight coil of icy emotions formed in his stomach and snaked through his innards.

Outside his tent, snow fell, drifting from the heavens like soft, frozen tears. From the gloom still persisting, sunrise was still a ways off, but the day was fighting to rear her head and pull them from the bleakness. And with each second, day's grasp on the world grew stronger. But Jared knew she ultimately would fail in that task—today, in more than one sense. The storm clouds above would only let the sun have so much of a hold, and today would mark a dark stain on history.

Men bustled past, the majority in clanking armor, most too lost in their own worlds and worries to notice him. Most failing to remember Bernot was dead—and that he was now Commander. So uncommon was any kind of acknowledgement that it was easy to forget the position he now held.

Glancing down the muddy path winding through the rows of tents, Jared spotted Mahogen. As always, the

Alvor moved with more grace than was naturally possible; he was beautiful.

As Mahogen passed by, Jared grabbed his arm, pulling him into the tent. The prince was surprised to the point of starting to reach for his weapons. But, realizing it was Jared, he relaxed.

"I know what I want." Jared pulled Mahogen into a kiss. "I don't want to die today knowing… knowing I felt something for you, but you didn't know. That… I didn't give what I feel a chance."

Mahogen smiled and they shared another kiss. "I am glad you finally know yourself."

Unsure of what to say or do next, Jared gave Mahogen a curt nod and headed toward the command tent.

As he walked, he felt lighter, blessedly so. Maybe Sola and Lunos would not seek to punish him for the perversion he had given into. Maybe it was as Keegan said, love was love.

Then he recalled what lay in wait for Keegan and the knots in his stomach clenched painfully enough to evoke an involuntary grunt. And he remembered he would be the source of it. It was enough to make him weep; but thousands of people looked up to him now, time could not be afforded to doubting himself.

Waiting inside the command tent were the rest of the leaders, clad in armor and scowls.

He must have been starstruck or shown his doubt for Atlia coached, "Do not waver. You have to let her go."

The ties in his stomach cinched tighter. "I know." And while he did know, he didn't like it.

"I expect to see all of you back here tonight," Eoghan said calmly. "He who dies is going to regret it even in the afterlife."

The quip was meant to dispel some of the tension, but it only worked to thicken it.

Personally, Jared could feel the words squeezing his heart, as if to suffocate him. "May Sola and Lunos see us through," he muttered.

"They will," Eoghan said, self-assured.

Then, silence. Whether they had nothing to say, or the atmosphere didn't allow it, he couldn't tell. Yet, the silence spoke for itself, whispering their doubts, fears, and worries and promising they would come true.

Studying the relief map of their world and where their forces stood, Jared found himself grounded. They would prevail. There was no other choice.

A soldier pushed into the tent, an update spewing from his lips.

"What do you mean there are dragons flying toward us?" Jared all but screeched.

"There are dragons flying toward us," the man reiterated timidly.

Ezadeen was at the front line and Jared took a moment to relay the situation to her and hoped it was all just a giant misunderstanding,

They are not any dragons I know, Ezadeen said. Her words were haughty as if the dragons flying toward them were beneath her.

Jared balked for a moment before grabbing a spy glass and heading to the front line, muttering curses under his breath.

Sulle landed just as he reached the line of waiting soldiers, Keegan sliding from his back tiredly. With every second, that tiredness dripped away, replaced by anxiety. "Done," she told him in what might have been the quietest voice he'd ever heard her use.

Jared didn't respond, instead putting the spyglass to his eye. The details of the dragons were hard to make out, but they bovestun weren't dragons. What he saw was a strange culmination of beasts; they had the head and wings of birds and the bodies of massive cats. And he definitely didn't like the looks of five of them coming straight at them. He pulled the eyeglass away to see Keegan squinting at the creatures on the horizon with a puzzled look.

"Well?" she probed, hoping for elucidation.

He offered her the spyglass; leave it to her to know the things he did not.

She scanned the sky for hardly a second. "Griffins."

He groaned. There'd been rumors that the Alagards possessed griffins, and now there was proof. No wonder their sigil was a griffin. "If they become a nuisance, I'm going to need you and Sulle to take care of them," he said.

"I'd rather not," Keegan responded.

"I'd rather not fight," he snapped, "but I don't exactly have a choice. Neither do you. That's an order." He felt bad for being so harsh, but war called for no quarter given.

«««   »»»

Soldiers marched forward, their timed footsteps going *thump, thump, thump*. It seemed there was no end to their forces as they filed past him, even if Nico knew that wasn't true.

The rest of the griffins were hardly more than misshapen birds on the horizon, and he envied them. He knew he should take his current orders as a blessing, but he hated being left behind. Hated feeling useless, like a child.

Though Braxton's orders were to not fight, he wasn't sure *what* he was supposed to do instead. And what he could not do was *nothing*. "There has to be something we can do," he bit, more to himself but loud enough that Mara could hear him.

"I am sure there is," Mara said calmly. "But it's not what we were ordered to do. We were told to stay here."

"Royik what we were ordered to do."

"Fighting here means fighting for Kolt."

His frustration simmered. "Then let's fight for the Lazado."

"How?" Mara asked cautiously. "Kolt will find out and we lose our heads. As will Harker and Ima. And Braxton and the others."

He growled in frustration at the situation and the verity of her argument. "But I can't just sit here and... do nothing!" This was not how a man comported himself in battle. Or otherwise.

Mara was quiet for a moment. "How about this, we fly well above the fighting and act as scouts?"

"Let's go," he said, already climbing onto Harker. He would accept anything that didn't require him to be stuck on the ground.

Are you sure this is a good idea? Harker asked, rolling his shoulders.

Nico knew it wasn't, but he couldn't let the fate of the world be completely decided by someone else.

Chapter 33

Kade slashed at the man in front of him, his sword tearing through the man's leather armor like it was nothing. He wanted to feel pity for him, for trying to fight ill-equipped, but he was already up against his next opponent. He quickly relieved the next man of his life as well. Kade felt no remorse—it was kill or be killed. This was war.

He could've been fighting for minutes or hours, it was hard to tell. Not even the sun in the sky offered a shred of grounding. He'd already lost count of the men he'd dispatched. And of the times he'd thanked Sola for deeming his life worth continuing.

Beside him, Icella and Reven fought wildly, no man managing to last long against either of them. Icella moved faster than raging water while Reven stood sturdier than a mountain. Together, the three of them were nearly untouchable. But he knew that would change as fatigue set in and their luck wore thin. At some point Lunos would curse them.

To his left he spotted Sulle, which meant Keegan was close by. So far, he'd watched the orange dragon tramp through the battle erratically; there had to be a reason behind his movements, and most likely it was Keegan's stubborn nature and impulsiveness.

The dragon fell into their little circle of chaos and Kade watched Keegan fight—though, it was more like working, as The Queen Killer hadn't even been pulled from its scabbard.

Kade was awestruck as he watched his sister; a man dropped his sword, put his hands on his head, and began walking through the battle. Another followed him. Then another. He watched the line of men march themselves to awaiting soldiers to have their hands bound and be led farther into enemy territory. He wanted to say Keegan's way was royiken stupid, but it was bovestun effective.

Kade couldn't remember a time Keegan had practiced manipulation since they were in Suttan—what felt like decades ago at this point. Yet, by her current skill in the art and given how rarely he'd been in her vicinity while training, he figured he must've just been unaware of her practice. From the way her face was devoid of emotion, manipulation was taking a lot of her concentration. And from the sweaty sheen on her brow, a lot of energy too. But his sister was stubborn. Likely the only person stubborn enough to be able to pull this off en masse.

A man tried to sneak up on his twin, and Sulle dipped his head to snap him up in his jaws, the crunch of bones and armor almost worse than the quickly cut off scream. Keegan flinched, her shoulder hunching and it was obvious she was biting the inside of her cheek, but she didn't falter in her task.

As much as Kade wanted to toss her over his shoulder and carry her off the field, she was holding her own, and desperately needed—every person was. He turned back to his own problems and realized there was a lull in attacks. Though he wouldn't admit it aloud, he was glad for the reprieve.

Men continued to fall before him, their blood watering the ground. His mind turned off and he fell into a rhythm, parry, slash, hack, next. The pattern was only broken when he heard a startled and pained scream, one that rattled his bones. He stabbed his opponent in the gut before giving his attention to the source.

Keegan held the side of her neck, blood oozing and dribbling between her fingers. No man stood near her, and he worried at the cause of the wound. As they both scanned the fray, Keegan was thrown forwards. The crunch of metal was grating against Kade's ears as his sister was propelled into Sulle's side.

Between her shoulder blades stuck an arrow. Given the fact it had managed to punch trough the diamond layer of her armor, it had to be spelled. Yet, the diamond appeared to have done its job, taking the brunt of the hit; only a small portion of the arrow, if any at all, had made it through the plating.

Kade looked fervently for the archer, almost missing him, not expecting to find him in the sky. He immediately recognized Braxton riding the bronze griffin, his black hair a blot of darkness in the snow falling around him. The prince already had another arrow notched and was taking his time aiming. At his sister.

Kade raced toward Keegan, throwing up an earthen shield as Braxton tensed in preparation to release the bowstring. When he came to a halt against Sulle's body, his heart skipped a few beats; an arrow tip was all but touching his nose, the bolt embedded in his earthen shield. He was incredibly lucky; it should've gone straight into his head.

"Get to the sky," he yelled, increasing the thickness and height of his shield.

Keegan didn't need to be told twice and scrambled onto Sulle, blood running over her armor in growing veins that splashed onto the dragon's orange scales.

As Kade lowered the shield to allow Sulle to take flight, the dragon released a stream of fire at Braxton and the griffin, forcing them to seek safer spaces. Even though not in the path of the flames, he could feel the scorching heat on his face like a slap.

Unfurling his wings, Sulle extinguished the flames and propelled himself into the air. Droplets of water began to fall, melted snow, and the people around Kade were thrown to the ground from the downdraft. Most of the Lazado knew what to expect as the dragon took wing and were able to use the advantage to dispatch their opponents—though, in some cases, it was the other way around.

Scanning the sky, Kade was surprised to find Braxton still nearby. Was Keegan not his target? He searched for Sulle and found the orange dragon heading south where soon they would be surrounded by nothing but grass. Worry flooded him when he saw a silver-sided griffin chasing after them. The rider had streaming black hair and Kade didn't need to see the horn stubs to know it was Vitia.

Jared, he called, *we need dragons. Now! Keegan's in trouble.*

Jared was slow to respond, no doubt in the middle of his own problems and fights. *You agreed to let her go. Remember?*

Letting her go and letting her die are two very different things!

Worry and confusion came through the mental contact.

Vitia's chasing her and Braxton's already used her for target practice.

Where are you?

He sent a mental image of his location.

Headed your way. Don't move.

He didn't respond, instead dealing with a man who had the horrible idea of charging at him.

«««« »»»»

Braxton had not expected to find Keegan on the battlefield. That was a lie; he had known she would be there, but had hoped his vision, dream, whatever, was wrong. But they never were. He hated what he was about to do, but it was her life or so many more—so many of those he cared about.

Slowly, he drew back the bowstring, the tautness of the string telling him it was about to snap if he was not careful, one of Kolt's accursed gifted arrows aimed and ready to bring pain.

He wants her alive, Myrish reminded him.

Though it might not seem like it, this was not meant to kill. With luck it would serve as a warning to get somewhere safe—so he could have plausible deniability. So he did not have to do what he had been ordered to. So Keegan might live and find a way to depose his brother.

He let the arrow fly and was happy when it buried itself up to the fletching in soil. It looked like he had missed if only looking where the arrow had landed. He could not see the blood from his lofty position, but knew it was there, now seeping into the earth as Keegan grabbed at her neck.

She stood there, as if unbelieving someone had injured her. Sola and Lunos, he wished she was smarter.

He prepared another arrow and let it soar, aiming to have it scrape against her shoulder harmlessly. Then, the worst possible thing happened; Keegan moved ever so slightly, and he cringed as the arrow punched through her armor, propelling her into the side of an orange dragon. The arrow appeared to have hardly made it through the metal plate, so her armor must be spelled like his arrows—or coated in diamond, which was the likely option as diamonds were a better protection against spelled weapons.

He noticed a figure racing toward Keegan and recognized Kade, his auburn hair distinguishing him. That, and having seen him around the castle for so many years, his face was not one he was likely to forget too. But maybe it was not him, he did not get a good look at the man's face—at least that is what he would tell Kolt.

Something whizzed past his ear and Braxton watched an arrow imbed itself in the earthen shield Kade created as he rushed to Keegan's aid. Whipping around, he found Vitia with a bow drawn behind him. He immediately recalled the second tube of spelled arrows Kolt had and cursed the fact that he had given them to Vitia.

Old grudges died hard. In Kade's case, it was keeping him alive.

"You're supposed to kill him!" Vitia seethed. She reached for another arrow but grasped at air.

He gave himself an inch to hang from. "I cannot prove it was him."

The angered growl Vitia gave was enough to raise the hairs on the back of his neck. If he was not careful, next time she might be coming for him.

Myrish lurched to the side and where they had just been become nothing but scorching flames. He thanked the old gods the griffin was not as easily distracted as he. A few of Myrish's feathers caught fire and he quickly patted out the flames.

Thank you, Myrish said, flying higher to escape the heat radiated from the dragon's maw.

Closing its mouth, the orange-colored dragon took to the air, Keegan on its back. Finally, she was doing what he needed her to do.

Vitia and Niyth had followed them upwards, and fury contorted the Alvor's face as she watched Keegan escape. "If you won't kill Kade, I'll have to do it myself.

That is after I make his life a Hiell," Vitia snarled, urging the silver griffin after the dragon.

"Kolt wants her alive," was all he had time to say before Vitia was too far to hear him.

Should we follow? Myrish questioned.

Not yet.

««« »»»

As the seam on Keegan's neck closed, her energy waned. By the time it was fully healed, she was exhausted and coated in blood. Hunched over Sulle's neck, she would've taken a nap if she thought she could get away with it. Keegan would've loved to deal with the arrow in her back, but it was deeply lodged in the armor, and moving her arms too much sent a jolt of fire radiating from the wound.

Thankfully, the arrow hadn't fully punched into her body, though it might've been better if it had. The tip sat flush against her back and sliced into her skin with every movement. Already a steady trickle of blood made its way down her spine like a never-ending shiver.

She was about to use magic to dislodge it when Sulle jerked to the right and let out a vicious roar, both in pain and anger.

Another behind us, the dragon said, banking sharply to the left now, almost unseating her.

Keegan twisted to see Vitia and a silver-fletched griffin giving chase. The last inch or so of the dragon's tail was missing, streaming hot blood onto their pursuers like gruesome stars.

You gonna live or do you want me to heal it? she asked.

I will be fine. We need to lose them though. Hold on. Sulle flipped onto his back and began to plunge toward the ground.

A scream escaped Keegan's lips and every muscle in her body tightened as it fought to hold on. Keegan didn't doubt that Vitia chased after them, the sneer on her face a telltale sign she thought she'd bested them.

Opening his jaws, Sulle released a stream of fire that matched his hide and quickly pulled out of the freefall, righting himself. Keegan had never been happier to have something solid underneath her butt.

As the flame dissipated, showering them in a deluge of melted snow, Keegan looked to make sure Vitia and the griffin had fallen back. She saw nothing and wondered if they'd gone up in smoke.

Just as she began to relax, something crashed into Sulle, and the dragon let out a wounded bellow.

Bastards came from below, Sulle said, rocketing further into the heavens.

Looking down, she saw the griffin dropping away doused in blood. *How bad?* she asked fearfully.

I have had worse.

Keegan wanted to call the dragon out. No one ever said they'd had worse and had had worse… at least not from the movies she'd watched.

Vitia and the griffin began to close in again.

Keegan didn't want to fight, but if her hand was forced, so be it. And Vitia deserved it. Reaching for the air paika in her throat, she created a vacuum around the now red-mottled griffin.

The beast gave a terrified shriek and began to plummet to the ground. Just before they hit the earth, Keegan released the magic, letting them land safely. Hopefully, it would serve as a warning that today was not the day to trifle with her; likely the message would be ignored.

Sulle beat his wings heavily, endless grass and river plain stretching underneath them, blanketed in varying degrees of snowfall. Looking back, a thick crimson trail marked their flightpath. This was worse than Keegan had thought.

We may have gone a little too far from help, Keegan noted.

There was no response from the dragon.

Sulle?

The dragon's wing stopped beating and they began hurtling toward the ground.

If she screamed, Keegan couldn't tell against the air roaring past her ears. She reached out to Sulle, pleading for him to beat his wings again. The ground was sickeningly close when he pulled out of the freefall.

I need someplace to land, he said weakly.

Without hesitation, Keegan crushed the earth paika and raised a plateau. No enemy from the ground would be able to reach them there.

Sulle shakily glided onto the plateau, collapsing as his feet touched down, digging troughs into the earth.

Keegan clambered from his back, feeling her stomach sink as she saw the gashes that raked across his abdomen. It was a bloodied mess, and she almost missed the sword protruding from his breast.

"Jesus," she muttered, placing a hand on the wounds and letting magic begin to flow. She wouldn't be able to do much, but she could buy them time. Maybe. Desperately, she sent out a call to Jared and Kade.

I am fine, Sulle lied through his teeth. His eyelids were beginning to droop.

"Let him die," Vitia called from across the plateau.

Keegan whipped around, though her hand on Sulle's stomach didn't move, never stopped sending healing power to him. "Fuck you!"

Sulle opened his maw in preparation to bathe Vitia in fire, a glow already coming from the back of his throat.

"Shut it," Vitia said. There was the grating sound of breaking bone and Sulle's head dropped to the ground lifelessly.

Keegan assumed the dragon's neck had been snapped given the way it twisted at an odd angle. She felt her heart stop painfully but the fire that had once lit Sulle's eyes had been transferred to her—and it was burning brighter than ever. Turning quickly, she drew The Queen Killer, fully intending to bring forth the sword's color from Vitia. "You bitch!"

A switch flipped in Keegan's mind, and she lost control over her body. She charged at Vitia, pouring all of her emotions into a feral scream, raw passion and magic guiding her limbs. She didn't recall actively reaching for her magic, but there it was. It knew what to do and she trusted it.

A fireball began to form between them, and it wasn't until Keegan was within striking range of Vitia that she realized she'd made a mistake—and what a big one it was.

Her body froze mid-stride, falling completely under Vitia's control. Knowing she was playing a dangerous game, that she couldn't maintain the fireball for much longer without consequence, she tried to release the energy but couldn't. From the mirth barely hidden on Vitia's face, this was her doing. The Alvor didn't understand the ramifications of her actions but would shortly.

Keegan watched in horror as the fireball grew and grew and grew. When it finally grew tired of being controlled, it exploded outwards, violently throwing her across the plateau.

As Keegan hit the ground, excruciating pain radiated across her body, reverberating in the depth of her bones.

The arrowhead fully pushed into her flesh, scraping against her spine, drawing a permanent reminder in bone. Her head rang and the clouds and snow above swam sickeningly in spirals laced with colors. Even once the world stopped rotating it was still a maze of stars, colors, and blurs that pounded in her eyes and danced in her ears. She told her body to move, but her synapses were silent. It seemed an eternity before she was able even to let out a strangled groan.

From her dazed position, Keegan watched Vitia struggle to her feet, lurching sideways and landing on her hands and knees. Seeing the blood dripping from her ears, Keegan knew why she was having so much difficulty. But soon enough her equilibrium would be restored and that would mean a world a hurt for Keegan.

Slowly, her neural connections lit up, like a highway in the early morning—sluggish at first but then rushing and vibrant—and she was able to make small movements and take in the pain fully. Vitia was similarly recovering, regaining the ability to at least stand.

In the blast, Keegan had lost The Queen Killer and she painfully moved her head to look for it. She found it lying mere feet from her.

Turning onto her stomach made her feel like death itself was clawing at her bones. The scraping of the arrowhead against her vertebrae as she moved didn't do her any favors, limiting her motion if she wanted to stop the shooting pains that arched down her back. Each inch forward was agonizing, and her fingertips were just brushing the pommel of The Queen Killer when a force pulled her backward by the ankle.

As Keegan watched the sword slip from her grasp, her hopes of surviving going with it, she gave up. She couldn't muster the energy to fight. What was the point?

Darkness covered her eyes and she felt herself being forced onto her back, a scream coming from her lips as the arrowhead scraped along her spine again. Vitia fumbled to remove her chest plate, the cold winter air whisking away the warmth given by the previously trapped sweat.

Her world returned to light, and she stared up at Vitia, who stood above her with a sword poised to end life. Stomach shifting like it would on a rollercoaster, there was pain as Vitia drove the steel into her body and into the ground underneath. After a moment, her stomach settled, and Keegan was shocked to find hardly any blood seeped around the edge of the blade imbedded in her.

"You're wanted alive," Vitia mumbled, stumbling back toward the silver griffin.

It took Keegan longer than it should've through the pain and throbbing in her head to realize what the Alvor had done. Vitia had shifted her organs to be able to stab her without doing catastrophic damage. And now she was stuck like a skewer.

She would've tried to remove the sword, but her body decided to be uncooperative again, her limbs heavy as stone. All she could do was watch as Vitia rummaged through the griffin's saddlebag.

Keegan tried to crush the earth paika, but it seemed to be coated in a layer of grease, making it impossible to grab hold of, let alone break. When she tried to use the other elements, the same was true. Something was blocking her magic.

"Why?" she groaned as Vitia returned, two golden bracelets, slajor manacles, in hand.

"Because my king commanded it. But more importantly, it will hurt Kade."

Keegan knew the slajor manacles were going on, and there was nothing she could do to stop it.

"I'm surprised you haven't tried escaping," Vitia said placidly, drawing out the inevitable, basking in it.

Keegan gave her a flat look that said she had tried to escape... and failed.

The Alvor smiled haughtily. "Seems ether straight into your bloodstream keeps you down."

Keegan gave a confused look, trying to recall when or even how ether might have gotten into her system.

"My blade is soaked in it," explained Vitia, chest puffed out in pride.

"Aw," Keegan responded conceitedly, "the first and last creative thought you'll ever have!"

Vitia's smile faltered and she stooped to clamp the slajor manacles onto Keegan's wrists.

The metal was cool and its effect instantaneous.

Chapter 34

Jared, Kade called franticly, *where are you?*

In the middle of something, was the response he got.

Kade gave it a few seconds before trying again. *Where are you?*

The response was curt and frustrated. *Still in the middle of something!*

In the distance he could see red rain falling underneath Sulle. Blood. They were royally royikox.

His next opponent, the most experienced of the day, pressed him, blade flashing in the snow and sunlight. Kade blocked before pushing back, the bodies littering the ground only making this all the more perilous.

Where are you? Jared came.

In the middle of something, he growled, stepping inside his opponent's guard, and raking his sword across the man's throat.

Given a moment to step away from battle and take in his surroundings, he was dismayed to find only Aron remained in the vicinity. He pushed aside his worry for Reven and Icella; they would be fine—they had to be. Just as Keegan had to be.

Kade sent Jared a mental image of his location.

Headed your way, Jared responded.

Aron used the moment of reprieve to pull arrows from the fallen around him and said, "Keegan is in trouble."

Her message must have been sent to all of them.

Spotting a Merwoman struggling nearby, Aron notched an arrow and felled her opponent. She gave a nod of thanks before jumping into the next battle.

"I know," Kade said, picking his way over, dispatching a man in the process. *Where are you?* he asked Jared.

Look up.

He barely had time to do so before two dragons dropped beside them. The ground trembled as the dragons landed. They snatched up enemies nearby, dousing the area in blood, screams, and flames.

Get on, one of the dragons said impatiently, snapping up another man and flinging him into the chaos around them. Kade cringed at the sound his body made when it hit the ground.

Kade raised a pillar of earth that would put him close enough in height to the dragon's back so he could do as instructed.

"What about me?" Aron called, shooting another arrow into the heart of one of Kolt's men.

Safely between the dragon's shoulder blades, Kade saw Jared sitting on the other dragon, drenched and peppered in as much blood as the rest of them.

"To your left," Jared said as the dragon he rode unfurled its wings and took to the sky.

Kade had just enough time to see a wolf tackle a man and rip his throat out before the dragon beneath him leapt into the air, making him nearly impale himself on one of the spines running down the ridge of its back. Now in the sky, he had to keep reminding himself to not look down—not the easiest of feats. He scanned the sky for Keegan and Sulle but couldn't find the orange dragon anywhere.

Out of the corner of his eye, he noticed a plateau in the distance that hadn't existed before. *Over there,* he directed the dragon.

This can't be good, Jared mumbled.

From what Kade could tell, the silver griffin, and presumably Vitia, were the only Vosjnik on the plateau. He was about to say it could be worse when Sola and Lunos took that as a challenge.

Hearing a caw behind him, Kade looked back to find four griffins whizzing toward them, all but colored streaks and blurs in the air. He cursed and tightened his grip on his sword, reaching for his magic.

I've got this, Jared said. *Go help Keegan.*

Jared and the dragon might be able to hold their own for a while, but soon it would be them being handled. But Keegan was in more imminent danger.

Knowing he had finite time to do something before the Vosjnik cut off their route, he urged the dragon toward the plateau. *Try to come down in Vitia's blind spot.*

I am a dragon, she snarled, *stealth is not exactly something I do!*

Even so, the dragon dipped down to the river plain, grass and snow sweeping into their wake in a fleeting storm. Reaching the face of the plateau, the dragon banked upwards sharply and landed on the edge silently.

Kade clambered off, which was more like sliding down the dragon's slick scales than anything and looked toward Jared. Eight on two didn't exactly seem fair. *Go help Jared, I can handle Vitia.*

The dragon didn't hesitate and leapt back into the sky, releasing a roar that had griffins and riders pausing for the barest of moments. In seconds, the dragon was invested in the fray.

Turning from the aerial battle, Kade was faced with the body of Sulle, still oozing blood from the shredded remains of his stomach, and a griffin lazily licking blood from its paws like a cat. He slowly inched forward, ready to render the silver beast useless.

Without looking up, the griffin said, *I am not going to stop you from killing her. In fact, I encourage it.*

Deciding to leave the beast alone as a potential ally, Kade crept toward Vitia; the Alvor was too busy tormenting Keegan to notice him.

Hot blood, spiked with rage, coursed through Kade's veins. Vitia's torments would cease.

As Vitia straightened up from leaning over his sister, he felt no remorse in shooting an earthen spike through the back of her neck that came out her throat just underneath her chin. Blood dribbled from her mouth in a steady flow, dripping onto Keegan's face. His sister wiped it away, but more kept coming.

"I told you I'd kill you," Kade said, coming into Vitia's view.

There was a fleeting moment of panic on Vitia's face before her eyes glassed over and her body slumped. And that was the end of that. He grabbed her by the shirt collar, removed the spike, and tossed her body aside like a rag.

Kade had imagined her death feeling righteous, instead, he felt nothing. Her death wouldn't bring back Cassidy. The only thing it did was prevent her from hurting more innocent people in the future—and that he could live with.

Looking down at Keegan's blood-splattered face, she was still working to process things. It was then he noticed the sword in her stomach and felt his heart sink. If she wasn't dead yet, she would be soon. He had caused wounds like this before and had never seen anyone survive. Not without a magically gifted healer nearby.

Like the one he had just killed. Like the one that was the only healer for probably several miles. Like the one that was their only chance of Keegan surviving.

"You look like you've seen a ghost," Keegan said finally. Though pain burdened her words, it wasn't the kind that said one was dying.

"You- you," he stammered. "Why aren't you dying?"

She raised her eyebrows in mock shock. "Geez, I'd've thought you'd be excited about that! Vitia shifted my organs before stabbing me, so everything's intact. Which means this sword is gonna be a right *bitch* to get out."

She already had a plan. Of course, she did. Kade couldn't help but shake his head.

"You'll be fine on your own." He gave a snide grin, "I've seen you worm your way out of worse."

Keegan held up a hand showing him the slajor manacles. Before he could complain, she added, "Vitia soaked her sword in ether, too. Apparently, if you put it straight into my bloodstream, it does the job."

Groaning, he asked, "How do you want it done?"

"Okay, you're gonna have to use metal magic. All you have to do is dull the edges of the sword so we can pull it out without my insides becoming confetti."

He was barely listening, his eyes drawn to the battle in the sky. Blood fell like rain and the dragons didn't seem to be doing well.

"I'd love to, but we've got bigger problems," Kade said, bracing as the dragon he'd ridden slammed into the plateau, skidded across the ground, and crashed into Sulle's body. Slowly, the two dragons—both now corpses—tumbled over the edge. There was a moment's silence before a shattering thud marked the end of their fall.

In the sky, Jared and the other dragon were still fighting, though two griffins had pulled away, presumably to dispatch him. "Stay here," he commanded

Keegan, grabbing his sword and walking to meet the Vosjnik.

Keegan shrieked, panic heavy in her words, "Wait! Kade! Come back here!"

《《《 》》》

Keegan watched her brother run to meet the descending Vosjnik and griffins and let her head fall back, immediately regretting the action as pain lanced through her skull. While she understood the need to deal with their enemies, she wasn't exactly looking forward to remaining a skewer. But without the ability to do something about the situation, sit there she would.

From her position, it was difficult to see much of what was going on, making it easy for Braxton to saunter over unnoticed. He seemed to have been spared almost entirely from the casualties of battle and she envied him. She might've called to Kade for help if she thought it would do anything.

"Don't," she said as Braxton wrapped a hand around the hilt of the sword, "that'll kill me." God, she felt like the stone from the legend of King Arthur.

"Who says you are wanted alive?" Braxton asked. Cruelty didn't suit him, and it was easy to see it was a façade.

"Well, given the fact Vitia gave me these bad boys," she responded, showing him the slajor manacles, "and told me I'm wanted alive…"

"Fair. If I cannot pull it out, what would you suggest?"

"Can you control metal?"

"Hardly on my best day and definitely not while wearing this." He held up a hand to show her the manacle he wore.

She didn't see one on his other wrist and gathered a single manacle must act as a dampener rather than an inhibitor. "You're gonna have to try. It's just like earth magic, just with a substance a lot less malleable."

"Earth is not metal."

"Look, I don't have the time to explain the science of it; just try. All you have to do is dull the blade. It won't be fun on my end either way, but one means I'm dead and the other means I'm pissed off and in pain."

Braxton's expression said he was contemplating just pulling the sword out—possibly to save her greater pain in the coming future. But she'd take her chances; she couldn't help herself if she was dead. Yet, there was no doubt if she survived this, things were only going to get worse—*far* worse.

"If you want me to die, go ahead, rip it out. If you want me to live, *do as I say*," Keegan snapped, not liking the indecisive look on the prince's face.

In the end, Braxton decided the fat lady hadn't sung. He placed a hand gently around the blade and concentrated. Eventually, he pulled the sword from Keegan's abdomen before she could protest.

There was a sharp pain as the blade sliced through her. When the sword was fully removed, she looked down to find she wasn't bleeding as badly as she should be. She placed a hand over the wound in an attempt to staunch the hemorrhaging—little good it would do realistically.

Braxton gave her a sympathetic look for all of half a second before pulling her to her feet. The movement made her feel like her innards were liable to try and slip from the gash in her belly and back. Once on her feet, a knife was placed at her throat, forcing her chin upwards.

At some point, Jared had joined the fray on the plateau. The odds still weren't in their favor, but it certainly increased their chances of walking way. Though, likely not in Keegan's case. And maybe not for

Jared and Kade either if she was successfully used as leverage.

She and Braxton stood there while Jared and Kade continued to fight against four of the Vosjnik. "Try yelling at them," Keegan suggested, realizing they'd never be noticed until one side had defeated the other. She was beginning to feel lightheaded, though couldn't tell if it was from blood loss, tiredness, or head trauma—or a culmination of the three.

Braxton took her advice and called for everyone to cease fighting.

Keegan clenched her eyes, the booming of his voice next to her ear causing pain to erupt and the world to begin spinning more than it already was.

It took Braxton a few tries before anyone noticed. Once someone did, getting the others' attention wasn't hard.

When Kade finally paused, Brennian took the opportunity to send him sprawling with a well-aimed punch to the jaw. Kade quickly pulled a dagger from his boot, not prepared to give in yet. Jared, on the other hand, dropped his sword and nonchalantly held his hands up.

"Keep fighting," Keegan urged, staring at her brother. For as long as Kade fought, it would buy her time—for what... she was still working on that.

As Braxton worked to make it seem like he'd do her harm, pressing the knife into her neck, enough so that blood would well from a seam if he pushed any further, she felt along her cuisse for the micro indentation. When Keegan pressed down, she gave a groan to hide the telltale click of a hidden knife popping out of place. No one noticed as she hid it against her wrist.

"Let her go," Jared said robotically.

"You know he can't do that," Keegan said, willing Kade to do something besides stand there and look angry.

"Just like he can't kill me. Not yet anyway." As she finished speaking, she drove the dagger into Braxton's hip.

The prince let out a ferocious yell, writhing in pain, causing her to release the knife, leaving it imbedded in his side.

She only realized how much trouble she was in when she felt the knife at her neck drop and the world spin around her. Slajor manacle or not, Braxton was pissed, and she was going to feel the full, unadulterated force of it.

The twisting world jerked to a halt, and she was slammed into something solid that hadn't been there before. The arrow in her back scraped against her spine and she screamed. The cry prolonged itself as a force shoved against her shoulder, shattering the bones within its vicinity.

A hand grabbed her throat and applied pressure. Her feet were lifted from the ground as all sense fled from Braxton. Her feeble attempts to break free weren't going to be enough, but she had to try.

It didn't take long for darkness to encroach on her vision, and it was an effort to simply hang there under Braxton's mercy.

Then, the world dropped, sending her into freefall. When her body hit the ground, she was able to see a pair of feet, two pairs, struggling. She willed herself to fight the darkness, but her strength had fled.

«««« »»»»

Aron watched Kade and Jared fly away and cursed them for leaving him with nothing but a wolf. But it was better than his own two feet. And should the wolf ever find out he wished for a dragon… he did not want to imagine what would happen. His neck and spine throbbed from where

Braxton's arrows had hit Keegan, but he was able to push past the sensation. Mostly because there was no choice.

The wolf gave a ferocious snarl as she ripped through a man's throat while he stared into the distance.

I have not got all day, the wolf barked, blood dripping from between her teeth.

Quickly, Aron slung his bow across his shoulders and climbed onto the wolf's back, twining his fingers through her thick black fur.

They tore through the battlefield, screams of terror and death chasing after them like leaves on a windy day. Occasionally, the wolf stopped to help a friend in need, splattering her fur and Aron further in red.

He quickly lost sight of the dragons and it felt like a lifetime before they reached the outskirts of the battle. Looking into the distance he could see a newly formed plateau, but who knew how long it would take to reach it.

Aron pointed toward the plateau and the wolf took off.

A sudden pain exploded across Aron's abdomen, making his head swim and his grip on the wolf's fur tightened as he struggled to keep in daylight's grasp. Carefully, he threw up a wall to keep Keegan's pain from incapacitating him as well.

Faster than he could have imagined, the wolf closed the distance to the plateau, the world a constant blur around him, which was amplified by what Keegan was feeling; combined, it made him sick to his stomach. Thankfully, there was nothing in his belly to retch up.

Slowly, the shadow of the plateau shrouded them in mild twilight and the wolf slowed. *You are on your own from here.*

He slid off the beast's back, and thanking her, stumbled to the face of the rock wall, Keegan's pain delaying the commands given to his body. It was worse than being drunk.

The wolf hardly spared him a second glance before racing back toward the battle. *Kill the bastards.*

Staring up the face of the plateau, he cursed. Everyone forgot he possessed no magical abilities—which was easy to do when you looked at who he spent his time with. With nothing to be done about the situation, he began to climb. He had never considered himself a good climber, but Sola and Lunos gifted him in this moment and slowly the top of the cliff drew near.

A slicing pain cut through his stomach again and he lost his footing, debris clacking against the rockface. Desperately, he pulled himself onto a small ledge, his life still flashing before his eyes. Taking several steep breaths, he steadied himself before continuing to climb. Pushing through the pain brought a hazy film over his eyes, but he told himself there was no choice and he was able to continue inch by painful inch.

Now at the lip of the plateau, Aron paused, knowing better than to jump into anything without knowing what was happening. Peering cautiously over the edge, it seemed he would not be jumping into a fight; Kade and Jared had been beaten. And Keegan was held captive.

Blood dripped down Kade's chin from a busted lip while Brennian held a sword to the small of his back. Rage brewed in Kade's hazel eyes; he was not ready to give up and was likely plotting ways in which to give reign to Lunos. Jared, on the other hand, was at ease, his hands held up in compliance. Braxton held a knife to Keegan's throat. She was like her brother, unwilling to submit, and he watched her stealthily pop one of the hidden knives from her cuisse.

Knowing Keegan was going to put that knife to use, Aron sprang into action to make the best of her chaos. As he pulled himself over the ledge, there was a ferocious cry of pain from his brother; looking, he saw the knife protruding from Braxton's hip.

Rationality left Braxton and he spun Keegan around, slamming her into a wall he raised.

Aron felt Keegan's entire shoulder splinter and his own arm felt heavy and impossible to use.

Still seeing red, Braxton placed a hand on Keegan's throat and lifted her. She feebly kicked and clawed at him to no avail.

Knowing she would not have long before succumbing to asphyxiation, Aron ignored the effect of air deprivation on Keegan and sprinted across the plateau. He meant to tackle Braxton, but it was more like stumbling into his brother as his falsely oxygen-deprived brain began to lose strength. But it did the trick.

Aron tried to grab the knife in Braxton's hip, but could not get his fingers around it, almost as if there was a force preventing him. His brother quickly gained the upper hand and slammed his head into the ground. Stars and colors flared across his vision and by the time the world cleared, he too was routed.

"Oh, brother," Braxton said quietly, "I wish you had not done that." Looking at the Vosjnik, he ordered, "Bind their hands."

Chapter 35

Even from up in the clouds, Nico could hear the screams of the dying, like waves on a beach during a storm, that plagued the battlefield. They made him cringe, want to crawl into a dark hole. But that wasn't what a man did in battle.

On Ima, Mara sat, eyes locked on the bloodshed happening below, her face pale as the snow floating around them.

Nico caught motion out of the corner of his eye and watched from afar as a morphing block of chaos formed in the sky.

What is that? he asked, already urging Harker to investigate.

Nico, Mara called after him, *Come back! I don't think that's—*

He shut her out. None of this was a good idea, but he was too far invested.

Getting closer, he identified four griffins and two dragons. He watched as one of the dragons had its throat bitten by Crowlin and dropped to the ground, momentarily pulling the griffin landward with it. The dragon careened toward a plateau, but Nico's attention was already focused on the remaining dragon, spotting the rider on its back. He almost didn't recognize the rider—so much had changed in two seasons—but it was Jared.

Before Nico could react, a force slammed into Harker and the griffin screamed in fright as he began cartwheeling through the air. Once Harker settled, Nico looked back to find Ima pulling away.

You can't help, Mara said, maneuvering Ima between he and the aerial battle.

I have to! That's my brother!

You can't, was all she said.

He could. And he would.

Nico fully opened his mind to Harker, and the griffin obliged his wishes, pulling in his wings and dropping toward the ground like an arrow. He knew they'd have to lose or incapacitate Mara and Ima before doing anything, and he preferred it not be the latter. But he would do it for Jared without a third thought.

Ima dove after them, her black eyes glinting with frustration in the weak wintery sunlight.

Nico pushed Harker through various loops and dives in an effort to make the girls fall back. When they'd first started training, the hatchlings had been equals, but now Harker was almost a foot taller than his nest mate. However, being smaller and lighter gave Ima an advantage when it came to agility. Nico knew the air was where Ima and Mara excelled, but there was one place he always beat them.

He urged Harker toward the ground, the griffin never balking for he knew what Nico had in mind. At the last second, Harker leveled out and though Ima tried to imitate him, she was moving faster than the golden male and collided with the earth. Through a spray of soil and snow, Ima gave a shrill cry that hurt Nico's ears, but he didn't have time to worry about them right now. Jared needed his help more than they did.

Looking back to the sky, his heart dropped as he watched the dragon his brother rode falter. After a moment, the dragon seemed to pull itself from Lunos's grasp, unfurling its wings to descend onto the plateau.

Jared dismounted and the dragon made to take to the skies again, releasing a spurt of fire. It succeeded, but only just, before the effort was too much and it plummeted to the ground, dead.

Though Harker raced toward the cliff, they were a fair distance from it and Nico feared they wouldn't be fast enough. As that spark of doubt began to pervade his mind, a lump stuck in his throat. He worked to push the worrying thoughts away; Jared wouldn't have survived this long without some kind of skill and an old god looking after him. He had to believe those two things would keep him alive a little bit longer.

Suddenly, Harker banked to the left and Nico almost lost his seat. He precariously found himself hanging onto the rim of the saddle, one leg hoisted above his head half off the saddle. With a strength he didn't know he had, Nico righted himself and hunkered low on Harker's back, his heart racing in his chest.

What are you doing? he demanded frantically to the griffin.

Keeping you safe, Mara said through Harker's mind.

Nico reeled; he'd known Mara was powerful, but to speak through another's mind while controlling them…

Fight her! Nico implored the griffin, choosing to believe determination could trump Mara.

Harker strained to shake free of her control, his movements erratic as two minds fought to control one body. In the end, the griffin's wings were not his own and they did Mara's bidding, slowly bringing them back to where the girls had crashed into the snow-covered earth.

Feeling like he had no other choice, Nico reached for his own magic. *I'm sorry,* he told Mara. *I never wanted it to come to this.*

Confusion emanated from her, but only for a moment before disappearing along with her control. He felt sick to his stomach, knowing what he'd done. But it'd been necessary. He had to help Jared.

Did you kill her? Harker asked, picking up on his guilt.

No. I knocked her out, Nico admitted timidly.

How?

Rock to the head.

Concern for Mara and Ima was pushed from their minds as Harker raced toward the plateau again. As the griffin landed hastily, Nico jumped from his back, rolling to keep from breaking his neck.

Getting to his feet, Nico's heart sank. Guthrie had a sword to Jared's neck while his hands were bound behind his back. Kade was similarly restrained by Brennian. Across the plateau, Keegan lay at the face of a wall, blood seeping in a growing rivulet from her stomach. Braxton had a man with black hair pinned and Nico wondered if this was the third Alagard brother he'd heard about; the resemblance between them was striking if they were related. There was no saving his brother or anyone else it seemed.

Spotting him, Braxton said, "Stop him," to no one in particular.

Dax stepped forward and grabbed Nico's arm, twisting it behind his back; it instantly took him back to a similar time. He had been younger then, weak, and unable to save his mother. He was stronger now, more experienced, and he would save Jared.

Nico fought against Dax's grip but was unable to break free. "Let him go!" Nico yelled, half a command, half a plea. His shoulder throbbed, the joint warning him of what would happen if he didn't stop thrashing.

"I cannot do that," Braxton said, catching a length of rope Dax tossed him. He forced the man he was pinning onto his stomach, tying his hands behind his back. He approached Nico, "I am sorry."

"Don't be sorry, do something," he begged.

In the background, Jared looked like he'd seen a spirit. Tears began sliding down his cheeks and he fell to his knees.

"Get him out of here," Braxton ordered Dax.

Nico bucked and fought as Dax struggled to drag him toward where Harker stood, his eyes exuding confusion, concern, and sympathy. "No!" He finally managed to break loose but didn't get far; a blinding force hit the side of his head and he remembered nothing more.

««« »»»

Jared didn't resist as Guthrie wrenched his arms behind his back and bound them; this was all part of letting Keegan go. He just hoped he and Kade were also wanted alive. They were in much better shape for facilitating an escape—if they were given a later. And if not… then this was the stupidest thing he'd ever done.

He wasn't surprised when an ether-soaked rag was held over his face. The air was sucked from his lungs in a burning gasp, leaving him breathless and in pain. His magic wasn't slow to seep away, and a horrible feeling wrenched in his gut as it slipped from his grasp, like he was losing a limb. As he coughed and wheezed, Dax and Brennian set to restraining Kade, and it was several painful minutes before he was finally cowed.

To his right a golden griffin landed on the plateau and skidded across the ground. Something—someone—leapt from its back and rolled to break their momentum. When the person stood, his heart froze.

Nico was alive, well, and had grown. The hair on his jaw had begun to show and soon he'd need to learn to shave. Jared felt a constriction in his chest as he realized

Nico would likely learn from a stranger rather than family.

Braxton noticed Nico and ordered, "Stop him."

Dax was quick to react, and Nico fought against him fiercer than a beast caught in a trap, yelling, "Let him go!"

"I cannot do that," Braxton said, catching the length of rope Dax tossed to him. He forced Aron onto his stomach and bound his hands. The prince left Aron where he was and went to stand before Nico. "I am sorry."

"Don't be sorry, do something," Nico begged.

Jared fell to his knees, tears sliding down his cheeks. If he was to be taken alive, he was certain Nico would be forced to do him harm and he didn't know who would be pained more. And if not, his brother didn't deserve to see him die; he'd already seen too much horror for one so young.

"Get him out of here," Braxton ordered churlishly.

Nico wrestled against Dax as he was dragged toward the golden griffin. "No!"

His brother managed to break free from his captor's hold, taking a few steps before Dax's fist met his temple and he toppled over. Without a word, Dax scooped Nico up and draped him over the griffin's back.

"Head back," Braxton ordered the Vosjnik. They gave him confused looks but clambered onto the griffins when the prince roared, "That was an order." Just before the griffins took to the sky, he added, "Niyth, stay behind."

Aron began trying to stand. As he made it to his knees, earthen spikes rose from every direction and pressed around his neck.

A moment later, Jared found himself in a similar position.

"Kneel," Braxton said, approaching Kade who'd been much quicker to find his feet.

Kade snarled and spat on Braxton's boot.

Sighing, Braxton came behind Kade and kicked him in the back of the knee. Kade stumbled forward and too found spikes at his throat.

With them all restrained, Braxton took the time to assess his own injuries. A pained grunt escaped his lips as he pulled Keegan's knife from his hip with a sick squelch. The wound dribbled blood but he didn't bother trying to stop it. From the looks of it, it was a flesh wound; it was a shame Keegan had only aimed to injure.

Braxton walked across the plateau and picked up Keegan's bloody sword. "Who solved the riddle of the Queen Killer?"

"It was Keegan," Jared answered. Her power might be a threat, but her knowledge could be a tool. And he was willing to give any incentive to keep her breathing.

"Impressive." Braxton marveled at the weapon before taking the sheath from Keegan and slinging the belt over his shoulder. "I hope one day she can reclaim it. I truly wish none of this had happened. Please know that I was only trying to keep Nico and the griffins alive."

Jared wanted to hate the prince but couldn't. If this man was working to protect Nico—whom he had no reason or duty to do anything for—he owed him a debt. "I understand. I can only hope one day I am able to hold my brother again."

"So do I," Braxton said quietly. Taking a deep breath, he headed toward his own brother, lowered the earthen spines, and made him mount the silver griffin.

Jared was surprised Aron didn't fight back, as if he trusted Braxton to deliver him to Sola rather than Lunos. Maybe they would live to see the other side of this.

"Follow the others," Braxton instructed the griffin.

The beast took to the sky, and they watched it melt into the snow-showered horizon.

There was a tense moment of silence before Jared realized something. With only one griffin left, he and Kade were not going to leave this plateau.

Jared had never imagined it was his duty to die, but if it meant his family and Keegan survived, he was ready. Dare he say he might even deserve it for willing let Keegan go to the enemy. But that didn't mean he'd go quietly or try to prevent the inevitable.

"It doesn't have to be this way," he said.

"I wish that were so," Braxton said regretfully, "but this has been the only way since my father died. And this is the only way to protect your brother. He is not blood, but…"

"Protect him, since I can't," Jared requested, his voice barely more than a whisper.

A lump seemed to be stuck in Braxton's throat as he nodded in response.

"And what about my sister?" Kade rasped desperately, his eyes wide and akin to a cornered animal's.

Guilt flooded Braxton's eyes as he said nothing and went to stand behind Jared. Taking the knife that had once been part of Keegan's armor and later resided in his hip, he placed it against Jared's neck.

Jared could imagine the prince pulling the blade along his throat. How the blood that would flow down his neck would be warm and run like velvet. And how it would feel to choke then finally succumb to Lunos.

The line of steel against his throat was cool and slick. It was fitting that Keegan's weapon would be the one to end his betrayal. Jared closed his eyes so whoever found him wouldn't be haunted by his glassy stare. He felt something press against his palm and thought nothing of it until Braxton stood stock still, as if waiting. When Jared investigated, it was a knife, tucked into the prince's boot.

When Jared didn't move further, Braxton pushed his foot closer to his body. Slowly, Jared pulled the knife from the prince's boot.

"It will be more torturous for you both to know Keegan will not die here," Braxton said abruptly, walking away, as if recalling something important. "She will die, painfully, likely at the hands of Kolt." He picked Keegan up and slung her over the remaining griffin's back.

The prince took his time securing Keegan to the bronze beast, giving Jared plenty of time to saw through his bonds. Wrenching his hands free, he dove toward Kade and sliced through the ropes restraining him.

Noticing they were finally free, Braxton swung onto the griffin, urging it into the sky.

Both sides had been deliberate in their betrayal. Braxton had a reason for letting them escape, just as Jared had one for letting Keegan be taken. But the better question was, would their sacrifices be worth it in the end?

Jared watched as the griffin became a blot in the distance, shame and guilt pounding against his body. The deed was done, but was Keegan truly going to survive? Would this ensure the future of the world? He'd taken a blind chance and could only hope they prevailed.

In anger, Kade took the dagger that'd been their salvation and hurled it fruitlessly at Braxton. He knew it wouldn't do any good, but the pointless act helped relieve guilt. When it missed by thousands of feet, Kade gave an anguished scream, every emotion the man had ever refused to acknowledge coming forth.

A striking force against his jaw caused Jared to stumble. Turning toward Kade, he stared at his fist the moment before it connected with his nose. Several more times Kade hit him, screaming curses and insults. Jared didn't stop him; he deserved it—for willingly letting his friend be taken. But he would do it over if it meant she survived, that all of them survived.

When Kade was finished, Jared's face had gone numb, and he was content to stare up at the falling snow. It was coming quicker now and there was a chance this would be his death shroud. They were far from the battle, and no one knew where they'd gone. The plateau's escarpment wouldn't be kind to them on the way down and it was a wonder Aron had managed to scale it. They would have to wait for rescue, or until the ether wore off—or until they froze.

Chapter 36

Though it was a small victory, Braxton would count his blessings where they came. He could plausibly say he had tried to kill Jared and Kade. There would be some form of punishment, no doubt, but he would accept it, knowing there was still a glimmer of hope.

Myrish quickly caught up to the others and Braxton noted Mara's absence, but assumed she was doing as instructed—not participating in battle—unlike Nico.

"Tell them to land," he called to Myrish, the slajor manacle again preventing mental communication.

The griffins descended toward the river plains slowly, circling like vultures. Though the sun was hours from casting them into the despair of darkness, he was not about to expedite the inevitable.

On the ground, everyone was slow to dismount, their movements stiff, as if realizing the gravity of what they had accomplished. There was no cheering though; they had thwarted Lunos and that itself was celebration enough.

The journey to Agrielha would take several days—if he stalled; plenty of time for something to go wrong—or so he hoped.

He felt Keegan shift and placed a hand on her back in preparation to stop her from sliding off the griffin as she regained consciousness. When she groaned, there was no doubt she was coming to. Braxton wondered if she was going to fight and if he should have restrained her. It was all a fine balance when it came to sabotaging himself.

Keegan seemed to quickly realize the predicament she was in, for the knuckles of the fingers she twined through Myrish's feathers turned white and she didn't try to throw herself off the griffin's back. Though maybe the latter was because of her injuries. Still clinging onto the griffin, she slowly slid down, her feet unsteadily finding solid ground. When she released her hold, her body gave out and she hit the ground with a pained scream.

Before Keegan could get to her feet, Brennian was dragging her away by the hair. Almost literally as her battered body refused to support itself.

"Let her go," Braxton said quickly. As he dismounted, his hip roared in pain.

Brennian gave him a confused look before doing as instructed.

Another cry came from Keegan, and she curled into a ball, left arm cradled against her chest, while her right hand pressed against the seam in her stomach.

As Braxton approached Niyth, Aron began streaming curses at him. It was hard to let them roll off his back. Never had he thought he would receive such hate from his brother. "It is either I fight you or I tend to Keegan," he finally told Aron.

Aron immediately quieted and clenched his jaw.

Braxton knew that look—his brother would do anything to save Keegan, just like *he* would do anything for Nico and the griffins. Aron let himself be pulled from Niyth's back and Braxton created a post to which he could be tethered. Later, when the others had fallen asleep, he would loosen the ropes and see if Keegan had taught his brother a thing or two about ingenuity.

Turning back to the girl, he was alarmed to find Guthrie and Brennian with their swords to her throat. The two were so afraid of her that a bead of red tricked down her neck.

A wordless cry for help rested on her lips while her eyes begged for swift mercy. He had heard a lot about Keegan—heard the fire in her hair did not just reside there, but it might simply be a story. While there was red in her locks—and not just blood—no fire burnt in her eyes, or her heart. She was broken and scared. This was the girl he had met back in April—not the savior of the world.

"Stand down," he ordered.

Guthrie and Brennian obeyed, giving him confused and angry glances. They had seen what this girl could do, especially when cornered and considered powerless. They had every right to be wary and afraid, but with her injuries and the slajor manacles, she was exactly that, cornered and powerless.

"Find something to do," he commanded the staring members of the Vosjnik, kneeling beside Keegan. "A fire would be nice. Maybe tend to your injuries?"

"Just kill me," Keegan told him quietly. Her voice was weary. "That's the end goal anyway, ain't it?"

"My brother wants to kill you himself." He had not thought any more fear could permeate her features. "Let us focus on something else. Your injuries—"

"Are bad," Keegan cut him off, shifting and barely managing to stifle a groan. "But I'm sure y'all have injuries to deal with, too. And what would be the point; y'all plan on killing me soon anyway."

He was shocked by her concern for the rest of them. "Why do you care… about us?"

She shrugged as best she could with one shoulder, wincing.

"What can I do for you right now?"

Keegan raised her eyebrows as her gaze flicked to the side.

"*Aside* from releasing you."

"Bandages, hot water, a sling, and remove the fucking arrow in my back."

"That can be managed. If I leave you here, do you promise not to run?"

"I honestly don't think I *can*," she returned with a minute shake of the head.

Hoping she might try anyway, Braxton gathered bandages and tore a blanket to fashion into a sling. Taking snow, he packed it into a pot and set it on the edge of the fire. When he returned, he said, "We will start with the arrow."

Cutting a small v from the nape of her shirt, he was dismayed to find her back was a waterfall of red. It was hard to tell where the arrow was, but eventually found the entry point by wiping away the gore.

Gently, he inspected the wound, pulling apart the flesh to try and see inside. The arrow was buried deep. He was going to need more hands than he had... and more magic than he was currently capable of. "Nico," he called.

The boy was quickly at his side.

"Have you ever worked with metal?" Keegan asked, a fearful look in her hazel eyes.

"A little," Nico answered.

"Okay, that's fine—great, actually."

"Do you want me to practice on something else first? Prove I can do it."

"Worst you can do is kill me." Under her breath she muttered, "Which might be really helpful right about now."

Ignoring the comment, Nico stood over Keegan. He held out his hand and his face took on a look of immense concentration. Without warning the arrow shot out from her back, sailing off into the plains, accompanied by a scream.

Keegan took deep breaths to regain her composure while tears glided down flushed cheeks. "The hot water."

Nico fetched the pot, while Braxton wiped away the fresh blood. Thankfully, the bleeding quickly stopped; with no good way to bandage the wound, they would be forced to leave it uncovered.

The next thing they needed to deal with was the puncture to her abdomen. Though the puncture did not look bad, it was impossible to say that they would not find Keegan dead come the morn; infection was their greatest concern here.

Braxton could have bound her torso with her sitting down, but he could do a better job if she stood. Through the entire process, she leaned heavily against Nico, as if standing were painful.

When she was allowed to sit again, she said, "I think my ankle's broken."

"When did that happen?"

"Who knows?"

"Let us deal with your shoulder and then I will take a look at it."

"Don't. My boot's doing it more good on than off."

Moving on to her shoulder, he carefully cut away her left sleeve. "How so? I cannot set your ankle with a boot on." Braxton felt his stomach churn as he looked at her shoulder; it was so deformed he was afraid to call it a shoulder. He reached out a hand to feel it.

"Don't," Keegan snapped preemptively, tensing and shying away. "Keeping the boot on will act as a quasi-splint. And if we take it off, the chances of getting it back on are slim to none."

He motioned to her shoulder, "I… I am not sure what I can do for this."

Keegan sighed and glanced at her shoulder. The longer she stared at it, the more a green tinge colored her face. "The *one time*," she said in barely a whisper, "Vitia would've been helpful." Steeling herself, she looked Braxton in the eye. "I don't think there's much we can do. Just help me immobilize it."

She set about giving instructions on how to position her arm across her chest, her hand at the opposite shoulder, and how to wind the bandages around her body and arm to immobilize the joint. Her knowledge of what to do was shocking and made him wonder how she had come by the information.

When done securing her arm, he said, "You know I have to restrain you."

"I'm not going to run. Can't really," she added, wiggling her foot. By the grimace she gave, she regretted the movement.

"Even so…" He thought for a moment. "Best I can do is have you sleep against a griffin. Stop touching them at any point…"

"I can agree to that," Keegan said tiredly. She seemed to have aged over the course of the day.

Scooping her up, he took her to Crowlin.

As they approached, the dark gray griffin unfurled her wing, allowing Keegan to be placed against her side. Then gingerly, she wrapped her wing over the girl like a mother hen.

«««« »»»»

Through the swirling gray clouds and falling snow, the sun was hard-pressed to give them light, and her ability to do so faded with each second as she sank lower beneath the earth. The world around Lucas was doused in colorless atrocity aside from the vibrant stains that made them thank Sola for her blessing and bringing horrid visions to the fronts of their minds. He trudged through the gore that had become the ground, doing his best to ignore it, but it would still haunt his sleep—for many years to come… if he were that lucky.

Part of him wanted to pretend he hadn't caused a measure of this tragedy. But there had been no choice—aside from death. And while what he had done might haunt him, he would not regret it.

Other survivors and victors were also dazedly walking across the battlefield. Some called out for friends desperately. Some found them and knelt beside them in their final moments. Others closed the eyes of friends so they might be spared from seeing more violence. The rest said nothing, simply working their way back to a place to sleep, forget, survive.

Lucas found himself amongst the first group; though he didn't call out for friends and family, his eyes scanned every face he stepped over, praying they weren't his brothers. It wasn't long before he stopped seeing the faces, stopped trying to look for Carter and Jared amongst the fallen, instead hoping they'd be waiting for him. It wasn't long before he stopped seeing at all, letting his body mindlessly forge a path.

Suddenly, a hand grabbed his ankle, stopping him in his tracks, nearly making him fall. He was about to shake it off, leave the wounded to someone else, when he saw to whom it belonged.

He dropped down to his haunches, a renewed vitality rushing through him. "Carter!"

His brother tried to say something but the only thing that came forth was a dribble of blood that trickled over a well-marked path from the corner of his mouth.

Another man laid atop him, and Lucas worked to shove the body off, his feet scrabbling to find purchase in the muddy, churned up earth. When he finally had his brother free of the dead weight, Lucas saw the red slick across Carter's torso and felt bile rising in his throat. "Help! Somebody, help!" he screamed frantically.

Several people began picking their way over, some with more urgency than others.

"You're not going to die," Lucas said, taking his brother's hand.

It shook; Carter didn't believe him.

It was hard for him to believe it.

It seemed years before help reached them and all sound had fled from the earth, leaving them in the pristine limbo between Sola and Lunos. There was a quick discussion amongst those who had come and then hands were picking Carter up, carrying him toward help. But only the old gods knew if they'd be fast enough.

«««   »»»

The dragon's feet had hardly touched the ground before Kade was sliding off its back. No one stopped him as he stormed through the camp. Currently, it was all he could do to keep his emotions bottled… to keep them contained to his own head. There was though the distinct possibility they weren't in check, and everyone was giving him space so they might retain their heads.

He desperately wanted to punch Jared but doubted he'd make it three feet once someone realized he intended harm to their leader. And he'd already done exactly that, and it hadn't made him feel any better. In fact, it'd done the exact opposite; now he had to see Jared's pathetic face and know that *that* was his fault too. Part of him knew Jared had made what he thought was the only choice, what was right. But that didn't lessen the anger, the hurt, the guilt. They had still betrayed Keegan in what was potentially the worst way feasible.

And he was donpox at so many others, too. Caius for marking his sister for death. Braxton for being too weak to do something about Kolt. Keegan for being such an easy target. Sola and Lunos for everything else.

So much guilt and hate pounded in Kade's veins, he might as well have drowned in it. But for as much as he wanted to place the blame on everyone else's shoulders, *he* had let it happen. When everything had come to a head, *he* despaired and given up. *He* let this happen. This was *his* fault.

Storming into his tent, he wiped away a tear that had managed to slip past his fragile shell. He tried to hold back the rest, but the dam had burst. Kade sank to his knees, agony ripping at his heart. Keegan and he may have been like oil and water—but she was family, *his* family. And he had willingly failed her. He was alone. And it was his fault. This was like losing his parents all over again, but, somehow, it hurt worse.

"Kade," a quiet voice said from the twilight darkening the corners of his tent. "Sola and Lunos…"

"Get out," he snarled, rising to his feet. He couldn't let Icella see him like this. *No one* could see him like this.

The Mermaid slowly came from the shadows. "No."

Spittle flew off his lips. "Get out!"

He took gasping, ragged breaths as Icella approached him, no hesitation, resentment, or pity in her eyes. She inspected him visually before wrapping her arms around him.

"Keegan," he choked.

The tears returned in a torrent, and he sank to the ground again, Icella going with him. It helped; she was a safe shore in a storm, a hand in the darkness pulling him toward the light.

He wasn't sure how long they sat there, but not even the chill of winter was enough to move him. And he was exhausted—the kind that left him completely uncaring and practically comatose.

When his sobs subsided, Icella pulled back slightly. Gently, she wiped his cheeks with her thumb. "Let us get you cleaned up; you are covered in blood."

He didn't react, too afraid of what horrible new emotion his guilt would bring or what self-accusation would come from his mouth. But he would deserve every destructive word.

Icella pulled a tub—where it had come from, he had no idea—to the center of the tent and had it filled and steaming in seconds. She had been... prepared. Maybe not for his breakdown, but for the gore and blood.

The Mermaid endeavored to pull him to his feet, struggling to do so with him acting as a dead weight. Yet, she managed. As she gracefully undid the clasps of armor, she spoke soothing words; what they were he hadn't the slightest, but they helped him enter a kind of trance—one where thinking ceased. Where he could just exist. As each piece of armor was pulled away, Icella put them down quietly, as if afraid the sound would break him. It would take far less than that to destroy him.

As Icella pulled his breastplate off, he was forced to look at the Tavin sigil. Keegan had chosen wrong. She was the hawk that never gave up. He was worthless.

He didn't stop Icella from removing his clothing. She was already seeing him in his darkest hour—what did it matter if she saw his body? His worthless human body that lived for a blip. His worthless body that had given his sister to the person trying to kill her.

When he was stripped bare, Icella gently led him to the tub, her hand warm against his, her eyes never leaving his, making sure he didn't feel taken advantage of. It raced across his brain that this was just one of many ways men and women were different. She helped him into the water, and it was blessedly warm and soothing. His mind refused to think past that. It wouldn't let him enjoy this.

Maybe it would never let him enjoy anything again. It would be deserved.

Standing at the foot of the tub, the Mermaid disrobed. There was a point in Kade's life where this would've... *excited* him. There was a point where this would've been an ultimate conquest. Now, it was nothing.

He was surprised to find that beneath the blue scales and fins, Icella was surprisingly human. And beautiful. Not the kind of beauty that came from the outside, the kind that came from knowing who you were. His eyes couldn't help but roam along her body, admiring it, but he couldn't enjoy it—not in the sense he usually would've. Not here in his darkest hour.

Icella slipped into the water beside him with hardly a ripple, a rag in her hand. "You do not bear this alone."

"But it was me who let her go. I was fighting for her. I might've told Jared I'd go along with his plan, but I was never going to."

"What changed?" Icella asked, gently wiping blood from his face.

"I don't know." Tears came again.

Icella pulled him close, put his head on her shoulder. "Shh, it is all right."

"Some part of me hoped Braxton would do it then and there—make it painless. Maybe I thought it'd be better for her rather than having to face who knows what. I should've kept fighting."

"And you will," Icella said, continuing to wipe the blood and grime from his body. "Letting her go was the only way to fulfil the prophecy. This is how she lives."

"What makes you so sure about that? What makes you think *any* of us will survive?"

"Sometimes you just have to have a little faith," she said, ever so gently kissing his forehead.

Chapter 37

Jared watched Kade storm through camp and would've loved to follow his example. But he was a leader now; storming away was likely something he could never do again—in public, at least. Taking a deep breath that stung the open wounds on the inside of his nose, he turned and headed into the command tent.

He knew he was a bloody mess, more from Kade's beating than anything else, but he wanted to show the other leaders what they'd done. He wanted them to see a visual representation of both his and Kade's emotional state. It was only a shame that he was the canvas. No, it wasn't.

The other leaders were already in the command tent, wearing the blood of their enemies like trophies. No remorse haunted their eyes; the victors rarely had regrets.

He slowly walked over to the three-dimensional map displaying their forces. Silently, he stared at it, something unnamable bubbling in his throat. Anger overwhelmed him and he slammed his hand onto the table, flinging pieces off the table. "ARE YOU HAPPY!"

Atlia visibly flinched, but no one responded or moved. He didn't think they dared to.

He continued to storm, sending pieces flying across the room and ended his rage by flipping the table. "Are you royiken happy?" he repeated, finding the nearest chair, and sinking into it. He covered his eyes as tears began to drip from his eyes, the salt bringing a bright burn to the inside of his nose.

"No," Atlia said, daring to brave the tempest. "None of us wanted this. But it was the right thing to do. The only thing that saves everyone."

"There's always another way," he mumbled. This couldn't have been the right choice. He had royally messed up. He couldn't get the image of Keegan out of his mind, totally beaten, her body broken and misshapen. And her fear, by the old gods, it had been palpable.

"But it is the way we have chosen," Eoghan said, rising and beginning to pick up the pieces from the war map. "And now we need to figure out what to do next." Gently he righted the table and began depositing handfuls of pieces haphazardly.

"I don't care," Jared mumbled.

"This is your war," Okleiy reminded him.

He suddenly saw red. "This was your plan!" he snapped. "Figure it out yourselves."

No one stopped him from stalking out, though someone must've started to because Atlia said, "Give him time. Today has been one of his hardest."

Making his way through camp, he focused on his anger. If he didn't, he'd see the true consequences of war and he wasn't sure he could handle having that culpability placed on him as well. It was bad enough he'd bear the guilt of giving Keegan up for the rest of his life. Any more and he was likely to lie in the mud and snow and see how long it was before winter claimed his life for Lunos.

In his tent, he found Mahogen, blood clumping strands of his hair together, making it look like bark weeping sap. There was a heavy tiredness in his green eyes, the kind that wouldn't be dispelled by sleep—time, and a lot of it, was the only thing that would remove that stain.

Mahogen breathed a sigh of relief upon seeing him. The Alvor walked quickly toward him and taking his face in his hands, paused only for a moment before delivering a kiss that cleared Jared's consciousness for as long as it lasted.

He was a leader now, and it meant making hard decisions. He'd made a hard decision already... but the next one was easy.

"They will find a way to accept it," Mahogen whispered.

Jared realized he was referring to what they were doing, what they wanted—the one thing humans as a society would always shun. But he wanted the words to refer to the spark of an idea that was growing. As he thought on it, and it continued to gain substance, he realized they'd find a way to accept it, because there was little anyone could do to stop him.

"I'm sorry," he said, pulling away. "I have to go."

Sadness formed a lump in Mahogen's throat, the kind that arose from not understanding, from believing you were the problem. To stay it, Jared kissed him again, to let him know this wasn't about them.

Rushing from the tent, the temperature seemed to have dropped dramatically in the few moments he'd been away from its claws. He shivered beneath his armor but didn't turn back for a cloak—he wasn't sure there was time.

Bursting into Kade's tent, he wasn't prepared for what lay inside. Kade's eyes were red and puffy, and he clutched a pillow like a piece of driftwood in a storm while Icella gently stroked his drying hair.

"Get out," Icella said calmly, quietly so as to not break the spell holding onto Kade. Yet the fury in her words was visceral.

The fact Kade didn't move or even glance in his direction belied his turmoil.

Ignoring the Mermaid, he snatched the pillow from Kade's arms saying, "Get up; we're going after Keegan."

«««« »»»»

As Keegan awoke, her mind was startlingly confused. Some kind of giant eagle wing kept her pressed against something amazingly warm. A part of her never wanted to leave the cocoon—as if it were the only thing keeping her alive.

Still dazed and half asleep, she tried to turn onto her side to see if she could dream a little longer and let out a scream as pain racked every inch of her body. Some parts screamed louder than others, mainly her shoulder and stomach, but everything still croaked and groaned and pleaded for death. With the pain, every horrible detail of the day past flooded back.

Then, the griffin's wing was suddenly moving, revealing the bright morning sunlight, made brighter still by reflecting off the new fallen snow. She somehow managed to raise a hand to shield her eyes.

"What is wrong?" Braxton asked, worriedly crouching beside her.

How he had so quickly appeared at her side, Keegan couldn't say.

"Everything hurts," she managed, calming herself enough to not try to flee. Not that she realistically could with her injuries. What she wouldn't give for a heavy dose of Advil… maybe morphine—definitely morphine.

Seeing there was no immediate danger, Braxton relaxed and left to continue packing bedding and supplies.

Looking around, Keegan saw most of the Vosjnik. They were in decent health given yesterday's events, and aside from Vitia, Mara and the fire elemental were also missing. Aron was tied to an earthen post and his eyes oozed sympathy whenever they held her gaze and fury whenever they landed on one of the Vosjnik.

Heaviness sat in Keegan's stomach; she knew where they were headed—and it didn't take a Blind Prophet to know it. There was no avoiding her fate. And, in all likelihood, no cavalry was coming. As slow as the army moved, they'd never make it to Agrielha before her execution. And with Jared as the Lazado's new leader and Kade deemed too important, they wouldn't be allowed to attempt a solo mission.

Nico handed her a small bowl of stew. It was warm, giving a false sense of hope. Resting it on her legs, she picked at the meal with little gusto. What was the point? Her time was limited.

"How long will it take…" she questioned, unable to finish the sentence.

"Two days, maybe three," Nico responded, handing her a waterskin.

She brushed the skin away. "I'm fine."

There was one thing she could do to make sure she never reached Kolt. All she needed was two days—likely less. It wouldn't be fun, but it would be better than whatever sadistic end Kolt had planned.

Thinking nothing of her refusal, Nico walked away, and cautiously approached Braxton. He hung around the prince, clearly wanting to say something, yet terrified to do so.

"Is there something wrong?" Braxton finally asked Nico, as he collected Keegan's still full bowl of stew. The prince considered it a moment before bringing the bowl to his lips and draining its contents.

Nico was pale and he barely managed to nod his head.

"Well, speak. What is it?" Braxton demanded, wiping his mouth.

Quietly, as if keeping the deed secret would relieve him of fault, Nico said, "It's about Mara. I hit her in the head with a rock to knock her out yesterday because she was stopping me from helping Jared. I'm worried…"

"She is alive. Mara is strong," Braxton reassured him with a hand on the shoulder. "As is Ima. I'm sure they just missed us in the dark and are on their way back to Agrielha as we speak."

"But what if they're not? They could be captured, or… or frozen. Or—"

"Or alive. If Mara and Ima are not at Agrielha, I will be the first one coming back to look for them."

Keegan bit her tongue; Nico was the only one not aware it was an empty promise. If Kolt held true to the callous and crass person Keegan remembered him as, the king would leave Mara and Ima to whatever fate had befallen them—and not think twice about it.

Nico nodded, not entirely placated. "Promise?"

"Absolutely," Braxton said. "And we will talk about what you did later." With a sigh he added, "But right now, get ready to leave. They day is short, and we will not be able to cover much ground."

It was a bold-faced lie, but Keegan didn't mind. She needed the extra time Braxton was trying to give her for her plan to fall into motion.

She needed time to ensure she never fell into Kolt's hands alive.

«««« »»»»

Mara's body was stiff—thankfully from sleeping on the ground rather than cold. Nestled against Ima she was quite warm, enough to have sweat beading in the small of her back.

Ima? she tested, praying the griffin hadn't given up overnight.

I survived, the hatchling answered.

Mara breathed a sigh of relief—likely to be the last one for a long time. They may have survived the night, but they were still a long way from true safety. Winter could claim them at any time if they didn't find proper shelter soon. And they were still close enough to the Lazado that should anyone see hide or hair of them, captives they would likely become.

Slowly, Ima unfurled her wing, allowing Mara to greet the day. They were surrounded by nothing but white for as far as the eye could see, piled almost a foot high. She brushed the snow off Ima's body and turned her attention to the griffin's wing.

There was no doubt it was broken—it was more a matter of how badly. Ima lay quietly while Mara felt along the fore-bone, giving a hiss of pain every so often. From what she could tell it was broken in at least two places. Nature would not heal this well—likely at all. In any other creature, this would be a death sentence.

But Ima had something her wild cousins didn't: a human.

Mara was about to voice her concerns and discuss their options when something in the sky caught her eye. It appeared to be… a bird? No, it was moving too fast, all but eating the miles as it streaked across the white covered world. As the silhouette continued to approach, it doubled. Then she recognized the creatures; dragons.

Whether they wanted help from the Lazado or not, they were getting it… as well as whatever the consequences of that help were.

In any other circumstance, Mara would've suggested they run, for griffins were faster and more agile than dragons, but Ima's wing prevented any such ideas. Their only option was to hide. If they had more time, they might've been able to bury themselves beneath a snowdrift—but there would still be no hiding their tracks.

The dragons were exceedingly close, and she could see one was yellow, the other red. Mara said a small prayer to Sola and Lunos that they'd be overlooked, and for a moment she was heard.

Then the dragons began to drift down from the heavens, circling like the predators they were. Their wings lifted the snow as they came within feet of the ground, swirling it about blindingly; Mara shielded her eyes until it settled once more.

What do you want? she asked, opening her mind to dragons so they could communicate.

"Mara?" a surprised voice said.

A man slid down from the yellow dragon's back and once he stopped moving, she realized it was Kade Tavin. She wasn't sure if this was a good or bad thing.

"What are you doing here?" another voice asked.

She looked to the other dragon and the second man on its back. They had encountered each other before as well... Jared was his name; he was Nico's brother. Even if she'd never seen Jared before, nor known his familial relationship to Nico, the evidence was obvious in the structural features of their faces and bodies.

Kade studied Ima, seeming to realize the griffin would act defensively if he got too close. "The griffin's wing is broken."

"We'll send someone to fetch the griffin," Jared said, "the girl comes with us."

Mara saw no reason to be separated from Ima. And where were Kade and Jared headed? "I won't go anywhere without Ima," she said defiantly, brandishing a dagger. She was at Kade and Jared's mercy, but a little confidence could go a long way.

"You don't have a choice," Jared returned. There was nothing malicious about the words, though they were spoken as fact.

Growling in both pain and defiance, Ima pushed to her feet, feathers rising on end. The dragons responded in kind, though their scales remained flush against their bodies. Mara hated to admit it, but with the smoke trailing from the nostrils of the red dragon and the static thrumming around the yellow one, they were much scarier. Ima felt the same, for her ears flattened against her head and her tail tucked between her legs.

The griffin will make a good bargaining chip, one of the dragons said.

With a broken wing, how do you expect it to get there? the other returned.

"Carry it," Kade said simply. "Now let's go, we're wasting time!"

"What makes you think I'll go with you?" Mara snarled.

Deciding to be prepared, she sent a tendril of thought out. From Kade she was met with a thick wall, one that would take weeks or months to surmount. Jared's wasn't as strong, but with Kade to back him up, she wouldn't be able to break through his wall and take control of him fast enough. And that still left the dragons; she had no grandiose notions she could ever beat them in a game of mental fortitude.

"Come with us, or we kill you now," Jared said, his sword whispering as it was pulled from its sheath.

You wanted to live, Ima said, *do as they say.*

«««« »»»»

Aron ran his tongue over his cheeks, his lips, willing saliva to be secreted. He could feel the coolness left behind. Yet no matter what he did, the dry, sticky feeling persisted in the back of his throat.

As Braxton led him over to the earthen post he would be tied to for the night, he said, "Can you give Keegan some water?"

"I just gave her some," his brother said dismissively.

"She did not actually drink."

"And how do you know that?"

As Braxton wound a rope around him and the post, Aron tried to come up with an explanation that did not allude to their empathy link. Braxton might not put two and two together, but if Kolt caught even the smallest whiff, he would figure it out—and they would be in a world of hurt. Aron stared at Keegan and saw the signs of dehydration.

"Look at her," he said, "she does not look well."

"She is severely injured," Braxton argued.

"Look past that."

"I… will admit I have seen her look better."

"And she has not relieved herself all day."

Braxton raised an eyebrow.

"She usually needs to go every few hours."

His brother gave him a blank look, likely questioning why he was so familiar with Keegan's bathroom habits, before walking toward her and grabbing a water skin. "Drink."

With her good arm, Keegan brought the waterskin to her lips. Aron watched as her throat bobbed like water flowed down it. But he did not feel its cooling relief.

When she handed the skin back to Braxton, she wiped beads of water from her lips. She seemed exhausted beyond compare, her head lulling to one side and her eyes glazed over.

His brother weighed the waterskin before offering it back to her. "Drink."

"I did," Keegan said weakly.

Braxton knew she was lying, and his face said it.
Weakly, she shook her head. "I don't want any."
"Drink."
"No."
Braxton looked over his shoulder. "Dax."
The water elemental stepped forward.
Aron felt Keegan bite the inside of her lip, understanding the threat his brother presented her with.
"No," she reiterated.
Sighing, Braxton handed Dax the waterskin.
The water elemental had the skin's contents float.
"Last chance," his brother warned.
Keegan remained stoically silent.
Braxton let out a heavy breath from his nose, motioning for Dax to proceed.
Dax shot the water toward Keegan in a fluid stream and Aron gagged as the water forced itself down her throat.
The water elemental relented, and Keegan took rasping breaths, water sloshing in her stomach like a roiling ocean. Aron felt the bubble rising in her throat as she hunched over and divulged the watery contents of her stomach.
"Drink," Braxton told her, offering the water skin he had commandeered from Guthrie.
She shook her head, still hunched over, her stomach clenching and forcing her to dry heave.
"Drink, or he does it again."
Keegan looked at Braxton with pained eyes and slowly accepted the waterskin. Shakily, she brought it to her lips and Aron felt cool water slide down her throat.

Chapter 38

Lucas forced himself to take a breath, the air sticking in his throat like glue. Around him, people bustled by, yet no one noticed him—or rather, paid him much attention.

Having gotten Carter to the hospital after the Battle of the Solstice, Lucas was dismayed to find his brother unresponsive and feared the worst. The rush of nurses who took Carter had only affirmed the idea he was set to meet Lunos. Then, Lucas was told to leave.

He hadn't wanted to go, but there was hardly any space for the wounded and dying as it was—the same was true now, several days later, even after so many had slipped away to meet Lunos. Out in the cold again that first night after the battle, and away from the stench of death, numbness had overcome him.

Lucas couldn't account for his time after that and at some point in the early morning, he awoke, not in his own tent but in Jared's. He must have come here, assuming this is where his brother would be. Likely, he had gotten tired of waiting and crawled into Jared's bed to wait him out.

Searching the gloom when he awoke, he found he was still alone. Lucas took it to mean Jared was already in the hospital tent, putting his position to use, ensuring that everything possible was being done for their brother.

His stomach in knots, Lucas forwent breakfast, and at the hospital was once again turned away. And Jared hadn't been there. Lucas knew he should be worried. Why was Jared nowhere to be found? Lucas could only hope Jared was busy dealing with the duties of a leader. If not, there was no conceivable alternative aside from what he feared most.

Lucas couldn't recall what he did for the rest of the day, he just remembered waking in Jared's tent yet again the next morning. And the process repeated.

Now, three days after the battle, he was finally allowed to see Carter. And it was that sight that was making it hard to breathe. The wound to Carter's stomach had been cared for, even partially healed, yet he still looked pale, so weak. And had yet to reawaken.

"Prognosis?" he managed to get out. The word felt foreign, heavy, deadly.

"We won't know for sure until he awakes," the nurse said, gently guiding him into the chair that had been brought for him. "If he wakes."

"He will," Lucas insisted. He wasn't giving Carter another choice.

«««« »»»»

Through the falling snow, the castle of Agrielha stood out like a structured shadow, offering no hope or warmth in its imposing mass. If Braxton had not known where to find the griffin stables, they would have been forced to circle the castle until the snow relented.

Out of the blizzard, warmth began to seep into Braxton's body, melting the snow accumulated on his shoulders and hair.

The Vosjnik quietly slipped off the griffins and led them to stalls, all glad to be out of the storm.

He helped Keegan off Myrish then let her lean against a post before attending to his bronze beast. Sweat covered Keegan's face, despite the chill—an obvious sign infection had set in.

"Give them a minute," Braxton ordered the rest of the Vosjnik once the griffins had been tended to.

The Vosjnik gave him confused looks, but when Braxton did not waver, they did as instructed.

"Go to her," Braxton told Aron when the three of them were alone, returning his attention to Myrish.

He was careful to angle himself away from Aron and Keegan, but not enough so that he could not watch them out of the corner of his eye. It was important that they felt like they got to say goodbye. At least it felt important to him.

Aron rushed to Keegan, who had managed to stay on her feet until then. As his brother reached her, Keegan's knees gave way. Aron helped her sink to the floor, unbidden tears streaming down her cheeks. He held her tight as she shuddered, likely wishing there was something he could do to fix the situation.

"I don't wanna die," Keegan sobbed into his chest. Her whole body shook.

Braxton's heart panged. Part of him wished he could stop what was to happen. Part of him desperately wanted to fling Keegan and Aron from the tower to save them pain, but something—call it hope—stayed him.

At her admission, Aron pulled her closer, stroking her hair, whispering, "Everything is going to be fine. I will not let anyone hurt you." It was a lie, a blatant one.

Aron began to rock, the motion likely comforting Keegan as much as it did him.

Suddenly, the door opened, and two guards filed in. The soldiers roughly worked to pull Aron and Keegan apart. When his brother clung to the girl, the guards struck him with no mercy or remorse.

"No," Aron screamed, "you cannot do this!"

But they could. Because they were stronger, because they had been ordered to, because the world was not fair.

Finding that even being beaten was not enough to make Aron release his grip, the guards recruited Brennian and Dax to help. It was only with the four of them together that they finally managed to separate Aron and Keegan.

Brennian and Dax retained their hold on his brother, pulling a struggling Aron from the room while the guards hauled Keegan to her feet, disregarding her injuries.

Aron fought and screamed and thrashed, but Keegan was silent. As if already resigned to the fate awaiting her.

Myrish shared a solemn glance with him before Braxton followed the commotion out of the stable. The hallway outside was eerie, cloaked in silence and fright.

Braxton found a third guard in the hall, hardly more than a child with the finest hairs gracing his upper lip. The boy held himself back, clearly wishing to be anywhere else, yet willing to do his duty as ordered. And that, Braxton could grant him.

"You," he said, "I have a different job for you. Take the boy," he nodded toward Nico, "back to my chambers and lock the door. He should not see what is about to happen."

The boy guard gulped and gave a subtle nod before turning and taking ahold of Nico. Though only inches shorter than the guard, Nico was hardly a match for him—especially when knocked on the head. His eyes took on a glass patina as he was easily led away.

As Braxton watched the youths stumble down the hallway, there was a clanging and he looked down to see Kolt's red gold crown dancing along the ground. Angered screams made him look up and he watched as Aron was forced down the corridor while Keegan was dragged, unable to support herself on a broken ankle.

He went to look at the crown again, but it was gone. A vision. Braxton pushed what he had seen aside as he followed after the guards. He could only hope Kolt had been toppled. Or that it would somehow happen soon.

《《《《 》》》》

The blizzard that had blanketed the world after the Battle of the Solstice was back, and with a vengeance. The biting wind refused to leave Jared any vestige of warmth and flung the snow about, blinding him.

The castle approaches, Thoren said, his second eyelid the perfect protection against the elements.

Jared wished his eyes were similarly protected. But he was not a dragon. And though he couldn't see his own face, he knew it was red and wind bitten.

Even with their second eyelids, Jared had no idea how the dragons could see clearly through the mass of snowflakes blazing around them. In any direction past maybe five feet, all he could see was an unending fury of white.

Any sign of the griffins? he called to the dragons.

Realistically, they had to rescue Keegan and Aron before they reached Agrielha castle. Once they were inside the protection of the castle walls, there was no way they'd be able to fight their way through whatever guards awaited.

I do not think so, Thoren responded.

Jared hoped that meant they'd overtaken the griffins somehow. He knew it was a lie, but he had to cling to the chance.

Raelin gave a mighty roar, spitting a stream of fire, the snow before him instantly turning to steam and water—what didn't evaporate immediately refroze and rushed to the ground as deadly shards and slabs of ice.

Where the ice struck, the earth gave a groan, as if mortally wounded.

There was a chance the inhabitants of the castle might think the noise was thunder, but he doubted it.

So much for not announcing ourselves! he seethed at Kade, who had no doubt played on Raelin's ego.

They were close enough to the castle that Jared could make out the illumination of the candles and torches within. It made him wish he was inside, talking and laughing with his brothers over a cup of something warm.

Sweeping around the castle, Raelin continued to release bursts of flame, half frozen slush slamming into the ground after each bout.

Through the raging storm, Jared espied a door.

Land there, he told Thoren.

The yellow dragon obliged, and it wasn't long before his legs were sinking into the accumulated snow. Raelin, with the griffin clutched in his talons, continued to rage around the castle, shouting spurts of fire whenever he deemed necessary. In front of Jared, Mara shivered, be it fear or cold or a combination, only she knew.

Seconds ticked by slowly with a painful thud of his heart against his ribs for each moment lost as they waited for someone to emerge. The thought that they were too late refused to banish itself and threatened to destabilize him.

Finally, a pale face dared to peek through the slit of an opening that could be managed against the snowdrifts.

Jared screamed to be heard over the storm's gusting wind, "You, there!"

The squall carried his words and the man's gaze snapped to him, eyes widening at the sight of Thoren.

"Tell Kolt we wish to parley," he continued. "We have the girl and griffin. He has an hour to meet us two miles north of the castle before we kill them." To drive home the façade, he drew a knife and pressed it against Mara's throat.

The face in the doorway immediately disappeared.

Sensing their goal was achieved, Thoren took to the sky and headed to where Jared had demanded Kolt meet them.

«««« »»»»

Keegan tried to keep herself composed as the guards dragged, pulled, and pushed her through the castle, her broken body making it impossible to do as they wanted. Her mind told her to curl into a ball and weep. Her natural stubbornness fought against those feelings, but it wouldn't be long before she lost; she didn't want to die.

She could hear Aron being pulled along behind her, fighting every step of the way. She respected him—for doing what she was too afraid and weary to do. But it wouldn't save her... or him.

Braxton walked before her ominously, restraining himself from looking back. From the way the muscles were corded in his neck, it was a difficult task. But she understood. If he didn't have to see the atrocity being committed, he could pretend it wasn't occurring. She loathed him for being so willing to let this happen.

Nico wasn't counted in the Vosjnik's number and Keegan was glad the boy had been locked away somewhere. He shouldn't have to see what was coming—hell, *she* didn't deserve to see what was coming.

Soon, she stood before imposing black doors, the figures of demonized griffins marring their surface. Braxton's self-imposed ignorance wavered for a moment before he pushed open the doors on near-silent hinges.

Keegan hung her head, not wanting to see what awaited her. The stones making up the floor slid by until they lurched up, almost meeting her face. She landed heavily on her knees and just managed to put out her functioning arm to steady herself. Her heart pounded at a furious pace and from the toll her injuries had taken, she might not be awake to witness her own death; wouldn't that be a blessing?

The world was deathly still, like the reaper presided over them and he who breathed first would breathe his last.

Tears dripped down her cheeks and became wet circles on the floor. She didn't remember starting to cry. Slowly, Keegan raised her head, realizing death wouldn't come until she looked it in the eye.

Kolt sat upon a gaudy throne, a simple, red gold crown resting on his blond head. He sat in what he thought was a regal and imposing position, but it only showed him as the monstrous child he was.

"Your prize," Braxton spat. "Now, release Nico from the spell you saw fit to plague him with."

Kolt laughed, the harsh sound echoing about the room. "You really are thick. I never placed a spell on the boy."

Though she was not sure what spell—or fake spell—they were talking about, Keegan could imagine anger and loathing curled Braxton's features as he realized he'd been duped.

"You do not have to kill her," Braxton said, throwing away his mask of naivety. "The slajor manacles have neutralized her."

Kolt stared his brother down, rising slowly. "She is still a threat. What she represents is a threat."

She could hear Aron screaming somewhere nearby, but also a million miles away. Everything was a million miles away. The only thing tangible was the rhythm of her heart, acting as the beat of the executioner's drum.

Her head lowered again, hoping against hope that if she ignored the monster in the room he'd go away.

A chill ran down her spine as she heard the scraping of a sword being pulled from its scabbard. Then, she felt its touch as the point was placed under her chin.

Kolt forced her to look up. "Beg."

Nothing but ragged breaths came past the constriction in her throat.

Anger flashed in Kolt's brown irises. He wanted to feel power, the kind that came from holding someone's life in his hands. As much as she wanted to give it to him, she couldn't.

With a sneer, Kolt finally pulled the sword away, letting her head drop heavily once more. Her hair fell around her face, blocking out the world in a curtain of ruddy brown. The fire that had once derived comment had died and with it, so would she.

There was a clamor behind her and at least two voices called for Kolt to stop. They would be ignored, for reason had never existed in this room. Reason had never been a friend to most of the Alagards.

Keegan felt the biting weight of the sword over her, just waiting to drop. Heat spread across her neck, as if she were receiving phantom pains from the future, and she wanted to scream. But couldn't. She could only let it all happen.

There was an almost silent swish of the throne room doors along the stone floor, and a booming voice demanded, "Wait!"

But it was too late. Kolt's sword was already whistling through the air.

The heat in Keegan's neck intensified and the world fell away.

Chapter 39

Braxton reached the griffin stable and was left to the many questions tumbling around his brain. Kolt was nowhere to be found—Keegan having disappeared with him. And poor Aron was left alone in a cell in the dank, dark, dungeon with more questions than everyone else. It had broken Braxton's heart to hear his brother's cries and accusations as he walked from the dungeon. Mostly because all of them were true. He was a coward.

He assumed the men on dragonback causing the commotion were Jared and Kade, but only time would tell. Braxton had not seen the dragons, nor their riders, so could confirm nothing. And given that only one soldier has seen the dragons, there were rumors it had been a mirage.

He was pulled from his thoughts by the door opening to reveal Kolt. Braxton still wondering why he put off the inevitable killing of Keegan; what did Kolt have to gain by it? Something told him he would soon find out.

Kolt had swung his sword and the soldier with news had been the only thing stopping Keegan's demise. Though Braxton was not sure that was entirely true. He could have sworn his brother's sword had made the barest of contact with Keegan's neck. Enough that she should be dead. But she was alive, and Kolt seemed to have gained a mysterious... notch in his sword. One that matched the curvature of a neck.

As soon as the guard had relayed his news, Kolt had ordered Braxton to prepare two of the griffins. Knowing it was better to do as told, he had slunk from the throne room.

Shockingly, no smug grin marred the king's features now; he was just as unsure as the rest of them. "Which ones are we taking?" Kolt asked.

"I am not sure any of them will consent to be ridden by you," he responded, refraining from spitting the words.

"I *will* ride one of them," Kolt said, earning a few dissonant clicks from the griffins. "I do not care which. Saddle them and let us go. Or would you rather the girl and griffin die?"

With the fate of Mara and Ima at stake, the griffins reluctantly settled. Myrish and Phynex were readied in what was likely record time. Easily, he swung onto the bronze griffin, his own anxiety matching the beast's.

Having mounted Phynex, Kolt urged her to the edge of the opening, snow howling outside. "You are to say nothing," he instructed, jabbing his heels into the griffin like he would a horse.

Phynex gnashed her beak, reaching back to snap at Kolt's foot, before leaping into the blizzard. Myrish was hot on her tail, the two of them becoming the only specks of color left in the world.

The distance to the rendezvous site passed in a literal blur. At first, Braxton thought no one was there, then he saw the masses of yellow and red.

Starting the descent, a whistling gust pushed against them, making every inch a battle. By the time the griffins landed, they were breathing heavily, foam at the corners of their mouths.

Kolt shielded his eyes as he slid from Phynex's back, and Braxton watched his jaw move, as if speaking. The snow and wind died, leaving them in a bubble of calm.

Outside, the storm still raged, demanding to be let back in.

"What do you want?" Kolt said coolly, turning his attention to the dragons and the person with them.

"Keegan and Aron for Mara and the griffin," Kade said. The way he spoke belied calm diplomacy, but Braxton could see the fire in his eyes. Something else was there too, but he could not name it.

"Where are they?" Braxton asked. Not seeing Mara and Ima, he feared they were dead already.

"No place you'll find them," Kade answered. "Do we have a deal?"

Kolt took his time answering, chewing on the decision. "Yes. Meet me outside the castle at sunrise."

Before Kade could respond, Kolt dropped the barrier separating them from the storm, making any response given impossible to hear.

«««« »»»»

The first thing Keegan was aware of as she rose from the depths of darkness was pain; her shoulder was a mangled mess and the seams in her stomach were in anguish. Not even in hell did one escape pain it seemed. Opening her eyes, she was prepared to be confronted with the fiery abode of Satan; instead, she was reminded of a castle—the devil had a misplaced sense of humor.

"Drink," a gentle voice said, pressing a cup to her lips. A hand slid under her neck and raised her head.

She drank greedily, not caring who was showing her the barest of kindnesses, and when the water was gone, finally turned her attention to the person. Relief flooded her as she gazed into Thaddeus's gentle brown eyes. Maybe hell wouldn't be so bad after all. *Or...* maybe she was still alive.

"I'd hug you, but..." she trailed off weakly. "It's good to see you."

"As it is good to see you," Thaddeus said, gently stroking her forehead, brushing aside a few wayward strands of hair.

"She is awake," another voice said. It might have been a question if not for the intonation.

Thaddeus nodded and stepped aside, revealing Alyck.

He was much the same, but his face seemed more haggard than she remembered. The Blind Prophet's expression was grim, foretelling of pain to come—granted, it didn't take a wiseman to know that.

Keegan looked between the two men, not knowing what to expect. Fearing what they might have to say if she was being honest with herself.

Alyck took the chair beside the bed and leaned back in a casual manner, if one could overlook the tenseness sitting in his chest. "There are some things you must know, for they have precedence in dictating the future. However, you will have to judge when it is time for these facts to become known to others... to my sons."

She didn't know much about the Alagard family but saw no reason Alyck couldn't've had children. Maybe his wife had died, and the boys were shipped away. Or maybe the mother had whisked them off to corners unknown to protect them against Caius.

Her mind was saved from further rabbit holes as Alyck took up his tale. "This all started with the first time my brother experienced a Nanagin. He was gone for almost a year. And when he returned, no one was aware of it for half a year more. Caius returned to a remote part of the northern Westerlies, where the griffins have domain.

"As you know, after coming back to this world, one boasts accentuated powers. Caius left Arciol as nothing but a telepath and returned as a telepath and spellcaster. From my brother's tales, if the mountains did not kill you, the griffins were sure to. But he survived.

"During his time in the mountains, Caius claims to have taken over the mind of a griffin, Iwin, and forced him to take him to one of the caves dotting the mountainsides. There, Caius began perfecting his control over the griffin, for he needed it to return to the rest of the world. And after six months, Caius had won, truly; he was too strong for the beast to battle in any capacity but with claw and tooth… or is it beak? Either way…

"Before leaving the griffin's territory, he stole fifteen eggs. Of those, thirteen were viable and have since hatched.

"After leaving the Westerlies, Caius came to the castle of Agrielha, seeking an audience with Seleena. She listened to his tale and while impressed, was furious he had stolen the eggs from the griffins. The griffins had an unspoken pact with the rest of the world; so long as they were left alone, the griffins would not leave their home. Aside from this, Seleena recognized that the griffins had done nothing to harm us, and Caius's deeds might be seen as an act of war. She ordered he return the eggs and make it known he had acted of his own accord. And to take whatever punishment, outside of death, that the griffins meted out. As for Iwin, Seleena never imagined Caius could have enough control over him to bend him to his will. No one knew Caius did not return the eggs until he took the throne many years later."

"I'm sorry," Keegan interrupted, "how does any of this have bearing on the future?"

Alyck ignored her and continued plodding along, "Supposedly having returned the eggs to their nests, Caius came back to Agrielha to beg forgiveness from Seleena. She forgave him, then asked him about his time in the other world. He was hesitant at first, professing it was a long story. Seleena invited him to take as long as it might, for knowledge was worth whatever cost of time.

"During the recounting of his time away, Caius learned I had survived. My brother immediately begged leave from the queen to seek me out, which was granted.

"It had been two years since I had seen Caius, and there were mixed emotions. A part of me wanted to blame him for our parents' deaths—"

"Wait, what happened to your parents?" Keegan demanded.

"A story for another time. But their deaths were an accident. And I was just happy to have my brother back, alive and whole. Not wanting to leave me to the life of a commoner, Caius invited me to Agrielha. I considered refusing, I had made a life, begun a courtship, but I was of the same mindset as Seleena—family is the most valuable thing we have.

As Alyck continued his tale, Keegan did her best to be attentive, to find reason behind the words, but couldn't, or maybe she was too blind. There came a point where Alyck's voice became monotonous, lulling, soothing. And through the pains of her injuries, they brought upon the desire to sleep.

"Alyck, you might wish to get to the topic of import before Keegan can resist sleep no longer," Thaddeus said, jerking her back to the present.

"At some point during his time with Seleena, before usurping her, Caius came to love her. When he became king, he placed a spell on her, freezing her in time, just as he did himself. Age would not be the death of them.

"He told the queen they would marry, and promised he would not force himself upon her, but would wait until she willingly gave herself to him. Because of his love for her, she retained her freedom about the castle."

Alyck paused, a lump in his throat. "And I was spurned. With Caius king and Angela Alaga dead, I was the only option to become the new Blind Prophet. I remember when my brother took my sight—it hurt, physically. It was like hot pokers were forced into my eyes. And the vision I saw as my sight was taken did not lessen the pain. I could see, but not as I once had; I was limited to what would be… what *might* be.

"With no country to rule, Seleena took to learning—in hopes knowledge could be used to return her people to the peace they deserved. No such thing happened, but she did find something else in the library.

"Our relationship was at first tenuous, both of us struggling to accept our new lots in life. Seleena was hesitant to ask the librarians for help, for fear they would report to Caius. And even though I could no longer see, I knew the library better than most. So, to me she entrusted her enquiries.

"I cannot recall when we realized our relationship had become something more than kindred souls. No longer was I there to simply help her find a book—and no longer was she there to keep me sane as visions drove me mad. We cherished each other and found ways to be together."

"Then Caius found out and wasn't happy about it?" Keegan tried.

"No," Alyck said with a glib grin. "I am not sure he ever knew. If he did, he never brought it to light. Then, I saw something—which made neither of us happy. Caius's reign would come to an end, but first a child had to be born."

"Me?" Keegan pressed.

"No, though your own birth was but a brick in the wall that needed to tumble down upon Caius. No, Caius's child needed to be born. Understandably, Seleena was not happy to hear this; or that Caius's child would someday take the throne.

"But there was something worse to come of this prophecy. The child needed not only be Caius's but also hers. I did not see Seleena for many months after this came to light, and when next I saw her, a ring graced her finger.

"For her people, she would marry my brother and bear him a child. But there were things she first asked of us Alagards. Of me, she made me swear I would not fault her in the decision and that our times together would not cease. Of Caius, she made him swear that when Lunos came for her he would do nothing to stop him. We both agreed.

"Within a year of being married, Seleena bore a son. He came into the world with a smile and hair as dark as his mother's. Two years later Kolt arrived. He was born with a frown and hair as light as his father's. Two years later… Aron. He was born crying, his hair dark as shadow, already in mourning.

"Seleena's last pregnancy was wrought with strife. She would not survive it. Lunos had claimed her life, but there were things she first asked of us before leaving. Of Caius, she made him swear to a Death Deal—he nor anyone under his command could harm her sons. Of me, she begged me to keep a secret."

Keegan's eyes widened in understanding. "They're not Caius's sons."

Alyck nodded. "Braxton and Aron are mine."

Chapter 40

Thaddeus heard the door to the antechamber open and close; it was time. He gently woke Keegan from her feverish sleep, which proved to be no easy task. Though he said nothing, his face must have spoken volumes for she was immediately tense and afraid.

He knew the girl wanted to ask if she was being taken to her death like a lamb to slaughter. Thaddeus wanted to tell her no but knew not what the future held—and the answer they both wanted likely would never be. Alyck might be able to provide an answer, but it had often been proven that not even fate could predict Keegan's path. The Blind Prophet might see her death today, but only Keegan could see it to fruition or demand that destiny change.

Looking over his shoulder, he saw two guards standing ominously in the doorway, Alyck and Braxton behind them. The Blind Prophet gave him the slightest of nods and Thaddeus stepped away from the girl, releasing her to the whims of the old gods.

Without hesitation, the soldiers hauled Keegan from the bed, oblivious to her pained cries.

Then, silence, a prelude to death.

For the first time, Thaddeus studied Braxton, trying to discern if Alyck had told the truth. He saw no reason for the Blind Prophet to speak falsely, but was the truth better or worse than the lie?

As Braxton started to leave, his father gently blocked his exit. "You will make a hard decision today. But it must be made. And no one will fault you for it."

《《《 》》》

The nurses claimed he got in the way—and during the day, Lucas conceded that. The hospital tent was a jumbled mess, rarely quiet, always anxious, full of bodies both moving and... dead. But nights were a different story. Then was a time of unnatural hush; Lunos, under the guise of darkness claiming lives, sparing others, all without a peep.

Since sundown, he'd been watching over Carter, ensuring his breaths remained even, that there was no sign he was in danger of meeting the god of death. With the dawn coming, he knew he'd have to leave, to sleep fitfully and dream he'd lost more kin.

He heard a mumbled groan and was immediately alert, pulled from the lull of silent waiting.

Carter opened his eyes slowly.

Lucas couldn't describe the relief that washed over him, only that he wished to cry at its beauty.

"Where am I?" Carter slurred, eyes darting about, trying to make sense of the surroundings.

Quietly, Lucas said, "The hospital. Do you remember the battle?"

Carter gave an imperceptible nod as his left hand gingerly moved to where he'd been stabbed.

Like a wraith, a nurse appeared. "Take it easy." She offered a kind smile then was gone again. When she returned, she bore a bowl of soup and a pitcher of water. In all the world, it felt like only the three of them were awake.

Gently, the nurse eased Carter up, folding the pillow behind his back. Taking the bowl, she placed it on his lap, the steam rising in curling wisps about his brother's face.

Not thinking about anything other than food—proof he was still the Carter of old—his brother lifted the spoon to his mouth. His hand shook violently, spilling the contents over his chest; the spoon soon followed the soup, making a dull thud as it hit the ground.

Uneasiness filled Lucas, but the nurse simply picked the spoon up, wiped it on her smock, and set it in Carter's hand again, as if to say, "nothing is amiss". And why *wouldn't* Carter be shaky after what he'd been through?

Carter must have felt the tension in the air as an obvious nervousness set about his features. Still, he dipped the spoon into the broth and lifted it to his mouth; again, contents and container came cascading down.

The spoon clean again, the nurse made no attempt to hand it back to Carter, instead, setting forth to feed him herself. In another time, another situation, this would have been a welcome dream for his brother.

A tap on his shoulder made Lucas turn, heart in his throat. Another nurse gave him a small nod and he silently followed her. She had two mugs of what smelled like borzan and pushed one into his hands, the warmth of the ceramic stilling his worries momentarily.

She pulled the tent flap back and Lucas wasn't sure where she was taking him. Outside, the air was frozen, its shards searing his lungs with each breath. Sunrise was soon to come, the barest hint of light hanging in the air. A promise of something better.

At first, the nurse said not a word, sipping her mug of borzan that steamed and clouded about her face. "The injury is worse than we suspected."

"How so?"

"Drink," she insisted before responding. "There's a chance your brother may not walk again... at least not without aid."

Lucas wanted to laugh; how could a gut wound prevent him from walking? "What do you mean?"

"From what I can tell, his wound is more than just a piercing of the abdomen. The blade bit into his spinal cord, too."

"So?"

"Some of the nerves were damaged."

"Have the doctor check again, I'm sure you're wrong."

The woman took another sip. "I am the doctor."

"Can't you fix him?" He was confused, life elementals could—*should* be able to heal any injury.

"Nerves... are a rare specialty. The only person I've ever known or heard of who could mend damaged nerves was Lyerlly."

Lucas didn't want to know the answer but had to ask. "What does this mean for Carter?"

"Like I said, it's unlikely he'll ever walk—"

Though he'd already been told this, the words felt like a slap this time. Irrevocable. Lucas stumbled, as if struck and eased himself onto a snowbank, his lungs unable to draw breath. Carter would never walk again. It was the worst-case scenario outside death.

"Let me finish," the doctor chided, kneeling beside him, placing a hand on his knee. "He might never walk again without the aid of a cane, crutch, or brace. And I say *might*."

His mind reeled, might was not an absolute. How could Carter both never walk again and yet also able to. "I- I don't understand." He ran a hand along his face, exhaustion amongst other things clouding his mind.

"The damage to his spinal cord wasn't enough to cause complete immobility. But it's enough that doing much of anything is going to be difficult on his right side. He's going to have to learn to use his left hand. We can try exercises to increase the strength in his right side, but he won't be as strong as he used to be. And it might get better on its own too—over enough time, that is.

"So, he could get better? You just said he could get better."

"Possibly. Sometimes the body mends nerves on its own. But it's rare, and it takes years, and lots of work."

"You can fix it. You have to fix it. That- that's what life elementals... do!"

"I'm sorry, there's nothing we can do—short term. Long term is another story. And trust that we are going to do what we can; but you must face the reality that your brother might be permanently crippled."

««« »»»

The two dragons stood out in stark contrast to the snow. Braxton spotted Ima lying on the ground beside the hulking reptiles and felt a trickle of relief wash over him. Then he noticed her wing, how she held it away from her body, and how it was angled awkwardly. He had no doubt it was broken.

His eyes never left the group, wondering at all the ways this could go awry, as Myrish finished descending. To start with, his gut told him Kolt was not going to relinquish Keegan alive—which meant Mara and Ima were likely facing the same fate. His mind raced to think of another way to ensure their safety... but there was only one option at the ready. And he abhorred to even think about putting it into action.

The second Crowlin's feet touched down, Kolt shoved Keegan from the griffin's back. The girl landed with a scream and made no attempt to move from the deep pile of snow. Her stillness brought an evil smile to Kolt's face.

Braxton glanced at Kade and Jared, fearing what retaliation they might take for even this small slight. The two shared a hard look before Kade pulled Mara to her feet brusquely.

"Are you ready to trade?" Jared asked calmly, clearly the diplomatic one of the pair.

Kolt stooped to pull Keegan to her feet. His fingers twisted tightly in her hair and held her head back, baring her neck to the old gods in a taunt. Mouth next to her ear, he snarled, "Yes. Only problem is, I have no intention of trading. No, she is going to die." Kolt threw Keegan forward into the snow again.

Braxton closed his eyes for half a second to stuff away the fear and anger that threatened to make him do something stupid.

When he opened them, Kade no longer clutched Mara and the girl was on her knees before Jared, as if tossed aside. The ex-Vosjnik member was in the process of drawing his sword, the metal reflecting the weak morning light.

"I will kill them if you hurt her," Kade said in a low voice.

Kolt blinked a few times, face unreadable, before shrugging. "What do I care?"

A knife twisted in Braxton's heart and a spray of blood danced across his vision before fading. Keegan would die—as would Mara and Ima alongside her—and there was nothing he could do to save them. Nothing that would not have dire consequences.

Then, he knew he was wrong; the blood he had seen did not belong to Keegan, but to Ima. Humans did not bleed purple. Helplessly, he watched as in fury Kade raised his sword. He wanted to cry out, join Mara's pleas that the griffin be spared, but could muster no sound.

When Kolt did not beg or plead, Kade brought the weapon down without hesitation. Braxton did not want to watch a friend die, but his gaze remained. The sword fell so quickly; it was like time stopped and sound faded away.

Then it all came roaring back; panicked voices cried out and a wounded beast yelled. It was almost too much to bear. But he could bear it because Kade had not meant to kill, not yet; he had sheered Ima's broken wing from her body. And now, it sat in the snow, seeping purple blood.

Mara became inconsolable and screamed all the obscenities Braxton had never imagined she knew, tears running down her cheeks. To keep the girl from rushing to the griffin's aid, Jared wrapped an arm around her waist.

The smell of iron finally reached his nose and a surge coursed through his throat. Braxton turned away, acid already burning his mouth, and divulged the contents of his stomach. Brought on by the burn in his throat, salty tears watered his eyes.

When he returned to his feet, wiping his mouth, Kolt gave him a disgusted look. "Pathetic."

Mara was now limp and weeping in Jared's arms, giving him the ability to return his focus to them. "Just as you will surely kill Keegan, we will kill them. But they are valuable, so let us trade."

Kolt raised his eyebrows and laughed. "What use is a griffin with a broken wing? At least that could have been healed. Now, it is entirely useless! The only thing of value left is the girl. And I do not want her." Kolt nodded toward Keegan lying placidly on the ground and ordered Braxton, "Kill her."

The words did not instantly register as Braxton's attention was still on Mara and Ima. Though Ima might never fly again, he could save her life if he could stop the bleeding. Already he was thinking of what to do. Packing snow over the wound would numb the pain and the lessen flow of blood. Then someone would have to get Rohan.

Kolt shouting, "Kill her!" brought him back to the moment.

A heavy stone weighed on his chest, making it hard to breathe. Two paths lay before Braxton, and he had to choose. Silently, he turned to his brother, a lifetime of hate flooding his heart.

"Kill her," Kolt snarled, a dangerous fire in his eyes. "Now!"

Desperately, Braxton wanted to disobey, but his body was no longer his to command. The Queen Killer slipped slowly from its sheath at his side, malicious and evil. Gulping, he stepped toward where Keegan knelt, miraculously calm, resigned to death.

He looked to Kolt, silently begging for a reprieve that would never come. Suddenly, it was all clear. There was nothing good about Kolt—no compassion, no love. His brother was an evil the world needed to be rid of. And that sneer, Braxton never wanted to see again—because he knew its presence signified someone else was in pain.

His fingers tightened their grip on the sword, as if trying to strangle it. "No," he said, stepping forward and driving the blade into Kolt.

Confusion crinkled Kolt's face, and his lips wavered in disbelief. The expression morphed to pain as Braxton pulled away, the Queen Killer squelching as it slid through Kolt's chest.

The king fell without a word and silence embraced the world. Good or bad, Braxton could not yet tell. A reflection blinded him, and he was reminded of the slajor manacle he wore. And those Keegan wore.

He knelt beside Kolt, grabbing his brother's hand, and wrapping it around the bracelet. Under its maker's touch, the manacle became pliable, and Braxton slid his hand from its cruel grasp.

Free at last, visions danced before his eyes unrestrained. He could make no sense of the millions of shards of colors and sounds. Then, in an instant, they were gone, leaving him once more in a gray reality. Of his earth magic, it was like the ocean was gently lapping at his toes, reminding him it was here, ready to do his bidding—eager to be put to use.

Taking a breath and feeling unburdened for the first time in his life, Braxton dragged Kolt the few feet to where Keegan lay, prone and unmoving. He hoped her condition was not permanent.

He forced his brother to remove her manacles as well, then stood towering over them both. "Goodbye, brother. I hope the afterlife is not kind to you."

«««« »»»»

Kade watched Braxton slowly look to Kolt, then ram the Queen Killer into the king's chest without a hint of remorse. He wasn't sure who was more surprised, Kolt or the rest of them. Forcefully freed of the sword, Kolt collapsed to the ground, blood oozing from the fresh wound and from between his lips. Braxton wasted no time using Kolt's limp hand to remove the slajor manacle he wore, then doing the same for Keegan.

Assuming Braxton would not oppose them, Kade raced across the expanse of snow, the depth of the drifts making him work twice as hard. He knew Keegan wasn't dead, but she also wasn't far from Lunos's clutches. Kade recalled the wounds and injuries she'd sustained during the Battle of the Solstice and imagined none had been tended to. Reaching his sister, he rolled her over and felt relief upon seeing the faint rise and fall of her chest.

He felt a gaze boring into him and looked up. Braxton's face was red, partially from cold, but mostly from anger.

"Don't," Jared headed the prince off, reaching them. "I don't agree with what he did, but let's try to prevent further bloodshed. Yeah?"

It was plain Braxton wasn't inclined to agree, but Jared had given an order, and Braxton was a good soldier—he needed someone to lead him. Though maybe he was straying from that precedence.

Jared continued, "Braxton, I'll need you to come with me to make the castle's soldiers stand down."

"I have more important things to worry about," the prince growled. "Ima—"

"Will be looked after by Kade," Jared cut him off.

"No, Keegan's my only concern," Kade contradicted. "I can deal with the soldiers while Braxton tends to the beast."

"You caused the problem with Ima, you will deal with it," Jared snapped. "That's an order." *Do not contradict me,* Jared raged, *Now is not the time. If you wish to brawl later, I'll happily do so. But for now, DO AS YOU'RE TOLD!*

Kade cringed and realized while Jared had only been Commander for a few days, he was already proving this was a role he'd been destined to fill.

He grumbled as he trekked through the snow again and wondered if he would take Jared up on his offer to brawl later. Approaching the griffin and her rider he could see Mara hadn't bothered to free her hands and was awkwardly holding them over the stump at Ima's shoulder—the snow around them was soaked, fingers of purple rivulets showing just how much had been lost. Tears streamed down the girl's face and Kade knew she feared for her friend's life as much as he feared for his sister's.

Viscous bile rose in Kade's throat as his no longer anger-agitated mind heeded his actions. The griffin had been innocent, another pawn used by the Alagards to subjugate the world. And now she would die—or at best be forever grounded. And it was his fault alone. This would never have happened if he hadn't let Keegan go. So much would be different if he'd been stronger.

He forced the dark clouds of thought away; he could dwell on them later. For now, he'd been ordered to see to the griffin. Setting his mind to the task, he instructed the girl, "Move."

Mara's red-rimmed eyes turned to meet his and darkened with fury.

Kade was ready when she flung herself at him, aiming to claw his face. He grabbed her wrists and held them steadfast. "If I'm fighting you, I can't save her," he said. He would save the griffin… or do his best to. He didn't want to make promises he couldn't keep, not even to himself.

The tide of hate ebbed away from Mara, and she sank down, sobbing.

What point is there to saving my life? Ima asked. *I will never know the touch of the clouds again.*

Kade gulped. *There's always a point. And I'll do what I can.*

Doing your best is not a guarantee.

It is all I have to offer.

Shutting her out, Kade went to a snowbank and took an armload of snow. Kneeling beside her, he packed it into the wound. It quickly turned to purple slush at the warmth of her life force. As the snow was sullied, he discarded it, replacing it with virgin white.

Chapter 41

Aron could not feel Keegan or her pain and was not sure what that meant. If it was death, he could not take that loss. Nor could the world. But he still had hope; from Eoghan's story of his own empathy link, it would be painfully clear if Keegan had met the god of death. So then why could he not feel her pain?

As he paced across the small cell, he wanted to remain positive, wanted to hope Sola and Lunos had other designs for them. But his mind always wandered back to death. The inevitable.

It had been only a night since his forced return to Agrielha, but in that time, he felt as if he had aged. His bones ached and he was inexplicably tired.

There was the sound of the lock being opened and a spear of fear shot through his heart. Lunos was coming for him. Kolt had done as he saw fit with Keegan and now it was his turn.

Then, Jared stood in the doorway, saying, "She's alive."

Peace, or a semblance of such, returned to his mind. Alive. But for how long? Aron recalled her injuries and her stymied attempt at meeting death. "Where is she?"

"Rohan's—the doctor. I take it you know where to find him. Go to her," Jared commanded.

From Jared's garb, thick pants, well-worn boots, and a heavy cloak, items needed to survive the cold winter temperatures, he must have plans to leave Agrielha soon. "Going somewhere?"

"Not yet… maybe. Or maybe not for a while," Jared answered.

The uncertainty of the answer was acceptable given that chaos reigned. As it had since Keegan had appeared in their lives.

Nodding, Aron slipped past the leader of the Lazado. It was not until he was well clear of the dungeons that he became aware of a pressing matter. If Jared was able to free him with a key, did Kolt no longer rule?

It had to be. Then what of Braxton? Jared knew Braxton's hand had been forced all his life and Aron chose to believe his eldest brother was still alive. Maybe a captive, but alive. Braxton deserved that much.

As much as he probably should have been asking questions, Keegan was his first and only priority now. There would be time to figure out what had happened to his brothers later.

The taking of Agrielha must have been peaceful as Rohan's door was closed and the halls outside his workspace silent. A blessing. Both for those who had been spared and for the fact the doctor could give Keegan his undivided ministrations.

Knocking on the door, he was bid to enter.

The room was warm, despite the windows being wide open to let in the numbing fingers of winter. A sweaty sheen coated Rohan and the only form of greeting he gave was a flick of the eyes upward to see who had entered. On the table before the doctor lay Keegan, a sheet covering her from ribs to shoulders, leaving her stomach bare.

He wanted to ask how she was, but from her condition it was painfully clear; she was in hands that could undo the damage, but it would take time.

"What can I do to help?" Aron asked, closing the door. Whatever energy he had, he would give it away willingly—even to the point of death.

"Nothing," Rohan grunted. "She's not likely to die."

"My energy—" he started.

"While I thank you, I'll decline."

"But—"

"Concern yourself with politics and leave the healing to me. If I need you, I'll call."

Aron knew she was in good hands, but… he owed her. And he loved her.

Rohan glanced up and his features softened. "Take a seat; at the very least you can tell me how each injury happened. That is, if you know."

«««« »»»»

Walking from the dungeons, Jared began a mental list of the things he needed to attend to: Nico, Ima, the other leaders… His head throbbed from the effort it took to come up with every menial thing he needed or wanted to do to set the world right.

Finally, he had enough and began to curse, even going so far as to kick the wall. He'd been spurred by the heat of the moment—and Keegan's dire need—and it was a wonder things had gone favorably. But now he had to face the consequences. And to do so, first and foremost, required communication with the other leaders. It would've been an easy task… had he thought to bring the Looking Glass shard with him. But time had been of the essence and his thoughts had been on more important things.

"What has you all trussed up?" Braxton asked, materializing from the shadows.

The idea that Braxton had been spying, or worse, intending to harm him, flashed across his mind. Then logic waylaid alarm; if Braxton's intentions weren't in their favor, Kolt would still be alive… Keegan would be dead.

"I need to contact some people," he said, unsure of what Braxton knew about their campaign—and not inclined to make him any the wiser if it could be avoided.

"I would say use the Looking Glass," Braxton answered, "but I doubt your friends have access to one."

"You'd be wrong. Where is it?"

The prince, or ex-prince, began walking through the corridors, leading him to an out of the way, nondescript room. Inside was a full-length mirror. The only thing marking it as a Looking Glass was that the entire room was dedicated to it.

Bernot had once shown him how to use the Looking Glass shard and Jared knew to speak the names of the other races in the Old Language. The effect should've been instantaneous, but instead, all that stared back was the inverse of himself. Maybe not all Looking Glasses operated the same?

"How does it work?" he demanded.

Braxton opened his mouth, but instead of sound, he furrowed his brows. He remained that way for several moments. "I am not sure. My father simply waved a hand before its surface."

Repeating the names of the other races, Jared waved a hand in front of the mirror. Nothing changed. He tried again, instead sending the words out mentally. Still nothing.

Braxton took a hesitant step forward, and knowing he wished to try, Jared stepped aside. When he received as much luck, Braxton said, "Maybe it only works for my father."

"Maybe so," Jared growled.

What was he to do now? He could hardly fly back to the river plains, leaving the castle under the care of Kade and Aron. Kade… was a mess, guilt-ridden and driven by anger. Aron's only true concern was Keegan and that she survived. And having seen what Braxton was capable of, Jared wouldn't be surprised to find his friends dead upon his return—though, perhaps not; Braxton had always been described as unlike his family, and his actions proved it. But Jared couldn't take the risk.

Then, he remembered Tahrin. She and the Western Front were a half a day's ride on horseback. It could only take less time by dragonback. And he had two of those at his disposal… well, if he asked nicely. One problem taken care of.

"I need you to go to the river plains and instruct your Commanders to stand down," Jared instructed. It would keep Braxton from doing any damage here should he so desire, and Kolt's… Braxton's… his? Commanders needed to know the war had ended, that no more blood need be shed.

"As you wish," Braxton responded, the taste of ash riding on the response. He clearly understood Jared didn't trust him left to his own devices near the seat of power.

«««« »»»»

The air was rife with tension, and word from Jared was doing nothing to lessen it. Three days without a leader had not been kind to the Lazado—men were starting to question if Jared was fit to lead. Thankfully, no one had stepped up to take his place, but without a good reason, Mahogen knew many would demand a replacement—and soon.

Eoghan was the last to join them, his shard of Looking Glass in hand.

"Proceed," Okleiy snapped.

Jared took a breath. "Kolt is dead, Braxton has surrendered."

Mahogen froze. From his shoulder, Adjran gave the warning of a scream, and he quickly resumed his pacing. He refused to leave the child in the care of anyone else, and the only way to get her to sleep was to walk with her.

"How?" Atlia managed.

"Kade and I came to rescue Keegan," Jared started.

There were some mumbled aggravations, but it had been assumed that that was where they had gone. Mahogen was thankful no one rebuked the human for being reckless.

"We captured a griffin and one of the Vosjnik on the way and leveraged them to parley with Kolt. Kolt met with us… though we now know he had no intention of making a trade. He ordered Braxton to kill Keegan…"

A unanimous breath was held. Kolt was cruel; it was now a question of if someone had intervened. Which they had, given that Keegan was alive.

"Instead, Braxton turned on Kolt. Then surrendered to us," the Lazado leader finished.

"And you left him alone?" Mahogen's father snarled.

The muscles in Jared's jaw tightened. "No. He has been sent to inform Kolt's Commanders of his death and the surrender. Kade and Aron are still at Agrielha where Keegan is receiving medical attention."

"So, our march was for naught?" Rangi said. Normally, the Buluo remained silent at meetings as events rarely affected him or his people, given they were still working to elect a leader.

"How far away are you?" Tahrin's man asked.

"Two days."

"Join us, for I have no doubt there are those who will still resist," Atlia requested.

"You are certainly right," Okleiy spoke, "but our goal has been completed. Whatever happens now is not a concern to the Alvor. The humans can decide the fate of their kingdom on their own."

There was a murmur of agreement from the others, though no one was as eager to pull their support outright.

The conversation continued, and while Jared was understandably unhappy about the inclinations of the others, he understood. Still, he had no intentions of being left outside in a snowstorm.

Eventually, all agreed a complete removal of support from the other races would not bode well for the start of a new era. So, they would remain, neither moving forward nor back. However, the humans would continue to Agrielha as quickly as winter conditions would allow.

It was a fair agreement.

The peace having been said and settled, Jared and Tahrin vanished from the Looking Glasses and the shards were put in pockets.

Knowing he was no longer needed, Mahogen grabbed his cloak and headed into the cold, making sure to wrap the garment tightly around Adjran. Walking back to his tent, his mind refused to stray from the fact Jared was in over his head. He had never ruled and had not been raised to do so. He would need a friendly face, one that could offer advice.

Immediately Mahogen's mind was made up. He would travel to Agrielha to offer whatever he could.

«««« »»»»

Nico wasn't sure… well, he wasn't sure. Something felt off about… everything. The whole castle was breathing easy—a feeling he wasn't familiar with here. Something had changed—something monumental.

He paused to look out one of the many windows and as far as the eye could see, the world was bathed in white, the declining sun reflecting off the frozen layer blindingly. It was beautiful in its own way—yet daunting. About to pull away from the sill, a blot of red caught his attention. A dragon. Headed straight for them.

About to sound the alarm, he decided against it. He was prisoner here and that dragon could be his salvation. Nico watched as the beast neared the castle and began to drift toward the whitewashed earth.

A smudge of brown atop the dragon's back alerted him to the fact they had more than one visitor. Given the dragon's flight path thus far, he was fairly confident he knew where it was going to land. Their guest deserved a welcoming committee, and certainly a helping hand in taking down Kolt. Which, now that he thought about it, he'd not seen hide or hair of the king all day.

Pushing away from the window, Nico quickly made his way through the halls, flabbergasted that no one else was the least bit concerned about the dragon's appearance. Something was afoot. But he could puzzle that out after welcoming their guest.

Behind the wooden barrier separating tame and wild, snow was piled in drifts several feet high. A single path led away from the castle, likely to the stables.

As the dragon grew closer, Nico had second thoughts. He didn't know who he was going to meet, and they might not recognize him as friend. Then he considered, what was the worst that could happen?

Pushing the door closed behind him, Nico immediately felt winter beginning to suckle the warmth from his exposed skin, raising the hairs across his body in a shivering wave. He waited by the door for the dragon to land, afraid his approach beforehand would be seen as a hostile action. The dragon took its sweet time, almost making him believe it wasn't going to land. The first sign of the beast's presence outside of a visual was a cracking wind that sent snow and ice flying through the air. Nico raised the hem of his cloak like a shield to keep from being sliced apart. When the storm abated, he was left with a glorious rust-colored dragon taking up the scene before him.

He'd seen dragons before, in the Battle of the Solstice, but not like this. There, they'd been bloodthirsty and fighting to stave off death. This one had not a care in the world and could just… beautifully exist. And he dared to consider it might be even more regal than the griffins. No, not quite—they stood on equal footing. What one lacked the other possessed, making neither the ultimate ruler of the sky.

Carefully, Nico began trudging through the now loosely packed snowdrifts. The dragon watched him warily but didn't react.

The man on the dragon's back hadn't noticed him and slid from the scaly beast, sinking deeply into the snow. He had to fight to pull his legs from its depths.

Under other circumstances, Nico would've laughed at his brother's situation. At the moment, he was simply glad Jared was alive, and here. And there was only one way he would be so carefree in proximity to the castle—somehow, someway, the Lazado had prevailed.

"Jared!" Nico called, wading through the snow, not caring about the details of how. He wanted to run, but winter insisted he took his time, and it made their greeting all the sweeter.

His brother looked him over, an almost confused expression on his face. It immediately melted to one of relief, then remorse, then happiness.

Standing between the dragon and the castle, their arms wrapped and tightened around the other. Nico was sure there was plenty to say, but he didn't need any words at the moment. This was enough.

««« »»»

It felt good to not have to chain Myrish to the wall upon their return, but Braxton was not sure the griffins would not steal away in the night. He was sure they had had their fill of humans, and rightly so, but he would miss them.

Freedom is there if we want it, Crowlin said, *but we have made friends here. Nor do we know the world of griffins. For the moment, here we shall stay. But one day... we may go. And it will be our choice.*

Braxton nodded, knowing he would be sorely sad when they finally decided to depart.

Night was falling, quicker by the second as the sun succumbed to the moon, though inside the castle, a permanent twilight was created by the torches lighting the halls. The gloom allowed Braxton to be trapped by his thoughts, something he wished to avoid. But alas.

Branshaw had been placid at the news of Kolt's defeat... and demise. There had been no rallying cry that they would fight for Braxton instead. He did not know the man outside his rank and occupation but had to wonder if war, battle, and death had been thrust upon him rather than a chosen path. Though this moment of peace might not last long if the rest of the country was not ready to submit to a new monarch.

Yet, even if there were those who were unhappy, winter would not make it easy to do much about it. A new king... or maybe queen, would be well in place before spring made rebellion possible. Braxton smiled at the thought; maybe for once this weight—to knock down those who sought to rise above his family—would not fall on his shoulders. But as much as he wanted to hope that, he knew it would never be so.

A face in the darkness caused him to jolt. Over the initial racing of his heart, he realized he was looking at the face of a dragon. But not a living one. He was gazing upon the dragon carved into the doors leading to the chapel of the prioress. Hardly dampened by the low light of the torches on either side of the doors, the white beast opposite its twin glinted.

Why was he here? What reason did he have to come to the hall of death? Then he remembered Kolt, and an acrid taste rose in his throat. He did not recall asking anyone to fetch the body, but the prioresses had always been a mysterious force, always knowing when death called someone away.

Guiltily, Braxton eased open the door bearing Sola, the black dragon of life, the hinges silent—he felt like they should have screamed, much like most of the living who passed between them did. The inside of the chapel was calm, deathly so. A single candle was afforded to light the entire room, strategically placed next to the stone platform.

Even in the dark, the form of a body upon the slab would have been distinguishable. With the meager light, it was malevolent. Or maybe it just appeared that way to him, because he had been the cause. Or maybe it was because of the monster his brother had been.

Normally, Braxton would have shut the door behind him, but not this time. To be closed in the room would make him feel claustrophobic, trapped… He didn't observe any signs he was not alone, but even so, he crept forward cautiously, like a child up to no good.

On the table, Kolt had been laid out, a sheet pulled up to his breast, hiding that which marked his mortality. His brother might have been asleep; the petrified, angry, and confused expression of his final moment had been removed from his features.

At the faint sound of footsteps, Braxton glanced over his shoulder. From the shadows came a prioress, though not the same one he had met when he had come to see his father's corpse. She was lithe and there was a nervous childlike air about her.

"It's good he's dead," she said softly, coming to stand beside him. "He was not a good man... or king."

Braxton wanted to rebuke her but could not. He could not think of a single kind, courageous, or noble thing Kolt had done. But did that mean he deserved death?

Carefully, the prioress pulled the sheet up to fully cover Kolt, then gave Braxton a gentle nod and disappeared back into the shadows.

Braxton was not sure she was gone, but at least he could forget she was there. Delicately, he pulled back the sheet to reveal Kolt's face.

What choices had his brother made, even the choices of those around him, that had made him such a hateful, spiteful person? Was there something he could have done? Or was Kolt always destined to be a despicable person?

He wanted to believe there had been a chance for Kolt to be a force of good in the world. It was better than the alternative. And the thought that his hope was likely not so, made him begin to cry. And, so, he wept for the brother that might have been, the one he would not have been forced to kill.

Chapter 42

Keegan's eyes blinked open, then quickly closed, the light too painful and bright. Even with her lids closed, the afterimage still burned against her retinas. As the stabbing pain subsided, she listened. Everything was… peaceful. Somewhere nearby a fire crackled. Light gusts of wind spun playfully past an open window. And she knew it was open because she could feel winter's hand caressing her cheek. An aroma, like that of dried plants permeated the air.

But none of this felt right. What had gone so disastrously amiss that, what she assumed was a peaceful scene, wasn't?

She attempted to raise a hand to rub her eyes and pain bloomed, the worst buds stemming from her abdomen and shoulder. Agony forced her eyes to open upon a dizzy and bright world. Panic rose in her chest, a feeling telling her she needed to flee. That sense only deepened when she felt hands pressing against her—keeping her pinned and prisoner.

Head swimming, eyes filled with cotton, mouth gritty with the feeling of sand, she started to resist. Little good it did her. She might as well have been paralyzed for how much she was able to move without excruciating pain lancing through her body.

Someone was saying her name, sounding alarmed, and her heart played on that. But there was something else, too… that person was trying to soothe.

Realizing resistance was futile—for the moment—she stopped fighting, letting her body relax into whatever it laid upon. Slowly, she brought her eyes into focus, clearing away the cobwebs covering them. She would've loved to take in the room, but two faces hovering over her were all she could see. One she recognized, the other she did not.

"Aron?"

"I am here." A pair of hands stopped pinning her down and instead gripped her hand, as if it was the only thing keeping her there. "I am here."

"I should be dead." The words came naturally. Her mind was confused and couldn't recall why she should be dead, but she knew it deep in her bones.

Aron's face didn't show surprise.

"How?" she managed to ask. Her vision was starting to fade, her body doing what it thought best to protect the mind from pain.

A mix of emotions danced on Aron's quickly blurring face; someone had died. And if she was alive…

"Kolt… is dead," Aron finally managed, explaining why grief and joy fought for a hold over him.

Everything was near black now, her body unable to withstand its hurt any more. But she had time to say a final thing before reentering oblivion. "Good."

«««« »»»»

The dragon slowly drifted toward the castle, never flapping her wings as the ground inched closer. Though Mahogen had not reached out and forewarned anyone of his arrival, he was sure Jared would be there to greet him. Seeing the lone figure of a man, contrasted heavily against the snow, he knew he was right.

The brown dragon landed gracefully, hardly jolting Mahogen, and thankfully not waking Adjran from her light sleep. The back of a dragon had not proved to be the best nursery, and the child was, rightfully so, sleep-deprived and cranky.

Thank you, Mahogen told the dragon, sliding from her back to land lightly in the snow.

Jarshua, who had spent the ride in a fur-lined pouch, wiggled from the bag with a joyful yip. Tail wagging furiously, relaying his thoughts of being on the ground again, the pup began to romp, forging furrows in the snow like the trail of the world's fastest snail. As he frolicked, he snapped at lumps in the powder, sneezing as the cold danced in his sinuses.

Preemptively, Mahogen sheltered Adjran—who was swaddled against his chest to keep his hands free—in the folds of his cloak as his hair began to whip around his face when the dragon took to the sky again, heading west toward Lake Romann. The snow was slow to settle, creating a fleeting shower that had a kind of magical charm to it. A large lump showed where Jarshua was buried and with a wiggle, the pup's head burst from the maw of white.

Mahogen was still lost in the scene's gayety and the gently drifting flakes when he felt hands pulling on him. Lips met his, and his shoulders relaxed.

When Jared pulled away, Mahogen said with a smile, "It is good to see you, too."

Jared laughed and kissed him again, conveying emotions words could never name. They could have stayed there all day had Adjran not fussed.

"Where is everyone else?" Jared asked, ushering them toward a door.

"What do you mean?" Once inside, warmth immediately began to seep into Mahogen's body, defrosting bits of him he had not even realized were cold.

Jared's eyebrows furrowed and disappointment tinged his words. "No one else came with you?"

Mahogen chuckled. "We cannot read your mind. Well… I cannot. You never asked that anyone come. You are lucky I recognized you were going to need help."

Jared tucked his chin in admonishment, akin to a scolded child. Oh yes, he was going to need all the help Mahogen could give. And likely more.

"Still," Mahogen teased, "I do have some idea of what you want… sometimes." He fished the Lazado's piece of Looking Glass from a pocket.

Jared stared, mouth slightly agape. "Have I told you you're amazing?"

He could not help but chuckle and bite his lip. "Not today."

They easily bantered the entire way through the castle, Jarshua plodding along beside them, occasionally stopping to sniff at a random object before bounding to catch up. Mahogen did not know where they were headed but when they stopped, they were inside someone's chambers—likely Jared's. Or so he hoped.

The room certainly had not belonged to a king, but it was… cozy. A fire crackled in the hearth and a bed big enough for two was piled high with thick blankets. A bookshelf, laden heavily, stood next to a neatly organized desk. Jarshua headed toward the fire and plopped down, tongue sagging from between his teeth. Little whisps of steam began to unfurl from his damp coat as he drifted to sleep.

"I'll have to get a bassinet for Adjran," Jared said, "unless you think having your own rooms would be a better idea."

Mahogen was silent for a moment. As much as he wanted to stay with Jared, he knew how humans reacted and with the turmoil, maybe it was better if they kept up platonic appearances. Just for a while, as much as that would hurt. Before melancholy settled in, he answered, "For now, I think that would be best. And that way you have an escape from Adjran when she decides to wail. And when Jarshua decides to howl."

From the look on Jared's face, he knew what Mahogen's concerns actually were. "Of course. Please, feel free to relax here for a while and I'll have some rooms set up for you. Now, before I have another talk with the other leaders, what exactly should I be asking them to send?"

"Well, for starters, you are going to need more men that are yours. The castle guards are fine to keep on retainer, but they should be outnumbered by those loyal to you."

Jared's eyes widened, then he clenched them shut. "I'm such an idiot!"

Mahogen chuckled. "No, just inexperienced. And wanting to see the good in others—which is not a bad thing."

Jared had a thought. "I do not want to make too many of our men travel here; what do you think about bringing in the men from the Western Front and sending the other races back to Jims?"

Mahogen mulled over the idea. "I think that is best. Show the rest of your kind you want peace, but also protect yourself without making a huge show of it."

"What else?"

"Well, a spellcaster, or two, would be nice. You will need to get into contact with the city lords at some point and they can help with that."

"Will this Looking Glass not be able to reach them?"

"Under normal circumstances there would be no issues. But Atlia's Looking Glasses were spelled specifically for you leaders, I think."

"Ah. Anything else?"

"A few smiths would not go amiss. Your brothers. Keegan's guard. Any supplies that can be spared—you could rise high in the minds of the commoners by redistributing those amongst the needy of the city proper."

"Thank you," Jared said, giving him another kiss before dashing out the door.

As Jared's footsteps faded, so did Mahogen's smile. Jared had a duty to his people and to the world. Many things would come first. He pushed the thought away; he too had a duty to the Alvor people, but they would make this work, even if it was only stealing the barest of moments when the old gods allowed it.

«««« »»»»

The smell of hay and damp was prevalent—and somehow claustrophobic to Braxton. The inside of the stables was dim with wintery light, pale as if suggesting the inhabitants should peacefully hibernate. Most of the split doors had been closed against the storm that had now passed. Though the grooms were supposed to see to their charges daily, the current conditions did not make them inclined to do so. But the horses were content, most dozing or munching on plentiful hay.

But Braxton was not there for the horses. And he wished he was not there at all.

Taking a big breath through his nose, he made his way along the alleyway, a harsher smell, one indicating the stable hands had mucking to do, mixed with the scent of hay and dust. As he walked, the only sounds he heard came from the horses, a few snickers, a whinny, a snort. The closer he got to the back of the stable, the quieter and eerier things became.

Cautiously, afraid to break the palpable tension in the air, Braxton peered into the stall. Plenty of hay covered the floor, more than any other stall had been allotted. Granted, in this case the hay was for comfort rather than consumption. Stains of purple were splattered here and there, potent amongst the dried yellow stalks.

This was not his first choice of locale, but what choice was there? Without two wings, Ima could not fly to the griffin stable. And to go through the castle, the narrow, winding staircases and the men at arms—it would not do. This was the only option; and he hated to see her here amongst the landlocked. He hated to see her despise life. But most importantly, he hated Kade for taking away Ima's one source of true freedom.

But there was nothing he could do about it—nor could anyone else; not unless they discovered the ability to reverse time.

"Mara," he said softly, making the girl start.

Her eyes were red and puffy, salt lines marking her cheeks. Dejection was all he could see in her eyes—that and anger.

"Are you hungry?" he asked, forcing himself to step into the stall. He willed the tray in his hands to not wobble.

A wall of misery settled on his shoulders the longer he stared at the girl. Soon he too would gladly curl up in a corner and weep if he could.

Mara said nothing and returned her attention to Ima, the two of them sitting in silence, curled against each other.

Carefully, Braxton sat beside the girl, making sure to place the tray of food where it did not seem like he was insisting she eat. And then joined them in their silence.

Without realizing what she was doing, Mara began to pick at the food, nibbling half-heartedly at first. He wished the same trick would work for Ima, but she was beyond gentle prodding.

"You should come sleep in the castle for a night," he suggested. "Warm up a bit."

No response.

"I know Nico would like to see you."

He knew instantly that was the wrong thing to say.

"He can burn for all I care," Mara snapped vehemently.

Nico had told him why they were in this situation. And while it was not what Braxton would have done, he could not blame the boy for acting in the moment—doing whatever necessary to protect his family.

There were many things he could have said, all of them logical, to prove Nico deserved forgiveness but they had not reached that stage. And that was fine—Mara and Ima were entitled to their rage. For now.

Knowing there was nothing else he could do, he pulled Mara against him, sheltering her against his warmth. As she began to cry, he stroked her hair, knowing she would eventually burst from the darkness, but that Ima might never be so lucky.

««« »»»

Lucas wanted to rant and rave, call Jared a bastard, but he actually understood—and agreed—with his motivations. Keegan was important and had needed saving. But why did it hurt so much? Likely because his brother hadn't even bothered to say goodbye—or let him know of his plan. Jared would pay for that later, but Lucas did understand.

"So, he wants us to go to Agrielha?" Lucas repeated, just to make sure he'd heard correctly.

Though Jared had become the Lazado's leader, little had changed in how their family was treated, revered. Some days he liked being one of the many, some days he hated being on the outer edge of the light, and some days he wished Jared's position could do more for them.

"Of course, he does!" Elhyas snapped. "He probably would've taken you outright if things hadn't been so dire."

That made him feel better. He hadn't thought his brother needed to leave straightaway to have any chance of saving their savior. His heart hardened at the thought that Jared didn't know about Carter; then began to thaw. He was requested in Agrielha because Jared had succeeded in saving Keegan—and she might be the only person who could put Carter right. Now there were two reasons to go and none to stay.

"We'll go," he said. "Though… Carter might—*won't*—be able to ride a horse."

"Horses wouldn't be able to get us to Agrielha before spring. No, we're going by dragonback," Elhyas told him nonchalantly.

His blood chilled, recalling the one time he'd been unfortunate enough to find himself in the sky. The sickening sight of the earth so far below had his stomach churning even now. "Is that…" he started.

"The only way?" Elhyas finished. "Yes. Pack your things, we're hoping to set off in a few days."

"Why not now?" Lucas asked past the coils in his stomach as the guard rose.

"We have provisions to gather. Things to arrange." Elhyas started toward the door, then stopped. "We're trying to round up a few smiths to go as well; think you can convince that grizzly friend of yours to come along?"

Lucas doubted it. "I can certainly try."

"Please, do. Jared asked for him by name."

That took him aback. "Why?"

"Said he needed someone who would call him on his vito. And he needs someone to keep Keegan in line."

Lucas laughed. "Can anyone do that?"

Elhyas sighed, shook his head, and left. They both knew from experience Keegan was beholden to no one but herself. And maybe the old gods.

The world became quiet now that Lucas was alone. Normally, Carter would be with him, or at least not in the hospital tent. Lucas shook his head to beat back those black thoughts. Keegan would be able to fix him. She had to.

Reinforcing the belief that nothing was impossible when it came to Keegan, he rose and went to seek Waylan. He almost laughed; before now, he never did anyone's bidding—aside from his father's. Now, he was taking orders from Jared—not that he minded; Jared would always have his family's best interests in mind—and the interests of so many more at heart.

The winter sun, weak as it was, offered a surprising warmth. Though not enough for him to shed layers, the feeling of her touch on his cheek was resplendent and it buoyed the hope growing in his chest.

Lucas hadn't been to see Waylan since the battle, Carter having taken up all his waking hours, and nightmares his sleeping ones. Now he wondered if Waylan was alive. He smiled, imagining the conversation the smith might have had with the god of death—and how Lunos might have given him back to the living just to be free of him.

Long before he arrived outside Waylan's tent, he knew at the very least the smith had survived. The din of the hammer on steel rang through the day like the clear sound of a bell.

The tent was much the way it had been before the Battle of the Solstice, minus the clutter of hastily made weapons. Lucas took a moment to take it all in, waiting for Waylan to acknowledge his presence. He was left waiting longer than he would've thought—and liked.

"Kind of you to finally check in," Waylan growled, stalking him past to grab a set of tongs.

"I'm sorry," Lucas opened before explaining about Carter.

Upon hearing about Carter, Waylan's haughtiness dropped away to be replaced by genuine concern. And it helped that Lucas apologized. Then, he got to explain why he'd finally come to see the smith. And to tell him of Jared's request.

"Sure, I'll go with you," Waylan said casually, taking Lucas aback. "I've always wanted to tell a king to fuck off."

«««« »»»»

Nico was surprised his boots weren't entirely soaked through at this point, but that just spoke to the quality of the leather. If someone had asked him a year ago if he ever thought he'd have boots this nice... However, he knew they wouldn't remain dry forever; actually, very soon he would start to feel the chill, even if he kept pacing. He knew what he had to do but had no desire to do it. This was entirely his fault, and if he could take it back, he would. But he couldn't, no matter how sorry he was.

Sooner or later, Harker said, sprawled out and completely comfortable in the thick layer of snow.

Desperately, he wanted to scream—but that would alert Mara and Ima to his presence. If they weren't already aware.

Sooner or later, Harker repeated, licking a paw.

The griffin was right, but that didn't make it any easier. He hadn't meant for any of this to happen; all he'd wanted was to make sure Jared survived. And he still had trouble processing how much damage he'd done.

Steeling himself, he walked a final lap before forcing himself inside the stable. To his shock... or maybe dismay—Harker followed. While he wanted the griffin as moral support, a part of him didn't want the griffin to see Ima at what would be her lowest low... or witness any of the well-deserved anger that was about to be heaped onto him.

The inside of the stable was stunted, as if trying to take a breath but unable. Maybe it was just him. Harker nudged him forward and he took a tentative step.

He'd heard what Kade had done, hadn't wanted to believe it, but had heard. It didn't prepare him for what he saw. The cut was clean, precise... and the guilt he felt pushed at the back of this throat.

Nico could stand at the stall door all day and not say a word. He could stand and weep for the rest of his life. He didn't have to reach out to Ima to know how much pain he'd caused.

Harker, not even pausing, approached his nestmate.

Ima didn't notice him at first, but when she did, it was hard to miss the longing in her glossy eyes. Both for connection with him and for what he was still capable of.

Harker carefully preened at her neck, rubbed against her cheek—mourned with her, letting her know that she would always be a child of the sky. Gaining acceptance, Harker sank into the hay beside Ima, his wing carefully wrapped around her as the two nuzzled together.

Nico saw hope—not that Ima would ever fly again but that she could lead a full life. He felt a tugging on his arm and realized Mara was pulling him away from the tender moment.

She led him through the stable and back into the gaze of the pale winery sun. There was no anger in her features.

Hope flourished in his breast. It did not last.

Fury quickly contorted Mara's features, the warmth of her hair turning to a raging fire—one that would burn and scar. The transformation was monstrous, and all Nico could do was watch in horror as her fist barreled down on him. There was a crack as her knuckles connected with his nose. Tears immediately welled in his eyes as his hands reached up to feel the damage—and create a protective barrier. But he needn't have worried about further attack; at least not yet.

Mara stood, eyes transfixed, as if she couldn't believe her punch had landed. Disbelief was slow to fade, but when it did, the fire returned. "This is your fault," she screeched, pulling her fist back again.

Nico only had a few choices. He could take her hits—he certainly deserved them. He could strike back. He could block and dodge. None seemed right, but he had to do something.

Tears dripped down Mara's cheeks, but for once in his life—and likely the last and only time in his life—he had an idea of exactly what a woman wanted. He stopped Mara's punch and pulled her close.

She fought, slapping his shoulders, pushing against him.

And still he held tight.

Slowly, Mara calmed and let herself be held.

"I'm sorry," he said quietly as she sobbed into his chest.

She proffered no response.

He would be forgiven—certainly not now, but it would happen.

Chapter 43

"Well," Rohan trailed off, stepping back, an unsure air about him, "that should do it."

Tentatively, Keegan flexed her fingers, rolled her knuckles, twirled her wrist, flexed her elbow. So far, no pain. Rolling her shoulder, she felt nothing at first. Then a twinge that made her wince, but not enough that she couldn't move her arm. And even raising and lowering her arm, moving it at most angles, proved fruitful. It was a drastic change from what she'd been able to do—or rather, had *not* been able to do—a few days ago.

Sighing and taking on a downtrodden countenance, Rohan placed his hands over her shoulder once more. It wasn't long before he pulled away. "There's not much more I can do. I'm sorry. I don't know why, but it's as if parts of the bones are... just gone!"

A small part of Keegan wanted to be mad, to rant and rave, be angry she would have a bad shoulder. But that wasn't fair to Rohan; he'd done his best. Hell, she couldn't even be mad at Braxton—she'd stabbed him first.

Her silence seemed to unsettle the doctor and he began rambling about all the reasons he could do no more. Keegan didn't let him get too far before easing his conscience.

"I can keep trying," Rohan said. "Don't know what it'll do, but I can."

Aron opened his mouth and Keegan quickly cut him off. "I've taken enough of your time. The fact I *have* a shoulder again is damn impressive. If I have a few twinges when I move wrong, so be it."

Rohan gave her a terse smile. "I'm sorry I can't—"

A sudden howling gale, like that of a hurricane, blasted through the air.

"The hell was that?" Keegan asked, sliding from the exam table. From the stunned looks on Aron's and Rohan's faces, they hadn't a clue either.

Pushing open the window, Keegan was assaulted with a puddle of color below. She had to blink a few times before she could focus against the glare off the snow. "Dragons?" she muttered, unsure of their consequence.

Then she noticed the people sliding from their backs, a few hunching over to release the contents of their stomach.

She felt body heat against her back and realized Aron and Rohan were peering over her shoulder. The warmth increased as Aron wrapped his arms around her waist and leaned his head on her shoulder.

"I hope this isn't more wounded," Rohan grumbled. Thanks to her, he hadn't had a break in days.

"Doubtful," Keegan said, noting the unhindered way in which the people below moved. "And besides, I can always help."

"Not yet," Rohan huffed, reaching past her to pull the shutters closed. The temperature in the room immediately rose.

"I got two arms that work," she chuffed. "Mostly."

"And muscles that have atrophied and bones that may still be weak," the doctor said. He came to the table and picked up a discarded loop of cloth. "Here."

"A sling? Seriously?"

"At least for a few days," Aron said in an attempt to help Rohan. "What can it hurt?"

"Fine," she conceded with a deep sigh. "Now let's go see who's here!"

««« »»»

The new year was upon them, bringing optimism and a fresh start. Jared hoped the men from the Western Front would arrive today; it would certainly be fortuitous.

"Spotted on the horizon," a servant said, popping his head in the doorway.

Jared nodded his thanks, refraining from laughing—only days ago a horde of dragons on the horizon would've set the inhabitants of Agrielha into a lather.

Knowing it'd still be some time before the dragons, and those riding them arrived, he grabbed his cloak before leaving his room. The reports could wait—not that he was in a rush to read through them anyway.

Walking the subdued halls of the castle, he wondered if he should have *anyone* else with him. He chuckled to himself when he realized that would be no easy feat—well, it would be hard to have someone he trusted at his side. Keegan was still recovering, and Aron would likely refuse to leave her side—which he encouraged; Keegan left alone usually led to difficult situations.

He couldn't imagine Braxton would be welcome—even if his intentions had proven true, so far. Kade was… he had no idea where Kade had holed himself up; he had to fix that later. Mahogen would be with Adjran, and it wouldn't do well to submit the child to the chill. Nico would be in the stables with Mara and Ima; he likely would hear the commotion and come see what it was about on his own. He couldn't truly count on anyone to be standing behind him today. It was a strange feeling.

His musings were more encompassing than he imagined for he suddenly found himself standing before a door. Taking a breath, he pushed it open, inviting the cold to fight against the boundaries of the castle.

The world outside was bright and pristine, a cheerful winter day. Jared imagined himself hurling snowballs with his brothers, laughter ringing in the air. Before the illusion shattered and the shards cut and sliced him, he reminded himself that world was dead, and tucked the happy memory away. On the horizon, a blot bobbed amongst the clouds. Dragons.

It wasn't long before the shots of color gained detail and pulled from the heavens. Oddly, only a small portion of the horde, fifteen, chose to alight. No doubt someone would eventually explain. Even so, he telepathically called into the castle to ask for assistance in bringing in supplies—whether he was heard… he'd soon know.

The downdraft from fifteen sets of wings was heavy and he had no chance of withstanding it, finding himself pushed face first into the snow. Luckily, he wasn't held there long, but still arose gasping for air. Where he now stood was a crater, the loosely packed snow having been blasted in all directions—aside from a vaguely human shaped mound where he'd been held against the ground.

Many of the faces on the dragons' backs were a green tone and their owners were quick to find their feet on the ground once more—some landing on knees to spew the contents of their stomachs. Spotting Lucas and Carter amongst the men, Jared rushed toward them.

He pulled his brothers close, a stone in his stomach he hadn't known existed disappearing. "It's good to see you."

"And you," Lucas replied. "We need to see Keegan."

Jared pulled back laughing. "You? Need to see Keegan? I can only imagine what for!"

A second of anger flashed across Lucas's face, his eyes darting toward Carter.

Jared looked his younger brother up and down, noticing nothing amiss, even if he leaned heavily against Lucas. "Is something wrong?"

Lucas opened his mouth, but the words choked him.

"I was injured in the battle," Carter said. "My spine was... damaged. We need Keegan to see if... if she can help."

The situation must be severe if Lucas was willing to seek Keegan's help.

Hearing a noise behind him, he turned, glad to see several guards and servants tentatively stepping outside. Many faces blanched at the sight of the dragons.

A man showing the least amount of fear said, "You asked for assistance?"

"Yes. Please help everyone get their things inside. Keegan's guards," Jared said, pointing them out, "are to be given full access to the castle. I need a spellcaster sent to my chambers as soon as possible. And Waylan should be given rooms near the forge and complete access to it."

"Yes, sir."

It was amazing how no one questioned him. Not so long ago, he wouldn't have been able to make any of these demands.

Turning back to his brother, he found Carter now had a crudely crafted crutch under one arm. Seeing it made the situation all the more real and his throat constricted. "Let's get you to Keegan."

"No need," Lucas replied. "Here she comes."

«««« »»»»

Keegan had certainly seen better days, but Lucas didn't doubt she'd also seen worse—especially of late. Though not fully formed, dark circles lined her eyes, and she moved stiffly. Her arm was obviously injured as it was in a sling, though he couldn't imagine someone hadn't immediately seen to it. So that begged the question of why hadn't it been healed? Was the injury so bad it *couldn't* be healed?

Some injuries were stronger than magic and it seemed even Keegan was no exception to them. If even their savior had to bear some insults, it didn't bode well for Carter—and Lucas couldn't bear to believe his brother might remain crippled. He forced the thought from his mind; Keegan would be able to fix Carter.

"Lucas," Jared called.

From the concerned looks he was getting, he hadn't heard anything that had been said over the last several minutes. Lucas mumbled a pleasantry to Keegan, hoping that would satisfy everyone, and let silence sit over them.

Ever the astute one, Keegan zeroed in on Carter. "What happened?"

Carter's eyes flicked over to Lucas and Jared picked up on the tension.

Jared began pushing Carter toward the doorway, "Please, come inside. I'll have some borzan and cider warmed for us. And food prepared if you're hungry."

Lucas knew the tactic well; stalling was a habit in the Sieme family. But for once, he didn't mind. If Carter could be healed, what were a few more minutes and food and drink in their bellies? And if not, what was a few more minutes of hope?

As they made their way to the dining hall, Jared sent servants scurrying about, orders for whatever food was presently available and mugs of warm cider and borzan.

Never in his dreams had Lucas imagined their family would have this kind of power. Then again, he would've guffawed at the events of the past half year if he hadn't lived them. It made him wonder what else the old gods had in store for them. He hoped it was good after all the loss they'd suffered.

The dining hall was massive, truly deserving of a king. But it was also cold and uninviting—lonely. At the door, Jared said a few words to Aron who had joined them. Whatever was said, Aron didn't like, but obeyed, retreating to a window just outside the doors that looked over the snow-covered plain and settled into a position that alluded to having been taken often before.

Carefully, Jared pulled the doors to the dining hall closed. From side doors, servants appeared, food and drink in hand. Duties completed, they were dismissed.

Privacy, Lucas realized. And what a gift it was. Even if it smothered them.

Jared cleared his throat, and yet, still no one spoke, no one moved.

"It's my back," Carter said quietly, staring fixedly at the plate before him.

"The fact you're walking at all is good. But I imagine it's serious if Lucas has sucked up his pride and is asking for help," Keegan said kindly. "What exactly happened?"

"I was stabbed."

Keegan lowered her chin, as if expecting him to continue. When he didn't, she sighed and launched into a series of questions—most of which Carter wasn't able to answer. She rose, saying, "I'll see what I can do, but no promises."

She had Carter lean forward and gingerly lifted the back of his shirt. Lucas knew there was no visible damage to find. Keegan trailed a finger down Carter's spine. Just below his ribs, she stopped and placed her palm flush with his skin.

When Keegan finally pulled away, a sense of peace settled over Lucas. Until she opened her mouth.

"I'm sorry." She didn't need to say anything more.

"Don't be sorry, fix him," Lucas barked.

Keegan looked taken aback. "What the—"

"It's alright," Carter cut her off. "You tried. We were already told it might be impossible."

With a contrite look, Keegan looked back at Carter. "There might be some hope. With some physical therapy and time, you could regain coordination and movement."

"And you will adapt if not," Jared finally spoke. "And you have friends and family who will support you no matter what."

Jared wasn't wrong, but Lucas desperately needed Carter to be whole again. His brother shouldn't have a permanent reminder of everything they'd fought for, everything wrong with the world. It wasn't fair.

"Come on," Keegan said, "I'll introduce you to Rohan. He might have a trick or two up his sleeve that I don't." She helped Carter from his seat and began walking him from the dining hall, their arms interlocked.

Jared lingered for a moment, then stood, his chair scraping against the stone floor. "He'll be okay. We all will."

Once everyone had left, Lucas let the tears fall.

«««« »»»»

Closing the door, Braxton was glad to banish the cold from his bones. Walking through the dim corridors of the castle's lower levels, he rubbed his arms to quicken the return of feeling to his body. With the sun having just set, most of the castle's inhabitants were likely sitting near a hearth, enjoying food, a warm drink, and merry company.

He very much wished to partake... but doubted he would be welcome. The guards who had once owed allegiance to Kolt were likely to believe him just as brutal as his brother. The guards who owed allegiance to Jared were unlikely to trust him. And the Children of Prophecy were likely to be the worst aspect of each. He could not blame them.

Had he not viciously killed Kolt? And what about all the horrible things he had done under commands from his father and brother? But seeing he had turned on Kolt, did that not prove he was a traitor, that his loyalties were changeable? Though they were all wrong about him, he did not blame them.

In his room, he called for a servant and asked for dinner to be brought to his chambers. The girl did not say anything other than, "Yes, sir."

Likely, the staff and servants thought of him as lazy and entitled. But there existed a few who had seen glimpses of the man behind the mask he wore every day. Yet, he doubted they would speak up and break the notion he was anything but a ruthless pawn.

The serving girl soon returned, a plate in one hand, a mug of ale he had not asked for in the other. At least some still saw him as human—worthy of small kindnesses.

"Thank you."

She dipped her head and left.

But not human enough. There would always be the stain of the monsters in his family borne on his name.

Glumly, he stared at the plate. Of its own accord, his hand picked up the fork and stabbed at the food. At least his own body knew the truth, knew the ordeals he had faced and the hard decisions he had made. All in the name of a better good.

Taking a breath, Braxton forced all thoughts from his mind and… existed. He did not hear the screams of the wind outside, nor feel the warming aura of the fire in the hearth, nor taste the food in his mouth.

His head bobbed forward, and he jerked back to reality. Or something that resembled it.

He was in the throne room, alone.

Warily, he cast his eyes about, looking for danger. There was none. He was utterly alone.

It was then he noticed the throne. A red tinge began to creep into the gold while a whisper called, "Ravliean. Ravliean." The color continued to darken, then dripped from the throne's surface. It was not until the tang of iron assaulted him that he realized it was blood.

Braxton propelled himself backwards and fell. As quickly as his drop began, it ended. Wheezing, he rolled away from the fallen chair, his chest burning as he struggled to take a breath.

When he could finally breathe again, panic settled over him. He could not imagine a bleeding throne boded well.

Chapter 44

The stables had become a safe place. There the world didn't see Ima's disfigurement. Nor did it see their sorrow and anger. Really, it didn't see them at all. And Mara liked it that way. For the first time in her life, she could just be.

Braxton wasn't to blame and therefore was begrudgingly welcome to sit with them. He often tried to coax them into conversation, and always failed. But Mara appreciated the gesture. She was still whole in the eyes of the world—even if she didn't feel it. But what Kade had ripped away from Ima had been taken from her too in a way.

Do you think Nico will come today? Mara asked.

Nico wasn't completely forgiven yet—but he was truly remorseful. He had neither foreseen nor meant for this to happen. As much as the results of his actions stung, even Ima had come to forgive him—not that she'd been inclined to inform him of that yet.

I hope so, Ima responded. *Just because I am a cripple does not mean you need bear the burden, too.*

Because I love you, I will, she told the griffin stubbornly. When Ima was ready to reemerge into the world, she would be by her side.

Ima tensed and Mara assumed someone was approaching. Though the door was closed, the griffin had a way of sensing when someone approached—smell, Ima had explained.

Mara considered standing to open the door but decided against it. Nico would barge in, Braxton wouldn't take no for an answer, and the servants who brought them food left it in the corridor.

Straining her ears, Mara was able to convince herself she could hear the person shuffling through the stable, strands of straw scraping against the loose dirt that made the floor. Then came a knock; it was a tentative, shy sound. This wasn't one of their usual visitors.

Let him in, Ima bristled, the feathers at the base of her neck rising.

Mara couldn't fathom who was waiting for them to make the griffin react so. Opening the stall door, she found her answer: Kade.

A snarl escaped Mara's lips, her own hackles rising. "What do you want?"

Let him in, Ima repeated.

When Mara turned to look at the griffin, she had risen to her feet.

Warily, Mara did as the griffin asked. Kade was Ima's monster to confront—who was she to say when or even if she could ever face him? But something didn't sit right, something was about to go horribly wrong.

She reached out preemptively. *Braxton.*

Is everything all right? came his response.

Kade's here in the stables. I have a bad feeling...

I'll be there in a few minutes.

Bring Kade's friends.

Returning her attention to Kade, he had certainly seen better days. But hadn't they all? His eyes were sunken and dark rings were beginning to show underneath them. And where he had once stood tall and proud, his shoulders hunched as if he wanted to be overlooked.

"What do you want?" Mara demanded again, eyes flicking between him and Ima.

"To apologize," Kade said quietly. "I'm sorry. I shouldn't—"

Ima had been relatively calm until that moment, but the mere mention of his heinous act was enough to send her tumbling over the edge. Quick as the wind, the griffin lunged.

Mara was pushed aside, tumbling to the ground. Her head struck something, bringing lights and spots across her vision. When her sight cleared, she gave a choked squeak upon seeing Ima's beak clamped over Kade's arm. No blood flowed yet, but she could sense that was what Ima intended.

Your apologies will never be enough, the griffin screamed. *But your equal suffering will.* Having said her piece, Ima clamped her beak shut with a bone-breaking crunch.

For a moment, Mara was afraid the griffin had hurt herself.

Then came Kade's curdling scream and the warm spray of blood from the stump that had once held his arm.

«««« »»»»

Having been informed of Mara's request for their presence, Keegan, Jared, and Aron raced through the halls as if their lives depended on it—though it was more accurate that potentially Kade's did. At the door leading to the snow-laden outside world, they met with Braxton.

"What's this all about?" Jared demanded, slightly out of breath.

"Mara did not say," the prince responded, flinging open the door, "only that she had a bad feeling."

Though completely unaware of what situation they were about to thrust themselves into, Keegan was inclined to concur. When it came to the lot of them, bad feelings meant something, and usually not something good.

Due to the horses needing tending, and the stable's newest occupants needing food and company, a well-trodden path through the snow allowed them to continue at their frenzied pace.

Bursting into the stables, the horses began to prance about, picking up on their nervous, excited energy.

Keegan was halfway to Ima's stall when an iron tang all but slapped her in the face. Getting to the stall Ima and Mara had taken for themselves, she wasn't sure what was going on… or even what to make of the chaos.

The first person she noticed was Mara. The girl was half-leaning against the wall near the door, stripes of blood, as if from arterial spray, splashed across her face and body. Horror was written on her face, and it seemed as if she was too stunned to move.

Her attention was next drawn to the back corner, where, surrounded in ruddy stalks of hay, a teal griffin Keegan knew was Ima, was chewing on something. It… almost looked like… an arm. Then she noticed Kade, collapsed just to the right of the door.

"Jesus, fuck," she exclaimed, kneeling beside her brother. It *was* an arm Ima was chewing on.

She quickly placed her hands over what had once been Kade's arm—what was now a truncated stump. With the entire limb missing below the elbow, she knew at least one artery had been severed, which explained his state of unconsciousness. Magic immediately began to flow, and she didn't consciously notice Aron running down the hallway to vomit, or Jared blanching, or Braxton rushing to check on Mara. All her focus was dedicated to Kade.

Absentmindedly, she instructed someone to retrieve Kade's arm—a sentence which felt alien and almost laughable. Some part of her knew no one moved, but she didn't care. She had to worry about stopping the bleeding; and, while not ideal, he could live without an arm.

Kade was lucky; whatever… whoever had removed his arm had done it cleanly. With no ragged ends to the bone or blood vessels, stopping the bleeding was at the very least manageable.

"Someone get me his fucking arm!" Keegan yelled, finally having the chance to think past the first stages of treatment and panic.

"Uh…" Jared mumbled, tucking his chin as if he too was going to be sick.

Keegan looked over her shoulder at the griffin, and it finally well and truly hit her what the beast was chewing on. Now *she* wanted to be sick.

Fair is fair, came the griffin. There was no satisfaction, anger, pride, or any emotion in the words. They were just an explanation, a truth.

Keegan gulped to keep back the bile rising in her throat. "Jared, Aron," she said tentatively, "I'm gonna need you guys to carry Kade. Braxton… could you get his arm?"

Feeling Mara was in no immediate danger, Braxton began to creep toward Ima, like one might with a dog that had their shoe.

Ima's hackles raised and she released a bone-chilling hiss.

"I think he is going to have to live without it," Braxton whispered. "Or more of us are going to lose limbs."

«««« »»»»

The world swam around Kade… yet didn't move at all. Suddenly, he gasped, like a fish out of water, and bolted upright. His body felt feather light, as did his mind, almost as if he were drugged. Hands were suddenly on his shoulders, pushing him down.

"Where am I?" he groggily asked, fighting against whatever forces sought to control him. He lost.

"The infirmary," a familiar voice he couldn't place said.

His vision blacked and when he came to again, things were less muddled. He recognized where, and even when, he was. A fire crackled nearby, providing warmth. His body still felt strange.

A cup was pressed to his lips, and as cool liquid slid down his throat, he fully came to. Rohan stood above him, his dark skin tawny in the dim light, looking almost shadow-like. He remembered something pressing against him, then nothing else.

Kade awoke with a start, his mind alert, yet completely confused. Looking around, he knew he was in Rohan's infirmary—yet he couldn't say why. His head felt light, and as he tried to sit up, someone approached and forcefully insisted he remain prostrate.

"Here, eat," the doctor pressed a small bit of bread to his lips.

Though it had no flavor, Kade ate ravenously. "Where am I?" he finally managed, even if he knew the answer.

He was given a response—the predicted one.

"Why am I here?"

Silence greeted him, then a voice said, "Um..."

He recognized it, but only in passing. Focusing his gaze on the speaker, he saw Jared. No, merely many of Jared's features. So, not Jared, a relative. His mind worked, struggling to place the person. Carter, he finally realized.

"Why am I here?" he demanded again.

Feeling an itch along the back of his neck, he raised his left hand to scratch it—except, his hand never touched his neck. He could feel his fingers, flex them, yet inexplicably, they felt foreign, as if they were nothing but thought.

He glanced at his left side and was cognizant enough to recognize his shoulder and bicep were wrapped in bandages. He wanted to look at his hand, see the damage, but someone was stopping him. "What happened?" Kade demanded furiously.

Rohan explained, but he didn't hear it.

He couldn't recount how many times his question was answered, and how many times his mind refused to comprehend.

"Kade?" Carter said, limping toward him.

He turned to the Sieme brother.

"Look at me. Take hold of my hand."

Nothing would've normally possessed Kade to do so, but somehow, he felt a kind of strength lending itself to him—a strength he needed to comprehend what was going on... what had happened to him. The fingers of his right hand tightened around a palm, grounding him to the present. And he was forced to listen and comprehend.

Tears began to drip down his cheeks.

Something wrapped around him, giving him warmth he didn't know was possible. Soothing words were said. Soothing thoughts were forced into his head. All too soon, as if in a dream, he was lowering down, down, down. All too soon, darkness, another form of nightmare, was overtaking him once again.

《《《 》》》

"Jared..." Mahogen said, tentatively broaching the subject, "it is time." They had had this conversation just about every day. Yet nothing came of it. And with what had just happened to Kade, this needed to be taken care of sooner rather than later.

"I know, I know," Jared repeated, raising his hands heatedly as he paced across the room. "But…"

All of Jared's fears had been voiced, and Mahogen had countered them all. Yet, he was still afraid to broach the subject.

"The humans cannot survive without a leader for much longer. Even if you only appoint yourself in the interim…"

"I know!" Jared angrily cut him off. "Just—"

"Being in charge is a lot harder than you thought," Mahogen finished as Jared exasperatedly sunk into an armchair.

He sighed. "Yes." There was a moment's pause. "Especially after today."

The loss of Kade's arm had been quite the topic of conversation. And many had concluded he was no longer in the running for the throne. Not that Mahogen believed his name had ever been mentioned in that regard.

"Keegan would be a good option," Mahogen said. Whether or not he believed that was irrelevant.

"Too much an outsider," Jared argued, rubbing his temples. "Maybe next—"

"No," Mahogen cut in. "It needs to happen this week. Tomorrow if possible. You have been able to survive off passive leadership while winter is here. But once the snows melt, every city lord will be looking to claim their own kingdom. And maybe a few heads."

Jared looked like a scolded child, crouched in the armchair as he was. "I know."

"Then do something about it!"

When Jared was slow to respond, Mahogen rose from his own chair and lithely crossed the room. Gently he took Jared's face in his hands. "It will not be easy but is has to be done."

"I know."

"You say that yet refuse to act." When Jared avoided his gaze, he could not help but smile. "You, and Keegan, and Aron, and Kade will figure it out," he promised, "but you have to open the conversation."

"I know."

Mahogen smirked. "Is that the only thing you are going to say today?"

Jared opened his mouth to respond, then smartly shut it. His lips pursed into a simpering grin. "No." He paused and sighed. "When Kade is well enough, I will formally hold a meeting."

Mahogen closed the little bit of distance between them, their lips meeting. "Good. And I will hold you to it. Now, the hour is late, we should head to bed."

With a deep breath, Jared nodded. His eyes were glazed over, his mind ruminating on more than most people could fathom.

Mahogen gently kissed his forehead and let him stand. He hoped for a kiss in parting, but with everything weighing on him, Jared was too focused on shuffling along to see the longing in his eyes.

When alone, aside from Adjran in her crib and Jarshua beside her, a chill swept into the room, reminding him how empty life could be without love. The fire in the hearth crackled wearily, giving just enough warmth to stay Lunos's hand.

Silently, he blew out the candles and crawled into bed. Even the mattress and sheets were ice cold in shared sorrow. Some days it was hard to remember Jared had more on his plate than most did in a lifetime. Some days, Mahogen wanted to be selfish. Some days, he wanted humans to be more understanding. But only time would let any of those wishes come to pass.

As he tossed and turned, sleep avoided him and the hate he harbored for not being able to share it with Jared burgeoned. But that was just a matter of yet. One day they would. At least he hoped so.

Suddenly, the door burst open, and a shadow raced to the bassinet where Adjran lay sleeping peacefully.

Mahogen was on his feet in an instant, a dagger in hand shortly thereafter.

"It's me," Jared said, moments before the dagger would have been used to do damage.

"What are you doing here at this hour?" Mahogen demanded, his heart rate slowly leveling. "It has to be near midnight."

At the sudden disruption to the night, Jarshua bolted awake and gave a small yip. Thankfully, it was not loud enough to wake Adjran.

Jared bent down and ruffled the pup's ears to show him no harm was coming to his Harang. "I just remembered... today's the day."

Mahogen's eyebrows furrowed. "What are you... Oh!"

Adjran had been in their lives for thirty-five days exactly. If Sola and Lunos saw fit to bless her with elemental abilities, they would manifest today.

But Mahogen did not believe she was going to be so blessed, given Jarshua had chosen her to be half of a Harang. A pairing that shared a lack of magic.

"Any signs of fever? Discomfort?" Jared asked hopefully, despite logic.

Even before the markings appeared on an elemental's wrist, there were signs. To an unknowing person they looked like sickness. But to those who knew better, the timing was no coincidence.

"No," Mahogen said. "She has been her normal self."

In the dark, it was hard to see Jared's shoulders sag, though whether of disappointment or relief, he was uncertain.

There was a slight shuffle and Mahogen hoped Jarshua was returning to sleep. If the pup decided now was the time to be awake, Adjran would follow suit… meaning so would he. And they would all suffer come sunrise.

"I suppose she will have to get things done the regular way," Jared said, a glint of white near his mouth the only sign he was not upset. He reached into the bassinet to caress the child's face. "I know many people, little one, who never needed magic. You'll be in good company."

Seeming to hear him, Adjran gave a sleepy coo, though did not rouse from the sweet dreams dancing in her little head.

Gently running his thumb over the child's forehead, Jared whispered, "I should head back to my own room."

Past the lump in his throat, Mahogen answered in the affirmative. Then thought better of it. "Maybe you should stay the night… just in case the timing is off. Bernot and Lyerlly were both brimming with magic, I *almost* believe it impossible their daughter should not be as well."

"Perhaps you are right." Quietly, Jared went to the door and closed it.

Mahogen was already in bed, waiting. He felt the mattress shift as Jared settled upon it. Then a body was pressed against his.

He smiled and slowly drifted to sleep.

Chapter 45

Awkwardly, Jared paced back and forth across the room while his friends watched, concerned glances jumping between them. He'd hoped it would take Kade more than three days to recover. None of them knew why he had asked them there. And after only three days since Kade's… incident, they probably didn't have a guess that would land close to the truth either.

Fighting past the constriction in his chest, past the finality this discussion would have, Jared broached the subject. "We need to decide who's going to lead… us. Humans, as a whole."

Keegan muttered, "Damn well took you long enough."

"So… who's going to lead us?" he reiterated.

Keegan was the first to respond. "Well, what kind of government do you want?"

"What?" Kade asked. Though still recovering from the loss of his arm, and enjoying the effects of some numbing herbs, Keegan demanded he, and everyone else, act as normal, claiming it would speed his recovery. For her sake, or maybe his, Kade was going along with it.

Though no longer pale and on the brink of death, there was a hollowness in Kade's eyes. He knew what he'd lost, and in turn the limitations put on him. It was a humbling parallel with Ima; while she would never fly, he would never… now that he thought about it, there was nothing Kade couldn't do, though plenty of things he would struggle to do. But those feelings, at least for Kade, were stuffed into a place of darkness. For now, Kade was just dealing with the physical loss; later would come the implied costs.

"Well…" Keegan started, "we can continue with a monarchy or, there's democracy. Or even meritocracy. And republics. And democratic republics."

Jared only knew what one of those was—and could only image how complicated all the others were.

"What are those?" Aron asked bravely.

Keegan raised a brow. "Which ones?"

Jared's head spun as the conversation continued. There were merits to each form of government as much as there were pitfalls. Honestly, there seemed no best choice. He was aware of the others discussing their options, but all he could process was placing one foot in front of the other.

At some point, someone called his name to bring him back to reality.

"What do you think?" Aron asked.

"I… haven't been paying attention," he admitted.

This spurred Keegan to re-explain. And for him to not pay attention once again.

The pattern repeated itself several times before Keegan shouted exasperatedly, "We might as well keep it a damn monarchy for all y'all're worth. At least for a little while until things settle down; then maybe we can talk about it becoming something else."

Unwilling to admit he *still* hadn't been paying attention, Jared nodded. As long as he didn't have to make the final decision, he was all right with whatever happened. As long as he didn't have to lead an entire country. His stomach clenched at the thought.

"Jared. Jared!" Keegan called. "What are your thoughts?"

He hated to admit he didn't have any. That he was happy to let someone else deal with this. And as he had that thought, his gut clenched. Bernot had seen something in him, deemed him worthy enough to lead after his demise. He owed himself that faith. But leading an army of rebels was drastically different from running a country.

"We're just asking for your opinion," Kade finally spoke up. "I wouldn't put you on the throne, and I can't imagine too many would be happy about it if we did."

It should've been an insult, but it steadied him. "Honestly, I think we should incur as little change as possible for the moment. Times have already been tumultuous. Most will seek the familiar."

"So, monarchy," Keegan reiterated. "Now, who do we crown?"

He glanced between Aron and Kade, hoping—praying—they wouldn't throw his name out... even if Kade had already pointed out he wouldn't get a warm welcome from the populous if that somehow came to be.

Eventually, seeing they weren't going to offer any ideas, Keegan began spouting nominations.

Jared was inclined to agree with all of them—as long as they weren't him.

Once Keegan opened the flood gates, Aron and Kade were more inclined to discuss and nominate. Yet after what felt like hours, they hadn't come to a consensus. They could think of no one who would lend themselves to the commoners, the lords and ladies, and the other races. There was always an insurmountable rift.

Keegan said finally, "You can't please everyone but pissing them off is a piece of cake."

As their conversation dwindled, their wells of ideas running dry, Jared noticed Keegan had become increasingly quiet—as if she wasn't saying something. "Keegan, you've still got one last idea, don't you?"

She took a breath, avoiding their gazes. "I do... but I don't think any of y'all will be particularly fond of it."

"How bad could it be?" Kade asked, going to cross his arms. The motion quickly set off his balance—both mentally and physically—and brought a green tinge to his face.

Slowly, Keegan said, "What about one of the Alagards?"

««« »»»

Heat flooded to Aron's ears as Kade laughed at Keegan's suggestion of putting either he or Braxton on the throne. Kade was not wrong... but it still hurt.

Keegan shot her twin a harsh glare, though it did nothing to stymie his laughter.

Once Kade settled himself, Jared said, "With all that Caius has done over the past two centuries, I can't imagine anyone would be overjoyed at the thought of his children sitting on the throne."

Aron felt a pit in Keegan's stomach, and the guilty look on her face said she knew something they didn't.

"Keegan..." he said worriedly.

She looked at him, pity and indecision dancing in her eyes. For several seconds she remained silent, as if struggling to find words. No, not struggling to find words, struggling to find the *right* words. "I don't think this was how he wanted you to find out."

Aron's eyebrows creased. "Find out what? Who are we talking about?"

Ignoring his questions, she turned to Jared. "What if they're not..." she gulped, "*his* children?"

A dead silence hung in the air. The posed question was simple; the implications behind it were anything but.

And what the question implied… a rabid chill ran down Aron's back.

"If they're not Caius's, then whose?" Kade exclaimed.

"Alyck's," Aron mumbled, looking the truth fully in the eyes.

When Keegan did not correct him, the room began to spin. A part of him wanted to deny he was Alyck's son, a part of him was glad, and a part had known all along.

He had always assumed he and Braxton just looked more like their mother with their black hair and blue eyes. And looking at her portrait, it was easy to believe. But now he saw he and his brother for what they were, a mix of both their parents. And he understood how the secret had gone undiscovered, for of course Caius's children might share features with their uncle—the same or similar ones that their "father" had.

Keegan avoided his gaze. "Yeah, Alyck's your father."

He half listened as Keegan began to explain the truth, and how she had come to learn it. But what did it matter—the truth was fact, and nothing could change it, not even the circumstance of its knowledge. All he wanted was silence, time to… process. And once Keegan was done talking came more discussion, more questions.

At some point, they must have come to some decision for silence enveloped the room—what it was though, he could not say.

"Aron?" Keegan prodded gently, placing a hand on his leg.

Her touch burned, and acid rose in his throat as he felt like she had slapped him. Brusquely, he brushed her aside and stood. He could not stand the looks Jared and Kade were giving him. Pity. Suddenly, it felt like a stone pressed against his chest, making it hard to breathe.

Quickly, he took his leave. His legs carried him of their own volition, seeking out the one place where he might find peace. The one place he was just Aron.

««« »»»

Carefully, Braxton pushed open the door. Though the snow was piled deep atop the castle, someone had already made the effort to escape to this little sanctuary. Stepping into the biting wind, he saw Aron standing at the edge of the gable.

Using the path his brother had forged, Braxton joined him. "I believe congratulations are in order."

Though Aron did not respond, the way his shoulders and jaw tensed said everything. Together they stood, only the whistling of the winter wind making a sound.

"What if I do not want it?" Aron finally whispered, his words almost undecipherable as they were sucked away by the breeze.

Braxton could not help but smile. He acutely recalled how similar feelings had constricted his own chest not so long ago—amongst other worries. "Unfortunately, I do not think this is something you have much of a choice in. Besides, not wanting the throne is good; it means you deserve it more than anyone else."

Aron gave a snort, the warm puff of air clouding around his head momentarily before dissipating. Then, a sigh. "I was not raised to rule; you were. Why do they not give you the throne?"

It was a valid question. With it coming to light that Caius was not their father, Keegan had told him both of their names had been tossed around but one factor set them apart.

"Because…" Braxton began, "you showed you were willing to stand up for what is right." It was kinder than admitting he himself had been too afraid.

"I do not think I can rule. I… Jared would be better suited."

"I do not think so," Braxton said, draping an arm over his brother's shoulders. "Jared knows the sentiments of the common man. And he has only been a leader for a short time."

"That is still more experience than me! And whose sentiments do I know?"

"For sentiments, well, you know how the lord thinks but also what the commoner needs. And our claim is greater than Jared's, as sons of Seleena."

"If we had been Caius's sons, our claim would have been only useful for house arrest or execution," Aron spat.

It was hard to argue truth. Taking Aron's shoulders, Braxton turned his brother to face him. "Look, there is no right answer as to why they chose you. But just like Bernot saw something in Jared, your friends see something in you."

Aron was still stiff, disinclined to believe he could be a king.

"And no one said you have to rule alone. Fa- Caius may have chosen to do so, but you can appoint advisors; and one day you will have a queen." It was miniscule, but he could tell some of the weight lifted from Aron's shoulders.

"You think I can do it?"

"I think this is what you were born to do." After the words left his mouth, he realized they had not been a lie to make this easier for his brother.

Aron gulped, then nodded.

A grin tugged at the corners of his lips. "Come on, we cannot have the new king catching pneumonia." He was shocked by the easy smile that creased Aron's face. A little faith went a long way.

Braxton fully encased them in darkness as he closed the door to the passageway and immediately, there were the sounds of Aron descending confidently. He followed behind, not nearly as easily, but without falling into one of the many traps.

Coming to the end of the passage, he sensed Aron hesitating. "You will be a good king," he promised. Braxton reached out and placed his hands on Aron's shoulders, giving a comforting squeeze.

The light from the torches in the hallway was blinding for a moment and, ever a creature of habit, Aron peered from the doorway cautiously to make sure the way outside was devoid of life. Satisfied they were alone, he slipped back into the realm of reality. He did not look back to see if Braxton too reentered the world of high expectations, and mindlessly made his way along—likely still lost in confusion at the turn of events.

Braxton said a quick prayer to the old gods that his brother would live a happy life. He doubted he was heard, but one never knew. Then, bracing himself, he stepped into the light and immediately regretted it. What he saw, he could not decipher, but it could only mean death and horror. As he was forced to watch, his fists clenched, nails biting into flesh.

He dug his fingernails deeper into his palm and his eyes snapped open, the vision vanishing. Ragged breaths heaved at his chest, emphasizing the horror he believed to be coming for them. He blinked and was faced with the gore once again. The throne, in all its golden glory, was red—blood-red. But it was not just the color of death, it *was* death. Blood oozed from every crevice in the worked gilds, dripping, screaming, dying.

A disembodied voice whispered, "Ravliean. Ravliean."

Though his nails dug deep and deeper still into his palms, that pain was nothing to what he *knew* was coming. And that pain was not enough to dissuade the vision from blinding him from everything else.

Every time he blinked, the vision returned, fraying his nerves further. But as Thaddeus had pointed out so long ago, there might be many meanings. Yet, he knew exactly what this was supposed to mean.

He desperately wanted to scream and rage, to knock about papers and furniture. But his fury would not change the outcome.

Sinking against the wall, he put his head between his knees, rocking back and forth as tears began to fall. How could the old gods decide they deserved this fate? Why did he deserve this madness? To know what the future held… But maybe not.

Pulling himself together, or a semblance thereof, Braxton rose and marched through the castle.

Arriving at the door he needed, he unintentionally slammed it open, cringing as he imagined this was all too often how Caius had greeted his brother.

Moving faster than Braxton thought possible, Thaddeus was almost instantly in the antechamber. He must have looked how he felt for the man was quickly ushering him into their sleeping quarters.

A cup of something warm was placed into his hands. He wondered if they had known he was coming or if this had been intended for one of them.

"Braxton," Thaddeus prodded quietly, "what have you seen?"

He did not need to blink to see the weeping throne. Just thinking about it made him shake his head.

"We cannot help if you do not tell us," Alyck said, kneeling beside him.

And yet, he could not bring himself to utter what he knew the vision meant. So, instead, he asked, "Can we change the future?"

Thaddeus and Alyck shared a glance. This was not to be an easy answer. Either in explanation or in the fact it was not what Braxton wanted to hear.

Sighing, Alyck said, "Not usually."

He had known this would be the answer... but he had hoped. Yet, there was still a chance, for Alyck said *usually*.

"But," Alyck continued, "I do know one person who is constantly changing what should be."

"Keegan."

"Yes. Even the smallest actions from her can have drastic effects. Though, knowing what will cause a change... or what the change will be..."

"You fear for Aron?" Thaddeus said quietly.

Braxton nodded. It was all he could manage.

"Then, fear not. Whatever horrid thing you see, I know Keegan will not allow it to befall him. Besides," Alyck continued, "Aron will live a long and prosperous life. Of all my visions, that is the only one that has never changed."

"Then what does it mean?" Braxton demanded, before explaining what he saw.

"You are right, nothing good," Thaddeus said. "But outside that... we will not know until it has come to pass."

Chapter 46

Keegan looked him up and down before reaching out to tug on Aron's tunic. Having smoothed down the fabric, she stepped away satisfied. Compared to a week ago, Aron had come a long way, most importantly in confidence, and now, he truly looked ready to become king.

His clothing was simple, but refined and elegant. The trousers were an inky black, with nothing in the way of adornment. His shirt was a pale blue, made of silk, and appeared to flow like water across his body, while gold threading at the collar and cuffs gave it a royal feel. The boots just looked like boots to Keegan, but she knew they were made of quality leather.

Smiling, she returned her gaze to Aron's face. He had forgotten to shave this morning, but she thought the little bit of scruff made him appear more… rugged? manly? mature? ready? maybe a combination of such?

Watching his Adam's apple bob, she realized she'd been drinking in his form for a little too long and now he was worried. "Relax. You look amazing. Don't be surprised if I get into a few catfights today." When his eyebrows creased in confusion, she amended, "Don't be surprised if I've gotta fight off a few suitors."

The little bit of humor did the trick and color returned to his face. But it didn't last long. "Are you sure I can—"

"Surer than anything," she cut him off. "Aron, I wouldn't have suggested you if I didn't think you were what this world needs right now. They… *we* need someone who has seen the… mistakes Caius made—and won't repeat them."

"But what if I don't make the right choices?"

She sighed. They'd been going in circles with this conversation for days. As frustrating as it was, she would've proposed the same hitches and hiccups in his shoes. "You'll never make everyone happy. Never. And you *will* make the wrong choice sometimes. But there are people here who are willing and ready to help you. And willing to shoulder some of that blame, if need be. You might be a king, but you're not alone up there."

A moment of silence. "Actually, I… I was thinking about that."

Keegan cocked an eyebrow.

"I am alone up there… because…" carefully, Aron reached into his pocket, "I do not have a queen." Gradually, he lowered onto one knee.

She wanted to say something, probably needed to, but was too stunned to do anything but stand there. Of course, she loved Aron, but they were only twenty. Yet... she'd seen how short life could be.

Aron stared up at her expectantly, and slowly worry formed in his features. "Will you? Marry me, I mean? And is this right? You only talked about this custom once."

Hearing his questions knocked her out of her stupor. Flinging her arms around his neck excitedly, she said, "Of course!"

Aron held her tight, all the words he could've said conveyed in the gesture.

When he finally released her, she pulled him forward into a kiss. She longed for more than that, but they had a coronation to attend. As he slipped the ring onto her finger, Keegan gave an excited giggle; her heart bubbled and seemed to turn to daisies.

Looking down at the ring gracing her finger, there were too many emotions to put the feeling into words. Some of them were good; she was ecstatic to know she would one day have Aron as her husband. But some of them were bad; her family—adopted family—would never get to celebrate with her, and she didn't doubt the customs of this world would be contrary or alien compared to the ones she was accustomed to.

"Do you like it?" Aron asked sheepishly in reference to the ring.

The main gem was a marquise cut diamond with two emeralds set on either side of a silver band. It was simple and beautiful—it was perfect.

"Aron, you could've made a ring out of grass, and I wouldn't've cared. But yes, it's gorgeous."

Smiling, he pulled her into another kiss. And with that kiss, her fears for the future melted away. She and Aron had done the impossible time and time again. Nothing could stop them.

«««« »»»»

If seeing a blood-drenched throne every time he blinked was not unnerving enough, Braxton had begun to notice small losses of control over his magic. Again. It was always something small, a few cracks in the wall, earthen objects flying across the room, dust covering everything, but it made him uneasy all the same. He wanted to believe this was caused by the stress of the vision, but the pit in his stomach said it was something else—something worse. And that there was nothing he could do to stop it.

Taking a breath, he closed his eyes mistakenly and the blood-drenched throne flitted across his vision. His hand tightened around the hilt of the Queen Killer.

Having taken it from Keegan at the Battle of the Solstice, he had genuinely intended to return it to her when circumstances permitted. But she had not wanted it, claiming it belonged to him. And that it might need a change in name since it did not just kill queens.

He hated that the red color of the sword reminded him of the life he had taken, but he saw it as a reminder too. Sometimes blood needed to be shed to create a better world.

Looking out the window, Braxton realized he had left himself very little time to get to the great hall for Aron's coronation. And he *would not* be late for that. Forcing his worries and the image of the bleeding throne away, he frantically made his way through the castle.

Even as he all but ran through the halls, it was hard to not notice how empty everything felt. Had this been what it was like during his own failed coronation? Or was there something nefarious afoot?

Everyone is in the great hall, he told himself. Who would want to miss this moment in history? Alagard had killed Alagard and was being replaced by an Alagard.

Flashes of the bloody throne continued to cloud his vision as he pushed forward against the anxiety. Gritting his teeth, he refused to stop and give the vision credence. If he kept moving, maybe the event would be delayed. Aron would be a great king, noxþ everyone and everything that suggested otherwise. Royik any god that sought to make it otherwise.

Eyes watering and swimming as they fought against the vision, Braxton almost missed the flurry of movement along a side corridor. Normally, he would have assumed it was just a servant or a page or any of the many other inhabitants of the castle. But something seemed familiar. And out of place.

Pausing, Braxton stared down the stark hallway, willing the phantom to return. Shaking his head, he decided it was just another vision. It would not be the most disturbing thing of the day.

He was about to continue on when there was a blinding pain in the back of his head. He was roughly aware of falling forward, but not much else.

《《《 》》》

The doors to the great hall opened slightly and Jared watched Keegan slip in. She was the last to join the congregation, likely having been helping Aron put the final touches on his ensemble as only a woman could. She quickly made her way down the central aisle, a spring in her step. He smiled; it was good to see her in better spirits. Especially after all the hardship of late.

She slipped into the seat beside him, the deep rosewood pink fabric of her dress splaying elegantly around her like a flower. Beadwork and embroidery embellished the bodice from the hips upward. The slender sleeves stopped at the middle of her forearm. He'd never seen her in pink before, and doubted he would again, but the color suited her.

From the hardly restrained grin on her face, she was excited about something. Subtly, she showed him her left hand and his eyes were drawn to the diamond and emeralds on her finger.

"Congratulations," he whispered earnestly, gently squeezing her knee. He would have embraced her if he thought they wouldn't be judged by the lords and ladies who had come for the coronation; right now, they needed to be in their good graces.

Keegan's grin grew brighter, and she gave him a gentle nudge with her elbow. "Hey, you'll be next."

He wasn't given time to respond as the doors to the hall were thrown open to reveal Aron and the officiant.

Jared knew he should be paying attention to the history being made, but Keegan's words held more weight than likely intended. He truly cared for Mahogen, but until Keegan had said it, he'd never thought about marriage. About how humans would always scorn them. While he hoped the human world might become more accepting eventually, he didn't hold much hope for it happening in his lifetime.

But with Aron as king, would he be needed to lead the Lazado? If not, he could easily live in Edreba—where they *would* be accepted. What about his brothers? Would they be as understanding and loving as Keegan? His mind mulled over the sudden desire until Mahogen gently nudged him.

"You might want to pay attention," the Alvor said quietly, gently rocking Adjran to keep her asleep.

Looking to the dais, they were truly about to crown a king.

The priest picked up a bowl of ash. "Rule with the fierceness of your brother," he started, drawing a line of ash along Aron's upper lip.

A noise caught Jared's attention and he tuned out the coronation. He was about to think it was nothing when it came again. This time he wasn't the only one to hear it. A few lords looked toward the doors, nervous expressions on their faces. Surprisingly, a few of them looked… excited?

The room became silent and there was no mistaking the sounds. Battle. The cries of the wounded and the ring of steel on steel filtered into the room.

«««« »»»»

Through the silence shrouding the hall, the sounds of fighting could be heard coming from the corridor.

Tensely, Aron rose to his feet, utter dread in his stomach. No sooner had he risen than the doors burst open, inviting pandemonium in.

Aron did not notice the skirmishes that started, his eyes were locked onto Caius's—or, at least, someone who looked very much like him. Whoever it was stood dead center in the doorway and from the look in his eyes, was going to enjoy hunting him down.

"We need to go. Now!" Keegan snapped, pulling him from his stupor. When and how she had reached him, he could only guess.

Part of him wanted to ask how they were going to escape; the only way in was currently blocked by a ghost. But as usual, Keegan had a plan and had already set it in motion.

He blindly followed as she led him around the back of the throne and was surprised when she opened a hidden door by pressing a stone in the wall. There were even more secret passageways than he knew of. And thank the old gods it was so.

Without a torch, Keegan was forced to produce light to see by and the only way to do so was via fire magic. It was hardly a few seconds before she was forced to release the magic and send them cascading into darkness once more. He could feel her palm stinging and burning, but her mind was focused elsewhere, dulling the pain.

"What are we going to do?" he dared ask, his voice sounding shatteringly loud.

"Run," Keegan answered simply, bringing forth another flame into existence.

Due to her issues with fire magic, she never held it for more than a moment, creating a staccato effect. But it worked, and that was all that mattered.

"What about the others?"

"They know how to get out," she promised. "Right now, we need to worry about us."

As the next flame popped into existence, the light fell upon a terrifying face. The ghost had found them, followed them.

"Yes, you do," Caius said, the low light only accentuating his malevolent grin.

As the light disappeared, the sounds of a scuffle broke out. Aron knew he should step in, but being completely blind, he was as likely to damage as he was to help. And even if he thought intervening would do any good, he could not get his feet to move. His mind was too wrapped up in the fact that his father—his *uncle*—was alive and back with a vengeance.

The decisive sound of a head slamming into the wall brought him out of his stupor. And by the reflected pain in his own skull, he was not dumb enough to believe Keegan had come out on top.

A faint glow began to grow, and Aron was forced to squint. "You... are dead!"

"No, just sojourning in Mexico," Caius sneered before lunging forward.

Chapter 47

As much as Kade wanted to question where Keegan had taken Aron, he didn't have time to. He brutally thrust his dagger into his opponent, then wrenched it out, bringing forth a splatter of blood. He would've preferred to be using a sword, but it wasn't exactly feasibly with one arm… yet. Besides, though he might now be one-handed, that didn't make him any less deadly—as he was quickly proving to those who now discounted him; he still had magic and something to prove.

Stopping to survey the hall for a moment, he knew they were fighting a losing battle. Most present hadn't thought to bring weapons—who would've thought the coronation would be the stage of a coup? Again. And they were heavily outnumbered. Spotting Reven, he fought his way to his friend's side.

"We need to go!" Reven said, dispatching a soldier.

"Obviously! But where?" he snapped, blocking an attack and retaliating.

"Did you n't get the message from Keegan?"

He *had* received a mental image from his twin but hadn't been able to decipher it. From what he could tell, it was a wall somewhere in the castle. Though not just any wall, there were plenty of clues to tell him exactly where it was now that he thought about it. "What's the significance?"

It 's where a secret passageway is, Reven explained.

"Then we need to go. Now!"

Reven snapped the neck of the man he was fighting. "No, I was thinkin' we should go on a picnic!"

Scanning the room, Kade saw some of their friends and allies were missing. He assumed they had made it out—or been felled. It was hard to tell which. "Get to the passageway, I'll start sending people to you."

Reven didn't answer but pushed through the chaos to the now gaping double doors.

As his friend went, Reven grabbed Mahogen, who clutched Adjran to his chest in a now blood bespattered blanket. Together they left the hall, cleaving a pathway through their enemies, Jarshua hot on their heels.

Kade put them out of his mind and continued to hack, stab, and slash. At some point he found himself fighting beside some lord clearly loyal to the Lazado. He quickly told the man how to get to the passage then continued through the chaos.

He lost track of who he told about their escape route, but knew it was no significant number. The skirmish was nowhere close to being over, but if he waited any longer, he wasn't likely to see the end of it. Screams and cries slowed the world, and as much as he wanted to do something about it, it would only mean death for him. What he'd done wasn't enough, but it was all he could do.

Heaviness sitting in his stomach for those who were going to be left for the vultures, Kade pushed from the hall. Fights filled the hallway, but it was nothing compared to the crowded great room. As he fled, those he came across that he could help, he did; and he sent them toward the passage.

By the time he made it there himself, he was blood-soaked and weary, the dagger immensely heavy in his right hand.

Reven breathed a sigh of relief upon seeing him.

"How many have made it through?" Kade asked.

"Not enough," Reven said quietly. "They 're all waiting about a hundred yards back. No one wanted to go on their own."

"Take them wherever this tunnel leads," Kade said. "I'll wait for any stragglers."

"Are you sure that 's a good idea?"

He knew it wasn't, but after all the atrocities he'd committed weighing on him, he felt obligated to try and do some good. "No, but I'm going to do it anyway. I'll only stay another five minutes."

He could see the fear in his friend's eyes. "Fine."

The fear came from the fact that if Kade wasn't five minutes behind them, no one would come back for him—simply because they couldn't afford to.

"Be safe."

Kade nodded, not wanting to make his words a promise he might not be able keep.

«««« »»»»

Lucas's breaths came heavily, but he didn't stop. He wasn't sure how he'd made it out of the throne room, but he was thanking Sola and Lunos with every fiber of his being that he had. Now he hoped they'd smiled as favorably upon his brothers.

When the fighting had started, he'd seen a flash of castle in his mind. It hadn't been until Kade told him about the hidden passage that he realized Keegan had told them how to escape. And he berated himself for not thinking of it sooner. He knew of at least one alternative route out of the castle, thanks to his assassination of Caius… who might not actually be dead. If Keegan had been a little clearer, more would've survived; but with how many people she needed to give the message to… it was hard to blame her for being hasty and vague.

Lucas zipped around a corner, the soles of his boots losing traction. He recovered quickly and within seconds was at the wall. It was already a crack open; either someone had been careless, or they were waiting inside. Or the enemy had gotten here first.

Carefully, he pushed against the wall. Someone grabbed the front of his tunic and slammed him against the wall. Though his head was ringing from becoming acquainted with the stone, he prepared himself to fight; there was no need.

"Glad you made it," Kade whispered.

Lucas nodded, giving his heart a moment to calm. "Have my brothers come through?"

"Don't know," Kade said, peering through the doorway. "Were any friends following?"

"I don't know."

Several tense seconds passed before Kade stepped back into the passageway, gently closing the door, shutting them in an impenetrable darkness.

As the scent of iron assaulted his nose, Lucas asked, "What are you doing?"

"We've waited long enough; we have to catch up with the others."

"Others?"

"Yeah. Reven got a handful of people in and started on already. I've just been waiting for stragglers."

"Know who they are?"

Kade shook his head. "Only people I can say for a fact are waiting for us are Reven and two Lazado soldiers."

Lucas desperately wanted to press, demand answers even if Kade didn't have them.

"We'd best get going."

Lucas heard the sounds of shuffling and assumed Kade had started through the passage. "No torches?"

"Sorry, I was a little busy trying not to get killed!" Kade snapped.

«««   »»»

They reached the end of the tunnel and there was nothing to do but wait. And with no light, they had no way of knowing who was there and who was not. Adjran was quiet in Mahogen's arms, either asleep or somehow knowing to make a sound meant death. Thankfully, Jarshua had only been inclined to give a meek whine once during their trip down the dark passage.

There was the sound of someone walking into another person. Two others had already joined their group in this fashion, so he was not inclined to panic. Yet.

"Kade?" Reven tested.

"Yeah, it's me," came his response. "I've got Lucas with me."

"Thank Sola and Lunos," came Jared's voice from his left.

Mahogen released a pent-up sigh, shoulders sagging in relief. He was mostly glad Jared had made it because he loved him, but as the Lazado's leader, without him, they would succumb quickly. And they would have to start their crusade all over again.

Voices began to call out, asking if friends or loved ones were there.

"Quiet," Kade snapped. "We don't know where we are or who waits for us outside."

"We're in an inn's basement," Reven said. "I already checked. No idea which one, but if we can talk quietly, I can open the door and let in a little light. Can we do that?"

There were a few murmured responses followed by the faint sound of scraping. A gentle light penetrated the gloom and Mahogen was able to see in total there were only about twenty of them.

Suddenly, from behind them came an excited cry, "I see a light!"

Instantly their weapons were drawn. Thankfully, there was no need for further bloodshed.

"Where did you come from?" Reven asked in way of greeting to Icella, who had been leading the other group.

"From the passageway. How did you get here?"

"Same as you," Kade answered, after he'd given her a hug. "But how? I shut the door."

"Wait, where was the doorway?" Hernando asked, pushing forward.

As they continued to talk, it became clear there was more than one way out of the castle. For some reason, Keegan hadn't given them all the same escape route.

"How did she even know about the tunnels?" Hernando asked, running a hand along his face, smearing blood across it in the process.

"I sent her and Reven to explore them," Jared explained. "I didn't want something like what Lucas pulled to happen. Seems Keegan spent more time on the project than I thought."

"Not that Caius needed the tunnels," Icella mumbled.

"That was Caius," Kade said. "Noxþ! I was hoping it was a trick of the eyes."

As the humans continued to discuss the whats and the whys, Mahogen let his mind wander. He knew they needed to focus on the next step; it was only a matter of time before someone found them.

"We are safe here," a man's voice said, as the doorway was pulled completely open from the outside.

Jared let out a stream of curses.

Mahogen placed a hand on his shoulder to stop him from berating the man before he had the chance to explain. When, or even how, the man had managed to slip from the passage without anyone knowing was going to remain a mystery.

"My father is the mayor of Agrielha city," the man began.

"Doesn't explain why you'd be so asinine as to give away our position," Kade snarled.

"I am known in every inn in this city. My face is not something out of the normal; no one would blink twice if they saw me. We are in the Golden Feather—a part of the Lazado's supply train. We will be safe here. Well, some of us."

"What do you mean *some*?" Hernando asked.

"The landlord only has room for a few in the hidden attic, but he is already sending runners to the other inns that are part of the train. We will find you safe housing." What the mysterious man left unsaid was if they would be given passage out of the city.

Mahogen glanced at the humans. Those in charge still bore scowls, but none were stupid enough to contradict what the man had done. Safe harbor was invaluable. And in more ways than one, this could be helpful. With enough Lazado or friends throughout the city, they could raise the people to rebellion.

It was quickly decided their group would split and in twos, threes, no more than fours, and taken to safe houses. He—and by extension, Adjran—Jared, Icella, Lucas, Kade, and Reven, would stay with the mayor's son as his family had the largest safe house in the city. And hopefully as proven loyal subjects to Caius, they would not be suspected of harboring fugitives.

Mahogen did not want to go along with the plan but did not see much of a choice otherwise. Quietly he said a prayer that they would not soon meet with Lunos.

«««« »»»»

Cautiously, Jared watched as the others of their escape party were handed off to runners who'd guide them through the city. He didn't like the uncertainty of everything, but they didn't have a choice.

His group, Icella, Lucas, Kade, Mahogen, and Reven would be the largest, and hardest, to get out of the tunnel. They needed their leadership together—and he needed those he loved under one roof.

While they were waiting for Massyn, the mayor's son, to figure out how to get them out, Lucas pulled him aside. "We have to go back for Nico and Carter."

Jared felt his heart sink, only now realizing they were missing their younger brothers. His first instinct was to tear through the tunnel and fight his way through the castle until he found them. But he couldn't do things like that anymore—not when the entire Lazado, if not the world, was depending on him. Logic had to dictate his actions now.

"Keegan said she found three tunnels," Jared started, "So far, we've only found the survivors from two; they could easily be in the third group. And who knows if Keegan found more escape routes."

Lucas crossed his arms in a fashion Jared knew well; his brother knew he was right to be cautious and patient but didn't want to admit it. "I can't not know they're okay."

"Sonny, you think we all do n't have people we 're hoping got out?" Hernando asked. "You going back could put all o' us in dragon's fire."

"There has to be something we can do!" Lucas seethed in a whisper.

"I might have a way," Kade said sheepishly. "As long as I have the door to the tunnel open, I can search for Carter and Nico telepathically. We'll know their fate one way or another."

"And if they're alive, we can help them get out," Lucas said.

"And, if Nico and Mara were out in the stable, they might not be discovered for a while. We could send a runner to get them," Kade continued.

Jared didn't want to say it, but they couldn't mount a rescue mission. With any luck, Carter and Nico's relation to him would keep them alive if they had been captured. And maybe they could find a way to blend in with the castle's inhabitants if they still possessed their freedom. Well, not Nico; he was well known by Caius. "No. If they can make it to the passageway, we'll get them through. But I won't send anyone back to the castle."

Lucas immediately opened his mouth to argue.

"I love them, too, but we can't sacrifice *anyone* at the moment. They're smart, they'll figure out a way to blend in or get out."

"We have got a wagon," Massyn said, suddenly reappearing. "We can take four now."

"Mahogen, Reven, Icella, and Lucas," Jared said. "No arguments; we don't have the time."

«««« »»»»

The atmosphere in the room was oppressive. Thaddeus and Alyck both knew what should have happened, but by the fact Alyck sat there seemingly fine, something had gone disastrously amiss.

There was no roaring anger this time. No cursing of the gods. Just silence. As if Alyck had given up.

A fire crackled in the hearth, ostensibly the only sound in the world. As logs splintered in the blistering heat, Thaddeus could feel his heart and resolve cracking too. "Did you know?" he finally asked.

Alyck rubbed his eyes tiredly. "It was one of many possibilities."

"Was there anything we could have done?"

A shake of the head. Silence once more.

"What do we do now?"

Alyck took a slow breath. "Same as always. Hope. Pray. Survive."

It was not the answer Thaddeus wanted to hear, but he had expected it. Locked in their little world as they were, their only power was words.

"The final strike is coming," Alyck said, pushing from the chair to stand by the fire.

««« »»»

Caius made himself comfortable on the throne before nodding at the men waiting below. Aden, the new lord of Bouyne after Caius had killed his father, stood to his left, blood-splattered and smug. No doubt there would be contention between the lord and Braxton—but a little incentive and competition never hurt anyone.

His son was hauled in, a mildly dazed expression painted on his features; be it shock or from the blow to his head, it was hard to tell.

"You," Braxton managed, fully finding his feet, "you died!"

The guards tentatively released his arms.

"Did I?" Caius responded with a chuckle. "Not even the old gods can stop me. Besides, did you think I would miss your twenty-fifth birthday? No, I was just enjoying a little… R 'n R as the other-worlders say."

Braxton shook his head in disbelief, eyes searching the floor as if for a clue as to how this was possible.

"Come, stand by my side while I deal with the Child of Prophecy."

A hard-set expression changed Braxton's features. "No. You have no place in this world anymore."

"Tsk. Do not be stubborn. Come."

"No! I freed us from the scum of our family once; I will not go back! I did not kill Kolt just to put you back on the throne."

Caius knew Kolt had been violently deposed, but this was new information. There was a part of him that longed to return Braxton the favor of a knife to the back... but another part was immensely proud. One day Braxton would take the throne, and to lead well he needed a backbone—which apparently, he was finally developing. But that was something Caius now had to mitigate while *he* still reigned.

Casually, Caius rose from the throne and examined his nails. Then, he teleported across the room, the new gift given to him by his Nanagins, his fist slamming into Braxton's jaw. He loved his accentuated powers. "Put me on the throne! *I* have reclaimed what is rightfully mine. *You* had nothing to do with it."

He smirked, seeing some of the fire leave Braxton's eyes. Oh, yes, he could still be controlled. Slowly, he walked back up the dais, motioning for his son to follow.

Unsurprisingly, the boy trailed, coming to stand at his right side, eyes downcast.

Caius gave another nod to his men and the first of the traitorous lords were dragged in. He had no desire to show clemency, but they had believed him dead, and the war lost. They would lose their titles, but as long as they swore allegiance, their lives could be kept. And as suspected, living was the greatest incentive.

He smiled again, motioning for the last problem of the day to be brought forward. Out of the corner of his eyes, he watched for Braxton's reaction. His smile grew as the color drained from his son's features.

Aron fought and pulled against the soldiers holding him; his youngest had grown in his absence. There was an audible cracking sound as Aron was pushed forward onto his knees. Unfortunately, Caius could tell nothing was broken—he would just have to do it himself later.

Turning his attention toward the girl, he was disappointed to find she was still unconscious. He must have slammed her head into the wall harder than he thought. But there were ways of fixing that. "Salts," he demanded.

The guards must have been anticipating this for smelling salts were produced in mere seconds.

The girl took a heavy breath once the salts were placed under her nose, but it still took several seconds for her to regain consciousness and a minute more to gain full awareness. And that moment of clarity only truly came when she looked upon Aron.

Slowly and carefully, Keegan looked toward Caius. She did an excellent job of schooling her features, but it was impossible for her to erase all signs of fear. No, he could smell it, wafting off her like the scent of a flower.

"You're going to kill me," she stated, grabbing a dragon by the tail. "Just get it over with."

It was not until he said, "All right," that an uproar rung about the hall. Aron had to be physically restrained with a knee in the back—and even then, he shouted and cursed... and pled.

Braxton gave a vain attempt to persuade him otherwise, but it was halfhearted and ineffectual.

Part of him wished the girl fought back, but she did not. Two reasons for this existed; one: she sought death, or, two: she was familiar with slajor manacles and knew there was no surmounting them. He had placed them on her himself back in the tunnel behind the throne but was not sure where another set could have been found to be forced upon her for her to know precisely how they worked. Then it hit him; Kolt. At least he had done something right.

Keegan remained stoic as Caius rose and pulled the gun from his waistband. As expected, she seemed familiar with the weapon. But unexpectedly, she seemed relieved this would be the method of execution.

Coming forward, he placed the muzzle to her forehead. The girl closed her eyes, clearly at peace with what was about to happen.

Caius smiled to himself. "I will kill you… but not just yet. I still have a use for you."

Keegan's eyes snapped open and true fear clouded them as her breath hitched.

It was hard not to laugh as she and Aron were pulled from the room. Returning to the dais, Caius settled himself onto the throne smugly. This was going to be fun.

Bonus Material

Choosing a Name

Looking out the hospital doorway and seeing the long line of men, Lyerlly's patience failed. She turned to the nurse at the next station. "Take over, please."

"Yes, ma'am," she said dutifully.

Lyerlly was long past the comfortable point of pregnancy. Her back ached by the time she went to bed and swollen ankles had become normal. Often, by midday she was exhausted, while hunger had her eating larger portions. But she would not complain; to soon be able to hold her child would be worth all of it.

Walking through the halls, a feeling of anxiety arose in her breast, one that begged her to remain in the safety of this about to be abandoned again city. Lyerlly placed a hand on her stomach; for as much as some small part of her felt the need to stay behind, her—their—place was beside Bernot.

Stepping outside, the autumn air was refreshing, and the sun warmed her skin, kissing it softly.

If she did not pay attention, it was easy to miss the signs they were preparing to depart. It was easy to forget they were at war.

Strolling through the courtyard, Lyerlly began to forget her aches and pains. Happening to glance up, she noticed Bernot and Atlia on the rampart. Her husband leaned on the parapet, worrying his knuckles.

Waiting until the Merqueen left her husband to brood, she took her time climbing the stairs. She could see over the city and beyond to where the majority of their forces were camped. Compared to a week ago, their numbers seemed to have been cut in half. If she did not know the army had split four ways, she would have worried.

"I am sorry," Bernot said, sensing her approach. "I promised to let you go with me wherever I went. But I worry for you, and for the baby." He was referring to their fight earlier. He had asked her to stay behind.

Lyerlly had been mad—furious—but she ultimately knew it came from a place of love.

Coming to stand beside her, her husband wrapped an arm around her shoulders.

"I will let you know when it is time to worry," she promised.

They stood together silently for what seemed an eon and yet hardly a second. Lyerlly knew when they left this moment, the world would change. They would change.

"Have you thought of a name?" Bernot asked.

She smiled. "Not yet. Have you?" It was one of the few lies she had told her husband, but she did not regret it. Many women thought of what they wished to name their children years before they would be blessed with the chance. But those names were secret, often holding childish dreams or whispers of people better left behind.

"If it is a boy, I would like to name him Parshin, the Old Language word for peace," Bernot said.

Lyerlly mulled the name over and it seemed to find a place in her heart like a key. Yes, a wish for peace in a tumultuous time. Yet, there was strength in the name too, for to choose the path of peace required a will not all possessed.

"And if it is a girl?" she asked, reaching to twine her fingers with Bernot's.

"Adjran, after the word for fighter."

She felt a jerk in her stomach and pressed Bernot's hand against her belly.

"Our little Adjran," Bernot whispered.

"Yes, our little Adjran."

What Keegan Learned

It hadn't been one of the shortest days or kindest days, and Keegan was simply glad it was over.

She paused outside the dining hall, weighing her options; she could either head to the mess hall and see if she could scrounge up a seat, or join the leaders and other important people in their own private dining room. Both had their pros and cons. Tired and grouchy, she chose the latter, not in the mood to have her ears assaulted with crass and gaudy songs from the soldiers.

Eoghan greeted her warmly with a smile and a nod as she entered the private dining hall but didn't pull away from his conversation with an Alvor she didn't know. There were only a handful of other people spread out amongst the small tables, leaving her with ample options to sit alone.

Filling a bowl to near spilling with a beef broth, Keegan took a seat in a gloomy corner, finally feeling the tension in her shoulders beginning to lift.

As she raised the spoon to her mouth, Cataline barked, "What did you learn today?"

"Jesus, fuck," Keegan muttered as the Buluo slid onto the bench next to her. "Can't I eat in peace!"

"Absolutely. Once you tell me something you learned today."

Jarshua, who had been gnawing on a table leg next to Jared a few tables away, bounced over to Ne'Khole, his tail wagging excitedly.

Ne'Khole, still in her wolf form, sat on her haunches, and, with an aggravated expression, let Jarshua lick her face affectionately. Though sentient, Jarshua was still a wolf through and through. And a young one at that.

"I didn't learn anything," Keegan said, leaning back in her chair. "All you and Ne'Khole did was beat up on me all day."

"Then you do not get to eat," Cataline said easily, taking a bite of her own meal.

"Hypocrite," Keegan muttered audibly.

"Today I learned Ne'Khole found her first gray hair in human form," Cataline offered.

Ne'Khole growled at her Paranath, making Jarshua pull away in fear she was growling at him. The wolf was quick to lower her head and give a soft whine of apology to the pup.

"I learned you're an ass," Keegan said.

"Used that for lunch three weeks ago."

"I learned you've got a damn good memory?"

"Breakfast nine days ago."

"Jesus." She paused to think. "Fine, I learned I'm not pregnant."

Cataline all but spat out her food, choking. Across the room, Eoghan burst into a deep laugh while most other people seemed to not have heard her comment.

Knowing Cataline couldn't stop her now, Keegan dug in, slurping down the broth a spoonful at a time. If it'd been any cooler, she might've simply drunk from the bowl.

The second she heard Cataline take a decent breath, she created a wind shell around herself; it was a good measure, too. The gust Cataline sent with the intention of slamming her head into the table sailed harmlessly over her, instead lifting some human's plate of food into his face.

Keegan had to pucker her lips to keep from laughing; she felt bad for the man, but the sight... "Also learned you're predictable."

Ne'Khole let out as best a snicker she could in wolf form, earning a scowl from Cataline.

The Will to Survive

Mara's eyes opened groggily as the cold frosting her lashes fought to keep them closed, potentially forever. Her entire body was chilled, and she had to have been lying there for quite some time given the layer of snow covering her. But where was she? As she pushed herself upright, a pain throbbed in the back of her head like a ceaseless drummer.

Twilight was coloring the heavens in dark hues of blue and orange and thankfully the sky held no red memories of the horrors it had witnessed today. Looking around, she saw Ima lying a few feet away. The griffin wasn't moving, and her heart skipped a beat as she feared the worst.

It will take more than a fall to kill me, Ima said, still unmoving. There was pain in the words though, as if she wished the fall had delivered her to Lunos.

Why haven't you gotten up? Mara asked, pulling herself fully from the white blanket shrouding her. Approaching the griffin, she gently brushed the snow from Ima's face.

What point is there?

What do you— Mara noticed Ima's wing; it was stretched out beside her, flush with the ground. *It can be fixed,* she promised, remembering the time she and her father had nursed a sparrow with a broken wing back to health.

Ima was calm, seeming to have already accepted her fate. *This is a death sentence.*

No. Get up. Now!

Ima let out a huff, sending loose particles of snow dancing through the mist of her warm breath to land lithely again a few inches away. *Darkness has fallen. If we survive the chill of the night, I promise I will rise.*

A sharp pain in Mara's gut said the griffin was just telling her what she wanted to hear. But the promise had been made—and she would make sure Ima fulfilled it.

With a nod, Mara acknowledged their agreement. And their predicament. Besides, there wasn't much more of a choice.

Ima unfurled her good wing, inviting her closer. *Come. My body is made to withstand the coldest temperatures the sky can offer.*

Before going to lean against the griffin, Mara removed her armor; here, it would not protect. And she wanted no reminder of what she had been forced to become—of what she might further be forced to endure.

Where are the others? she asked as Ima lowered her wing.

Gone. I tried to call out to them, but no one heard.

Gone where? Mara couldn't imagine they'd been forgotten. Nico... Her jaw clenched, remembering this was his fault.

Gone west. Back to Agrielha.

West was also where the army's camp was. Braxton might not be aware of what had befallen them; but surely someone would come looking for them once they realized they were missing.

But, if the Vosjnik had gone back to Agrielha, then they were alone—truly alone, and helpless, in enemy territory.

Survive the night and everything else is tomorrow's problem, Mara told herself. Some small part of her almost hoped the morrow wouldn't come.

The King's Return

A bell sounded and Caius recognized it as the doorbell—a wonderful invention that was so much more pleasant than incessant knocking. It was one of the many wonderful things he had come to love in this new, advanced world that existed in parallel to his own.

"I will get it," he called to Angel—wherever within the house his friend was.

Caius calmly walked through the mansion, its opulence no longer a wonder. He could not explain it, but it almost seemed like static thrummed in the air. Opening the door, he found Miguel—one of Angel's men—outside, bloodied and battered. Caius was about to refuse him entry, for the wounds were superficial, a cut to his eyebrow supplying most of the blood on his person.

But before Caius could so much as get a grunt out, the Mexican quickly shoved his way inside, slamming the door shut behind him.

"Angel!" There was terror in Miguel's voice. Something bad was going down, or he was a magnificent actor.

Angel came down the stairs, all but running when he saw Miguel. "¿Que esta pasando?"

What was going on? A very good question to be asking.

Miguel was not given time to respond before bullets began streaming through the foyer, shattering glass and cracking wood and plaster.

They all quickly ducked into another room, Angel pulling a gun from his waistband while Caius flipped a table to give them cover. It didn't feel like it would do much in the way of protection as bullets pierced and shattered the windows like paper, but anything was better than nothing. He reached for the gun Angel had insisted he keep in his own waistband, then thought better of it and left it where it was hidden.

The rain of bullets stopped for a moment before quickly starting up again with renewed vigor. Then they stopped once more, and the doorhandle turned. Whoever was outside, began trying to kick down the door. Thank the old gods for Angel's auto locking door.

"¿Quién esta ahí?" Angel called, peering from around the side of the table cautiously, gun aimed at the entryway.

They were given no answer.

Then, there was the telltale click of a hammer—except, it had come from inside the house. He and Angel turned, dread in both of their features.

Miguel held a gun to Angel's head, the barrel aimed between his brows. "Cambia mi mente," he said.

If Miguel could be swayed, they stood a chance of making it out alive.

"Si estás aquí, tu mente ya está decidida," Angel said, offering no resistance.

Angel was correct, there was no reversing the course. If Miguel backed down now, Angel would kill him for even thinking about killing him.

"Aunque debo preguntar por que," Angel said softly.

Yes, they did at least deserve an explanation.

"Mi mujer," Miguel answered.

It was a universal truth that people would do anything to keep their beloveds alive and do anything to give them vengeance.

Staring Angel in the eyes, Miguel squeezed the trigger.

Angel fell back against the table, blood dripping from the small hole in his head. At least it had been quick.

"Lo siento," Miguel said, gently closing the fallen Angel's eyelids. Turning his attention to Caius, he said, "Tú, no siento pena por."

No love lost here.

Caius clenched his eyes and waited for the bang that would precede his introduction to Lunos. It came. And then it came again. And again. But he was not dead.

Opening his eyes warily, he saw Miguel emptying his clip into something behind him, a petrified look contorting his features. Caius looked behind himself, saw a gaping chasm, and knew exactly what it was.

Before Miguel could reload the gun and try to kill him—again—Caius dove through the rift and felt himself land on grass, though it was exceptionally cold. He was home, but he was not going to be going anywhere anytime soon as he felt his energy sapping away.

H. C. Kilgour

Pronunciations and Translations

Characters

Aden Kota [ay-den ko-ta]
Adjran Bællar [adj-ran bay-lar]
Alyck Alagard [al-eck al-ah-guard]
Amathya Rubel [am-ath-ee-ah rue-bell]
Angela Alga [an-gel-a al-ga]
Aron Alagard [ah-ron al-ah-guard]
Aros [ar-ohs]
Arthur [ar-thur]
Atlia Mahiako [at-lee-uh mah-he-ack-o]
Auckii Wealsh [auck-e well-sh]
Bastille/Darkheart [bass-teal/dark-heart]
Bernot "Bær" Bællar [bern-ot "bear" bay-lar]
Branshaw Appen [bran-shaw ap-pen]
Braxton Alagard [brax-ton al-ah-guard]
Breccan Schun [breck-an sh-oon]
Brennian Thandov [bren-ee-an than-dov]
Caius Alagard [kai-us al-ah-guard]
Caius Niranda [kai-us nir-an-duh]
Cataline Wind Breaker [cat-ah-line wind break-er]
Carter Sieme [car-ter sigh-m]
Cassidy Wungim [cass-ih-dee wung-im]
Crowlin [crowh-lynn]
Dax Ockloun [dax ock-lown]
Dunkirk [dun-kirk]
Elia [ell-e-ah]
Elhyas Wealsh [e-lie-as well-sh]
Eoghan Rubel [ee-oh-gan rue-bell]
Ernst Priesner [earn-st prize-ner]
Esen Bællar [es-en bay-lar]

Evard Poukyn [ev-ard poke-in]
Ezadeen [ez-ah-dean]
Ezekhial Dorehiem [ez-ee-ke-al door-e-hi-m]
Felix Isaacs [fe-lix iz-acks]
Garne Skaagg [garn-eh sk-ag]
Guthrie Urvent [guth-re ur-vent]
Harker [hark-er]
Hector [heck-tore]
Hernando Barnsed [hern-an-do barn-said]
Icella Bravano [ee-cell-uh brav-an-o]
Ima [e-mah]
Ilene Piscol [i-lean piss-cull]
Jared Sieme [jare-ed sigh-m]
Jarshua [jar-shoe-uh]
Jesus [jee-sus]
Kade Tavin [kay-d tav-in]
Keegan Digore [key-ghan die-gore]
Kolt Alagard [colt al-ah-guard]
Lucas Sieme [loo-cas sigh-m]
Lunos [loo-nohs]
Lyerlly Bællar [Lie-er-lee bay-lar]
Mahogen Ustor [mah-hog-en oos-tore]
Mara Foxire [mar-ah fox-ire]
Miguel [mig-el]
Myrish [my-rish]
Ne'Khole Sharp Tooth [knee-coal sharp tooth]
Nicandro Quolt [nick-an-dro qu-olt]
Nico Sieme [nee-kho sigh-m]
Nikita Sokolov [nih-key-tah sok-o-luv]
Niyth [nyth]
Noriss Ett [nor-is et]
Phynex [phe-nex]
Okleiy Ustor [oak-lee oos-tore]
Oxren [ox-ren]
Quin Qualazar [quin qual-az-ar]

Raelin [ray-lynn]
Rangi [rang-i]
Reven Broyker [rev-en broi-ker]
Rohan [rhow-han]
Seleena Vællar [sell-ee-nuh vay-lar]
Shiloh Laund [shy-loh lau-nd]
Sola [sol-ah]
Stalia [stal-e-uh]
Suki Vælar [soo-key vay-lar]
Sulle [sull]
Tahrin [tah-rin]
Taite Ault [tay-t auwlt]
Thaddeus Broyker [thad-e-us broi-ker]
Thahan Havidray [tha-han have-ih-dray]
Thoren [thor-en]
Vitia Gorell [vee-tee-ah gore-ell]
Vinson [vin-son]
Vladimir Putin [vlad-ih-mere poo-tin]
Waylan Piscol [way-lan piss-cull]
Zavier Tribianto [zay-ve-er trib-e-an-toe]

Places

Agrielha [ag-re-el-uh]
Arciol [are-see-ole]
Bouyne [boone]
Charlotte [shar-lot]
Cornelius [corn-eel-e-us]
Edreba [eh-dreb-uh]
Gortlin Tree [gore-t-lin tree]
Grenadone [gren-ah-dohn]
Grevasia [grev-a-see-uh]
Hamrick [ham-rick]
Jims [jims]

Ravliean

Lake Romann [lake roh-man]
Nueweba River [new-ebb-ah riv-er]
Revod [rev-od]
Suttan [sut-tan]
Ubëmble [oo-bem-bley]
Vercase [ver-case]

Old Language

Æeyi [aye-i]- he/his
Æayni [ay-ni]- him
Adjran [adj-ran]- fighter
Az [as]- I
Agno [ag-no]- old
Arse [are-s]- ass
Ayþ [ay-th]- the
Azole [az-ole-le]- god
Bastard [bass-tard]- bastard
Bokel [boh-kell]- long
Bovestun [bove-est-un]- bloody
Buna [boo-nuh]- fire
Bwint [bwin-t]- bitch
Cabre [cab-rey]- breaks
Ce [seh]- on
Cler [cler]- or
Dæ [day]- this
Deyfn [dey-fin]- race
Dognath [dog-nath]- spell
Donc [don-k]- piss (as in "urine")
Donp [don-p]- piss (as in "pissed off")
Evait [ev-ate]- live
Fayo [fay-oh]- by
Forsae [for-say]- future

H. C. Kilgour

Gexanlim [gex-an-lim]- shred
Ghæ [gay]- that
Granklo [gran-klow]- bone
Halnson [haln-sohn]- man
Herzo [her-zo]- place
Hiell [hi-ell]- hell (phrase, though more akin to a place)
Huschk [hus-chk]- skin
Hynak [hi-nack]- whore
Iruh [ih-roo]- for
Jonx [jon-x]- death
Jurvet [jer-vet]- meet
Kaythe [kay-th]- take
Korbæne [core-bane]- pact
Kunyi [coon-yih]- king
Malink [mal-ink]- remain
Moudise [mou-di-say]- promise
Nastor [nas-tore]- hell (phrase)
Naya [nay-ah]- no
Noxþ [nox-th]- damn
O [o]- a
Opida [oh-pee-dah]- bitch +7
Parshin [par-shin]- peace
Poegen [po-gen]- wield
Proytyct [proy-tict]- protect
Qalx [o-a-lx]- from
Quirse [qu-ir-say]- uphold
Rahm [ram]- more
Resy [res-i]- made
Rhæpn [rap-n]- who
Ri [re]- of
Royik [roy-ick]- fuck
Royit [roy-it]- shit (as in "give him shit")/fuck with (as in make fun of)
Sa [sah]- in
Sesuna [ses-oo-na]- serve
Soth [soth]- shall

Ravliean

Sugore [sug-or]- fuck (sexual)
Tansred [tans-red]- body
Twyt [tw-it]- twat
Tyth [tyth]- tell
U [oo]- to
Ube [oo-beh]- as
Undegthi [oon-de-ge-the]- male
Venot [ven-ot]- their
Vilet [vill-et]- word
Vito [vee-toe]- shit (as in "jack shit/piece of shit")
Vitt [vit]- shit ("oh, shit!")
Wedlonst [wed-lon-st]- forever
Wixne [wicks-ney]- and
Woth [woth]- will
Xao [sh-ah-oh]- any
Xye [zi]- is
Yiam [ye-am]- both
Yana [yan-ah]- bitch ("hurt like a bitch")
Zodonv [zod-on-v]- weapon

Word Endings/Tenses

-est- the most ("great*est*")
-ox- past tense ("play*ed*")
-en- present/future tense ("go*ing*")
-s- plural ("dog*s*")
-alb- more ("great*er*")
-u- feminine noun/verb ending
-i- masculine noun/verb ending

H. C. Kilgour

Russian

Chertov [sher-tov]- damn (masculine)
Chertova [sher-tov]- damn (feminine)
Cyka [soo-kah]- bitch

Peoples

Alvor [al-vore]
Arciolan [are-see-ole-an]- someone from Arciol
Buluo [boo-loo-oh]
Lazado [laz-ah-do]
Pexatose [pex-ah-tohs]- someone from the other world
Torrpeki [tore-pec-ee]
Vosjnik [voz-nick]- a group of the best in each of their fields

Other Pronunciations

Borzan [bore-zan]- coffee
Enishnom [en-ish-nom]- Torrpeki equivalent of moonshine.
Ether [eth-er]- agent used to temporarily inhibit magic use.
Harang [har-ang]- pairing of wolf and Buluo that both cannot perform magic.
Henshren [hen-shwren]- Buluo leader in times of war.
Koilk [koi-lk]- loincloth like item worn by Torrpeki.
Kojote [koh-joe-te]- a person who secrets elementals across the country to safety.
Migun [mig-un]- a poison.

Nanagin [nuh-nah-gin]- magical portal between worlds, specific in time in place to each person.

Paika [pie-kuh]- source of elemental magics. Differ in color and location based upon element.

Paranath [pair-ah-nath]- pairing of wolf and Buluo that both possess magical abilities.

Ramilla [ram-ill-uh]- a poison made from octopus venom and the nectar of the dogwood flower.

Reintablou [rein-tab-lohw]- Torrpeki leader in times of war.

Slajor manacles [slah-jur man-a-cles]- bracelets that permanently inhibit magic use.

H. C. Kilgour

Growing up, you were just as likely to find H. C. playing outside as you were to find her with her nose in a book. She particularly enjoys books focusing on worlds of magic and adventure.

Often joking that she's part mermaid, Haley pursued a marine biology degree from the University of North Carolina Wilmington, graduating in 2017. She then proceeded to attend the University of Miami earing a Master of Professional Science in marine conservation in 2019.

With an English father and an Italian-American mother, H. C. had a colorful upbringing in Charlotte, North Carolina, which she has accentuated by traveling as much as she can. She currently lives in Key Largo with her husband and two cats.

She says her biggest inspiration for writing is that she simply needs her characters to be quiet, so she can think. Currently, she divides her time between writing, scuba diving, her loving friends and family, and work.

Milton Keynes UK
Ingram Content Group UK Ltd.
UKHW022130051124
450708UK00016B/1271

9 798218 475963